# THE LITTLE VINEYARD IN PROVENCE

# THE LITTLE VINEYARD IN PROVENCE

## Ruth Kelly

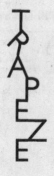

First published in Great Britain in 2019 by Trapeze
an imprint of The Orion Publishing Group Ltd
Carmelite House, 50 Victoria Embankment
London EC4Y 0DZ

An Hachette UK Company

5 7 9 10 8 6

A CIP catalogue record for this book is available from the British
Library.

All the characters in this book are fictitious, and any resemblance to
actual persons, living or dead, is purely coincidental.

ISBN (paperback) 978 1 4091 8530 7
ISBN (ebook) 978 1 4091 8531 4

Typeset by Born Group
Printed and bound in Great Britain by Clays Ltd, Elcograf S.p.A.

MIX
Paper from
responsible sources
FSC® C104740

www.orionbooks.co.uk

For my mum

# Prologue

'Yuck, that's bitter!' Ava spat out the grape.

Grandpapa laughed so loudly he was overwhelmed by a fit of coughing.

'That's because it's not ripe, child!' He patted his chest. Holding the red grape between his finger and thumb, he angled it to the sky. The bright sunshine streamed through it, turning the purple fruit a transparent shade of lavender.

'We must catch them at the perfect moment. That is why we have to keep trying them. Tasting them. Checking them for their sweetness. And then when they are ripe, we pick them!' he exclaimed with his typical French exuberance.

Ava giggled.

'But . . .' he waggled his finger. 'But there is only a tiny little window for this magic to happen.' He shrugged. '*Bouff*, maybe two, maybe three days. And if we get it wrong . . .' he paused.

She stared at him, mouth open like a goldfish, hanging on his every word.

'It is a disaster!'

He walked on, leaving her glued to the spot, first with shock and then curiosity as her mind began whizzing with questions.

'The grapes are only ripe for a few days, Grandpapa?' she called after him.

'*Oui!* Come along now.' The chalky dry soil crunched underneath his dusty shoes as he walked ahead. Every now and then, he would reach his hand out and touch the leaves with a soft caressing motion, as if he were stroking a beloved pet dog.

Ava followed closely at his heels, lurching from stop to start whenever her grandfather decided to test another grape.

Her freckles were developing by the second under the scorching afternoon sun.

Suddenly he turned and looked at her intently.

'I'll let you into a little secret, my dear Ava.' His voice lowered to a whisper.

Her eyes widened, waiting for him to reveal another nugget of wisdom.

'These grapes here,' he motioned his hands across the rows of vines. 'They are the heart of my vineyard. They are the oldest vines, and do you know what that means?'

Ava shook her head.

'It means, they are the strongest. Their roots have buried deep into the *terroir* so they can reach nutrients no other vines can get to.'

Kneeling down, and groaning slightly at the effort, her grandpapa wrapped his sinewy fingers around the trunk of the vine and placed his other weathered hand on the ground to provide some support. His rugged hands were covered in liver spots.

'*Très forte*, very strong,' he muttered, as he gave it a gentle shake. 'They drink the minerals and carry them through here.' He traced his forefinger up the trunk. 'And along here.' Ava watched with fascination as he drew a pathway to the fruits. He tugged another grape free, the vine shaking before springing back into place.

2

'And when it is ripe, it will add a perfect sweetness to my rosé wine like no other grape can.'

He placed the little red fruit into her palm. His bones creaked as he steadied himself back onto his feet.

She looked up at her grandpapa in awe, but his gaze was now fixed on the horizon. Eyes narrowed, he stared past the vines to her parents' car, which was speeding along the driveway, trailing a cloud of dust.

'Is everything okay, Grandpapa?'

His warm smile had evaporated. His bushy grey eyebrows pinched together with a frown.

'Grandpapa?'

He muttered something in French.

'Come on child, let's get you back to the house.'

# Chapter One

November 2017

Ava clamped her phone to her ear with her left shoulder, and used both hands to wrestle with the stiff lock on her front door.

Between the rain driving at her neck and her husband, Mark, yammering on in her ear, it was difficult to concentrate, but finally, the key shifted and the lock gave way.

She stumbled into the warmth, exhausted.

While Mark chatted through his day at work, Ava picked up the small pile of post from the doormat. She dropped the house keys into the bowl on the hall table, kicked off her damp ankle boots, peeled herself out of her drenched coat, unwrapped her flowery chiffon scarf, and hung them both on the set of hooks next to the mirror.

Ava grimaced at her reflection. She looked a state.

The sudden downpour on her walk home from work had turned her shoulder-length dark hair into matted clumps. Her mascara had bled down her face, leaving inky swirls across the apples of her cheeks.

She padded along the hallway in her damp socks to the kitchen.

The smell of last night's chicken korma still clung to the air but before she could think about airing the room, she needed a large glass of wine to wash away her stressful day at work.

It suddenly dawned on her that she had been on the phone to Mark for well over twenty minutes and he still hadn't got around to asking her how she was.

Ava clasped her mobile back between her ear and her shoulder as she unscrewed the cap of the Sauvignon Blanc. The white wine sloshed from side to side as she filled the glass just shy of its brim. She raised it to her lips and took a large gulp, the acidity burning her throat.

Mark never did have much of a clue when it came to choosing decent wine. All he cared about was getting a bargain. Two for one, twenty-five per cent off; if there was a deal to be had, he would have it. She threw an irritated glance across the kitchen at the two cardboard boxes of plonk stacked by the wine rack, still waiting to be emptied out.

'So, when do you think you'll be back?' she asked, interrupting him mid-sentence.

Mark had been away from home for three and a half weeks, having been sent up north by the construction company he worked for. They were building a motorway hotel near Leeds, she recalled him telling her.

'Not too much longer sweetheart, you know how these things can take time.'

But it wasn't like Mark to spend this long away without returning for the weekend. While Ava cherished a bit of time alone after twenty-three years of marriage, she was starting to feel the distance.

'Well I'm doing a big food shop tomorrow so it would be good to know.' She pushed him for a more concrete answer.

'Gimme a break, I'm under the cosh as it is, I can do without your nagging,' he snapped. Ava could imagine his cool blue eyes narrowing as he spat out the words.

She bit her lip, as she often did these days. Ava had learnt it was easier not to antagonise Mark.

Instead she zoned out, his voice turning into white noise as she started on the mail.

She used her forefinger to rip open the first letter. It was a money-off voucher for her favourite clothes shop. When was the last time she'd treated herself to something new? Any spare money they had was spent on their daughter Sophie, or used for long overdue repairs to their house.

But if Ava was completely honest with herself, she'd have to admit that she'd lost interest in caring about her appearance. She rotated between three trouser suits for work, and at home all she wanted to do was to slip into her M&S pyjamas and wrap herself in her long mottled blue cardigan, which Mark said resembled a dressing gown, and not in a good way.

She put the voucher to one side while Mark changed the subject from work to Sophie, who was in her first year at Birmingham University.

'Sophie rang today asking for a hundred quid to buy a dress for a party.'

Their daughter was a daddy's girl; she had her father wrapped around her little finger. It was Mark's fault – he'd caved in to her every demand since she was a little girl. That meant Ava was often unfairly left to play the villain, the mean mum who said 'no'. Meanwhile, Mark could do no wrong in Sophie's eyes.

Ava tore the next letter open as she replied.

'Sophie has dozens of dresses she's bought and not even worn yet. And . . .'

But she couldn't finish her sentence. The words were caught in her mouth as she stared at the numbers on the paper, in total disbelief.

Surely she must be imagining what she was reading? She closed her eyes and opened them slowly. But the numbers

6

were still staring back at her, on the crisp white letter from the building society.

'Yeah, but you know what she gets like if she can't have a new dress and . . .'

'Mark?' She interrupted her husband's monologue.

'Yeah, what's up?'

'This can't be right,' she muttered, turning the letter over, expecting the real figures to be printed on the other side; surely this was a mistake.

'What's wrong, babe?' His voice had a slight nervous tremble to it now, as if he were expecting bad news. 'Is everything okay?' He chased her for an answer. No question about it, Mark was sounding nervous, and guilty. After two decades together, Ava could read every nuance in her husband's tone.

'No, everything is not okay! The building society says we haven't paid our mortgage for six months!'

This was the moment where Mark should have jumped in and torn the bank apart for being incompetent idiots for sending out the wrong paperwork. Instead, Ava was left with a long disconcerting silence on the other end of the phone.

Dread gripped her stomach and she almost choked on the numbers as she read them out.

'They say we owe them £15,000 . . .'

Still nothing from Mark. His silence spoke for him.

With every word, Ava's voice rose an octave, growing in fury until she suddenly exploded.

'They are going to repossess the house! Are you listening to what I'm saying, Mark?'

Ava wondered if her husband had hung up, but then she heard the faint whistle as he drew in a long breath, and out came his cool, calm, wheeler-dealer businessman-voice.

'It's nothing that I can't sort out, you know, you've just got to stay calm.'

Calm – the word was like a red rag to a bull.

'We're going to be homeless and you want me to stay *calm*?'

Mark always had a way of twisting things around. Ava had spent the better part of their marriage apologising for mistakes that were really his.

'I wouldn't be in this mess if it weren't for you. I've spent all this money trying to keep you and Sophie happy and all it's done has got me into debt.'

Ava couldn't be more different to the flashy wives who demanded their husbands buy them show homes. She wasn't materialistic; in fact, *she* was the one who put everyone first, to her own detriment.

Although almost every breath had been punched out of her lungs from the low blow he'd socked her, she somehow managed to keep her composure.

'Where's the money gone, Mark? What have you spent it on?'

Deep in his selfish heart, Mark knew Ava wasn't the least bit interested in keeping up with the Joneses, and though he liked to come out on top in an argument and shift the blame onto her whenever he could, this time he had to concede. Mark couldn't talk his way out of this one. Finally, he came clean.

As Mark confessed how he'd lost tens of thousands on a failed property deal on the Costa del Sol, Ava's head started to spin.

She clambered onto one of the chrome stools dotted around their granite-topped breakfast bar and clung onto its edge as she waited for the nauseating whirling to stop.

Every few minutes she found herself repeating Mark's last word, as if that would somehow help the hopelessness of their situation sink in.

'Loan shark?'

'Yeah, that's right, I had to do something to find the money to invest in this property deal, didn't I? And then it went bust, so I lost it all.'

In her mind, the debt was stacking up into a huge Jenga tower, about to come crashing down and bury them.

'Who did you get the loan from?'

Mark cleared his throat. 'You don't need to worry about that, darling.'

Ava knew how this story ended.

'You haven't paid it all back, have you?' Ava couldn't even bear to think what the interest on the loan would be.

It was just as well Mark wasn't standing in front of her now or God knows what she would have done. Never in her life had she felt so angry, so betrayed and so let down.

And just when she thought it couldn't get worse, Mark revealed he wouldn't be coming home just yet to clean up his mess.

'I don't think it's safe for you if I come back. I don't want to bring trouble to our door. Look babe, I'm going to sort this out, just sit tight,' Mark promised. 'You know I love you, you mean the world to me.'

Ava's anger fizzled into nothing as the reality of having to deal with the mess on her own sank in.

'Please Mark, you have to come home, you can't leave me,' she begged. She couldn't fight the tears back any longer.

She tried to picture her husband's face – his rugged good looks, his cheeky grin, the dark bristle of his stubble – in a desperate attempt to bridge the distance between them.

'Stay strong for me, for Sophie,' Mark said, winding down the conversation.

Ava was sobbing now. 'Please Mark . . .'

Just as she was about to ask him when she would next hear from him, Mark told her he needed to go. And pouff, just like that, her husband, and the life they had been living, were gone.

She sat in stunned silence.

As she looked around her, at the kitchen they had filled with memories since they scrimped and saved to buy their two-bedroom suburban semi ten years ago, Ava had never felt so alone.

She grabbed her wine glass and tipped the remaining contents into her mouth, wincing with the sourness, but it didn't stop her reaching for the rest of the bottle.

Glug. Glug. Glug.

She stared blankly out of the patio doors, mesmerised by the rain trickling down the glass. Tears ran down her cheeks, her eyes glazing over as she drifted into deep thought.

How could this have happened?

She knew how Mark could have got them in such debt without her knowing: they had separate accounts and Mark handled the mortgage payments and the credit cards, while she took care of the gas and electric from what she earned working as a receptionist. A thankless job in a Range Rover showroom, dealing with snotty city types who moved to the shires, with more money than manners.

Her dream had always been to own a cake shop, baking everything from lemon drizzle to black forest gâteau, doing something creative and inspiring . . .

Slurp; she knocked back another large gulp as she wondered where her life had gone.

How could Mark have been so stupid as to gamble away all their money on some dodgy property development? Ava knew she'd married a dreamer but that's what she had liked about him, his big ideas, and for the best part of their marriage she believed that one day he would make it.

Her friends had warned her off him, promising her she'd be sorry one day, but she hadn't listened. When you're in love, you never do.

That's why Ava was now struggling to know who to call. She'd cut herself off from almost everyone she'd grown up with by defending Mark, and eating humble pie would be difficult.

She reached for her wine glass again. Slurp.

Ava was hoping the wine would make her feel numb. But it was only heightening her feelings of anxiety. Countless questions raced through her mind and she couldn't be alone for a second longer.

She picked up her phone, scrolling through her recently called list. There was only one name on there that she could turn to, someone who wouldn't attack her with a bunch of 'I told you so's'.

Emilia answered on the third ring.

'What's wrong?' she demanded. She knew her best friend too well.

Ava didn't know where to start. She sniffed, fighting back the avalanche of tears that hearing a friendly voice set off.

'It's Mark, he's really messed up this time.'

'Jesus. Are you okay?'

'Not really, can you come over?'

Thankfully Emilia lived close by. Ever since school, they'd made a pact never to be more than half an hour from each other. Emilia had to twist her husband, Paul's, arm to get him to agree to Surrey. But then she could be very persuasive, and persistent when she wanted to be, and had somehow managed not only to talk Paul into moving across the country but to settle down in the very desirable and expensive Esher.

Mark never had anything nice to say about Emilia, but Ava was sure that was because he felt threatened by her feisty spirit. Emilia refused to accept anything but the best in life, and as a result, she almost always got what she wanted.

Emilia would never have got herself in this mess, Ava reflected, as she prised two more wine bottles from the rack and wobbled her way through into the living room. She collapsed into the sunken sofa, her glass clinking against the bottle as she landed.

For a long moment, she lay there slumped, staring up at the ceiling, emotionally drained. She replayed the phone conversation with Mark, reliving the shock, the deceit; trying to remember the details of what he had said, and that's when the thought grabbed her:

She sat bolt upright.

If Mark had kept the mortgage debt a secret, what else was he hiding?

With a renewed energy fuelled by anger and alcohol, Ava charged across the living room to Mark's desk. She pulled open the drawers of the lacquered pine monstrosity, one by one, riffling through the contents, searching for clues.

A gym membership contract form, a parking permit, a box of paperclips, a stapler, an old Nokia 3210 that hadn't seen the light of day in ten years. She kept going, spraying the contents onto the carpet like a dog turfing up the garden for a bone.

She tugged at the bottom right-hand drawer but it wouldn't budge. She tried again, sending herself tumbling backwards onto her bum through misjudged force. Ava gave the drawer the death stare, then clambered back onto her feet in search of something with which to prise it open. She was like a woman possessed.

Ava returned from the kitchen, this time carrying a screwdriver. She'd never broken into anything before in her life, but she found it strangely satisfying attacking the desk, finally allowing herself to unleash her fury.

She stabbed at the lock, shook the drawer from side to side, gored it some more. Wood shavings flew through the air as she chipped a hole large enough to squeeze the screwdriver into.

'YES!' she exclaimed with delight as she managed to slide her weapon of mass destruction into the drawer.

With one almighty heave, she wrenched it open.

Ava's heart was hammering with adrenaline as she peered inside. She had a horrible sinking feeling she was about to discover something terrible. The Mark she knew wouldn't keep things under lock and key, but did she actually know him at all? The doubt crept further in with every passing second. Inside the drawer was a huge pile of papers and torn envelopes, as if someone had hurriedly shoved them inside.

She took a deep, calming breath and dived in.

But no amount of yoga breathing exercises could have prepared her.

With trembling hands, she pulled out statement after statement for maxed-out credit cards. £8,000 cash withdrawal made on the 2nd of February. Seven thousand pounds taken out of a Barclays account she never knew Mark had, only a few weeks ago. On and on it went.

The room started to spin so quickly, the numbers blurred into a thick grey mass on the page. Ava crumbled into a heap on the carpet, swallowing hard to stop herself from being sick.

Clutching her stomach, she closed her eyes.

How could Mark do this to her? Who was Mark? He'd gone from her husband of twenty-three years to a stranger in a matter of minutes.

The toxic cocktail of lies, secrets and cheap wine was sending Ava into a downward spiral. She curled herself into the foetal position and sobbed her heart out.

# Chapter Two

Ava yawned, stretched, rolled over, and nearly tumbled out of her best friend's single bed.

Remembering where she was, she scrabbled back under the duvet, and lay on her back like a squashed starfish, staring blankly at the ceiling, as she acclimatised to what her life had been reduced to.

It had been four months since she'd discovered her husband had squandered all of their money. The house that she loved, that she'd poured her everything into making a family home, had been repossessed and was up for sale. If that wasn't devastating enough, Mark was now living with Gabby from accounts. They were having a 'thing'. Something 'casual' they had struck up after he had interpreted her needing some space to reflect on everything he'd destroyed, as a break. Mark had sworn nothing had happened while they were together but of course that was a pack of lies. Wasn't it? Emilia had called it utter bullshit. But Ava wasn't sure about anything any more.

Her marriage, her life, was in tatters. She was staying in Emilia's spare bedroom, surrounded by mountains of bags and suitcases – the leftovers of her life, packed away in an ungodly mess.

As her eyes focused on a teeny spider crawling across the ceiling, Ava wondered if she could lie there for another year, until her life had somehow magically fixed itself. But Emilia wouldn't hear of it.

'Are you up yet?' Right on cue, a cry came from the kitchen.

Ava pushed herself upright and took a small breath as she mustered up the energy for a final shove off the bed. She clambered onto her feet, settled into the thick fluffy white carpet, and padded her way, bleary-eyed, into the kitchen. Her hair was probably skewered in all directions, but she didn't care.

As usual, Emilia was rushing around like a fly on amphetamines, and in spiked heels.

Ava trudged over to the breakfast bar as her friend whizzed past and weaved around her. Ava heaved herself up onto a stool, placed her elbows on the work surface and buried her eyes in the heels of her hands.

'Not today!' Emilia poked her in the side, jolting Ava so violently awake she almost buried her nose in the bowl of milk and cornflakes Emilia had plonked in front of her.

'You're going to be late!'

Ava hunched over her bowl, stirring it listlessly.

'You don't have to keep making me breakfast, you know.'

'I know!'

Emilia continued her manic morning preparations, knocking back another Nespresso as if it were a Jägerbomb.

'You and Paul must be sick of the sight of me.'

She slurped a spoonful of soggy cereal.

Emilia sighed, as though trying to curb her frustration.

'You know you are welcome for as long as you like. I've told you so a gazillion times.'

'I know. I just don't want to be in anyone's way . . .' Her voice cracked with the onset of tears.

Emilia softened. She rushed to her side, opened her arms and wrapped them around her friend, hugging her tightly.

Ava tried to fight her sadness. 'I'm fine,' she wriggled.

'No, you're not, come here.' Emilia held her even more snugly until Ava relented, softening into her friend's comforting embrace.

After a long consoling silence, she pulled back and took a deep breath, gearing herself up to manage another few spoonfuls of cornflakes and somehow get through the day.

'So . . .' Emilia crossed her arms.

'Have you heard from *him*?'

It was an innocent enough question, but having to say no made Ava feel ten times worse than she already did. Time apart was making her reconsider whether she had done the right thing.

She shook her head, gloomily. 'Everything is done through our solicitors.'

'That's good! You don't want to hear from him. It gives you the space you need to build yourself back up.'

Ava let out a little breath as something inside constricted.

Emilia flashed her a pointed look.

'You don't want him back, okay. Do you hear me?'

Ava shifted in her seat.

'You can't want him back, not after everything. God knows what *she* sees in him. It's not like he has any money. He's found someone to sponge off, good for him. I bet it won't last five minutes.'

Emilia had never been shy about hiding her contempt for Mark. Ava would never forget the very awkward dinner they'd had at Sergio's when Emilia encouraged her to follow her heart by enrolling in a baking course. Mark had almost choked on his carbonara, telling Emilia to mind her own business between his coughs and splutters. Of course that only served to antagonise Emilia more and the two locked horns until Ava finally had to speak up and reassure Mark she had zero plans to leave her receptionist job.

Ava loved how her friend was so defensive of her but the pep talks left her feeling more drained than rejuvenated.

'I know I don't say this enough, but I'm so proud of you.'

'What, really?'

'Yes! You've come so far, don't give up now. This is the worst bit. Breaking up with someone is scary. It can feel like your world has ended. It can feel like they have died! It can feel like you will never move on and you will spend the rest of your life in eternal misery.'

Ava frowned, unconvinced her friend was helping much.

'But you will be fine, I promise. Once you file for divorce, and you find what you want to do with your life . . .'

'Divorce?' Ava spluttered. 'Where did divorce come from? I'm just taking a bit of time . . . I mean . . . we're both just having a bit of time apart . . . I just . . .' she sighed deeply. 'Actually, I just don't know anything any more.'

Ava bowed back over her bowl, her mind scrambled with confused thoughts. Divorce sounded so serious, so final. Admitting her marriage was over was petrifying. What would she do without Mark? The thought of starting over at forty-three was scarier than the idea of being homeless, thousands of pounds worth in debt and preparing to forgive her husband for shacking up with another woman. It was even scarier than swallowing her pride when he finally came back to her. Ava had convinced herself Mark would be back after he'd realised the grass wasn't greener. Mark might not be the ideal husband, but he was all she'd ever known. Her identity hung on the life they had built together. If that disappeared, who would she be?

Putting up with crap from a man was something Emilia couldn't understand though, and struggled to empathise with, or even listen to. She marched over to the window, lit a cigarette and inhaled deeply with relief.

'I don't even know if he's managed to sort out all his debts,' Ava hung her head as it dawned on her how disconnected she and Mark had become.

'Who cares! Not your problem.'

'But if he's got loan sharks after him . . .'

Emilia cut her dead.

'Don't feel sorry for him.'

'I'm not.'

'And don't feel sorry for yourself.'

'Umm, can't I? just a bit.'

Emilia blew out a plume of smoke from the corner of her mouth, fanning it out of the window with her hand.

Ava scowled. 'You're not still trying to pretend you've quit, are you?' You should just be honest. I had secrets in my marriage and look where it got me.'

'Hun, it's just a fag!' Emilia stubbed out the butt into the shrivelled herb pot on the windowsill. She glanced at her watch.

'Christ, I'm late for work.' She pointed to the bathroom. 'And so are you! Go! Are you home for dinner?'

Ava shook her head.

'Sophie is back from university for the weekend, we're having dinner together tonight.'

'Oh lovely! Give her my love. She's welcome to crash here too.'

Crash was the operative word, Ava mused. Living like a student again, regressing to the life of her eighteen-year-old daughter – with a car crash of a marriage.

'Thank you, I'll tell her she can.'

Emilia jammed the last of her things into her Chanel handbag. 'Phone, keys, ciggies, gum.' She plunged her hand down the V of her tailored white shirt, rearranging the padding of her push-up bra to accentuate her assets even more.

'How do I look?' she stood back, her hands on her hips, modelling a pencil skirt, stilettos and a lot of cleavage. Her almost neon blonde hair tussled into a side parting in a sexy just-got-out-of-bed way.

Ava admired how her best friend was always stylish and groomed to perfection. She slid off the stool, causing her faded penguin-print pyjamas to almost slide off with her. She clutched the waist where the elastic had long gone and waddled towards the bathroom.

Emilia threw her one last cheerful smile. 'Don't give up, hun. Stay strong.'

The front door rattled shut and Ava's shoulders slumped in relief that she could stop pretending she had any will to go on.

She stared at the sofa longingly. *Nobody would notice if I just disappeared under the blanket and watched Netflix while devouring bags of crisps and chocolate for the rest of the day, would they?*

And then she sighed deeply as she remembered her thankless job and her arsehole of a boss.

As it turned out, eight hours sitting at the reception of Gary Lovett's Range Rover dealership on the high street, staring numbly at the murky sky and the people ambling past the showroom windows, was even worse than Ava had imagined.

When her boss Gary wasn't up-selling a four-by-four to some clueless city type, he liked to lean with his elbow across the reception counter and talk to her breasts as he recited his favourite motivational quotes. Today's gem was: 'If football taught me anything about business, it is that you win the game one play at a time.' Still staring at her tits he'd added: 'If you play your cards right, you'll be standing where I am one day.' He'd even managed to squeeze in a wink. Ava felt unclean just looking at him across the showroom floor.

She'd been watching the clock obsessively for the last hour. Counting down the minutes, counting away the seconds until home time. Precisely two minutes until freedom – Ava gathered her things, unhooked her mud-coloured jacket from the back of the swivel chair and just as she was making a break for it, her boss stamped a handful of letters on the counter.

Loosening his tie and collar with the other, he grinned: 'Off home are we?'

Ava double-checked her watch. Surely she couldn't have got the time wrong after all that clock watching.

'It's six p.m.,' she confirmed. But it turned out Gary was prying.

'A little birdie told me you're back on the market,' he raised his eyebrows up and down.

Ava glared at Gemma on sales who quickly looked away.

'I wouldn't say that. Last time I checked, I was still married.'

'But heading for a divorce?' He pushed his tongue into his cheek.

It seemed more of a statement than a question, Ava thought. She shifted uneasily in her chair but there was nowhere to hide in the goldfish bowl of a showroom.

'I'm not . . .'

'The key to running a successful business is knowing when to cut your losses.' Gary interrupted, patting his hand over his slicked-back hair to check it was still glued in place.

Ava rolled her eyes.

'Right.'

'And you don't want to miss out on a good deal,' he leaned in.

Ava wasn't convinced he was still talking about car sales. 'Okaaay then.'

She quickly shoved the rest of her things into her bag and rose to her feet, desperate to leave. She squeezed past her boss, who was giving her the once-over. As she made for the door, Gary shouted:

'I've got something you might like.'

She flinched. Closed her eyes and slowly opened them, taking in a sharp breath of patience.

'What's that then?' She turned to face him.

He was holding out a letter.

'It wasn't just Gemma who gave the game away. Redirecting your post here is a bit of a giveaway,' he tapped his nose, knowingly.

Ava smiled through gritted teeth, but as she went to grab the post, Gary snatched it from reach. Dangling it in front of her like a carrot.

'For goodness' sake,' she muttered under her breath.

'So maybe we could go for a drink sometime?' he waved the letter playfully.

'No.'

'Just a cheeky one after work?'

'Nope!' She motioned for him to hand over the ransom.

Finally relenting, he thrust the envelope into her hand. She stuffed it into her handbag.

'Think about it. I won't be available for long, you don't want to have regrets,' he called after her.

Ava shook her head wearily as she finally made contact with the door handle.

*Could this day get any worse?*

# Chapter Three

The drive to the Slug and Lettuce in town didn't take Ava past her old house on Acorn Close but she couldn't stop herself making a detour.

Slowing the car to a crawl, she approached Number 21 at the end of the cul-de-sac and then gently came to a stop outside the red brick semi-detached house with the For Sale sign outside.

She remembered the day she and Mark moved in like it was yesterday. He had kissed her passionately, lifted her into his arms and carried her through the white porch and across the threshold, her ankles, not so romantically, banging against the doorframe. Sophie was only ten and full of energy, running up and down the stairs, yelling at the top of her voice how she wanted her room to be turned into a palace with a mock princess bed and everything must be pink. Mark had of course agreed to everything.

As the enormous grey sky pressed down and the rain started to splatter across her windscreen, their once cosy home looked cold and unwelcoming. All that was left was an empty shell. The furniture they had scrimped and saved to buy had been sold for a fraction of its value to a second-hand store, while the rest had been unceremoniously thrown into a skip. Their favourite sofa was still for sale. Ava knew because she had checked last week. It was some sadistic ritual she had somehow got into the habit of inflicting on herself – revisiting the tatters of her happy past.

Well, happy wasn't completely accurate, but it had started out that way. A home full of hopes and dreams.

Ava had met Mark in her final year at college – he was the bad lad in her class who maddened the teachers because despite being clever, he refused to channel it into his studies.

Instead, Mark would spend his time planning schemes to get rich quick. She thought back to the nights they would hide away in his attic room at his parents' house. She would lie with her head on his chest, the purr of his gravelly voice in her ear, lulling her to sleep as he chatted through his grand ideas. She remembered the internet clothing brand where everything on the site was a bargain £10. Then there was the idea to open a nightclub in town, and then came the discounted wine shop idea when Mark heard a friend of a friend urgently needed to shift box-loads of New Zealand chardonnay from his warehouse.

Ava loved his energy and she was there to support him every step of the way and, in turn, at first, Mark encouraged her to make something of her creativity. Ava loved baking cakes, the more elaborate the better. She had planned to enrol in a cake decorating course but then Sophie had come along and everything changed. Between being a young mum and holding down a job, she'd quickly became bogged down in family life – keeping the household running, putting dinner on the table – and so her dreams were moved to the back burner until they eventually fizzled out.

Mark found a job with a construction company and threw himself into his building projects. Any leftover time he had, he gave to Sophie.

Gradually, so slow it wasn't at first noticeable, they became like ships passing in the night, parents to a beautiful daughter, but little more than friends to each other.

But that had been okay, because that's what becomes of all relationships, Ava had reasoned. Most of the wives of Mark's friends had sacrificed their careers for their family. Almost all of them moaned about their non-existent sex lives. Emilia was one of the few exceptions who had managed to keep both.

Ava blinked through the drizzle at Number 21, where she had tried so hard, on so many occasions, to create a home to keep her family together. She wiped away the tear that had escaped her eye. *What had it all been for?*

More tears appeared, bubbling out of the corner of her eyes and trickling down her cheeks. Too many to catch.

Her thoughts flitted between her old home and the house she envisioned Mark was now living in with *her*. It was probably immaculate, like a show home, full of cream soft furnishings, and she probably had one of those fancy ottomans where Mark could rest his feet after a hard day's work. Ava was now imagining her giving him a foot rub, showering him with attention. Giggling flirtatiously, her blonde curls tumbling in front of her face as she tried to catch his eye. Ava had created a whole persona for Gabby out of the Facebook pictures she'd been staring at, obsessively, for the last few months.

Her heart quickened inside her chest while her anxiety tightened it like a vice. The tears streamed down her face while her snot clotted her nose. She couldn't breathe. No air was coming in or out of her lungs.

She couldn't breathe.

With shaky fingers she desperately fumbled for the ignition key.

'Come on! Come on!' she wheezed, trying to get the window down, but it was all taking too long. Suddenly, she snapped the door open and exploded onto the pavement. Gasping with relief, she fell back against the car, surrendering to the cold and the rain.

She was sure Gill Baker's curtain at Number 23 twitched but she didn't care what the neighbours thought. She inhaled the cool damp air deep into her lungs, relishing the release of pressure from her chest.

A long inhale in and three counts out. Whoosh, into the grim evening air.

Within minutes she was drenched to the bone. The rain had soaked through her coat, saturating her suit jacket, sticking her white blouse to her skin like wallpaper paste. But for some irrational reason she couldn't pull herself away. As she looked on at her old home, Ava now saw past the imperfections, the problems, the heartbreak, and had an overwhelming urge to return to the security and comfort of her former life. All she wanted to do was crawl back into her old skin and start again.

The curtain at Number 23 was now violently moving back and forth as Mrs Baker pressed her nose against the living room window. Ava was sure she could hear the words 'What on earth is she doing?' Just as her husband opened the front door, sending out a triangle of light into the now dark evening sky, Ava's mobile started ringing.

It was the jolt she needed to get her back into her car.

She dived across the seat for her handbag in the footwell, the gearstick spearing her stomach, her feet dangling out of the driver's door.

'Hi sweetheart, I'm on my way!' She blurted breathlessly into the phone.

'I'm outside Auntie Em's. It's pissing down with rain. Where are you?'

Ava hated it when her daughter swore.

'I thought I was meeting you at the pub?'

'It was easier for me to dump my stuff first. How long are you going to be? It's cold and I'm getting wet and Em isn't home,' she whinged.

'That's because she's . . .'

'How long, Mum?'

Ava shut her eyes wearily. She wished, just once, Sophie would treat her with the same respect she gave her father. She loved her daughter but she hated how selfish she'd become. Ava wished she could be honest with her, tell her how much it hurt when she spoke to her dismissively, but she was too tired, too cold, too drained to put up a fight.

'Ten minutes, I won't be long.'

'Okay, hurry!'

As Ava shoved her phone back into her bag, still horizontal across both car seats, she noticed the letter had fallen out into the footwell. A large droplet of water trickled across her forehead, ran down her nose and hung at the tip like an icicle as she turned the envelope over.

Plop. The droplet landed on her name. Only it wasn't familiar. In fact, it seemed like a lifetime since she had read anything written in that language.

*Madame Chiltern.*

Her whole body stiffened.

Airmail from France. The stamp said the letter had come from Provence.

There was only one person she knew who lived there, and she hadn't spoken to him in over thirty years.

Her thoughts were startled by a loud clearing of the throat.

'Is everything okay in there?'

Ava craned her neck over her shoulder to see Mr Baker

hunched under his big black umbrella, peering down at her with a look of bewilderment.

'Yes, fine,' she squeaked, pushing herself into an upright position, pointlessly wiping the wet from her face with her saturated coat sleeve.

'Absolutely fine, nothing to see here,' She smiled with what she imagined were slightly wild, demented eyes.

'Right you are,' he nodded, taking a step back.

Embarrassed, Ava quickly closed the door, turned on the ignition, and put her foot on the accelerator. She tore off up the suburban street, away from her beloved home. The whole time, the white envelope on the passenger seat burned a hole in her mind.

# Chapter Four

**Provence, Summer 1985**

'I don't want to go!' Ava screamed until her little lungs rasped.

'Just do what you're told!' Her mum grabbed her wrist, fiercely, tugging her towards the car.

'Let go, let me go, GRANDPAPAAAAA!'

Her grandfather lunged for her but her mum thrust her body between them like a barricade.

'She's coming with me!' She hissed, inches from his face.

'Don't do this to the child, she needs to know.'

'Do you have *any* idea what he'll do to me?'

'What choice do you give me, I've tried everything else,' he held her shoulders but she shook him free, turning her back on her father, yanking open the back door of the battered maroon Citroen.

'Get in!' she barked at Ava.

'No, I don't want to leave Grandpapa,' Ava wailed, trying with all her might to wriggle free from her mum's grasp, but her fight was fruitless. Her mum shoved her into the back seat.

'Now wait here,' she pointed a finger at her face. 'Don't move. I'll be right back.' She slammed the door hard, the window rattling in its sleeve.

Ava's heart was hammering so rapidly, so loudly, she thought it would explode out of her chest. Yet she was too terrified to move, to even wind down the window to let air into the scorching oven of a car.

Instead, she watched in horror as her mum charged at her grandfather with the same pointed finger, jabbing it in the direction of his face, her mouth curled into a snarl.

Her eyes brimmed with tears as she watched her grandfather attempt to reason with her, holding his hands up with exasperation. Their voices were nothing more than angry muffles though the thick glass and steel doors. But her dear grandpapa was no match for the fury of her mum.

Eventually he stood down, taking a step back, shaking his head while her mum turned and marched towards the car. Her blue-and-white floaty dress clung to her thighs as she took long strides and she swore under her breath as she clambered into the driver's seat, violently slamming the door. Ava's mother sat perfectly still for a moment, breathing furious breaths, and then turned on the ignition. She crunched the car into gear, the tyres burning as she tore off back the way she had come. She ignored her daughter.

Ava twisted her body around, her fingers gripped over the top of the seat, her chin resting on her hands as she stared out of the back window at her grandfather, who disappeared into a haze of dust as the car tore up the dirt track.

Her mum sighed deeply. This time her voice was shaky with fear as she instructed: 'Not a word.' She then turned on the radio, drowning out Ava's sniffles.

**February 2018**

Sophie was perched uncomfortably on top of her small wheelie case in Emilia's porch, the fur-trimmed hood of her Parka jacket pulled over her head. She was scrolling impatiently through her mobile phone.

'What took you so long?' she demanded as soon as she clapped eyes on her mum.

Ava trudged up the garden path that carved the manicured lawn in two, modelling the drowned rat look again. Her hair was glued to her face, her skin sallow and blotchy and shadows crept away from her eyes. Her feet were making a ghastly noise as they squelched in her boots.

'And why are you so . . . wet?'

'Hi sweetheart!' Ava opened her arms to give Sophie a big welcoming squeeze.

'No, seriously, Mum, you're too damp to touch!'

'Thanks, darling.' Ava pulled the keys out of her bag and opened the front door of Emilia's expensive new-build.

Ava pointed to Sophie's military-style boots. 'Take those off, Auntie Em is very precious about her white carpet,' at which Sophie immediately rolled her eyes.

Sophie parked her suitcase in the middle of the hallway and made a beeline for the fridge.

'I'm bloody starving!'

'Oi, language, missy.'

Sophie pretended not to hear her as she rifled through the shelves of the fridge, picking everything out in turn and examining it.

'Doesn't she eat normal food?' she moaned, before settling on a bacteria-friendly yoghurt. She threw herself down onto Emilia's gigantic sofa, while Ava's thoughts returned to the letter in her hand. Half of her itched to open it, while the other half was fearful of what it might say.

She grabbed a hand towel, reappearing in the living room, scrubbing dry her bedraggled hair.

Sophie was now watching something on TV, her arms crossed. She had fully embraced the university shabby cool look with her hoodie jumper, ripped skinny jeans, her hair in a 'just got out of bed' messy top bun with tendrils hanging in front of her face. She looked up at her mum with her heavily kohl-outlined eyes.

'I don't like being here!'

Ava sighed deeply, as if her day hadn't been trying enough.

'Look, I know it's not ideal, but things haven't been easy, and . . .'

'I want our old house back. I know it's still for sale, can't you buy it back?'

'Honey, if only it were that easy.'

'Why can't it be that easy? Can't you find the money from somewhere? You must have something stashed away, I just don't understand how this could have happened.'

Ava and Mark had agreed to tell Sophie as little as possible about their financial mess to protect her. She didn't know the extent of her father's wheeling and dealing, how he'd even sunk to the depths of getting mixed up with loan sharks.

'And I hate that bitch dad is with. Gaaaaby. That's her stupid name, isn't it?'

Ava should have told her off for her swearing again but she decided to let this one go.

'She's got fake tits and she's had her lips done!'

Which was the moment Emilia walked into the room carrying a bag full of wine bottles.

'Who's got fake tits?' Emilia exclaimed, the bottles clinking against each other.

'Dad's new girlfriend. I hate her.'

'Ah.' Emilia exchanged looks with Ava.

Sophie picked up her mobile and returned to her scrolling.

'I don't know why you told Dad you wanted time apart, he wouldn't be with her if you hadn't said that,' she added, acidly, not looking up from her iPhone.

'Soph, don't speak to your mum like that,' Emilia shot her a warning.

'It's *her* fault! Dad says Mum's to blame. Why did you tell him that?'

There she went again, taking her father's side over her mother's. If anyone was to blame, Ava was, for not standing up for herself years ago. She felt all her resolve seeping away like a slow puncture. Emilia stuck up for her instead.

'Sophie, watch what you say. Don't believe everything your dad tells you. Your mum was right to take some time and he was with that tart long before that.'

Meanwhile Ava slipped quietly away into the dining room, her footsteps muted by the plush carpet.

'What? That's not true, is it?'

She sat down heavily in one of the cushion-backed chairs. Ava placed the letter on the glass tabletop and stared at it for a long moment.

'Mum?'

*It must be from him*, she thought. *Who else would be writing to her from Provence? But why now? Why after thirty-four years of silence?*

A sudden surge of adrenaline blasted through her as she ripped at the seal, excited at the thought that her beloved grandfather had finally got in touch. She removed the folded letter, shaking it free. That paper felt thick, crisp – expensive.

Her eyes locked onto the embossed letterhead of the French *notaire* – Sebastien Fabrice, and suddenly the bickering going on behind her slipped into the background as she read the words on the page.

Her face dropped.

It shouldn't have come as a surprise; he was ninety-three after all, but for some reason it did, and it was shaking her to the core. A sharp pain stabbed at her stomach, that horrible nauseous feeling when bad news catches you off guard.

'Mum?'

'Ava, hun?'

Ava looked around, her face the colour of the paper she was holding between her shaky fingers.

'Oh no!' Emilia gasped. 'What is it?'

Dazed, Ava replied softly. 'It's Grandpapa. He's died.'

She now had two voices coming at her. One consoling her, the other demanding answers to a flurry of questions that Ava couldn't quite decipher in her shocked state.

'I'm so sorry, hun,' Emilia whispered, tentatively.

'Is that the French great-grandfather I never met? Who you never talk about?' Sophie finally put her phone down and came towards her.

'Yes, sweetheart.'

Emilia was hot on her heels. 'On your mum's side?'

She nodded and mumbled something inaudible. She continued to stare numbly at the letter, her eyes glazing over while Sophie and Emilia took a seat either side of her at the table.

'Were you close?' Emilia asked gently.

Ava looked away, wistfully. 'We were once.'

'I'm sorry, Mum,' Sophie touched her arm.

'It's okay darling, thank you.'

Emilia peered over her shoulder. 'So, who is the letter from?'

'The *notaire.*'

Emilia stared at her blankly.

'The lawyers, it's an *Acte de Notoriété* . . . his will, confirming who his heirs are.'

Her eyes widened.

'It says my grandfather wrote me a personal letter.'

Emilia gasped. 'Bloody hell! Well, where is it?'

'Here!' Ava pulled out a second envelope from the original one. Only it was much smaller and faded yellow, as if it had spent years on a windowsill being bleached by the sun. It was unmarked except for her name, handwritten and underlined.

She held it between her fingers, the rough grain like sandpaper on her skin. She thought she could almost smell him, enmeshed into the paper.

Ava balked, suddenly afraid what it might say. Her grandfather's departure from her life when she was ten years old had been so abrupt, so shrouded in mystery, so upsetting. *Did the explanation lie before her now, finally?* She wasn't sure if she wanted to hear it.

Her mum had never again spoken of the day she had dragged Ava into the car and whisked her away from France. It had been like the elephant in the room for years to come.

'Are you going to open it?'

'Yeah Mum, what does it say?'

Ava's eyes flickered between her daughter and her best friend, and the old sun-beaten envelope she kept turning over in her hands.

'Do you want me to open it?' Emilia reached out.

Ava pulled it close to her chest. 'No, it's okay.' She took a deep breath and began gently slicing it open as if it were a historic artefact that might crumble in her hands.

She expected to pull out pages of her grandfather's handwritten scrawl explaining everything, but to her amazement there was simply a single sheet of paper.

Ava unfolded it, warily, while Emilia and Sophie studied her face for clues.

At the top was Château Saint-Clair's logo – a red cross. A tribute to the Knights Templar who had planted the vineyard hundreds of years before her grandfather took it over. Underneath that was the date; fifteen years earlier. Below was a great expanse of white paper and just a handful of sentences:

*My dearest Ava,*

*When you receive this letter, I will be gone.*

*Perhaps my spirit will live on in my beloved Château Saint-Clair.*

*I'm leaving my vineyard to you because I know you shared my love for it. I vividly remember our walks through the vines and when you walk there again, I hope you'll think of your grandfather sometimes.*

*With love,*
*Grandpapa*

Ava could almost hear her grandfather's voice, his strong French accent, gravelly from a lifetime of smoking cigars. She pictured him in his study, with a cup of black coffee by his side as the sunlight from the terrace streamed onto his desk. It would have been just after breakfast when he wrote her the letter, she imagined, as that was the time her grandfather always attended to his business.

It seemed a lifetime ago; the memories blurred by everything that had happened between then and now. The domesticity of her life with Mark and Sophie was so different to the magical summers she used to spend at the vineyard when she was a child.

'I can't believe it,' she whispered.

'What?' Emilia and Sophie both gasped.

'This can't be right.'

'What is it? Are you a multimillionaire?!' Emilia's eyes looked as if they were going to pop out with excitement.

'Come on, Mum, what does it say?'

Ava cleared the lump that had risen in her throat. 'It says I've inherited Château Saint-Clair.'

'A French castle?' Emilia spluttered.

'No, Grandpapa's house and vineyard in Provence.'

Ava finally looked up, in disbelief. 'What am I going to do with a vineyard?'

'SELL IT!' Sophie shrieked.

Emilia guffawed. 'Don't be daft. She's going to get drunk on all the fabulous wine.'

'I'm serious, Mum, sell it! You can use the money to buy back our house and get Dad back.'

'She doesn't want your dad back,' Emilia corrected her.

With the adrenaline of the anticipation over, Ava seemed to wilt back into the seat, still shaking her head with bewilderment and whispering 'Why me?'

Sophie started sniffling with the onset of tears. 'Please, Mum. I just want us to be a family again.'

That familiar feeling of anxiety returned, squeezing Ava's chest tighter and tighter. 'Honey, I just need time to—'

'Time to think? Just like you told Dad you needed time?' Sophie suddenly rose to her feet, pushing her chair back with such force that it nearly toppled over.

'Where are you going?' Ava and Emilia both chimed.

'To meet Carly.'

'Where are you staying tonight?'

'With Carly.' Sophie screwed up her nose. 'Because I don't have a home any more.' She spat out the words childishly, her tears having suddenly evaporated.

'I said you could stay with Auntie Em.'

Sophie blanked her mum's offer. As she turned to leave, her face crumpled again. 'Please Mum, please will you get our house back, it's *our home.*'

37

She slammed the front door so hard both Ava and Emilia jumped.

After a long restorative silence Emilia let out a whistling sigh.

'Wine?'

One hour later and three glasses down the hatch, Ava had revealed how she used to spend her summers at Château Saint-Clair helping her grandfather make his award-winning rosé. Her mum and dad would drop her off there and pick her up at the end of August. And then it all fell apart.

'Bloody hell, mate!' Emilia exhaled. 'So you still have no idea why your mum dragged you away that day. It's a shame you can't ask her.'

Ava was just seventeen when she lost her mum to an aggressive cancer. Not long after, she met Mark. He had been her rock, putting her back together when she was broken with grief.

'Even if mum was still alive, I don't think she would tell me,' her brow knitted, 'it was this big family secret I was never allowed to mention.' She strained her eyes. 'My memory, it's all so hazy. I remember picking the grapes, the sunshine, the fun I had, but everything else is blurry.'

'And your dad? Would he know?'

'Ha!' she snorted. Ava hadn't spoken to him for almost as long as her grandfather. He'd walked out on her mum when she was fourteen. She didn't know where in the world he was, nor did she care to know. Ava clenched her jaw angrily at the thought of him and how he used to make her mum cry.

'And your grandmother?'

'I never had the chance to meet her. She died long before I was born. Grandpapa never remarried, he was too in love with her memory.'

Emilia knocked back another slug of wine. Wiping the traces from her top lip, she exclaimed: 'You own a bloody vineyard! Let's just stop to appreciate this for a moment.'

Ava gave her head a shake as if the full meaning of it hadn't fully percolated yet.

'What's more you own a vineyard that's won awards, that's made loads of money. You can start again.' She grabbed Ava's hands and shook them. 'This is your chance to start over!'

'Um, I . . .' Ava hesitated. The thought of venturing out into the world alone suddenly terrified her.

'What do I know about wine?'

'How hard can it be?' Emilia picked up her glass again, examining it millimetres from her nose so all Ava could see was a huge magnified eye. She swirled the pink liquid around, plunged her nostrils inside and inhaled deeply, noisily.

'Smells good to me,' Emilia tipped a third of her drink into her mouth, winced, and grinned. She puckered her lips joyfully. 'Yep, tastes great.'

Ava shook her head. 'I'm not sure. I know I should be excited but . . .'

But maybe her daughter was right. The vineyard could be a way of getting their house back. It could bring Mark home. The idea of starting over was so scary it was driving Ava to think irrationally, and act illogically.

'I'd better let Mark know the news,' she announced, reaching for her mobile.

Emilia lunged, sploshing wine everywhere.

'Wait!' She pulled the phone from Ava's hands.

'He should know, he's still my husband.'

'Think this through carefully.' Emilia stared into her eyes. 'Have you forgotten already what a mess he's left you in?

He's forfeited any right to know what's going on with you. Not to mention that woman he's dropped you for.'

'Thanks for reminding me.'

'I'm serious, hun, this is your inheritance and you don't want Mark getting his hands on it. He'll only fritter it away and you'll be left with nothing.'

Ava tucked a tendril of her overgrown fringe behind her ear, her eyes now glued to a spot on the floor.

'Ava?'

Emilia softened. 'Just do something for me. Go out there and see how you feel. Take a holiday. Just let yourself be! And I bet you won't want to come home.'

'I'm not fearless like you.' She shook her head. 'I don't have the strength right now.' Ava pulled her grandfather's handwritten letter close to her chest.

'I just don't think I can.'

# Chapter Five

'I can't believe you've packed everything into one suitcase!' Emilia stared in disbelief.

'What do you mean? I'm only going for a few days to do what you suggested, you know, see how I feel,' Ava mocked.

'You're going for a few days to *Provence*.'

Ava looked at her best friend cluelessly.

'To the Côte d'Azur?!'

She was still none-the-wiser.

'To the home of St Tropez, Nikki beach, Cannes. You should have packed at least three outfit changes a day! You never know who you're going to meet. You might bump into a hot French stud sauntering along the beach.'

She waved her ring finger in front of Emilia's nose. 'I'm m-a-r-r-i-e-d!'

Emilia scoffed.

'What?'

'Oh nothing, I just want you to look the best version of you.' She smiled innocently.

The tannoy bleated, announcing a final call for baggage check-in. A family of five suddenly sprang into life, sprinting across the airport concourse, dragging their suitcases behind them. There was noise and chaos everywhere.

Trolleys ramming into heels, people searching for their passports, kids screaming with the excitement of going on holiday. And all at an eye-wateringly early time in the morning. Ava was catching the first EasyJet flight to Nice simply because it was the cheapest one going. She didn't have the luxury of choice, Mark had made sure of that. She thanked her friend for dropping her off while it was still dark outside.

'Don't mention it, hun. I wanted to make sure you got on the plane! I'd be coming with you if it wasn't for my job.'

'And Paul?'

'Oh yeah, I forgot about him,' she winked playfully. 'Although he understands I'm a magpie to everything bling like the super-yachts in St Tropez.' Looking even more mischievous, Emilia added: 'Do you remember when we used to go out and get hammered?'

Ava smiled as she thought back to the nights they used to stagger home along the country lanes to their parents' houses, barefoot, their ridiculously high heels dangling by their straps from their fingers. Their attempts to flag down any taxi failing miserably because no one wanted two teenagers on the cusp of vomiting in the back of their car.

The past felt like another world to Ava now.

'Well, if you stay in Provence a bit longer and give me a little notice so I can take time off, we can go for a long overdue girly night out!'

Ava giggled at her best friend's persistence. A sweet girly laugh that so rarely bubbled out of her mouth these days. 'I'll be back before you . . .'

'What am I talking about?' Emilia interrupted, throwing her hands up. 'We won't need to go out, you own a bloody vineyard! We can raid your grandfather's cellar!'

'Right,' Ava's eyes lifted to the departure board for her flight to Nice, putting an end to Emilia's trouble-making.

'I'm going to miss you,' Emilia confessed, pulling out a box of cigarettes from her handbag, on hand for as soon as she walked out of the sliding doors.

'Bad habit!'

'I know, I know, but it's one of my few little pleasures in the morning, along with an espresso. It's not healthy to deny yourself what your body craves. Come here,' Emilia pulled her in for one of her comforting hugs.

They said their goodbyes by the luggage check-in desks, a moment of calm and silence amid the pandemonium.

'I guess I'd better get a move on,' she hung her head.

Emilia nodded. 'This is going to be incredible.'

'Really?'

'Yes! You're venturing into the heart of the stunning French countryside.'

'In winter,' Ava mumbled.

'In spring!' Emilia corrected. 'You're going back to a place where you once were very happy and where you can be happy again. This is it, I can feel it.'

Ava looked at her heavily.

'Honestly, trust me. What do they say, carpe diem!'

'Huh?'

'Seize the day, babe. This is your day.'

'God, you sound more like my boss by the minute.'

Speaking of her boss, Ava had managed to haggle three consecutive days off with the proviso she worked every Saturday for the next month. Gary was so ruthless, it was hard to believe he had a pulse.

'And I know it couldn't have been easy disappointing Sophie,' Emilia added.

Ava grimaced. 'She doesn't know. She thinks I'm going out there to get a valuation on the property.'

'Well, what's a little white lie . . .' Emilia fanned away the problem with her hand. 'And Mark?'

'I haven't told him anything. Actually, I still haven't heard from him.' Her shoulders sagged.

'Good!'

Noticing Ava's face drop, Emilia elaborated: 'I mean it's good for your current mission. Remember, you want to keep your cards close to your chest. I suppose Soph might tell him?'

'I asked her to keep it a secret for now, but . . .' she shrugged.

'Well there isn't much more you can do to stop her. But if he does come asking, keep shtum.'

Ava nodded.

'This is your time now. Just think about you.'

Ava squeezed out a smile.

'Be strong! Now go!' Emilia directed whilst tugging a cigarette out of the box with her teeth.

'Call me!' she shouted over her shoulder, already striding towards the exit, her voice muffled by the cigarette wedged into the corner of her mouth.


The thud of the plane wheels on the runway shook her awake. For a split second she had forgotten she was heading to France. No wait, she was in France now. She was really here, she thought, staring out onto the grey tarmac.

She massaged her spasming neck, which had been crooked against the window for her entire snooze. She took a long restorative swig from the dregs of her water bottle, washing away her desert of a mouth. She flicked the dry crusts from the corner of her lips and looked sideways. The man in the neighbouring seat was looking at her with utter disgust.

'Morning!' she squeaked. He grunted.

The seatbelt sign was extinguished and the scrabble for the overhead bags began.

Ava sank back into her window seat letting the madness pass over her, wondering if it was normal to feel so unenthusiastic about getting off a plane. She was in France. *En vacance.* Three whole days away from her dick of a boss and all she wanted to do was go back to sleep. This couldn't be right. Was she sick?

But despite a heroic attempt to quietly remain seated until the return flight home, the satsuma-skinned air hostess eventually prodded Ava into life, stabbing her fingers around her feet as she searched for rubbish. Ava handed her the water bottle and reluctantly heaved herself into motion.

She shuffled like a zombie along the aisle, towards the front exit. She yawned and stepped blindly off the plane – into a blaze of sunshine.

Ava blinked wildly, acclimatising to the glorious morning weather. It was a world away from the drizzle and murk of London. The sky was a vivid shade of blue and completely cloudless. As she clambered down the metal stairs onto the runway, a soft breeze kissed her skin. It was fresh and warm and smelt of the sea.

Overcome with the foreign feeling of warmth, Ava paused to undo the toggles of her duffle coat. She craned her head to the sky and closed her eyes, melting into the moment. She was almost enjoying herself when a mini suitcase rolled over her toe, jolting her back into reality.

'Oww!' she yelped.

'Pardon!' The French lady barely apologised, tugging at her stubborn wheelie case.

'Welcome to France,' Ava grumbled to herself.

\*

There was one café in the Arrivals hall in Nice Airport, and only two choices on the board – coffee and pastries. The menu reflected the typically French 'take it or leave it' attitude.

The woman serving behind the counter mirrored that vibe too.

'Madame?' she grouched, without a trace of a smile.

Slightly wrong-footed, Ava stuttered: 'Yes, I mean, *oui*, I mean, *Je voudrais un café noir, s'il vous plait.*'

It was hardly sophisticated French but Ava felt taken aback by the ease in which it flowed off her tongue. As if it had always been there, buried somewhere in the back of her mind from her childhood.

The dark-haired cashier stared at her expressionlessly before squashing her efforts. 'One black coffee. Anything else?'

Crestfallen, Ava pointed to the croissant.

She took a seat by the huge windows overlooking the taxi rank, and savoured her pastry. It probably wasn't any different to the one she could pick up in Pret but somehow it tasted 'French'. The butteriness of it, the way it pulled apart like candy floss. For a brief moment, all her problems slipped into the background as she was lost in a wave of gastronomic heaven.

But her joy was quickly followed by a sharp pang of missing Mark. It was more like a jab in the ribs, it left her feeling so winded. One minute Ava was savouring her croissant, the next she was thinking how she would have torn it in two so Mark could taste how delicious it was. *This should have been a little getaway for both of us*, she thought. They should be sharing the adventure together – exploring the French countryside, Ava showing Mark where some of her happiest memories were made.

Suddenly, Ava felt compelled to hear Mark's voice. The urge overcame any feelings of resentment or anger she still had.

She dug her mobile out of her bag and dialled her husband.

With every ring, her heart thumped louder in her ears. She was afraid he wouldn't answer her again.

Worse, Mark cut her off! The answerphone kicked in early and Ava quickly ended the call before she left an awkward squawk and slumped back into her seat, steeling herself not to cry. She knew it was completely masochistic, but no matter what she did she couldn't scrub the image of Mark with Gabby, who was obviously more beautiful than her, thinner than her, younger than her. The thought of her draped across his chest while they lay in bed, their fingers entwined, imprinted itself onto her brain.

'Go away! Go away! Go away!' Ava shook her head, trying to scatter the painful thoughts across the café.

But she couldn't stop her imagination from whirring, from conjuring up storylines until she was lost in a toxic cloud that felt so poisonous it made her feel physically sick. Ava pushed what was left of the croissant away.

Every part of her being wanted to send Mark a highly emotive message to provoke a reaction. To take his attention away from *her*. Or the business meeting, or the client he was schmoozing or whatever it was that was more important than trying to win her back.

She furiously tapped at her keys. Against Emilia's advice, she wrote:

*My grandad has died. I'm in France dealing with his estate. It's all very upsetting . . .*

Just as she was about to press send, her friend's voice snapped into her head, 'Keep your cards close to your chest for now.'

Knowing Emilia was right, she reluctantly erased the words and replaced them with an equally needy message, just with less information:

*I need you. Please call me.*

# Chapter Six

'Sorry! I mean *Pardon*. I mean, Bugger! Bugger!'

Ava smacked the indicator left and then right and then slammed on the brakes just in time to allow the car charging head on towards her to swerve out of the way. She could barely look at the driver who was cursing and shaking his fist at her.

'*Merci Monsieur*,' she smiled sweetly at him for reminding her she was now in France and had to drive on the other side of the road. She then sank into her seat, her heart hammering from her near-death experience.

Thank God she was still doing loops around the airport carpark trying to find the exit rather than on the motorway, she thought, trying to look on the bright side.

She took a deep breath and tried again. This time on the right-hand side of the road.

A few engine restarts and bunny hops later, she had somehow managed to survive the one-way system and several roundabouts to reach the turn-off.

She was actually getting the hang of this. It was such a small achievement but for some reason it gave her a huge burst of confidence.

Ava felt a rush of adrenaline as she pressed her foot down on the accelerator and glided onto the motorway.

It had been three decades since she was last in Provence and all she could remember was staring out of the car window, her nose rubbing smudge marks on the glass as she watched the fields morph into cities and back into fields again on the endless drive from Calais to the south of France. By the time her bickering parents had arrived at the vineyard it would have been dark and Ava would have been asleep.

She was seeing Provence with fresh eyes, the countryside covered in a blanket of glorious morning sunshine.

According to the sat nav, Château Saint-Clair was a forty-five-minute drive inland from the coast. With every passing mile the landscape seemed to transform into something more dramatic. The dry scrubland grew into greener, taller, more impressive truffle oaks whose branches were budding with spring leaves. The fields rose up into mountainous passes, scattered with olive groves. And as she turned off in the direction of the town of Flassans-sur-Issole, she was met with the magical sight of row upon row of grapevines.

This was the real heart of winemaking country. Almost every field that lined the meandering road was filled with orderly rows of vines, perfectly spaced apart, precisely tethered by wire and posts.

Now far away from the motorway fumes, Ava wound down her window and inhaled the fresh country air into her lungs. It smelt of leaves and herbs and a touch of lavender, although she might have imagined that bit, knowing she was also in the epicentre of the lavender-growing area.

The closer she drew to Château Saint-Clair, the quieter, more winding and narrower the roads became until Ava started to worry whether she was lost. She hadn't seen a house for miles, or a petrol station, or a living being. Had her grandfather really lived in the middle of nowhere for all these years?

But despite the thought of impending isolation for the next few days, Ava felt something extraordinarily foreign

– excitement. She was really, genuinely, heart-skippingly excited about see her grandfather's vineyard.

Everything at Château Saint-Clair had moved in sync, in a wonderfully relaxed sun-drenched way.

Ava had spent her days, from dawn to dusk, tearing around outdoors like a brazen tomboy. Her evenings would be filled with laughter and delicious food as everyone gathered around the table for supper. Her grandpapa was the heart and soul of the community and there would be a constant rotation of his friends, coming and going. Other winemakers, musicians, even local dignitaries. They would bring bread and dessert and mouth-watering home-made dishes – so much food Ava could barely lift herself from the table afterwards. It was the only time she could remember feeling happy growing up, feeling that she belonged to a family, the sort of loving warm existence her friends at school would describe.

It was painfully hard saying goodbye to her mum and dad that first summer, waving them off as their car disappeared down the long driveway. But over the years, as the fights between her parents grew worse, as they became more venomous and frightening, soon all she looked forward to were her summers with her grandpapa.

And just when she'd come to look on Château Saint-Clair as her only sanctuary in the world, it was snatched away from her.

Ava slammed on the brakes.

'This can't be right!' she muttered, punching the buttons on the sat nav with her forefinger.

It was telling her the entrance to the vineyard was a pothole-ridden dirt track up a steep hill overgrown with thorny-looking plants that would scratch her hire car to smithereens.

She drove on, ignoring the computerised woman's voice insisting she make a U-turn.

'*Attention. Vous avez passé votre destination!*'

She passed several more dirt tracks.

'*Attention! Attention! Attention!*' The woman's voice became increasingly persistent and irritating until Ava finally snapped and turned off her stuttering commands.

Now all alone, in the middle of nowhere, Ava reached deep into the archives of her memory to see if she could pick out anything that looked familiar.

But after several minutes of soul-searching, Ava had to admit defeat and begrudgingly took the irritating woman's advice, and made a U-turn.

As Ava twisted and turned her way back along the country lane, she began to regret not pulling into the petrol station for food supplies. At this rate, it was going to be dinner time before she got there.

She slammed on the brakes again, the gears grinding as she threw the car into reverse. She could have sworn she saw something.

The little Fiat 500 whined as it backtracked up the now all-too-familiar road and then came to a halt at a fork.

A victorious smile crept across Ava's mouth. It was half hidden by more of those thorny-looking plants, but it was her grandfather's swirly handwriting all right. 'Château Saint-Clair this way'. She remembered the afternoon he had carefully painted the lettering onto the white-washed wooden board. Ava had been itching to help, getting under her grandpapa's feet until he finally gave in and let her paint the top coat of varnish.

She shoved the car into gear again, indicating to her right, although Ava had no idea why she just did that considering she hadn't passed another car for what seemed like hours.

A flutter of excitement passed through her as she started off along the track. Every bend in the road brought back another memory.

She remembered it taking forever to reach the château but she'd forgotten the bumps. Ava put her rally-car driving skills to the test as she swerved around the potholes and bounced over the tree roots, leaving a cloud of chalky dust billowing in her wake.

She drove into a tunnel of trees, their branches arching over her, the sunlight dappling through the new leaves. Her heart skipped more than one beat as she saw the bright expanse of light ahead.

She was seconds from reaching the point at which the vines began. She remembered the fields she used to race through, sprinting up and down the rows of grapes until she ran out of puff and collapsed onto her back, staring up at the blue sky.

Ava squinted into the blinding glare.

But as her eyes readjusted, she continued blinking.

Had she made another wrong turn?

The vineyard that stretched in front of her looked like a bleak forgotten landscape.

The vines were growing at jagged angles. Some had fallen from their posts and were crawling along the soil rather than reaching for the sky.

She slowed the car, taking in everything that it wasn't any more. It looked sad, unloved and uncared for. It wasn't the place she remembered.

Her grandfather had kept the vines in tip-top condition. Of course he hadn't managed it alone, he always had a small army of people working for him, overseen by his head gardener, Bernard. Ava could remember Bernard clearly. Square-jawed, stubbly, rugged as the landscape and permanently coated in a dusting of the chalky earth. He used to tell Ava off for eating the unripe grapes.

'*Tu vas etre malade!*' You will get sick, he'd shout after her as she scampered back to the house. Ava would run to her grandfather for a consoling bear hug only for him to tease her that it wasn't the unripeness she needed to watch out for but the pips! 'They will grow vines in your tummy!' he would exclaim in his exuberant way. She would stare at him wide-eyed, her childish imagination conjuring up images of stringy vines sprouting out of her mouth and ears until he finally broke into a belly laugh.

'Don't worry, child. The grapes will not harm you, they are the nectar of this earth!'

His comforting words were like a protective armour and from then on whenever she was told off by Bernard, to his immense irritation, she would flash him a cheeky smile to say she knew better.

Ava never did get sick from eating too many grapes. In fact she proudly attributed her iron-clad stomach to those early years of acidity, pips and bugs, although it probably had nothing to do with that at all.

But as she drove on, her happiness dissipated. She began to dread what would be around the next corner, feeling resentful that her sunlit memories were being stamped out by what she was seeing now.

She took a breath as she turned into the courtyard, the sand and stones crackling underneath the tyres as she circled the great mulberry tree in the centre. *At least that was still there.*

Coming to a standstill, she wrenched up the handbrake, turned off the engine and sat quietly for a moment, deflated, vaguely considering whether to turn around before more happy thoughts were spoilt.

But the spring heat, magnified through the windscreen, soon flushed Ava out of the Fiat.

She shook her legs awake, stretched and pulled off her thick lilac cable-knit jumper, exposing her milk-white arms to the gentle sun. She tied the jumper in a knot around the waist of her jeans, and reluctantly made her way towards the house.

Ava thought it peculiar how the French call some vineyards 'château' when they are really little more than a country house. She supposed it added that feeling of grandeur and heritage associated with French wines.

All these years later, her grandfather's 'château', although considerably bigger than her semi in Surbiton, seemed smaller than she remembered.

The stone-walled house hugged the courtyard in an L shape. She circled the two-storey building, inspecting it as if she were a property developer. The gutters were loose, tiles were missing. The once emerald-green shutters were faded and mildewy. Several were broken and had holes, the edges jagged as if someone had hurled stones through them.

With no one else around, it felt utterly desolate.

Hesitantly, she carried on with her inspection, heading towards the pool at the back of the house. The walk there used to be Ava's favourite of all. She would pass half a dozen terraces, each tier like passing through an enchanted garden.

Closest to the house was the maze of knee-high hedges, which when she had been here thirty years ago were perfectly manicured, neat squares and rectangles surrounded by huge ceramic urns. Her grandfather collected animal statues and her favourite was the dancing hare in the fountain.

The hedges had sprouted into overgrown blobs. One urn was missing, another had fallen onto its side and the fountain had dried up. The once sprightly hare looked like it had contracted some incurable disease, its grey stone fur blotchy with patches of dark lichen.

Ava crossed her arms protectively as she walked on. She could hardly bring herself to look at the shrivelled herbs at her feet. The once magnificent kitchen garden had boasted every herb under the sun – sage, thyme, rosemary, tarragon, dill – separated by balls of lavender. The bouquet of scents would rush up Ava's nose when she rocketed her way down the cobbled path to the swimming pool.

After everything she had seen so far, it shouldn't have come as a surprise. Yet it still pained her to see the derelict pool. The place where she had playfully splashed around, where she had learned to swim, was now just an empty shell with a tide mark of filth where the water had slowly evaporated and a brown slush of leaves and grot lurking at the bottom.

The white sunloungers were folded and piled against each other, coated in mud splatters from the storms they had weathered.

As Ava's eyes flickered between the derelict pool, the overgrown gardens and the run-down house, a plastic plant pot cartwheeled past her in a gust of wind, like tumbleweed. Ava felt like she had walked onto the set of a Western, only in the Côte d'Azur.

She stood there in disbelief, wondering how the vineyard could have fallen into such disrepair in such a short space of time. The solicitors had told her that grandpapa had passed away three months ago. She was staring at years' worth of neglect.

She couldn't start a new life here. How? It would cost thousands to bring it back to its former glory. Ava swallowed the dreaded thought as she retraced her steps to the house, terrified of what lay behind the front door.

# Chapter Seven

Ava lifted the stone on the porch, relieved to find the key she'd instructed the *notaire* to leave out for her.

She turned the key in the lock and gave the door a push. It barely budged.

Tired, deflated and angry, Ava took out her frustration on the stubborn wood, which looked like it had become warped through the seasons.

She rammed her shoulder at the front door with all her might.

Miscalculating quite how much force she needed, Ava tumbled headlong into the hallway.

'Right then!' she muttered, dusting herself off.

She looked up and was surprised.

She had been expecting desolation, but the place didn't look so much run-down as put on ice, as if waiting for someone to arrive. Dust sheets covered everything. Wandering between the study and the living room she occasionally lifted the corner of a starchy white cloth to reassure herself the familiar furniture was still there. The brown leather sofa she would curl up on, the standing light behind her grandfather's reading chair, the antique chaise longue that Ava had been forbidden to lie across because it was only for grown-ups. And the floor-to-ceiling bookshelf that held an assortment of battered board games, incomplete jigsaws and her grandpapa's favourite novels; the ones he used to read to her at bedtime.

Despite being all alone, in a big echoing house where nobody would hear her, the silence was making Ava want to tiptoe. As she stepped lightly towards the kitchen, the place exploded with a sudden noise.

Ava's heart almost jumped out of her chest with fright. She spun around to the sight of the cuckoo clock, crowing at her.

Bong. Cuck-ooo. Bong. Cuck-ooo.

It was five o'clock already?

But what puzzled Ava even more than how she had managed to lose track of time in what was fast becoming the Bermuda Triangle of Provence, was *why* the cuckoo was speaking to her. Someone must have kept him wound up, because she clearly remembered her grandfather cursing under his breath every time he had to wind up the clock.

A shiver went down her spine.

About time she put on her lilac jumper again, Ava decided, unfastening it from her waist.

She stepped blindly into the kitchen as she threaded her head through the oversized knit. As she brushed the strands of hair from her eyes, Ava was met with an even creepier sight.

There, on the big wooden farmhouse table where they used to share their family meals, was what she could only describe as a care package.

Neatly arranged in the centre was a collection of tins of food, a glass jar with teabags and a carton of long-life milk.

Ava gingerly edged towards the table as if the unlikely bundle on top might be a bomb waiting to detonate.

She paused before ticking herself off for being such a scaredy-cat and reached a more confident hand out to examine the contents of the cans.

There were lots of vegetables: haricots verts, petits pois, sweetcorn, cornichons and . . .

'What's this?' Ava held the large can up to the light. 'Roasted duck in a tin?' She'd never seen that on the supermarket shelves in Tesco.

She double-checked the table for a note, half expecting there to be a little handwritten sign saying 'Eat Me' just like in *Alice in Wonderland* but there was nothing there.

*It was all very creepy.* Who had left out this food?

She opened the glass jar of teabags, stuck her nose in and inhaled the scent.

And who had been thoughtful enough to leave out British tea? An avid tea drinker, Ava was a master in distinguishing the difference between the European and English varieties. She could smell Tetley leaves a mile off.

There was also a tin opener, a plate and a knife and fork, all laid out neatly. For her? Or was someone else in the house?

Something in her gut was telling Ava it was all for her. But judging by the fact no dust had settled on the plate, or the tins, Ava deduced it couldn't have been left out by her grandfather.

Another, much more sinister shiver ran through her.

Not surprisingly, she was a little reticent about investigating the upstairs. But her rational head told her it was better to uncover the axe murderer now while it was still light, rather than in the middle of the night.

She went back to the hallway and peered nervously up the stairs. Swallowing hard, Ava placed a tentative foot on the first step. It creaked loudly under her trainer. Up she went, cautiously, making her way along the curving staircase to the second floor. The dark wooden steps, uneven due to years of use, moaned under the pressure.

At the top of the stairs was a huge white sheet covering what she remembered to be the mirrored oak cupboard where the linen was kept. Ava was grateful she wasn't a child any more as it could have looked like a towering ghost to an overactive imagination. She peered underneath, just to double-check it wasn't a giant wearing a dust sheet. Thankfully all was still as it used to be. She made a mental note to return to collect some fresh bedding.

The long corridor was dark but there was still enough daylight to make out the detail on the paintings lining her path. They were landscapes of the vineyard, oil paintings of sunsets and sunrises and ripe juicy grapes, all splashed with vibrant colour. It made Ava smile, as they captured the way she used to see her summers at Château Saint-Clair.

Three doors along and she was standing outside her old room. Ava turned the handle; the door groaned as if the hinges hadn't moved in decades. As she stepped inside, she held up her hand like a visor to the glare.

The golden setting sun was streaming through the big windows and onto the . . .

'What the hell?' Ava gasped.

She blinked twice, in disbelief at the sight of a beautifully made-up bed.

Ava looked around, apprehensively, expecting someone to appear at any moment shouting 'Surprise!'

But no one emerged from the shadows. It was just her, all alone, in a dismantled house that creaked and moaned, where her bed was made and her dinner laid out on the kitchen table.

Now it was dark, the temperature had plummeted.

Ava sat at the kitchen table, shivering, prodding the limp saturated vegetables and shredded duck with her fork.

Luckily the electricity and gas were still working but she had no idea how to switch the heater on. She wasn't sure if there was even a boiler.

She unhooked her duffle coat from the back of the chair and wrapped herself into it like a blanket. Sitting at the kitchen table where she once shared so many happy meals, eating warmed-up canned food in her coat, was sending Ava back into depression, and driving her towards that all-too-familiar feeling of missing Mark. She hadn't heard a peep out of him since she had messaged that morning. She was now staring at her phone, willing it to ping, contemplating whether to send him a follow-up text and then balking at the thought of feeling rejected again. It was unbearable. Ava knew she should feel furious at him for not responding to a message that clearly stated I NEED YOU. But instead, in her lonely, vulnerable, cold state, all she wanted was a hug.

With the thought of a long bleak evening stretching out in front of her, Ava decided to take herself off to bed early. She plonked her dishes in the sink to deal with in the morning and traipsed back up the creaky stairs to her bedroom.

She left the light in the corridor on, just as a precaution to ward off any ghosts that might be floating around the château. She climbed into bed and pulled the duvet up to her nose. With all her worries whirring around her head, Ava assumed she'd struggle to fall asleep, but as soon as her head hit the pillow, her eyelids grew heavy and rolled down for the night like shutters. She blindly reached her hand across and switched off the bedside light. Within minutes, Ava was sound asleep snuggled in her soft and lumpy but nostalgically comforting childhood bed.

*

They were stifled, but she could still hear that horrible asphyxiating sound of someone trying to strangle their sobs. Her ears were as sensitive as a mouse's, attuned to even the slightest change of vibration in her home. She crept along the landing, her bare feet padding across the swirly patterned carpet, past the buttermilk walls to the spare bedroom, where the door was ajar. Ava pushed the handle, just a smidgen, enough to see into the gloomy room. The curtains were drawn against the daylight and her mum was perched on the end of the bed, hunched over, her fingers shakily turning the pages of a book. Every part of her wanted to burst in and throw her arms around her mum's neck, hugging her, making her feel loved. But something much more powerful was holding her back. A fear that she would be walking into a secret place to which she hadn't been invited. A dark cave her mum insisted on returning to, each time leaving another piece of herself behind there.

The floor squeaked, Ava's heart almost stopped. Her mum swung her head around. She slammed the photo album shut and hissed: 'What are you doing here?'

Ava looked at her blankly.

'You can't tell your father I've been here,' she warned, slipping the book underneath the bed with fear in her voice.

Ava nodded.

As soon as she saw the dusky red cover she knew it was the album of Provence. Tentatively, she asked: 'When will we see Grandpapa again?'

Her mum looked away.

'Mummy?'

'You need to forget your grandfather. Your life is here now, with me and your father.'

'But Mummy?'

'Please, Ava,' she insisted.

*But Mummy. But Mummy. But Mummy*, the words were caught on repeat. Ava lurched awake from her nightmare.

For a moment, she had absolutely no idea where she was. She was in a dark, creaky, mothball-smelling room, covered in a film of sweat.

She threw the sheets off, only to be hit with a similarly distressing whoosh of cold air.

'Bloody hell,' she squealed, hiding back beneath the duvet. Suddenly she sobered up to the reality of her situation.

It was 3.30 a.m. and the temperature in the room felt like it had plummeted to sub-zero, and there seemed to be some strange noise coming from downstairs . . . *Oh my God, there it was again.* Ava pushed herself upright, her heart thundering.

Almost too afraid to listen, she was frozen to the spot with fear and cold, unsure what to do next, and there is was again. *Oh my God, Oh bloody hell* . . . Ava dived back under the duvet.

She could hear the sound of her panicked breathing in her ears.

But a feather duvet wasn't enough to insulate her from the sound of whatever the hell was going on downstairs. The noise echoed through the house, up the stairs, along the corridor, into her room . . .

Ava's imagination was running wild. But cursing and panicking, she soon realised, quickly used up all the oxygen and she was forced to come up for air. She rose out of the sheets, gasping.

She sat there panting for a moment, her eyes flickering left to right as she scanned the room for murderers or ghosts or

63

strange people who lurk around in the countryside making beds and laying placemats.

Did she lock the front door? She couldn't remember.

There were two choices. Hide in her room and hope for the best. Or find out what was making that noise.

There really was only one sensible option, but something inside Ava was willing her to be brave. She reasoned if she didn't go and have a look, she wouldn't be able to get back to sleep with that racket going on.

She counted herself down from three and threw off the bedspread, sending a whoosh of cold air against her skin. Ava wriggled her feet into her trusty Ugg Boots, which she had packed as her replacement slippers, and put on her jumper over her PJs. Armed with the torch on her phone, she was now ready for anything.

Ava felt safe under the protection of the corridor light but the warm glow had all but disappeared as she reached the bottom of the stairs. Her heart was thudding in her chest as Ava stared into a pool of inky blackness. She was used to suburbia, where the street lights shone through the living-room window. But the countryside was something else. It was so pitch black she could barely make out her hands in front of her.

She jumped almost an inch off the ground as the banging returned. The whole house shuddered, the window panes rattled, the roof creaked and moaned and enough was enough . . .

Ava steeled herself, flicked on her torch and began her journey across the living room in search of the light switch. Caught in the beam of her torch, the dust sheets looked like ghosts floating around the room. She wanted to yank them all to the ground, but first things first.

The banging grew louder as she neared the kitchen.

Her heart hammered more wildly as she stepped closer to what could be her final minutes on earth.

In one swooping motion, she smacked the switch on the wall.

As the kitchen burned into brightness, Ava wanted to scream 'GOT YA'.

But she would have found herself talking to the furniture as she realised the banging was nothing more than a loose shutter.

She pressed the palms of her hands into her eyes and let out a tension-relieving 'Arrrrrrgh'. She then burst into a fit of slightly delirious laughter.

Still smiling, Ava opened the window above the sink and reached on her tiptoes to grab the flapping shutter. She fastened it, closed the window and breathed a sigh of relief.

'I can handle this being alone malarkey!' Ava applauded herself for her bravery. If someone had told her a week ago that she would have been investigating strange noises in the night in a creaky house in the middle of nowhere, she would have thought they were having her on.

She poured a glass of water to relieve her parched mouth, took an enormous gulp and then almost choked as her swallow reflex froze.

*Oh God, Oh God, what was that?* she screamed internally as she sensed something move behind her.

Her eyes watered as she tried to suppress a fit of coughing and spluttering. But her fight was futile as she was forced to give in to her heaving chest, water spraying from her nose and mouth, everywhere.

Ava wasn't sure what she was more devastated about, the fact that she was about to meet her murderer or that her final moments would be spent with snot and water dribbling from her face.

She spun around to face whatever was lurking behind her and let out an involuntary ear-piercing scream.

# Chapter Eight

Ava didn't know who was more frightened, the tiny dormouse or herself.

Both were frozen to the spot, eyeballing each other.

The mouse twitched its nose, tilted its big satellite-dish ears and then scuttled off behind the fridge.

'No wait!' Ava called after it. 'I'm sorry!'

*I'm sorry?* she mouthed, shaking her head in disbelief that she had just apologised to a mouse.

What was happening to her? She'd spent less than twenty-four hours in the countryside and she was already going round the twist.

*I know what's happening, I'm getting signs!* The flashbacks, the nightmares, they were all saying, walk away! No, not walk, run! She needed to bury the past, she needed to sell Château Saint-Clair. Yes! Sell, sell, sell! The more her internal monologue ran, the more hysterical she felt.

What was she thinking believing she could start a new life here? It was madness! She should have never listened to Emilia. She should have trusted her gut instinct and done as her daughter asked. Well, it was okay, she was going to do that now. She was going to sell up, buy her old house back in Surbiton, and try and fix her marriage. Ava grabbed her mobile and began frantically googling estate agents nearby.

'Damn!' The phone signal had mysteriously fallen away. Another sign! She angled her mobile to the left, to the right, and then when that didn't work she clambered on top of a chair, balancing precariously as she stretched her arm up above her head. When that failed she dashed back upstairs to try from her bedroom. At some point, at some ungodly hour, when her eyes became too heavy to read the screen any longer, she must have passed out, clutching her phone.

Not surprisingly, she spent what was left of the rest of the night tossing and turning, lurching awake with visions of mice crawling all over her. She woke with the sheets tangled around her legs and her body splayed diagonally across the bed, her hands and feet dangling off the sides.

She slid off the bed. Amazingly her feet landed inside her fur-lined boots. She stretched, bending from left to right in a slow aerobic movement, her body stiff and achy from her night of drama and broken sleep.

Ava glared unkindly at her bed head in the dressing-table mirror, zooming in on her dark circles and wrinkles. She was her own worst enemy. Even if everyone told her she looked stunning she would find some flaw with herself. She turned her back on her reflection and combed her matted mess with her fingers, tying her hair back in her go-to loose top knot.

Leaden-footed and woozy-headed, she made her way downstairs, seeking caffeine like a heat-seeking missile. She entered the kitchen with half an eye looking out for the dormouse, as strangely, Ava still felt bad for scaring it. The tiny furry creature felt like her only friend right now.

She plugged in the kettle and clicked the switch. As the water squealed its way to boiling, she washed up her plate and cup from last night.

Ava turned to grab a teabag from the table and let out another involuntary glass-shattering scream.

'Arrrrrrgh!' came the response from the elderly woman in the kitchen doorway, holding her hands in the air with fright.

'Arrrrrrghhh!'

'Arrrrrrrghhh!'

It was a bizarre scream-off; they were both as startled as each other.

And then the room fell into complete silence as the penny dropped and they both worked out who the other was.

It had been three decades since Ava had seen Madame Chevalier. Although time had aged her grandpapa's house-keeper, her features hadn't changed. She still cast the same stern, slightly disapproving look, her mouth dragging down in the corners. She even dressed her hair in the same tightly braided ponytail. She was a stocky woman, her apron stretched across her large chest and her wide hips. She wore the same lace-up black shoes and ankle socks combo under her calf-length skirt.

Madame Chevalier grumbled: *'Tu m'as fait peur, mon enfant!'*

'I've scared *you*?' Ava managed to translate. She considered pointing out she was no longer a child but thought it best to drop it. She remembered Madame Chevalier's waspish tongue and no-nonsense approach to life. Formidable would be a good adjective to describe her. The housekeeper had adored her grandfather though, always sweet as honey when he was in the room, her eyes filling with instant warmth. And then she would turn on Ava, mostly deservingly, for leaving her toys out or food wrappers on the furniture or for running across the house in mucky shoes. Ava was particularly guilty of that as her boots were permanently covered in soil from the vineyard.

Unsure of how to greet a sort-of old friend, Ava stuck out her hand awkwardly.

Madame Chevalier stared at her implacably, not taking it.

She then lurched forward, grabbing Ava firmly by her shoulders and briskly planting a kiss on either cheek.

'In France, this is how we greet someone!'

'Yes, of course, it's been so long!' Ava smiled apologetically.

Now the ice had seemingly been broken, Madame Chevalier went into overdrive, buzzing around the kitchen like a trapped insect, flying between the fridge and the sink and the larder.

'Sit!' she pointed to the chair. 'What would you like for breakfast?'

'How did you know I was here?'

Madame Chevalier placed her hands on her hips and matter-of-factly announced: 'Monsieur Bellavance said you would come.' Monsieur Bellavance was Ava's grandfather, and although Madame Chevalier had worked for him for years, she had never graduated to calling him by his first name.

Realising there was no further explanation to come, Ava took a sip of the tea that had been plonked in front of her.

The housekeeper carried on beavering away at the breakfast. She had brought some eggs with her and a baguette. She cut a few slices, releasing the scent of freshly baked bread into the kitchen. The butter hissed in the pan as she heated it up for fried eggs. Ava had forgotten how the French use lashings of butter with absolutely everything.

There was also a small selection of pastries in a brown paper bag. Ava stuck her nose inside to investigate: *pain au chocolat*, a croissant, a raisin and cinnamon swirl. Too much for one person to gorge on. Ava backed away.

Madame Chevalier caught her looking. 'Go on, help yourself. You could do with some fattening up,' she remarked, looking Ava up and down as if she were a turkey needing plumping up for Christmas. 'I bought them for you.'

More puzzled, Ava frowned and pushed for answers. Her grandfather may have warned the housekeeper he had left Château Saint-Clair to Ava, but that didn't explain how Madame Chevalier knew she'd arrived. She repeated her question, just rephrased it in a slightly different way.

'*Alors!* Bernard saw the lights on in the house.'

A smile erupted on Ava's face. 'Bernard is still here?!'

'*Mais oui!*'

And then the housekeeper's face fell. 'But he is not well. His lungs are bad, he struggles to walk, to breathe, all that hard work has caught up on him, it's not good.'

She shook her head forlornly.

'That is why the estate is in such a terrible way. Bernard tries, but it's too much for him to manage alone. And there is no money!'

A weighty silence filled the kitchen. Ava dropped her gaze, her eyes fixed on her mug.

Softly, she said: 'That's terrible, I'm so sorry to hear that.'

Madame Chevalier went into overdrive again, sliding the sizzling eggs onto a plate, scraping the leftovers with the spatula, the pan hissing wildly and the steam rising as she filled it with water to soak.

She plonked the fry-up in front of Ava and rattled on. 'And the problem is I can't be here all the time, I have a husband, I have three grandchildren who all need my attention.'

The corners of her mouth dragged even further downwards with weariness.

'Thank you,' Ava's voice was drowned out by Madame Chevalier as she continued her rant. Judging by the force and the speed it was delivered, Ava sensed the housekeeper had been waiting a long time to get things off her chest.

'It's too big a job for two people. Two people as old as Bernard and I.'

Madame Chevalier and Bernard both must have been nearing seventy now. Doing her best to be understanding, Ava said: 'Of course it is! Didn't my grandfather think of hiring more people to help you?'

But as soon as the words left her mouth, she regretted them. Madame Chevalier bristled. 'What makes you think we are being paid?'

Back-pedalling, anything to avoid the wrath of the formidable housekeeper, Ava tried to explain: 'I, I . . .'

But her throat constricted, her words became stuck in her mouth, and instead she squeaked: 'I, I just assumed.' She coughed nervously, wiping her mouth with the napkin. 'I assumed Grandpapa had made some financial arrangement.'

'*Non!*' Madame Chevalier almost recoiled with horror. 'We are here because this is our home!'

The words hung in the still air, the room suddenly filling with tension.

Ava shrank back into her seat. She felt like her ten-year-old self again being told off for misbehaving. Unsure what to do next, she nervously rammed a chunk of fried-egg baguette into her mouth. She could feel the housekeeper's gaze on her as she chewed her way through it, not daring to look up. Instead, she quietly mumbled between mouthfuls: 'I'm sorry, I didn't mean to offend you.'

There was another weighty silence and then the uneasy moment lifted as Madame Chevalier seemed to accept Ava's apology and got on with cleaning up. She snatched the now empty plate from under Ava's nose and carried on chatting as she took up position by the sink.

'It's fine, you weren't to know. Your grandfather was very kind to us. He gave us what he could. He left the lodge to Bernard and me, and Bernard now lives in it.'

The housekeeper squeezed a noisy blob of washing-up liquid onto the sponge.

'Your grandpapa's last years were spent in near poverty.'

'But I thought the vineyard was a success? I remember Grandpapa's wine winning all the awards.'

'That was a long time ago. He was sick for many years with cancer. He was such a proud man, he wouldn't tell anyone. He wouldn't ask for help . . .'

Madame Chevalier's voice cracked with emotion. She stopped scrubbing and stood perfectly still, her back silhouetted against the light of the window. Ava watched her shoulders heave up and down as she tried to control herself.

Regaining her composure, the older woman plunged her hands back into the soap suds and carried on scrubbing.

'It hasn't been easy.'

'It must have been very hard for you all,' Ava nodded understandingly.

And then on impulse, Madame Chevalier swung around, her long braid of hair swishing onto her shoulder. Wiping her hands dry on her apron, she blurted: 'That is why we are so happy you are here. You have come to rescue the château, Mademoiselle Ava!'

Ava's jaw tightened. Her breath caved into her chest as an enormous pang of guilt shot through her entire body.

She slid her gaze to the floor; anything to avoid looking Madame Chevalier in the eye. Quickly diverting the conversation away from the château, from her imminent plans to put a 'For Sale' sign outside the front door . . . 'It's actually Madame now,' Ava waved her ring finger, in a theatrically cheerful way.

'*Ah oui!* Your grandfather did say, I forgot.'

'Grandpapa knew I was married? But how . . .?'

The housekeeper smiled fondly. 'He knew everything about you. He loved you very much.'

So many questions were now bouncing around Ava's head. How did her grandfather know so much about her yet he hadn't made contact with her for all those years? How could he be certain she would return to Château Saint-Clair?

She was about to ask but Madame Chevalier got in first.

'He said more than anything he hoped you were happy. That you had found a wonderful man to love you. That you had a marriage nothing like your parents'.'

Ava could hear her grandfather's passionately energetic voice through Madame Chevalier's. The way he would have said '*amour*' with French vivacity.

'You *are* happy aren't you, Madame Ava?' The housekeeper looked at her intently.

She asked the question in such a way that made Ava wonder if Madame Chevalier needed to hear Ava was happy for her own peace of mind. To be reassured that all of her hard work, her loyalty, everything she had given of herself over the years to the château, had been worth it. That the person who was picking up from where her grandfather had left off would bring the same love and laughter to the place. There would be family meals around the table again, board games by the fireside, splashing in the pool, and that the vineyard would be returned to its former glory.

Ava smiled at her; possibly the least convincing smile ever.

# Chapter Nine

She didn't waste any time.

Wracked with guilt, Ava had raced into the nearby town of Flassans-sur-Issole to arrange a valuation of Château Saint-Clair so she could leave France as swiftly as humanly feasible. An appointment had been booked for that afternoon.

Unable to face Madame Chevalier, Ava decided to spend some time looking around the town. She stepped into one of the many cobbled alleyways meandering away from the high street.

The pastel houses with their bright shutters towered over her, one side hidden in the shadows, the other glowing in the late morning light.

Ava tilted her head up to the sky to see what life was above her. Someone's washing was flapping in the breeze, hanging precariously from string that looked like it would snap at any moment. Many of the taller buildings had balconies, adorned with herbs and blazing red flowers in terracotta pots. It all looked truly Mediterranean.

The alleyway forked into two. The path to the left turned into steps – far too many for Ava's liking – which climbed up to more houses and a church and a bright blue sky. She didn't hesitate taking the easier option down the hill, towards where she had parked the Fiat 500.

As she walked, she mulled over what Madame Chevalier had said. 'You are happy aren't you, Madame Ava?' The words resonated somewhere deep inside, in a place Ava wasn't sure she wanted to go to as it still felt too foreign, too unfamiliar.

The alleyway snaked to the left, curved to the right, past a grimy-looking sports bar, a hairdresser's with faded posters of 80s styles in the window, and a florist that was closed and looked like it had been that way for some time. Just when Ava was wondering where everyone was, she ran into three teenage boys outside a 7–11 shop. One was leaning against his moped while the other two had their heads together, sniggering at something they were watching on a mobile phone.

They barely noticed her as she trudged past. Their laughter faded as she turned another corner into what was fast becoming a rabbit warren of a town. She wondered whether she had taken a wrong turn somewhere. Just as her feet were starting to ache and she was cursing herself for going off the beaten track, Ava emerged into a beautiful courtyard.

In the centre was a fountain and around it were a handful of restaurants and cafés, their tables and chairs scattered across the cobbles, underneath a cluster of fig trees.

The buildings were much more colourful than the ones she had passed before. Clementine, mint green, baby blue, rose pink. The shutters were open and welcoming, painted either a darker hue than the colour of the building or something bright and contrasting. Her favourites were the canary-yellow ones above *Café Claude*.

A group of men were smoking and sipping coffee outside. They stopped and stared as Ava walked past, as if she were an endangered species they'd spotted on safari.

She supposed she might have stood out slightly in her overly wintry ensemble. For some unknown reason, which she was now deeply regretting, Ava had decided to layer up when she left for town. She was wearing her blue duffle coat, a chiffon scarf *and* a beanie hat with a red pompom.

She tugged the woolly beanie over her ears, self-consciously, feeling their eyes watching her back as she walked in the other direction. As soon as she had passed they continued their conversation, which sounded animated and gossipy. One of them erupted into a deep throaty laugh, hoarse from a lifetime of cigarettes.

Ava spotted a Spar shop where she could pick up some fresh milk – the UHT long-life stuff was killing her – and some nibbles for lunch. Just as she was daydreaming about melted brie on baguette, Ava caught a delicious waft of freshly baked bread. She looked up to find she was standing outside the *boulangerie*, its window laden with French delicacies. There were custard tarts, chocolate eclairs, and a strawberry-and-cream creation that made her stomach growl excitedly, telling her to go inside immediately and try absolutely everything.

It didn't take long to give in to temptation. The shop door jangled as she entered, like the old-fashioned stores in the movies.

Behind the counter was a woman who bore a striking resemblance to the sweet buns she was selling. She was round and cuddly and sprinkled in a light dusting of white flour. Her long curly eyelashes even had a coat of frosting. She was deep in conversation with an elderly woman, who seemed to be having a moan about a woman with 'loose morals', someone called Camille.

The baker broke away from her gossip and welcomed Ava with a beaming smile. '*Bonjour Madame! Vous désirez?*'

Ava wanted to reply, 'I would like all of it,' but realising that it would only lead to self-combustion, asked for the strawberry cream cake she'd been most lusting after, in her best French.

'English?' the woman asked.

'Yes.' Was her pronunciation that bad? Ava mused.

Nosily, the woman asked: 'Are you here on holiday?'

The old lady to her left leaned in, trying to catch the conversation. Both women were now staring at her.

'Um, not really,' Ava started, but then thought better of it, quickly realising she might be talking to the town's biggest gossips.

She smiled pleasantly and offered them a half-truth. 'It's just a flying visit.'

Hard of hearing, the old lady asked the woman behind the counter to repeat what Ava had said. In French, the baker shouted back, 'She's come to visit someone!'

Ava quietly laughed at her interpretation, now certain she was talking to the town's biggest gossip.

Not satisfied with Ava's closed answer, the woman tried digging for more information. Wrestling with the paper bag and the slice of strawberry cake, she pretended to casually enquire: 'How long will you be staying—'

But she didn't manage to finish her sentence as the door was flung open and a young man burst into the shop.

Jumping the queue, he turned around to Ava and said: *'Excusez-moi Madame,'* flashing her a clearly well-used charming smile.

But despite being mildly annoyed at his manners, Ava found herself moving out of the way and following that up with a little smile of her own, because it was hard not to notice how gorgeous he was.

He was very boyish-looking with his floppy dark brown hair and dimpled grin and Ava guessed him to be in his mid to late twenties. He had the classic French caramel skin that would ripen to an even more deliciously dark shade in the summer.

As he stood waiting for the woman's attention, he brushed his hair out of his eyes with a single sweeping motion.

He was wearing what looked like a waiter's uniform. Black trousers, and a white tailored shirt that clung to his every muscle, stretching across his chest and upper arms. A triangle of golden skin peeked out around his neck where he had left his shirt unbuttoned. He wore a single-beaded choker, the type of thing young people pick up when they go travelling.

He had a biro tucked behind his ear and a notebook wedged into his back pocket.

*Oh God*, Ava was now staring at his bum.

She shook her head, as if she were shaking sense back into herself.

It had been a very long time since someone had made her jaw drop, if ever. Let alone someone not much older than her daughter.

The baker at first pretended not to hear him but she too couldn't resist his presence and eventually relented.

'*Oui Jacques?*'

A quick exchange followed, and from what Ava could make out, the younger man was trying to twist the baker's arm into handing over her loose change and the woman was getting frustrated at the nearby restaurant for always cleaning her out of her much needed cash.

She popped the till open, sighing deeply as she examined the contents.

He flashed her another of his winning smiles. Her eyes flickered between him and the till and whatever he was doing seemed to work, because despite being put upon, the woman handed him a handful of loose change.

'*Merci Margot!*' he shouted over his shoulder, already halfway through the door. Ava peered through the window and watched him dart across the courtyard and into *Chez Paul*. She couldn't take her eyes from his athletic physique and stifled a giggle with her fist, as her laughter caught her off guard.

Without her realising, 'Margot' had been watching her, watching him. She nodded sagely, 'He's trouble that one!'

'Ah, right,' Ava said, unsure how to reply.

The pair exchanged cake and money and as Ava pulled the jangling door to, the baker wished her a good day with, if she wasn't mistaken, a hint of mischief in her smile.

# Chapter Ten

'This will have to go!' The estate agent lifted a corner of the sheet. 'And this too,' he said dismissively of Ava's grandfather's desk. Waving his hands around the room like an orchestral conductor: 'It will all have to go, no room for tat like this when we sell.'

*Tat?* Ava's heart felt speared – that was her grandpapa's furniture he was talking about.

He breezed through the living room, Ava trotting behind to keep up. Over his shoulder he remarked: 'There's a darling little *brocante* on Sundays in town, you should be able to get a few euros for these bits and pieces.'

*Bits and pieces?* Ava's eyes narrowed, the valuation was making her feel angry rather than relieved.

'Let's have another look at the outside,' he disappeared into the courtyard.

A tremendous clattering of pots and pans sounded from the kitchen where Madame Chevalier was cleaning up. That was the fifth interruption in as many minutes. Ava was convinced it was more out of protest than her butter-fingers dropping things.

Ava, now reluctantly, followed the estate agent out into the sunshine.

She caught him scrutinising the roof, his head lifted; his back was arched which only pushed his belly out more. Ava couldn't help thinking it resembled the bottom of a sagging sofa where all the springs had sprung.

Gustave Dupont, who, as it turned out, ran the only estate agent's in town, had thinning grey hair and a grey goatee to match, which he had clearly spent some time grooming that morning. He was a stocky man, with a thick neck that was being choked by a too-tight shirt and tie. A roll of skin folded over his collar as he lowered his eyes to meet Ava's.

So far he had seen the vines, the old dusty barn where her grandpapa would ferment and blend the wine in barrels, and the house.

Remembering there was one more place she could show him, Ava said, enthusiastically: 'I can take you to the cellar where my grandfather used to keep a selection of bottles from each year.'

It had been one of her favourite hiding spots when she was a child. Ava recalled the small room underneath the barn being musty and dark except for a tiny shaft of red light that would seep through the stained-glass window in the shape of a cross – the vineyard's logo. The tinted sunshine would glint across the row upon row of wine bottles in their racks. If she closed her eyes she could still hear the trickle of water that ran down the wall in the corner of the cave-like room.

Monsieur Dupont held up his hand. 'There is no need.'

Ava breathed in sharply.

She had wanted to like Monsieur Dupont because he was supposed to be the saviour of her financial crisis, but her goodwill towards him reduced every time he criticised Château Saint-Clair.

He took one last walk around the courtyard, examining the building and the fields from afar, while Ava examined his facial expressions, watching them morph into different grades of dissatisfaction until she could barely look at him a second longer.

She followed a foot behind in silence as Monsieur Dupont strode across to the mulberry tree, his phone pressed to his ear as he gave his colleagues back at the office a candid appraisal of what he'd seen. He shoved the mobile into his pocket and turned to face her.

Ava braced herself for bad news.

He unbuttoned his snugly fitting jacket, letting out a small breath of relief.

Clearing his throat, 'Madame Chiltern, you don't need me to tell you your grandfather's vineyard is not what it used to be.'

Ava nodded, grudgingly.

'And I was very much looking forward to seeing it. Even though it is one of the smallest in the whole of Provence at just ten hectares, it was once one of the most successful! Did you know its history spans hundreds of years, from the thirteenth century when it was founded by the Knights Templar?'

Of course she did. Ava had spent many a summer evening listening to her grandpapa retell the magical story, giggling as he re-enacted the past, pretending to be a knight clip-clopping along on his trusty steed with a walking stick for a sword.

Monsieur Dupont went on. 'The vineyard was also a resting place for large numbers of pilgrims venturing to the Holy Land. Following the French Revolution, the vineyard became the property of the nation and was then acquired by the Rigord family, passing from generation to generation.' He smiled. 'That was until your grandfather purchased the château in 1965 and gave this magical place, steeped in a history, a new lease of life.'

He cast his eyes across the fallen, tangled vines stretching up to the house.

'It is a shame. A very big shame,' he shook his head.

Ava's fingernails dug into the flesh of her palm as she clasped her hands involuntarily.

'I remember when your grandfather's rosé was the most sought-after wine in all the region. There wasn't a restaurant in Provence that did not serve it. It won awards, even the Golden Grapes. But now . . .' he shrugged.

Ava felt another rush of irritation. Did he really need to go on reminding her of everything it wasn't? Picking it apart, bit by bit?

She had an overwhelming urge to tell him to leave. But she couldn't before she knew how much Château Saint-Clair was worth. Although she was questioning by the second how the value was measured. She hadn't expected to feel so possessive and sentimental over it.

A lump had risen in her throat as she began to speak. 'So what do you think?'

Monsieur Dupont smiled, rising cheerfully to the climax of his discourse, the part where he got to talk numbers.

He rocked slowly back and forth on his heels, savouring the enjoyment of keeping Ava hanging on.

Ava felt like a contestant on Britain's Got Talent, suffering the agonising silence of the judges before they dispense their verdict.

'I am afraid, Madame Chiltern, that the vineyard is worthless.'

'Worthless?'

'*Oui*. Worthless.'

Ava bristled as he repeated the offensive word.

'It will be impossible for me to sell when the vines are sick and the house is falling down; why would anyone want to buy this?'

Her eyes narrowed.

'As far as I can see, you only have one choice, Madame Chiltern,' he said, thrusting a chubby finger into the air.

Ava felt her lips move as she mouthed, 'What's my choice?' but no words came out. She tried again, this time emitting a squeaky whisper.

Monsieur Dupont savoured his moment of power. After a weighty silence he looked up as he plucked his solution out of the sky. 'You can sell it for building.'

'Building?'

'*Oui*, for, how do you say this in English,' he chewed over his words. 'For making houses, many, many houses,' he moved his arm slowly across the horizon. His eyes were glinting with excitement.

Ava gulped.

Softly, she said: 'You mean, chop it up into plots of land?'

'*Oui!*' Monsieur Dupont replied, even more excitedly. 'We get a bulldozer and we get rid of the house, the vines, it all goes to make beautiful modern apartments.'

Ava felt physically sick, a rancid, bitter taste rising in her mouth as she listened to the estate agent explain how there was a huge market for tourists wanting to buy holiday homes near the Côte d'Azur.

'Big business, Madame, huge. This will give you a lot of money, millions. And I have a client who is very interested in this project. He is a respected man and will buy it from you, immediately. There will be no delay.'

Ava stood there in stunned silence.

'Or you can turn it into a working vineyard again!' Monsieur Dupont sniggered, as if that was the most ludicrous idea ever.

He shrugged.

'*Alors!* It's up to you. I know what I would choose.'

He then shoved his business card under her nose, before turning abruptly to answer his ringing phone.

Ava stood frozen under the mulberry tree, her brain humming with anger and shock. When she finally started to thaw, she felt someone watching her. She looked up to see Madame Chevalier glaring through the kitchen window. Their eyes met, the housekeeper giving her the death stare.

Another huge lump rose in her throat.

She supposed she was going to have to face the music. But not before she spoke to Mark. Ava was tired of dealing with all of this by herself. She hated making decisions at the best of times, let alone ones on this grand a scale. She needed Mark; he was still her husband, her rock.

Ava tugged her mobile out of her jeans pocket and turned her back on the housekeeper's glare, although she could still feel Madame Chevalier's eyes boring into her as she dialled the number.

She was going to tell Mark everything. The truth about why she had come to France, about inheriting the vineyard and the revelation that she would be able to buy their house in Acorn Close back.

Her heart was swelling with a mixture of excitement, stress and confusion – excitement that she would finally have money, lots of it, enough to solve all of her problems, enough to make their daughter happy, enough to lure her husband away from Gabby – surely the money would bring him back to her again? But stress and uncertainty at the emotional cost of selling the vineyard. It would be wiped from history. Everything her grandpapa had built, the past, gone forever. Ava tried to blank that part from her mind, muting the words of his letter to her, as she listened to the dialling tone.

'Pick up, pick up,' she said.

*Ring ring.*

'Come on, pick up.'

*Ring ring*

'PICK UP, Mark, you bastard!'

But the phone just kept ringing and ringing until the nauseatingly smug answerphone message kicked in, which Ava couldn't bring herself to listen to any more.

Crestfallen, she trudged back to the house. But she couldn't cry, or scream out in rage, she just felt numb.

She walked blindly into the kitchen where Madame Chevalier was still clanking things loudly.

For a moment, neither said anything, although Ava could feel the tension mounting as she watched Madame Chevalier grip the side of the basin, exposing her white knuckles.

Ava didn't want to be the first to break so instead she quietly counted down the human time-bomb in her head. Three, two, one . . .

'Who was that?' Madame Chevalier finally exploded. Her lace-up shoes squeaked violently on the tiles as she spun around to face Ava. Of course she knew full well who Monsieur Dupont was.

Ava sighed deeply, knowing there was little she could say that would pacify her grandfather's faithful housekeeper.

'It was an estate agent,' she replied quietly.

'What did he want?'

Lowering her head, Ava mumbled: 'He didn't want anything, it was me, I wanted to know how much Château Saint-Clair is worth.'

'*Mon Dieu!*' Madame Chevalier exclaimed.

Just as Ava was about to offer an explanation, a shadowy figure appeared in the doorway.

'Bernard!' Ava smiled weakly.

The gardener nodded in acknowledgement. His face was as thunderous as Madame Chevalier's.

They both glared at her, without saying a word. Ava felt like a tiny insect being examined under a microscope. A wave of guilt rose through her, turning her chest and neck red.

'What was I supposed to do?!' she blurted out.

Both Bernard and Madame Chevalier kept a disapproving silence.

'I'm in so much financial mess. This place is beyond repair and I have no money to fix it with. I thought I was coming to the beautiful château I remembered, not this ruin,' she babbled nervously. 'I've lost my home in England, my daughter wants me to buy it back, she wants us to be a family again,' she inhaled, 'because we are not a family any more, yes that's right, my marriage has fallen apart . . .' her voice wobbled.

She caught sight of Bernard and Madame Chevalier's sideways glance.

'And to make things worse my husband, who got me into this mess, won't even pick up my calls . . .' She yanked her phone from her pocket and slammed it onto the table as if that might strengthen her case.

'But it either goes to answerphone or he cuts me off and . . . and that's probably because he's with his other woman.' Tears collected in her eyes.

Madame Chevalier let out a little gasp of horror.

Now that she had started talking, she couldn't stop. 'Gabby, that's her name. And he blames me for it all, he says it's my fault he's with her because I wanted a break to think about the financial mess he'd left me in, but surely it was okay to be angry at him about that?'

Madame's eyebrows had shot up.

'I just don't know what's right and what's wrong any more. He won't pick up, why won't he just pick up the phone?' she cried, her eyes pleading with her grandfather's two most loyal staff for answers.

The next thing Ava knew, she had collapsed onto a chair and was sobbing, her head in her hands, her chest heaving for air, tears streaming down her face.

Bernard dipped his gaze.

Madame Chevalier softened a little. Ava felt a warm hand on her shoulder.

'Here, child, use this,' Madame Chevalier thrust a square of kitchen roll into her hands.

'Thank you,' Ava sniffed, then blew her nose noisily into the tissue.

Madame Chevalier tried her best not to look too disgusted at Ava's blast of snot as she took a seat beside her.

On the other side of the kitchen Bernard suddenly lurched forward as his body was attacked by a sudden fit of coughing.

Madame Chevalier turned her attention to her old friend. 'Bernard, move away from the draught!'

When he didn't move she bossed: 'Come, come,' with a shooing motion of her hand.

Bernard rolled his eyes as he limped away from the door and into the room.

Ava felt even more guilty at the thought that her decision to sell could leave Bernard without a home as she watched the frail old man struggle to walk, his breath laboured. He was still the Bernard she remembered – rugged, stubbly, smelling of the earth, with overalls covered in soil. But he was a shadow of his former self.

Ava cast an anguished look and whispered: 'I'm sorry.'

Madame Chevalier nodded, as if accepting her apology, her thorny exterior becoming more blunted.

'Why don't you tell us a bit more about what the estate agent said,' she asked more gently.

Ava proceeded to recount everything Monsieur Dupont had suggested, the choices she had been given, and how he had thought that turning Château Saint-Clair into sparkling new apartments was her only option.

'And you won't consider his idea of turning it into a working vineyard again?' she asked.

Ava stared at her blankly.

'I . . . I don't think he meant that as a serious option. In fact, he laughed when he said it.'

Madame Chevalier and Bernard exchanged glances again.

'*Pourquoi?*' they slipped back into French.

Ava continued to stare at them, bewildered.

'Why? Ummm, because I know zilch about winemaking. And more importantly, I have no money. How could I restore the vineyard when I barely have enough to live?'

Ava had a savings account which she had managed to keep just for herself. It was something small, a tiny amount she'd been hoarding for a rainy day, enough to buy groceries with – nowhere near the amount she would need to resuscitate the vines let alone start on the repair work to the house.

Bernard mumbled something under his breath from his corner of the room. Madame Chevalier fanned off Ava's reasoning with her hand, 'Just minor details!'

Although her argument was falling on deaf ears, Ava continued to make her case, hoping they might see reason. 'My daughter will hate me forever if I don't buy our house back. If she knew I had the money to save our family and I didn't use it. If I didn't try and get her dad back.'

She looked up, wearily.

'I have to sell,' she repeated. 'I have no choice.'

Madame Chevalier frowned. 'You always have a choice.'

'That's not true,' Ava said, although it sounded more like 'snot true' through her sniffles. 'Sometimes you just don't.'

Madame Chevalier stood up abruptly. 'Nonsense, child!' She sighed, like an exasperated mother.

She then stared at Ava, her face serious, her mouth more downturned than ever.

'Madame Ava, why are you going to all this effort for a man who doesn't even bother to pick up the phone when you ring him? We know you love the vineyard. Why would you let a silly little man drive a digger through it, destroy all its magic, all its beauty, for a buffoon of a husband who has run off with another woman.'

Bernard nodded again.

Ava was stunned into silence.

But Madame Chevalier hadn't quite finished.

'He knows you are in France?'

She shrugged. 'Probably, I'm sure Sophie has told him by now.'

'For all he knows you are in trouble, and you need his help?'

Ava dropped her gaze, ashamed. She closed her eyes for a long moment as she recalled her last message to Mark, which he ignored.

When she snapped them open, Madame Chevalier was still staring at her, looking less than impressed.

'Like I said, he's a buffoon! He cares more about himself than you.' She turned to Bernard. 'Don't you agree?'

Bernard squirmed slightly at being brought into the conversation but nonetheless nodded in agreement.

'See, Bernard thinks so too! Let him have this other woman, you will be much better off without him! Why would you want him back after he's been with her? And as for your daughter. She loves you, she will understand and want what's best for you.'

No one had summed things up quite as bluntly before. Only Emilia would have dared to deliver such an outspoken appraisal of Ava's situation. But the tough love approach worked. Ava felt as if she had been struck by a bolt of lightning, electrifying her awake after months of incessant worry and feeling sorry for herself.

Madame Chevalier shrugged.

'If you were my daughter I would tell you to tell him to . . .'

She turned to Bernard and asked something in French, which Ava couldn't understand. Bernard said something back and then the housekeeper returned to Ava.

'I would tell him, as my grandchildren would say, to "jog on"!'

Despite herself, Ava couldn't help but smile.

Madame Chevalier clapped a hand on Ava's back as if she were petting a dog. 'Now I must go and do things. But have a good think before you make a decision.'

The housekeeper signalled to Bernard it was time to leave Ava to her thoughts, sweeping him out of the door with her hands.

The room was now completely silent.

There wasn't even a drippy tap, or a creak from somewhere in the house to break the deafening lack of noise.

And then, as if on cue, Ava's phone pinged.

It was Mark.

# Chapter Eleven

Ava's heart leapt.

*I'm busy. What do you want?*

Ava stared at the message in disbelief. 'You bastard,' she muttered.

*I'm in trouble, I need your help.*

She typed and then watched in dismay as Mark read her WhatsApp message but decided not to respond. And then her phone pinged again.

*How's the vineyard? Hope you're not getting too pissed without me!*

It was Emilia, signing off with a winky face and two kisses.

*What a bloody good idea!* Ava thought, suddenly realising that she had spent almost two days at a vineyard and not even thought to try some of her grandfather's famous wine. What was she thinking?!

The chair screeched across the tiles as Ava rose to her feet, on a mission to raid the cellar.

She charged through the house, across the courtyard, through the length of the barn and down the wobbly stone steps to the cellar where there was a key hanging from a hook on the wall. One of those oversized antique bronze keys that would open the door to a secret world if it were in a children's fantasy film.

It may not have been a magic kingdom, but as far as Ava was concerned, what lay behind the door was just as good – it was going to take her to a place where she could forget her problems for an evening. She turned the key in the lock and gave the solid oak door a hard shove.

A smell of damp, dust and mustiness swooshed up her nostrils. She leaned back, fanning the earthy cocktail away with her hand. It was early evening and the light had faded, leaving the cellar in almost complete darkness.

Ava switched on her trusty mobile-phone torch. She shone the beam into the blackness, the light catching the particles of dust floating in the air. She swiped it from left to right, across the wine racks, and to her horror, saw that there was absolutely nothing in them.

Nada. Not even one dusty bottle for old times' sake. The cellar was desolate. Ava was now utterly convinced that someone had it in for her; that she must be the unluckiest person on earth to inherit a vineyard without a single bottle of wine in it to drink.

So where was the wine? Had her grandfather drunk the cellar dry? She supposed he had been too unwell to produce anything in his final years, and not that she was any sort of expert, but she supposed the vines were in too bad a state to be harvested. Which brought her back to Madame Chevalier's idea of resuscitating the vineyard – how could the housekeeper possibly think she could take on such a gigantic job?! Most importantly, how could she recreate her grandpapa's award-winning rosé when she had nothing in front of her to replicate?

Daunted by the choices that lay ahead, and feeling that these questions were too big to contemplate on an empty stomach, she remembered the courtyard she had stumbled across that morning. Any of those restaurants in town would be better than sitting by herself with her feelings. And she needed vino, quickly, to help with her dilemma. Just something to take the edge off her nightmare of a holiday.

The evening was chilly but the small round tables scattered across the square were full, with locals shoulder to shoulder, each dressed in warm coats and thick scarves, grazing on light bites.

Skinny plumes of smoke from their cigarettes rose into the air from every direction, streaks of silver against the dark night sky.

The only light flickered from candles in glass tumblers dotted across the tables and from a tired string of fairy lights looped around the branches of one of the fig trees. Ava wondered if it was meant to be there or a leftover from Christmas.

Even though she was wearing many layers, she suddenly felt exposed by the idea of eating alone in this tight-knit French community. Worse still, a woman eating alone. She hesitated for a moment, wondering if buying a sandwich would be a better idea. Her enthusiasm for sampling the local food and wine was dampening by the second.

But it was too late for alternatives. The shutters on the Spar shop were rolled down. She'd missed closing time by twenty minutes. The *boulangerie* was also shut. All tempting pastries had disappeared from the window. That left her with a choice of two restaurants.

Her eyes flickered between the similar-sounding billboards – *Chez Paul* and *Chez Monique*. Both had blackboards outside advertising their menu, but Ava felt too shy to walk through the nosy crowd to read them. *Chez Paul* or *Chez*

*Monique*? *Chez Paul* or *Chez Monique*, she ping-ponged, and then a hint of a smile danced across her mouth as she remembered why the former might be the better option.

As she threaded her way through the round tables towards the entrance, part of her hoped that the young guy she'd seen in the bakery that morning would still be on his shift, but she very much doubted it.

A burly-looking man who could have easily been mistaken for a bouncer greeted her at the door with a menu. He had a chubby face, shaved head, stubble and a thin gold chain glinting through his forest of chest chair. Clearly having your shirt unbuttoned into a deep V was the thing at this restaurant, Ava mused, as she recalled the much more appealing image of the young waiter's golden triangle of skin.

The man looked her up and down. 'English?'

Did she have something written on her forehead that said foreigner? Ava was starting to worry.

'Yes.'

'Table for one?'

Ava flinched. 'Umm, yes.'

'Follow me, love,' the man gestured her inside with a menu.

Love? The man was clearly a Brit too, Ava picked up a London twang. She wondered if he might be the owner, Paul.

She was now feeling deeply self-conscious and was imagining everyone's eyes watching her as she squeezed past their tables, even though they were probably far too engrossed in their steak and frites. She didn't dare look up from her feet, even though she had this surprising urge to see if *he* was somewhere milling around the restaurant.

She followed the man through the tiny room, noticing how he tidied up as he went along, rearranging salt and pepper pots, straightening cutlery on a mat, asking an elderly couple to his right if they were enjoying their meal in his best East London French. They nodded and grunted.

The man she took to be Paul placed the menu he was holding on a small table, pulled out a chair and gestured for her to take a seat. *It would have to be right at the back,* she thought, *because that's where the lonely single people get shoved.*

Ava hurriedly removed her coat and slid in, brushed the hair from her eyes and glanced up. The man already had a pen poised to paper waiting to take her order.

'I just need a minute.' Ava looked at the menu frantically.

'Take your time, love. What would you like to drink?'

'A glass of wine . . .'

'Red? White? Rosé?'

The man looked over his shoulder, distracted by a customer adding an extra chair to their table. His eyes had narrowed with irritation as he returned them to her.

'Rosé please.'

'House?'

'That's sounds great.'

It was a quick-fire round.

'Carafe?'

Which meant 'jug' but Ava only realised that after she'd said yes and he'd scooted across the room to moan at the people rearranging his furniture.

Now he had gone, Ava had time to unwind and absorb her surroundings. The air was heavy with the smell of rich food and heat coming off all the bodies squeezed inside the small space. The little square window behind her was misted up and even the bottle of cold water on her table was sweating.

The decor was cosy if unusual: France meets London pub. The walls were panelled with wood in a mock brasserie style punctuated by miniature lamps with green velvety shades. The decorations looked like they had been picked up from the Sunday morning *brocante* that Monsieur Dupont had mentioned; faded paintings of landscapes, a rusty brass bugle, some French flag bunting strung between the light fixings. For the more reclusive diners, there were two booths, upholstered in burgundy leather with gold studs.

As Ava glanced around, she noticed she was one of only two people eating alone. The other was an old man at the bar, hunched over his stew, shovelling the food into his mouth with one eye on the television screen overhead.

The rest of the tables were made up of groups or couples and almost all of them were older than Ava. Some were laughing over a bottle of wine while others stared into each other's eyes. One couple was glaring at one other as they sat in complete silence. At least she and Mark hadn't got to that stage, she thought.

She noticed the occasional sideways glance in her direction, followed by a whisper to their friends or partner. Ava couldn't help but imagine what they might be saying. *Look at that sad old lady eating by herself.* 'Old', there she went again labelling herself unkindly, but she couldn't help it. She'd been feeling that way since she found out about Gabby, since she'd started to stare, a tad obsessively, at her Facebook profile; since she'd decided she was on the shelf at forty-three.

This was the first time she'd ever had a meal out by herself, she suddenly realised. On the rare occasions that Mark took her out or she ventured to the Slug and Lettuce with the girls, she'd never stopped to notice who was sitting alone. It was as if those people were invisible.

She wished she was invisible now.

Ava pulled out her mobile to look like she was busy doing something.

Two messages. One from Emilia: *Are you still alive?! Call me.* The other from Sophie: *Are you going to sell the vineyard?* Followed by: *Could I please borrow some money? There's a gig that EVERYONE is going to this weekend, I promise I'll pay you back xxx.* Nothing from Mark.

She was staring at her screen when a basket of bread was placed on her table.

'And your wine, Madame . . .' A tanned hand reached across and picked up the wine glass.

*That didn't sound like the gruff cockney voice of the man who had shown her to her table.* Ava looked up.

She felt her cheeks flush red uncontrollably.

He smiled.

'Hello again! No pompom hat this evening?' the guy from the bakery teased.

She felt herself blush an even darker shade of red, probably something close to crimson now.

'No, no, it wasn't that cold tonight,' she spoke into her chest.

'Shame, it suited you.'

*He had to be teasing her now.* She didn't dare look up, even though her eyes were being drawn to him like a magnet.

He tilted the glass as he poured the salmon-pink wine. He placed it by her hand and then took a step back, straightening his body as if he were about to make a formal speech.

'This is a 2017 Château Ambrose rosé, an award-winning wine from our local vineyard. You will be able to taste the red fruit; the redcurrant, the raspberry.' He inhaled deeply. 'The flowers; lily and lavender and, of course, the citrus.' he paused and then smiled. 'And some melon too.'

Ava was taken aback. The way he spoke about the wine was so lyrical, as if he were reading her his favourite poem. And in perfect English too.

'Thank you.'

He wasn't finished.

'Its fruity fresh notes will complement many of our starter dishes, especially the seafood. I can highly recommend the mussels, Madame, they are marinated in a sauce which is a delicacy for the area.'

Ava loved the way his voice sung the word 'delicacy'. Still feeling extremely self-conscious she said, 'That sounds lovely, I'll have that.'

'And for your main course? *Vouz désirez?*'

*Desire?* Ava gulped. Flustered, she chose the first thing on the menu. The *Chez Paul* burger with chips.

'Would you like that rare?'

'Oh no, well done, thank you.'

He chuckled.

'*Bon!* My name is Jacques and I will be looking after you tonight.'

Jacques flashed her one of his winning grins. He tucked his biro behind his ear, his notebook into his back jeans pocket and turned.

*Don't look at his bum as he walks away, don't!* Ava couldn't help herself. She quickly cast her eyes around the restaurant to make sure no one had seen her gawping, and then took a cool sip of wine and smiled a secret smile to herself . . .

By the time her starter arrived, Ava had torn her thoughts away from the waiter's derrière and had returned to her dilemma about whether to sell the vineyard or not. Madame Chevalier's candid appraisal of her marriage whirled in her thoughts as she broke off a crusty chunk of baguette and dunked it in the sauce. She then swirled the wine in her glass before taking a sip.

She was expecting something sharp and vinegary; she'd grown so used to the wine Mark had been fobbing off on her.

But Ava was pleasantly surprised. The rosé was fruity without the acidic burn and it had an aftertaste that was actually nice. She nodded and raised an eyebrow involuntarily, as if having a conversation with herself.

Jacques caught her mid-gulp.

'It's delicious, *oui*?'

'Yes, it's lovely,' Ava quickly dabbed her mouth with the napkin.

'Monsieur Ambrose has created blends that are *très delicioux, très unique*, we are very proud to say he comes from this area.'

'You seem to know a lot about wine, well a lot more than me anyway, but that isn't hard.'

He shrugged. 'Ah *bouff*, not really, just *un petit peu*.'

Ava had a feeling he was holding back about something. Perhaps he was just being modest?

There was a short silence.

'Well, I wish I knew more about wine, I think it would help me . . .'

Jacques' head suddenly turned. The man who had shown Ava to her seat was signalling at him, grumpily.

'That's my boss, I must see what he wants, *un moment*.' He dashed off.

Ava was grateful for the interlude as it stopped her spilling her life story to a complete stranger. *What was she thinking?* She'd worked out that news travelled fast in the tiny town and she needed to figure out what her plans were before everyone else started asking questions.

When Jacques returned, he was carrying the thickest burger Ava might have ever seen.

She took a little breath as he placed it in front of her.

It was two patties high, the juice from the fried onions and melted blue cheese oozing down the sides, soaking into the doughy sesame bap. There was a small mountain of crispy cut chips on the side and a tiny salad of lettuce and radish.

'Another glass of wine?' he picked up the carafe.

Ava waved her hand across the brim.

'I'm driving, sadly.'

His eyes twinkled.

'That's a shame. There was another wine I wanted to introduce to you.'

Was he flirting with her? Surely not. Staring at the empty glass Ava wondered if the 2017 Château Ambrose was stronger than she'd realised.

But for some reason unclear to Ava, Jacques didn't seem to want to leave just yet.

'You mentioned you wished you knew more about wine.'

Ava frowned. 'Did I?'

'*Oui*, you were saying just now . . .'

Ava clammed up.

'That's right. I . . . er . . . I think it's a pity I'm staying in a region famous for wine—'

'—famous for rosé—' he corrected.

'—famous for rosé,' she smiled. 'But know nothing about the different wines, what is good, what is bad.'

'*Alors!* This can easily be corrected!' he raised his hands enthusiastically, his face lighting up. 'There are many places you can do wine tasting. The vineyards are closed in spring, but I know of a shop where you can try many wines.

'So many wines you won't know what to do!' he added playfully.

*Yes, I really think he might be flirting with me.* Ava thought, and then quickly rationalised this as him being a charming waiter who flirted with everyone to get extra tips.

Whatever moment they were sharing, it was broken by Jacques' boss

'Jacques, table four!' he hissed.

Jacques rolled his eyes to Ava.

*'Excusez-moi.'*

He then looked to the gigantic burger. *'Bon Appetit,'* he said, winking.

Normally, Ava wouldn't have thought twice about tucking into a burger that was the size of half her face but suddenly the thought of Jacques seeing sauce and grease dripping from her mouth made her cut it up into four bite-sized quarters.

The grumpy restaurant owner kept Jacques busy for the rest of the night, running between tables and the kitchen. She stopped looking at her phone and started watching him, as he rolled up the sleeves of his fitted shirt. As he ran his hands through his hair when it flopped in front of his eyes. When he flashed his incredible smile to whoever he was serving.

She'd become so enthralled by the sideshow, Ava found herself feeling disappointed when Jacques only had time to give her a quick *'bon appetit'* as he delivered her dessert of *crème brûlée.*

Ava was so convinced her eyes might give her away that she had to dip her gaze when Jacques finally returned to her table to hand her the bill.

As he placed the white saucer with the handwritten piece of paper in front of her, he asked if she had enjoyed her meal.

'It was delicious.'

'Good!' he replied, distracted, and then darted off to get her change.

Ava had put on her duffle coat and scarf by the time Jacques came back carrying five euros in coins, and so she resigned herself to the fact that whatever little 'frisson' they had shared earlier was over.

Jacques looked tired and harassed as he cleared the last of the things from the table, the half-full carafe, the breadbasket. Ava stood up to leave, secretly willing him to give her one last incredible smile, and then she would be on her way. *She should probably even pack her suitcase tonight*; her thoughts already drifting to the flight she needed to catch tomorrow.

'*Merci*, she said, one of the few French words she was confident saying.

For the first time since she had met him, Jacques appeared awkward. He stood there stiffly, a carafe in one hand, a woven breadbasket in the other. He shrugged and said: 'If you would like to try more wines, I can take you. I know the person who owns the shop in town.'

Ava looked at him for a second longer than she should have, wondering whether he was coming on to her or just being nice. Or worse, pitying her for being alone.

Whatever the answer, she knew she should say no to a stranger's offer to go for a drink, a drink of sorts anyway. But not before blushing first: 'Thank you, but I'm sorry, I'm not going to have time.'

There was a brief strained silence and then Jacques blinked his long dark eyelashes, recovered his poise and smiled. 'Another time.'

Ava suspected he wasn't used to being turned down.

She nodded goodbye and couldn't help notice he didn't give as much room as he could have for her to squeeze past. As she brushed his arm she caught a waft of his aftershave – he smelt fresh and citrusy, much like the rosé he'd recommended.

'*Bon soir, Madame.*'

'*Bon soir,*' she replied, slightly confused by what had just passed.

The restaurant door clipped the back of her shoes as it closed. She lurched into the now dark and desolate courtyard. The little tea lights had burnt out. Someone had turned off the string of fairy lights. *Chez Monique* was empty. All the shutters were closed.

She tucked her nose into her scarf and buttoned up her top toggles. It was freezing.

As Ava tried to remember the way to the narrow side street she'd parked in, she heard a loud clinking of bottles followed by an explosive '*Merde!*' followed by some giggles.

She peered down the alleyway next to *Chez Paul.* Silhouetted against the harsh yellow outside light were three people, and she stepped a bit closer to see who. Two women and a man. Taking another half-step as she didn't want to be noticed spying, she saw the man move out into the light and she realised it was Jacques, accompanied by two pretty young girls!

He was holding a crate of beer bottles in his arms as one of the girls leant back against the wall, giggling. Her hands were thrust deep in the pockets of her leather jacket, one trendy trainer raised flat against the wall. The other girl, who had long wavy hair that somehow even managed to look glossy in the yellow strip lighting, was staring at him coyly. He was clearly enjoying holding centre stage from the way he courted both their attentions.

*I knew it*, Ava thought as she observed his peacocking from afar. *He's just an outrageous flirt*. Although she couldn't help feel a slight pang of jealousy as she watched the three of them laugh together. She also suddenly felt incredibly old and unattractive as she looked on at the fresh-faced beauties, and then realised how bitter she was being, and stopped herself.

Ava buried her nose deeper into her scarf, hiding her face in flowery chiffon. She edged away, trying not to make a sound. Being caught spying would be highly embarrassing.

'*Madame!*' she heard the already-familiar voice call out behind her.

She flinched.

She pretended not to hear and kept walking.

'*Madame!* Wait!'

The sound of running footsteps grew louder and closer until she could hear his breathing behind her.

'I have something for you!'

Ava frowned. *Had she left something behind?*

Ava turned around, half cringing, a quarter nervous, a quarter excited about seeing his face again.

His hands were on his hips as he tried to catch his breath, his strong shoulders silhouetted by the lights from the restaurant.

She blinked, waiting for him to speak.

Jacques pulled the notebook from his back pocket and the pen from behind his ear; a grin growing across his mouth as he scribbled something down. He tore a page free and handed her the jagged piece of paper.

'Just in case you change your mind about the wine tasting.'

She glanced down at the note. It was a mobile number.

He smiled.

She blushed.

And then he ran back towards the restaurant.

She scrunched up her eyes and opened them again. *Did that really just happen?*

# Chapter Twelve

Ava slowly came around to the sound of the birds cheeping outside her window and the sunshine pouring through the gap in the curtains. There were no sirens bleating, no car engines revving, no radios blaring, just nature – floating into her bedroom. She hadn't slept so soundly in what seemed months, maybe even years. She peeled back the duvet and leisurely made her way downstairs.

Blinking into the bright light gushing through the living-room windows, she felt relaxed and happy and like a teenager as she replayed the events of last night. Of course she had no intention of doing anything with the number, that would be just ridiculous, she was old enough to be his mum! And Jacques had probably forgotten he had given it to her by now; a guy like that would have all the girls in Flassans-sur-Issole running after him for a date, but it was a nice memory to have, and to take away with her, and hang on a minute, Ava paused for a mental breath, as it suddenly dawned on her – this was the longest she hadn't thought about Mark since she'd arrived in France. She hadn't even checked her phone to see if he had contacted her.

She smiled triumphantly.

There she stood for a few minutes like a grinning mad person, until she was struck with a moment of clarity, looking around the large room with its ancient wonky walls and thick wooden beams at the dust sheets covering every inch.

'Grandpapa would have hated this!' she blurted, loudly.

Powered by a surge of new-found energy, Ava yanked at the cloth that had been suffocating her grandfather's favourite reading chair, releasing an explosion of dust motes into the air.

Once she had stopped sneezing, she studied the armchair, picturing her grandpapa with his legs crossed, his well-worn suede loafers slowly sliding off his feet. He was pouring himself a glass of rosé as he did every day at 5 p.m. as an accompaniment to a bowl of his favourite cheese biscuits. Ava had scurried to his side carrying an empty glass, which her grandpapa would promptly fill with one-third wine, two-thirds water, something Madame Chevalier would have thoroughly disapproved of. But she was busy in the kitchen cooking the lamb for dinner so Ava and her grandfather exchanged mischievous looks as the scents of butter and rosemary and seared meat wafted into the living room.

Desperate to reconnect more with the past, Ava yanked at another sheet, and then another. She was like a tornado spinning across the room, pulling sheets off left, right and centre, launching clouds of dust and memories into the air, everywhere.

Some were making her smile, others were making her sad and longing for what once was. As she traced her finger across the teak bookcase, she came to an abrupt halt. There, in three silver frames, were photographs that she never expected to see. Pictures of her, as a young girl, picking grapes and beaming into the camera.

So he had cared? For all those years, Ava had believed he'd given up on her. What else was she supposed to think? He hadn't once tried to contact her after that day she was dragged away. She grew to accept his indifference and in time forget he was part of her life. And there she had been, this whole time, smiling from his bookcase.

There was something else, sandwiched between two books, the corner jutting out. Ava tugged at the stray photograph. The back was marked August 1985. She turned it over and her eyes instantly filled with tears.

She touched the grainy image, her finger dipping back in time, transporting her to the moment her mum tried to get her to smile for the camera. She tickled her underarms and when that didn't work she let Ava borrow her huge Jackie-O sunglasses that swallowed half of her face. Ava remembered the smell of her mother's sweet citrus perfume as she hugged her tightly. Click. Click. Click.

'Madame Ava?'

Ava let out a little breath as she was thrust back into the present.

She dabbed her eyes and turned to face Bernard. He stood there, waiting for her to regain her composure.

She followed his eyes as they dropped from her face to the photograph she was holding. She wasn't sure if she imagined it, but they too seemed to light up when he recognised the captured moment.

Softly, he said, 'Your mother, she was a wonderful woman.'

Ava bit her lip to stop the tears. She smiled weakly at the old gardener. Clearing the lump that had risen in her throat, she said:

'I still don't know what mum and grandpapa fell out about. Why we never came back here. What could have been so bad we could never return?' She looked at Bernard, searching his face for answers. He had been working for her grandpapa after all, perhaps he had seen something, had heard something, she knew it was a long shot but it was worth asking.

His gaze dropped to the floor, and he suddenly seemed very uneasy. Ava felt bad for putting him on the spot.

'Sorry,' she breathed out sharply, annoyed at herself for revisiting a past that just didn't seem to want to be unearthed.

'Anyway,' she smiled. 'Was there something I could help you with?'

He nodded. And then began coughing so severely he had to sit down. Ava rushed to the kitchen to pour him some water. When she returned, she found him still gazing at the old photograph.

She handed him the glass.

'*Merci*,' he said.

She was the one now feeling awkward, as a strange silence filled the room.

'Was there something you wanted to tell me?' she tried prompting him.

He nodded, before taking a sip of water.

*This is like extracting blood from a stone*, Ava thought.

And it was then that she noticed his thumb and fore-fingers, gripped around the glass. They were horrifically disfigured, the joints swollen and bulging from what Ava thought must be arthritis. She couldn't imagine what pain he must be in and ticked herself off for being so impatient.

She started babbling about her evening to fill the prolonged silence, describing the food she'd eaten, the restaurant – but leaving out her '*frisson*' with Jacques.

Bernard cleared his throat. 'Madame Ava, I have an idea.'

'An idea?'

'Something to solve your problem . . .'

She smiled encouragingly, although scarcely believing he could have the answer to such a gigantic financial mess.

'I think you should enter the competition.'

She cocked her eyebrow. 'Competition?'

'The Golden Grapes. There is €50,000 for the winner. Your grandfather won every year until he fell ill,' his eyes narrowing. 'Now Château Ambrose has first prize.'

'Ah yes!' she yelped in recognition at the name, 'I tasted that wine last night!'

Bernard curled his top lip in disgust.

'It was okay, it was better than anything I had tried before, but . . .'

'It is terrible!'

'Oh, okay.'

'And Monsieur Ambrose is a thief! He has stolen the award from your grandfather. And I don't know why because he is a terrible winemaker and he does not know how to care for the grapes! He uses chemicals and machinery and all the modern trickery.'

Ava shook her head. 'Hang on a minute. Did you say, stolen the award?

'*Oui!* As soon as your grandfather was too ill to enter the competition, he took first prize.'

'Technically, that's not theft . . .'

Bernard's eyes narrowed. 'He had been waiting for the moment, like a praying mantis.'

Bernard's English was better than she first thought, Ava mused.

'He is desperate to win again, and he will stop at nothing to keep the title.'

'At nothing?'

'Nothing!' he stared intently at her. 'Trust me! He tried to beat your grandfather by bribing judges, by sabotage. I am certain he paid off the competition so he could win this year.'

'Gosh!' she exhaled.

Madame Chevalier appeared, with a broom. 'So will you enter the competition?' she pretended to ask innocently, not doing a very good job of hiding the fact she had been earwigging from the kitchen the whole time. 'Your grandfather would be turning in his grave if he knew Monsieur Ambrose had stolen his award.'

'Technically, it's not really stealing . . .' but Ava's voice petered off as she felt the full force of Madame Chevalier and Bernard's glare.

'But you're right, it's awful,' she corrected herself.

'Awful? Awful? It's a catastrophe.' Madame Chevalier's voice soared an octave higher. 'Where is your anger? You must fight for what is rightfully yours, for your grandfather's memory.'

Her words hung in the upturned room.

Ava looked around her, and the memories she had freed. She imagined some rich executive and his family standing where she was now in six months' time, in their sparkling white sterile apartment, discussing what inflatable they wanted to chuck in the infinity pool. It made her feel dead inside.

She pictured her grandfather's disappointment at dishonouring his legacy. She felt sick.

She then pictured her grandpapa's smile as she held the award for first prize. The pride on his face, the joy radiating from his eyes at seeing his granddaughter save his beloved vineyard. All she had ever wanted to do was make him proud of her.

With a new-found fire in her belly, Ava turned to her grandfather's most loyal workers. 'So how are we going to win this prize?'

Madame Chevalier clapped jubilantly while Bernard launched breathlessly into his elaborate plan, which he had clearly been plotting for some time.

'We will recreate the award-winning rosé.'

III

'But the vines? They look dead.' Ava exclaimed.

'They are not well, this is true, but they are still producing grapes, enough to make a small blend – a Cuvée. Maybe 3,000 bottles. Enough to enter the competition. We will need to care for them, nurture them, love them.'

'That's great, but, ummm, slight problem, I have no idea how to make wine!'

'You need to contact Jean-Marc in Paris. He is an oenologist.'

'A what?'

'An expert, a master in winemaking, you know? And he was your grandfather's close friend. He will recognise the flavours. The blend. He will be able to recreate the wine. He has an excellent nose, the best in all of France.'

'But what is he going to recognise them from? I've been to the cellar, and there are no bottles left.'

Madame Chevalier and Bernard exchanged glances. They both took on an oddly conspiratorial air.

'Your grandfather made one last rosé before he died. For his friends. He instructed I keep three bottles, just in case.'

Ava couldn't believe how cloak and dagger this was becoming.

'Well, where are these bottles?'

'Under lock and key, in a very secret place.' Madame Chevalier beamed proudly.

'Right. And how are we going to pay him, this Jean-Marc chap?'

'That is your job, to talk him around. I'm sure he will say yes,' Madame Chevalier encouraged her, with a confidence that Ava didn't feel was rooted in very much at all.

'And how are we going to nurture these vines? With all due respect, Bernard, this seems like too big a job for you.'

'You know how to prune?' Bernard asked.

'I had a bonsai tree which I'd occasionally snip leaves off.' Ava frowned. 'But then it died.'

'Then you can snip vines too.'

'Snippety, snip,' Madame Chevalier joined in.

'It is just at harvest time we will need help. But for now, we are okay just with us.'

'Jean Marc, how will I contact him?'

'You need to find your grandfather's address book.'

Ava looked at them blankly. 'And where is that?'

They both shrugged. '*Bouff!*'

It was like being handed a trail of breadcrumbs to follow. Ava raked her hands through her hair in frustration and with nerves at the enormity of the task, at the life-changing decision she had just signed up to.

She searched the house, opening drawers and rifling through cupboards. Of course it wasn't in the most obvious place, her grandpapa's desk, because that would be far too easy and nothing about Château Saint-Clair was simple, Ava was quickly realising.

'Think Ava, think!'

She tried to remember her grandpapa's hiding places, his habits, his daily rituals, what he liked to wear. That was it! Ava sprinted up the stairs and charged along the hallway to his bedroom.

It was the largest of the upstairs rooms and in complete darkness when she entered. Ava drew the curtains, flooding the high ceiling with light. It was as cluttered with antiques as she remembered it to be. Two tall mahogany cupboards stood like pillars either side of the window and next to that, an eighteenth-century wooden screen folded like a concertina into the corner. By his huge emperor-style bed, laden with antique white linen and bolstered with overstuffed pillows, was a side table with a hardback copy of *Great Expectations*, folded open like a rooftop. Beside that were her grandfather's reading glasses. She brushed them softly and then picked up the book. Its ancient spine creaked as she gently closed it to its resting place. She took a deep breath before carrying on with her search.

Her eyes traced across the uneven whitewashed walls, smothered in dozens of small-framed oil paintings and a large circular gold-dipped mirror. She'd forgotten he had a separate dressing room for his clothes that could be found through a tiny door at the back of the room.

Ava ducked, smiling at how much bigger the secret door had seemed when she was a child and wondering how her grandpapa, who was quite a large man thanks to his love of wine and rich food, had managed to squeeze through it for all those years.

A pong of stale cigarettes hung in the airless room, seeping out from his smoke-infused clothes. Other than that, it was a pretty little space, with a sink in the corner which had blue and white hand-decorated tiles and bronze candlestick holders screwed into the walls, a nod to the days when there was no electricity and Château Saint-Clair would have been lit up by candlelight. How romantic, Ava daydreamed, before reminding herself what she had come to do.

She began her search of the wardrobe, the hangers screeching as she scraped the items, one by one, along the rail: cuffed shirts, one in every colour, pressed trousers, waistcoats, until she came to the white linen jacket she'd been searching for. Ava plunged her hand into the outside pockets and then inside until, eureka, there it was, the bulging book, weighing down the fabric.

The cover was brown leather and looked like it had been thumbed a hundred times over. She slipped off the elastic band that was stopping it from bursting open, and leafed through pages overflowing with her grandpapa's spidery scrawl.

'Jean-Marc Chalifour, Jean-Marc Vanier,' she mumbled, trying to decipher her grandpapa's handwriting, wishing she had a surname to go on. 'Jean-Marc, Paris. Rue de Tivoli. *This has to be him*, Ava thought. Bernard had mentioned Paris.

Ava couldn't quite believe what she was about to do as she made her way back through into the bedroom. Ringing a stranger who supposedly had the best wine nose in the whole of France, who might not even be the Jean-Marc she was looking for. Back in Surbiton, she avoided like the plague anything that pushed her out of her comfort zone.

She swallowed her nerves and picked up the phone on her grandfather's bedside table. It was one of those 1960s models, the kind with the springy corkscrew cords that needed unravelling. It put up a good fight but Ava gave the receiver a hard tug. She felt butterflies as she dialled the number.

The background noise was so intrusive she could barely make out the voice at first. Clinking glasses, explosive laughter, it sounded like she had interrupted some sort of party. Ava glanced at her watch; it was only 11.30 a.m.

A high-pitched male voice exclaimed: '*C'est impossible!*'

'Um,' Ava hesitated. 'Is that Jean-Marc?'

'*Oui*. Am I speaking to a ghost? *Non*, this is not my dear friend Monsieur Bellavance?'

Ava suddenly realised her grandpapa's name must have appeared on his screen.

'It's his granddaughter, Ava.'

There was a long silence. And then suddenly an explosion of French enthusiasm. '*Oui, Oui, Oui!* So wonderful to hear from you. You are staying at Château Saint-Clair, it's exquisite isn't it?'

There was another deafening eruption of laughter from the party.

'Pardon, we are tasting a new wine this morning and it is just magnificent. It's fruity, buttery, velvety, just *mwah*.' She heard him pucker his lips.

Ava couldn't help giggle at his eccentricity.

'*Bon*, where were we? You were saying you are visiting Provence?'

'Not exactly,' Ava replied. 'I actually now own the vineyard.'

'*NON!*'

'Yes. And I need your help.'

'Me?'

'Yes, I want to enter the Golden Grapes competition, but I don't know how to recreate my grandpapa's rosé. Will you help?'

Jean-Marc let out a shriek so ear-piercing Ava had to hold the receiver at arm's length.

'Oh, this is so exciting. I know all about Monsieur Ambrose and his terrible wine. We *must* conquer again! I will help you. Of course I will. It would be *mon plaisir*.'

Jean-Marc was ridiculously over the top but his energy was contagious.

'I'm afraid I don't have any money but I can offer you some of the profits of the sale of the wine,' Ava suggested, suddenly finding her wheeler-and-dealer inner voice. Twenty-three years of living with Mark's 'Del Boy' had clearly rubbed off on her somewhere.

'Tsk,' Jean-Marc ticked her off. 'I will not hear of it. I will come as soon as I can.'

The conversation had been so brief and so whirlwind, Ava was seeing stars as she got off the phone. She fell back onto the bed, glowing with achievement, exhausted by the amount of effort it had taken to get there. Lying on her back, staring at the ornate ceiling, her thoughts settled.

'Oh my God!' She pushed herself bolt upright. *What was she thinking?* She'd become so swept up in the grand plan to save Château Saint-Clair that she had completely forgotten about her job!

'Bloody hell!' she yelped. She had a plane to catch in four hours' time.

# Chapter Thirteen

Did that really just happen?

Ava giggled to herself as she pruned another stem from the vines with the gigantic secateurs.

Did she really tell her boss to stick his job up his arse? She sniggered into her gardening glove. Bernard looked at her sideways, suspiciously.

She hadn't planned to tell Gary he was a lech, the words had involuntarily fired out of her mouth, right after he told her receptionists were ten a penny and that he could find a prettier, younger face to replace her in a heartbeat.

'And if you think you'll find your Prince Charming out there you're deluded, love, there are only frogs in France,' he'd spat down the phone. To which she had replied: 'I'd rather kiss a toad than you.' Ava closed her eyes, cringing at her brazenness. Where had that come from?

'The vines, the vines!' Bernard exclaimed, as Ava almost blindly clipped the wrong bud.

Bernard had been educating her that it was of the utmost importance she removed three out of every four new stems. That way the surviving vine would receive the lion's share of nutrients and send all the goodness directly into the grapes, making them full and juicy come summer time.

He'd been keeping a watchful eye over her all morning. They'd been pruning side by side, in a comforting silence.

Occasionally Bernard would speak to offer her nuggets of his wisdom, just as her grandfather used to do.

He reminded her how in its former glory, Château Saint-Clair boasted five varieties of grapes, but sadly, only two were salvageable – Grenache and Tibetan. Luckily they were the ones needed for the rosé.

Bernard went on to explain how special Château Saint-Clair's *terroir* was – the elements that come together to help create the perfect grape.

'We have the perfect hard dry soil,' he kicked the stony earth, 'low in acidity, high in clay. The right height above sea level – 220 metres,' he pointed into the distance, in the direction of the glamorous French Riviera. 'And the dry stone walls radiate the warmth of the sun during the night, feeding the grapes with heat.'

Ava listened intently, drawn to Bernard's knowledge, his unassuming manner and the strange affinity she felt walking across the familiar soil.

'The stone walls are very special because they were built by the Knights Templar and we are the only vineyard in Provence that has them.'

He looked visibly distressed as he noted how many of them were crumbling or had slumped into piles of rubble. He gave his head a little shake, breaking his train of thought, and turned his attention back to the vines.

Bernard tugged a leaf free and waved it under his nose as if smelling a glass of wine.

'The vines, they speak to me and it is my job to listen, to coax out their beauty.' He smiled as if the breeze had lifted him into the air and taken him to some heavenly place.

Still beaming, he added: 'They say that in the Middle Ages, Cistercian monks used to taste the earth in order to savour the vineyard.'

Ava's brow knitted. *Was he suggesting they eat the earth?*

'It is probably a legend.' He winked.

She let out a little breath of relief.

'But what it tells us is the importance of having an intimate knowledge of the land.'

His smile travelled up, across his weather-beaten face. Ava studied him closely, seeing him differently with her adult eyes. It must have been hard for him, being alone for all these years, giving his entire being to a plant rather than a woman. Ava found herself wondering if he had ever been in love.

Her thoughts flip-flopped back to her love life, or her disastrous lack of one. Mark would have hated this, she thought, as she twisted her body like a pretzel to reach a stray bud. He despised all things outdoorsy. The only way she could get him to go for a walk was to bribe him with the promise of a pint in the pub en route.

Ava breathed the fresh spring air deep into her lungs, forcing herself to look forward rather than back. She'd made her decision, as crazy as it was. She had no income, no secure future of any kind, no idea if her marriage was really over or if their time apart could breathe new life into it. All she had was pipe dream of winning the wine equivalent of the Golden Globes. Yet, for some unknown reason, it felt bizarrely liberating to live with such uncertainty for the first time in her life.

Sophie was furious with her and had been sulking since she told her the news that she wouldn't be selling Château Saint-Clair. Ava hadn't tried to placate her this time though. Something had shifted – she felt confident in her decision to follow her heart. *Sophie would forgive her, eventually, surely? She might even like coming here.*

Ava rose to her feet, arching her back, rubbing the base of her spine with her thumbs. Her jeans sported a filthy patch on either knee. Her white T-shirt was smudged with mud, her hair pulled back into a messy ponytail, but she didn't care. She felt sun-massaged, relaxed and a whole lot lighter since she had made up her mind.

'Bernard,' she said inquisitively. 'Remind me, don't we need white grapes to make rosé? I mean, how do you get the colour pink otherwise? In art class at school we were taught if you want to make pink you need to mix red and white together.'

'*Mon Dieu!*' He looked up to the heavens.

Ava blinked. 'What?

'I've got the memory of a goldfish,' she humoured him. Bernard had become a little prickly with age and from spending so much time alone. But Ava could tell underneath his gruff exterior he was a big soft teddy bear.

He straightened his back as he limbered up for his soliloquy.

'The grapes must be red. The colour pink comes when you press them. But not for too long, maybe only four hours they can sit in their juices, just enough time for the tannin to be extracted, to create the magic.'

'Oh wow,' she enthused, noticing how Bernard was secretly enjoying educating her.

'It is called maceration and it must be done when the fruit is perfectly ripe and at the specific temperature and for the exact amount of time, and . . .'

'And thank goodness we have red grapes left,' she said cheerily, snipping off another stem.

'*Oui*, thank God,' he sighed, before they fell back into their comfortable silence.

It did get Ava thinking though, about how little she knew about wine. If she was going to create this award-winning blend, surely she had to know more? Goodness knows how long it would take for Jean-Marc to travel down from Paris. I mean, it was ludicrous to think she could produce something 'magical' on her minuscule knowledge. In fact – what on earth was she thinking?

A mischievous smile danced across her lips.

What she should be doing was research. The only way she was going to save Château Saint-Clair was to saturate her mind with as much wine info as she could possibly squeeze in.

'You don't need to worry, Bernard!' Ava announced. 'I have an idea.'

'*Mon Dieu!*'

Ava's fingers hovered over the keys on her phone – suddenly feeling a lot less certain about her grand plan. *What if Jacques doesn't reply? He probably won't even remember who I am.*

She typed the message:

*Hi Jacques. It's Ava (with the red bobble hat).*

She frowned – no that wasn't how she wanted to be remembered by a hot young guy. She tried again, keeping it simple.

*I was wondering if that offer of a wine tasting is still open? Ava.*

Send? Her stomach somersaulted so violently she had to look away as she pressed the trigger. The message whooshed as it fluttered into cyberspace. She closed her eyes as the agonising wait began.

Within twenty seconds she had an answer. Ping.

*Of course! How does tomorrow 5 p.m. sound? Meet me outside the restaurant. Jacques.*

Ava stared at the message with a mixture of disbelief, dread and excitement. Tomorrow at 5 p.m. That gave her just over twenty-four hours to calm down and think like a grown-up, because that's what she was after all: much more grown-up and older than him, and married. She repeated the M word in her head to reinforce its status, shaky though it was.

Ava wondered if she should confide in Emilia. Her best friend would knock some sense back into her, give her a piece of her brutal honesty. As if by the powers of telepathy, her phone pinged again.

*Snogged any hot frogs yet?* followed by aubergine and frog emojis.

*She wouldn't be confiding in Emilia then! She would only encourage this madness.* Ava switched her phone off in an effort to rebalance her thoughts.

Five minutes later she turned it back on, just in case Jacques messaged.

# Chapter Fourteen

Half the contents of her suitcase were strewn across her bed and Ava was no closer to deciding what to wear. She cursed herself for not taking Emilia's advice and packing something decent. And then she stared at herself angrily in the mirror for getting so worked up over what was supposed to be a bit of educational fun.

'Who cares what he thinks of me,' she grumbled at her reflection. She grabbed her comfy, familiar, lavender jumper from the back of the chair and headed for the door.

Two seconds later, Ava was back in front of the mirror with her lipstick and mascara. She undid her ponytail and combed her hands through her hair, casting one last critical glance at herself.

She was hoping for a clean getaway but as per usual, Madame Chevalier appeared out of nowhere.

She immediately arched an eyebrow: 'Going somewhere nice?'

Ava shot her a look. 'No, just into town.'

Madame Chevalier nodded, her interest piqued. 'I see,' she waddled into the next room, leaving mischief hanging in the air.

Ava practically sprinted to the car before she could be quizzed again.

Two minutes later she was panicking about something

entirely different: the fact that her Fiat 500 wouldn't start. She tried again, the ignition chugging into nothingness.

'No, no, no!' she banged the steering wheel, accidentally stamping the horn with her fist, pumping a tumultuous noise across the courtyard. Her first response to her accumulating stress levels was to blame the rental company for giving her a dud car but that was before she noticed the fuel gage was on zero.

'Bugger!' she cursed, and then sank into the seat, closing her eyes with defeat.

Two seconds later her eyelids snapped open. She bounded out of the car and with an athlete's determination, sprinted back across the courtyard in the direction of her grandfather's tool shed. She even managed a wave to Madame Chevalier who was looking at her with bewilderment through the kitchen window.

She was certain she saw it when she was giving Monsieur Dupont the grand tour. Ava puffed, wrenching the giant barn door open.

It hadn't been a figment of her imagination. In the corner sat the green rusty bike with its woven basket, resting against the crumbly wall, in between her grandfather's worktop and his mountain of toolboxes.

She grabbed the handlebars, sending a small avalanche of dust to the ground.

'You won't get very far on that,' Bernard startled her. He pointed to the flat tyre, stamping out her enthusiasm.

'You've got to be kidding,' she flung her arms up, feeling as deflated as it looked.

Picking up on her disappointment, Bernard asked her if she needed a lift anywhere, to which Ava immediately replied, 'Yes!' She had less than fifteen minutes to get to the restaurant, but it was all okay now that Bernard had saved the day and was going to take her to town.

Ava's thoughts froze, as did her face, as Bernard drove into the courtyard on his tractor and trailer, grinning enthusiastically underneath his flat cap.

'I need to pick up some compost in town so I can give you a lift,' he shouted above the chugging vibrating engine.

Ava's gaze slid back to the kitchen window in time to catch Madame Chevalier stifling a giggle. She covered her amusement with a smile and a cheery wave.

'Just brilliant,' Ava muttered. Seeing the French countryside in an open-top vehicle had been on her bucket list, but this wasn't quite what she had in mind.

She cupped her hands around her mouth, yelling above the noise: 'Where am I supposed to sit?'

Bernard pointed to the trailer.

Ava grimaced. Not her idea of perfect transportation, but beggars couldn't be choosers under the circumstances.

Ava hoisted herself up, trying to blank out the fact her jumper was receiving a coating of manure or something similarly unmentionable. She crawled on her hands and knees towards the back of the trailer. Using an old compost bag as a seat, she pulled her legs into her chest, and tried to trick herself into believing she was being whisked away in an open-top sports car.

The tractor lurched forward, sending Ava flying.

'*Pardon!*' Bernard cried, as he started along the long drive. Ava gripped the sides of the trailer for dear life, her ability to imagine herself in a convertible diminishing by the second.

They bumped and bounced over the tree roots and rocks. The view had all the potential to be stunning, only it passed by in a blur for Ava, as she was vigorously catapulted up and down, her bum making contact with the compost bag for a second before she was hurled into the sky again.

'Are you okay?' Bernard checked on her as they turned the hairpin bend onto the main road into town.

Her bottom was killing her. 'I'm fine,' she shouted back.

She thanked God that Bernard was able to pick up speed now they were driving on tarmac, and from the force of the wind in her face, it felt like they were going along at a clipping pace, so quickly they might even get into town on time. Then a group of cyclists, in neon lycra, overtook them, ringing their bells and waving and Ava shrank into herself with embarrassment.

Bernard was enjoying every second of being the chauffeur though. He lifted his flat cap and shouted, jubilantly: '*Allez Allez!*'

The next fifteen minutes didn't exactly fly by, but Ava did eventually make it into Flassans-sur-Issole, and, amazingly, in one piece. What she didn't bank on though was for Bernard to drive right through the centre of town. When she accepted a hot young waiter's invitation to a wine tasting, turning up in the back of a trailer wasn't quite how she envisaged it would pan out. Her cheeks burned red as they chugged through the cobbled avenue towards the square. Bernard was continuously waving and shouting '*Salut! Bonjour!*' He seemed to know absolutely everyone. Ava, however, was slowly dying of embarrassment. As *Chez Paul* came into view, Ava's reflexes took over. She ducked, crouching so low she was practically horizontal in the trailer, much to Bernard's amusement.

'Are you okay?' He looked over his shoulder, smirking.

She gave him a cheery thumbs-up.

The tractor came to an abrupt stop. Ava prayed it wasn't outside the restaurant – that would just be a cruel twist of fate. As she peered, gingerly, over the top of the trailer, her eyes met with Jacques'.

She ducked, hoping he hadn't seen her, wishing the ground would swallow her up.

'Ava?'

She wanted to die.

'Ava, is that you?'

She slowly lifted her head above the parapet. 'Oh, hello!' she waved. She stood up, casually dusting off the mud and straw, doing her best to look like she hadn't been rolling around in the back of an agricultural vehicle.

In which time, Jacques had bounded from the entrance of *Chez Paul* to the trailer. He held out his hand, which flustered Ava more than everything that had just passed. His skin felt soft as she slipped her palm into his, but his grip was firm, and strong, and he smelt so good and fresh. She bumped her chest into his body as she landed awkwardly on the ground.

'Sorry,' she mumbled, to which he laughed. A deep manly laugh.

'What is it with you English? You love to say sorry.'

'Sorry . . . oh no . . . I mean.' Ava clamped her hand over her mouth girlishly. For some reason, being around Jacques reduced her to a giggling teenager.

Suddenly feeling a third wheel in the painfully awkward conversation, Bernard cleared his throat, loudly. 'I'm going now.'

She pulled her gaze away from Jacques.

'*Au revoir.*' She waved him off, trying to sound impressive with her French.

The tractor engine roared and she turned her attention back to Jacques, whose hand had moved to her face. *What was he doing?* She froze as he lightly brushed her cheek with his fingers. His eyes fixed on her.

'You have a piece of straw in your hair,' he pulled the strand out from behind her ear.

'Oh right, thanks.' She blushed, running her fingers through what she imagined was now a bird's nest of a bouffant.

Judging by his playful smile he was clearly enjoying her awkwardness. 'Follow me, we are late.'

It felt like the eyes of the whole town were on her as she crossed the square. Occasionally she lifted her gaze from the cobbles to Jacques, who was striding confidently in his drainpipe jeans, which had trendy rips at the knees. He was wearing a denim jacket with a furry sheepskin-lined collar and his tailored white work shirt had been substituted for a white T-shirt that was equally clingy in all the right places.

He glanced down at his watch. '*Merde!* We are very late.'

'Oh no, I'm sorry!'

Jacques smiled at her.

'I can't help apologising.'

'I'm not angry at you, it's my friend, he is very particular and we still have a little way to go.'

'Oh, I thought his shop was in the town?'

They turned the corner into a small courtyard behind the restaurant. He looked at her hesitantly, trying to read how she would take the news.

Ava stared at the moped.

On the positive side the helmet would hide her bouffant. She wasn't sure how she felt about another white-knuckle ride through the countryside though. *And where would she sit?* She panicked, studying the silver bike.

Jacques handed her his spare helmet. 'Get on!' His confidence gave her no time to magic up an excuse.

She clumsily lifted her leg over the seat, unsure where to place her hands, until it dawned on her that if she didn't hold on to Jacques, she might die. She wrapped them around his waist, his warmth instantly feeding into hers.

'So where are we going?'

'It's a surprise,' he said, kick-starting the moped. 'Hold on!'

Ava squealed as they sped off, roaring down the narrow road.

She gripped his waist tighter, her hands slipping underneath his jacket. She could feel his stomach muscles tensing as he weaved through the traffic.

The brightly coloured buildings rushed past her like a kaleidoscope. The rich cooking smells wafting through the open windows onto the street whooshed up her nostrils.

He took a sharp left down a side street, mounting the pavement, her body bumping against his. He slowed and turned his head. 'Are you okay?' His voice was muffled through his helmet and instead of answering, she squeezed him a *yes* instead. The sign language wasn't lost in translation though, as he joked: 'Okay we can go faster then!'

'No!' she squealed, but part of her was secretly enjoying it. It was frightening but exhilarating, putting her life into someone else's hands.

They whizzed up and down the steep streets, over a bridge with glistening water, so quickly her stomach dropped through her feet. They curled along *Avenue de Pamplemousse* until it widened into a main road. Jacques revved the motor and beeped the horn, celebrating the start of the open road.

They passed field after field of vines. Jacques pointed to a rocky outcrop in the distance, and suddenly made a sharp right, veering onto a bumpy dirt track. He suddenly burst into life, pointing every which way.

'Cherry trees.'

She gave him the thumbs-up.

'Olive trees.'

She imagined the spindly branches laden with olives at harvest time.

'And peaches.'

Ava's stomach rumbled. *Trying wine on an empty stomach – perhaps not such a good idea.* She had been so preoccupied with what to wear for the wine tasting she'd forgotten to have lunch.

The closer they drew the more enormous the rocky outcrop ahead became, eclipsing the setting sun. Ava's jaw dropped as she noticed the houses, which had been carved out of the mountainside. Jacques started to build up speed as they approached the zigzagging road to the top.

'Hold on,' he shouted.

She wrapped her arms around him even more tightly as they snaked their way up, slowing only for the hairpin bends. As they rose into the mammoth sky the vines shrank into thin green stripes that looked like they had been drawn on with felt-tip pen.

One last sharp corner and they were in the heart of the village, which was more like a fortress. Every building was decorated with turquoise shutters, every doorstep was adorned with earthenware pots filled with blazing pink pelargoniums. Jacques parked alongside the drinking fountain in the centre of the tiny square that was spurting crystal-clear water from the mouths of bronzed chubby cherubs.

Ava reluctantly released her grip on Jacques, and attempted her most elegant dismount despite having legs of jelly. Jacques slipped off the moped in one swift movement. He removed his helmet, ruffling his hand through his hair. Grinning, he said. 'How was that?'

It was the most alive she had felt in years. The wind in her face, the cold air thrusting at her from every direction, the warmth of Jacques' body against her chest.

'It was nice.' She shrugged.

He smiled, knowingly. 'Follow me, I can't wait for you to meet . . .

'Pierre!' he exclaimed.

The spindly man with a goatee beard and wearing small circular glasses was tapping his foot impatiently on the entrance step to *Vin du Domain*. Jacques greeted him with a brotherly hug and then turned back to her.

'This is my friend, Ava.'

'Friend', for some reason the word burned when really she should have been grateful he introduced her as a friend at all considering he'd only just met her. *For goodness' sake, Ava.* She kissed Pierre on both cheeks.

The shop was more like a cave – they dipped their heads to enter a candlelit cellar, packed, floor to ceiling, with wine racks. In the centre was a long chunky wood banquet table stained with wine rings and encrusted with wax. The place smelt of wax and wine and dust and cork and something deliciously sweet.

Pierre immediately got to work selecting wines from across the region. He brushed his forefinger across the bottles until he found one he liked the look of. He pulled it from the rack, the glass clinking as it slid out. He blew on the label, sending a cloud of dust into the air. He then nodded to himself, as if he was having his own wine tasting, and this one was satisfying him immensely.

Jacques leaned in and whispered: 'This is the best bit, watching him choose the ones he thinks you will like.'

She felt his breath, soft and fresh on her face.

'How does he know what to pick for me?'

'He has studied you, the way that you walk, the way you smile, the way you speak . . . he knows.'

Ava folded her arms, suddenly feeling a tad exposed. 'But I only arrived on your moped five minutes ago.'

'Just wait and see. One day I want to be as good as this.'

She looked at him sideways, intrigued by the ambition he showed.

Pierre carried on preparing for the tasting, placing a row of glasses on the table next to a silver bucket. He cleared his throat, announcing he was ready.

'So how do you know so much about wine?'

Jacques shrugged. 'Growing up around here, it's hard not to love wine. I didn't have the money to pay for university, so instead I went to the city to train as a sommelier in restaurants.' His eyes narrowed fractionally as if something had pinched his thoughts. 'It was hard work, not that I'm afraid of that, but it was a thankless job. I wasn't learning about wine, I was spending most of my time waiting tables and dealing with rude tourists and I was bored. I wanted more. I wanted to learn how wine was made, to really understand the process, you know? So I came back here.' He dropped his eyes. 'But it's not easy for a farm boy to get a job as a winemaker, there is a lot of snobbery.'

'A farm boy, huh?' Ava teased, trying to halt his mood.

He looked at her seriously and then his face cracked into that familiar, brilliant smile. 'Yes, I'm a farm boy. My parents live on a farm not far from here.'

'How nice!'

'I just want to make them proud. I've been working at a vineyard near here but it's not paid work so that's why I'm back waiting tables at *Chez Paul*.' He sighed, a little defeated breath. '*Alors*. One day though, I will make my own wine.'

Ava opened her mouth to speak; she was curious which vineyard, but Pierre was ready with a bottle.

'It is always good when you taste wine that you try from the lightest to the strongest. Usually white will be first, but I like to taste rosé, because it is the speciality of the region.'

He revealed that Provence was the oldest winemaking region in the whole of France. 'Wine has been made in this region for over two and a half thousand years, ever since the ancient Greeks founded the city of Marseille in six hundred BC,' he pulled the cork from the first bottle. 'And it is arguably the largest rosé producer in the country.' It made a popping noise as it felt the first breath of air.

He poured the pink nectar into the glasses, the bottle glugging merrily.

'This is the premium Black Label from *Château de Berne*. The rosé is quite a simple blend of two grapes: eighty per cent Grenache and twenty per cent Cinsault. There is more Grenache to give it structure and body. The Cinsault is not a dark grape so it is great for rosé, giving the light colour. It's to be drunk chilled, but not too cold. If it's too cold you will lose most of the flavours.'

Ava thought back to all the times Mark had buried a bottle of rosé in a bucket of ice. She felt slightly smug knowing he'd been wrong all along.

'If we look at the wine,' Pierre tilted the glass into the candlelight.

Ava and Jacques slanted their glasses.

'Just enjoy the colour, it is so nice, between pink and orange.'

'Salmon!' she exclaimed.

'*Oui!* This is the colour of Provence. Rosé from other areas is much darker. Provence rosé is pale and bright.

Bright means young. An old rosé gets dark and dull.' He smiled at his glass. 'Now smell the wine.'

Pierre closed his eyes as he stuck his nose inside the brim. He inhaled deeply. 'It's quite lively, a bit citrusy. Rosé is always citrusy, it makes it feel fresh.'

Ava gingerly dipped her nose inside.

'Don't be shy, really stick it in, like this,' Jacques dunked his perfectly shaped nose deep inside the glass.

She giggled.

'But if you have a strong citrus sensation, it is not a good sign, so beware, it will mean the wine will be too sour and dry.' Pierre inhaled again. 'Grapefruits!' he exclaimed. 'And if you want to aerate the wine, like this,' he swirled the pink nectar around in the glass, 'it will reveal more of its romance.' He dunked his nose in for a third time. 'I'm getting peach notes now,' he rolled his hand, 'and apricots, and also tropical fruits, mango.' He paused, thinking hard. 'And melon!'

*Extraordinary*, Ava thought as she took another whiff of what to her smelt simply like wine.

'And now to taste. Enjoy the freshness, the liveliness, the balance.' Pierre took a sip, making a funny sucking noise, closed his eyes with ecstasy and then, to Ava's horror, spat into the bucket.

'The best way to taste is to circle the wine in your mouth, stretching the wine. *Bon*, you try.'

Jacques perfected the technique first go, and somehow he managed to make it sound more like he was puckering up to the wine rather than slurping it.

They both turned to Ava.

She smiled sheepishly and took a sip. But her attempt to swirl led to a less than sexy dribble down her chin. Too embarrassed to follow through with a spit in front of Jacques, she downed it.

She couldn't bring herself to look at him as she wiped the spillage from her mouth.

'And now for the second wine,' Pierre gallantly moved on to the next bottle.

What followed was not a lot of spitting but excessive amounts of drinking – all on an empty stomach.

'Yessssh this is an elegant wine,' Ava slurred, as she drained yet another glass. Her head was growing lighter and groggier by the minute. She'd stopped noticing what she was drinking some time ago and was now much more focused on the way Jacques lifted his glass to his mouth, the way his bicep flexed, the way . . .

Jacques leaned in. 'To me what makes a premium rosé is the balance. The flavours, the colour. It's the art of making something very dry, very citrusy. But not aggressive.' He smiled. 'Something soft.'

She watched his lips move as he spoke.

'Don't you think?' He stared at her.

'Um, oh right, yes, definitely.' She hadn't heard a word he'd said.

'So you were about to tell me at the restaurant, why you wanted to learn more about winemaking.'

'Oh yeah, that,' she raised her eyebrows. 'I've just inherited my grandfather's vineyard and guess what?' She held her hand over her mouth, childishly pretending to hold in a secret.

Jacques was still digesting her huge revelation.

'I haven't a clue about wine!' She giggled.

'What is the name?'

Ava frowned; she could feel she was exaggerating all of her facial expressions. 'What name?'

'The vineyard. What is the name of your grandfather's vineyard?'

'Ohhhh,' she wobbled, her wine sloshing. Pierre was shooting her horrified looks. 'Château Saint-Clair.'

Jacques slapped his hands over his eyes. 'Are you serious? Château Saint-Clair won the Golden Grape award nine years in a row. I used to serve your grandfather's wine in the restaurants in Montpellier when I was a waiter. You are the luckiest woman in the whole of France!'

Ava stared at him, blinking. Swaying. And then she narrowed her eyes.

'How old are you?'

Taken aback, Jacques frowned. 'Twenty-seven. Why?'

'Ah-ha, that's what I thought,' she pointed her finger into the air, ridiculously.

Tired of listening to their somewhat disjointed conversation and Ava's lack of winetasting decorum, Pierre started to drop heavy hints that perhaps it was time to leave. Jacques grabbed Ava's scarf and jacket and gently began herding her towards the door.

The friends bowed their heads together as they whispered something to each other, which Ava took as a perfect opportunity to grab a few seconds of resting time against the wall, which felt so cool on her skin. Her leaning quickly turned into a slump. Suddenly, she felt Jacques' arm grab her waist firmly.

'Here's not a good place to take a sleep,' he winched her back onto her feet.

'But it's so nice and cold and comfy,' she fought against him, her control over her limbs vanishing at a rapid rate. Ava nuzzled her face into his neck as he half carried her out of the cellar into the chilly night.

Her nose still firmly implanted into his neck, she sniffed Jacques' citrusy aftershave that smelt an awful lot like . . .

'You smell of rosé,' she giggled.

'I do?'

She inhaled deeply. 'I'm getting notes of grapefruit, and mango, and . . .' She sneezed loudly.

'Sorry,' she hiccupped.

Jacques dabbed his skin dry.

'So how are you coping with running a vineyard?' he asked, trying to keep her talking as he figured out the huge problem of how they were going to get down the mountain on a moped when Ava could barely put one foot in front of the other.

Ava groaned. 'Well, I'm not really, I don't know about wine and I don't have anyone to help out . . . except Jean-Marc who is on his way down from Paris. He's promised he will be able to recreate my grandpapa's wine, but even then I don't know how we are going to win the award.' *Why had her voice become so high-pitched?* 'Anyhoo, that's me,' she blew out her cheeks, nestling back into Jacques.

The moped was metres away but all Ava could see was the fountain in front of her. Suddenly hit with a drunken surge of energy, she lurched free from Jacques' grasp and raised a very unsteady foot up onto its edge.

'We have to go, come down from there,' Jacques turned serious.

'But I like it up here, I can see everything,' she wobbled, her hands outstretched like a trapeze artist on a tightrope.

Back on earth, Jacques had assumed a rugby tackle position, light on his toes, ready to dive left or right depending which way she swayed.

'Please come down,' he beckoned.

'You know what, Jacques,' she wobbled. 'You're very serious!'

He sighed deeply. 'Just come down, Ava.'

'You know what, Jacques . . .'

'What?' he exhaled.

'I have no idea what your surname is.'

'Jacques Janvier. Now get down.'

Pointing at him and slurring. 'You know what Jacques Janvier, I'm feeling very, very hot and would love a little swim to cool off.'

'No, stop!' he shouted, but it was too late, Ava had launched herself into the fountain, trainers and all.

Jacques peered over the side to find her sprawled on her back in the ankle-deep water. She pushed herself onto her elbows. Her hair was glued across her face; her jumper, drenched. Her jeans were now a very dark indigo.

'Ooooh, what are these?' she said, rummaging round in the water. She picked up a coin and held it up between her thumb and forefinger, squinting, watching it sparkle under the moonlight.

'They are people's wishes. Now please get out.'

Another bedroom light turned on in the square. A shutter opened and someone shouted 'shut up', not so politely, in French. Ava carried on oblivious to the fact she was waking up the town.

'I'm going to make a wishhhh, I wish, hmmm.' She cleared her throat and tried again. 'I wish that I win first prize in the Golden Globes.'

'Golden Grapes.'

'Yes, the Golden Grapes, that's what I said.'

'*Parfait*, now put your arms around my neck.' Jacques bent over so she could reach. As her arms flopped around him he held her body tightly, hoisting her out of the paddling pool of a fountain.

'You're so strong,' she gurgled as he struggled with her dead weight.

They fell backwards onto the cobbles, Ava tumbling on top of him, turning his white T-shirt transparent with her soaking wet clothes, defining his every muscle. They stared at each other, not breaking eye contact, for what seemed like an eternity.

And then, with drunken courage and fuzzy reasoning, Ava moved her lips towards his.

# Chapter Fifteen

Nope, they didn't want to budge.

She tried once more to prise open her eyelids, which seemed to have been welded together.

Her tongue felt like she'd licked a carpet. Her mouth tasted rancid and there was something unmentionable encrusted in the corners.

If that wasn't bad enough, she could feel someone watching her.

As her blurry eyes slowly came back into focus, she noticed there was a stag, eyeballing her from across the room.

Her heart quickened. She tried to move but even the slightest shift of her head led to a shooting pain ricocheting off the inside of her skull. She flicked her eyes, left to right, absorbing her surroundings, the reality slowly sinking in that:

'This is not my bedroom!' she yelped. Even speaking hurt.

She was in a hunting lodge judging by the number of dead animals sharing the room with her. As well as the stag there was a bear rug and a stuffed wild boar in the corner.

Her gaze slid from the taxidermy to the bed she was in, which wasn't her own, that and the fact that she was wearing nothing except her underwear.

Suddenly the door burst open. Ava yanked the white sheets up to her neck as Jacques breezed into the room in his uniform clutching a tray with two cups of coffee and croissants, filling the air with an aroma of freshly ground beans and baked bread . . . all of which turned her stomach.

But Ava wasn't sure if it was the smell of food that was making her queasy or that she couldn't remember a single thing from the night before past the third wine bottle.

'Here, drink this, it will help,' he passed her a cup.

She reached out an arm, still clutching the sheet firmly to her face with the other, wincing with pain as she propped herself up against a pillow.

He smothered a smirk with his cup as he drained his coffee in two gulps. He placed it back on the tray and shook out his legs energetically, as if he were about to go for a run.

'I must get ready for work, I'm late, Paul will kill me if I don't open up on time. The croissants are fresh, you will like them.' He turned to open the dramatic floor-to-ceiling velvet curtains, and then paused, realising the sunshine would only hurt Ava more. With much kinder eyes he said 'How are you feeling?'

'Fine,' she pushed out a smile, pretending to enjoy the coffee. Her head felt like it was going to explode.

There was an elephant in the room, lurking somewhere between the bear and the boar. Ava finally broke the awkward silence before he turned to leave.

'There's something I need to ask you,' a flush of red spreading from her neck to her cheeks. 'I was just wondering . . .' she cringed. *Why did she have to be so English about these things?* 'I was just curious, umm, why am I just wearing my underwear?'

He grinned at her.

'Did . . . we . . .?'

'*Non!* Come on!' he exclaimed.

Ava laughed, hysterically, suddenly feeling foolish. 'Of course we didn't, silly me, ignore that last question.'

'I had to take your clothes off because they were wet.'
Ava looked puzzled.
'You don't remember taking a swim in the fountain?'
*Oh God*, her head started to throb ten times more.
'You were also sick.'
She stared at him, horrified.
'You know, throwing up,' he demonstrated.
'Yes, yes, I know what that means.' Her cheeks burning even more crimson. A hazy flashback of lying on top of Jacques came into view. Her moving into kiss him, and then the vomit rising in her mouth. She wanted the earth to swallow her up, immediately.

'Was I sick on you?' she squeaked, not really wanting to hear the answer. Dread gripped her stomach as she tried to read his expression.

'No, don't worry.'
She breathed out.
'But I needed to get you out of your clothes in case you got a cold. I'm sorry.'

'You're sorry? I'm sorry, I feel so ashamed.'
Shame didn't even cover half of what she felt though. She was mortified, certain Jacques would never look at her the same way again, if he looked at her again at all. She felt sick and sad, the worst combo with a hangover from hell.

Jacques smiled at her with what she interpreted as pity. His gaze shifted to her hand, still clasping the sheet. 'I would never try to kiss a married woman.'

With all that had happened since she had left England, Ava had momentarily forgotten she was married and that she was wearing a ring.

'Oh, yes, right,' she said, looking to the gold band on her left hand.

'Is your husband staying with you at the vineyard?' He suddenly seemed a little awkward.

Ava cringed as it dawned on her how desperate she must look to him. He probably thought she was some lonely housewife who would stoop to any level just for some attention. So she tried to remedy it by inferring she was much more single than her wedding band implied:

'He's in England. We're not speaking.'

'Oh, I see.' He pinched his bottom lip between his teeth.

Perfect! Now she was desperate . . . with marriage problems, clinging to any man who paid her attention, misreading an innocent winetasting as a date. Unsure where to go from here, she burbled: 'It's fine, I'm fine. We're taking a . . .' she paused. 'We're not really together,' she hesitated, 'we're sort of separated.' She sighed as she struggled to assess what her relationship status actually was. 'It's complicated.'

He looked at her with a hint of concern.

'I'm okay, nothing to see here,' she grinned ridiculously, hiding the hangover tears that were now prickling her eyes.

'I must go,' he smiled and then edged towards the door.

Ava bit her lip, devastated at how she must be coming across.

'Just rest, and leave when you like. Pierre said he would take you back into town.'

'I'm really sorry,' she said again.

'It's fine.'

He slipped from view.

'Hang on!' she called after him. The most obvious question of all . . .

'Where am I?'

He poked his head back around the door with one of his big smiles.

'My uncle Fabian's house. He likes hunting.'

'I can see that,' Ava's brow furrowed.

'Hunting wild boar is a big thing around here, they eat the grapes and . . .' Jacques trailed off as he noticed Ava's disapproving expression.

'He loves making whiskies and liqueurs,' he pointed to a bottle of peach schnapps on top of the dresser. Just looking at alcohol sent a wave of nausea rolling through her.

'But he is away on business so you can relax here for as long as you like today. Just put the key underneath the stone by the front door. Anyway I really must go. *À bientôt*,' he called out from down the hallway.

As soon as she heard the front door close, she slid back onto the bed, gravity pulling the tears from the corners of her eyes, streaking the sides of her face with mascara.

She didn't know if she was crying most because she had nearly spewed over a hot guy who she clearly liked more than she thought, because she was in a world of pain, because she was stuck in a room full of dead animals or the fact that Jacques had seen her in her most unsexy underwear. And to make matters even worse, she now had war paint striped down her face.

Within seconds her mood had shifted again, this time to bad-tempered, as she rapidly pedalled through the stages of a hangover.

She glared at the wild boar.

'What are you looking at?' she grumped. 'Thought so!'

'Owwww!' she clutched her temples.

'The house is still for sale.'

'Sorry, what's that, sweetheart?' Her head was pounding so hard she could barely hear what her daughter was saying. She closed her eyes and slowly opened them.

'*Our* house, it hasn't been sold yet.'

Ava sighed deeply.

'I checked.'

'You checked?'

'I asked Carly's mum to drive past and the For Sale sign's still up.'

'Oh honey.' Of all the moments for Sophie to pick a fight. 'I thought we had been through this.'

There was a long silence on the other end of the phone.

'I thought I'd explained the situation, I'm not buying it back.'

'Well what about a new house?' she snapped.

Ava didn't have the resolve to deal with such a highly emotive conversation while navigating a stonker of a hangover. Even her shoes clacking on the cobbled street were sending tremors through her head.

She turned the corner that opened onto the town square, and froze. It was market day.

'Honey, can I call you back?' She stared at the hundreds of people milling around. Her headache graduated to migraine status.

'Honey?'

But there was no reply – Sophie had hung up.

Ava couldn't believe it. Her daughter had actually put the phone down on her. What she should have done was call her back and give her a good telling-off about manners and respect. But instead she blinked several times in disbelief and let out a high-pitched whimper, not too dissimilar to an animal dying a slow painful death.

On any other day Ava would have embraced the local market with open arms. She would have perused the stalls, sampling local delicacies, gathering mouth-watering ideas to introduce French cuisine into her home cooking.

But today, the sight of a tray overflowing with pigs' trotters, a tank crawling with crabs and the stench of pongy blue cheese was sending her over the edge. Every few leaden footsteps she paused to swallow back the contents of her stomach before she could continue.

She could see the illuminated sign for the pharmacy up ahead, flashing like a beacon hopefully promising a hangover remedy. The only good thing about the corridor of stalls was that it obscured her view of *Chez Paul*. Her feeling of humiliation had intensified as the day had gone on and her hangover had worsened. She now also had 'the fear' to contend with, the alcohol-induced anxiety about what you did the night before. She was sure Jacques had dampened down his version of events to save her dignity, he seemed a gentleman like that. The mention of his name sank her heart. She wouldn't hear from him again after her moonlight fountain performance – no chance. Why would he want to spend time with some forty-something woman who couldn't handle her booze, who was having something kinda complicated with her husband?

Her thoughts were punctured by the ginormous pair of knickers that were being waved in front of her like a flag. Her gaze travelled from the pants to the stall holder – a stocky man wearing a beret and green wax jacket, shouting what sounded like the French equivalent of two for a pound.

Her eyes were steered to his stall with the red awning and a mountain of supportive underwear in beige, light brown and various shades of grey.

'*Très belle, Madame*,' he dangled under her nose the knickers that would reach past her bellybutton, his bushy moustache twitching up and down like a caterpillar with excitement.

*It's a sign! She was on the shelf, destined to a life of solitude wearing enormous knickers.* Ava admitted defeat in her fragile state. The pushy stall holder had packed the twin pack into a carrier bag before she had time to change her mind.

'Twenty-five Euro, *s'il vous plaît.*'

She repeated the amount, spluttering with shock.

'*Oui!*' he held out his grasping hand impatiently.

Ava didn't have the energy or the fight left to argue. She accepted the daylight robbery and returned to her original mission of putting an end to the pain that was penetrating her head like a drill.

Her stomach screamed at her again as she saw the fat dripping off the skewered chicken in the rotisserie oven and why did the oyster stall emanating fishy smells have to be last, just when she was hanging on by a thread? She bit down on her fist as she made those last agonising steps, bowling herself through the door of the pharmacy.

She stood absolutely still for a moment practising deep yoga breathing, until the pharmacist approached from behind, gently asking if she was all right.

Ava nodded, exhaling a weak: 'Yes, thank you.'

She turned around to face the woman, who was strikingly beautiful. 'Can I help you with anything?' Her voice was soft and lyrical, like the French actresses Ava had watched in films. Her dark hair was frizzy and wild, a halo around her face, making her petite features seem even more delicate.

She looked out of place in a small rural pharmacy, her stylish outfit screaming Champs-Élysées rather than Flassans-sur-Issole. Her sexy hourglass figure was accentuated by her green pencil skirt and a pussy-bow blouse, nipped in at the waist by a black belt with an oversized gold Gucci buckle. Ava imagined her wearing oversized sunglasses as she sipped an espresso in a chic terrace café in some uber-trendy part of Paris.

'Would you have anything for a hangover?' she asked, sheepishly.

'Of course.' The pharmacist smiled knowingly. Her eyes ran over Ava, trying to work out what she needed. She sashayed in her heels across the small store, but instead of grabbing a box of paracetamol, she pulled out a tiny glass bottle containing pink liquid.

'This will help,' she handed it to Ava. 'Take all of it in one go.'

Ava stared at the bottle that looked more like a poisonous potion from a fairytale than a remedy.

'It's okay, I made it myself.'

Ava's eyes opened a little bit wider.

'Drink.'

She took a deep breath and downed the fluorescent liquid in one.

'Eugh!' she recoiled. 'It's disgusting! What is that?'

The woman laughed. 'It's the grape extract that makes it bitter. It's only natural herbs and spices, a little of lavender, saffron, turmeric and a special something else.'

Ava dared not ask what.

The woman studied her face. 'I haven't seen you before here, have you just moved to the area?'

'Into Château Saint-Clair, my grandfather's vineyard.'

'Ahhh, so you are the woman they are all talking about.'

Ava's brow knitted.

'Don't worry,' she touched Ava with her slender hand, 'everyone knows everyone's business, nothing is secret in a petite ville. I more than anyone should know that.'

The woman drew a pained breath. She then straightened her back as her thoughts shifted. 'My name is Camille, and I am here if you need anything.'

Her huge smile was warm and magnetic and immediately put Ava at ease. She had a disarming way about her that invited you to tell your life story. Her eyes ran over Ava again. 'Are you okay?'

Something as simple as the kindness of a stranger was enough to open the floodgates in her fragile state. Ava's bottom lip wobbled, tears pooled in her eyes and before she knew it, she was sobbing her heart out on the shoulder of a virtual stranger, explaining her life story between dog-like wailing.

When she had calmed enough to stop hyperventilating, Ava pulled away, wiping her nose on her sleeve. The one good thing was that her hangover had finally started to dissipate.

'So Jacques, you like him?' Camille asked.

'Yes, I mean no, I don't know, I . . . I feel guilty for liking him.' Suddenly panicking she had said too much, Ava spluttered: 'Do you know him?'

She smiled. '*Mais oui*, there are not many handsome men in this town so he is memorable.'

'Please don't say anything,' Ava clasped her hands together.

'Ha, who would I tell? They are not interested in what I say, they are too busy gossiping about me.'

Ava raised her eyebrow questioningly. 'About you?'

'Yes, of course, a single woman of my age, living alone in the countryside, the women assume I am here to steal their husbands.' Her tone hardened, her beautiful features took on a brief mask of sadness. She fanned the thought away. 'Let them think that. They need me as I have the medicine,' she winked.

Ava suddenly saw an ally in Camille.

'I wish I could have your confidence.'

Camille frowned. 'What is this talk? You are beautiful,' cupping her hand around Ava's face. 'Your skin is exquisite, your big eyes will swallow any man, all you need is a little bit of *Je ne sais quoi*,' she flitted her delicate fingers into the air like she was spreading fairy dust.

'Je ne what?'

'Mystery, allure.'

Camille's gaze slid to the thin plastic bag Ava was clutching. 'You have been shopping?'

'Oh no, that's just something from the market.' But before Ava could hide her purchase, Camille was rummaging inside. She dramatically turned her head away in horror, and then gingerly came back for a second peek, just to check she hadn't imagined its contents.

'*Mon Dieu!* You can't be serious! A woman of your beauty should not be wearing those monstrosities,' she held up the tummy tuck pants by the tips of her fingers as if she might catch something from them.

'You must be swathed in the finest lingerie, at all times,' she instructed.

'Even if I'm not dressing up for a man?'

'Especially if you are not,' she stressed. 'If you wear beautiful underwear you will feel sexy, like a woman,' she shimmied her hips as she ran her hands over them. 'And you will be able to smile to yourself knowing what is underneath, with that hint of . . .'

'*Je ne sais quoi*,' Ava finished off her sentence, smiling.

'Listen, we will go shopping one day soon and you will come home feeling,' she paused, her eyes twinkling, 'transformed.'

'You'll do that for me?'

'Of course.'

Impulsively, Ava grabbed her new best friend, holding her tightly, her eyes brimming with gratitude.

They swapped numbers. Ava paid for her magic hangover potion and took two more bottles just in case she might need them in the future – she was going to be making wine after all. Camille popped an extra remedy in the bag as a gift.

'It's lavender oil, made by the monks in the monastery not far from here.'

Ava unscrewed the lid on the miniature bottle and took a sniff. The smell was heady and sweet and delicious.

'It will help you sleep. Just a few drops on your pillow at night.' Her enchanting smile returned. 'For when you worry too much.'

'Thank you, for everything.'

'*De rien*. I will see you soon.'

# Chapter Sixteen

For the first time since she'd arrived in Provence, the sun had been swallowed up by vast grey clouds threatening rain. Ava cuddled her arms across her jumper as she quickened her step across the market to the rendezvous point she'd just arranged with Madame Chevalier.

As she shuffled through the bottleneck of people by the cheeses, a hushed silence fell across the stalls. Everyone seemed to stop what they were doing and stare at something, or somebody.

Suddenly the crowds parted and a couple, who looked like they had stepped out of Hollywood, sauntered towards her.

The man was in his late forties and impeccably dressed. He wore a white linen jacket, jeans and deck shoes, his designer sunglasses hooked into his open-necked shirt. His greying hair was bright against his youthful tanned skin. A real silver fox. Ava's eyebrow went up.

'*Salut!*' He shook the hands of the people he passed like a film star on the red carpet. '*Salut!*'

The woman clinging onto his arm with ruby-red talons for nails wore an almost identical outfit. Skinny jeans that made her legs go on forever, a navy tailored blazer with gold buttons and a serious amount of cleavage on parade. She had a lion's mane of long blonde hair. Her lips were glossy red. Her eyes were hidden behind cat-eye-shaped sunglasses. Her Louboutin heels clacked on the cobbles.

She strutted beside him, pouting, as if she were on an imaginary catwalk.

Ava stepped aside to let them pass as he was clearly the local celebrity, or perhaps the mayor or . . .

'Victor Ambrose,' the man stopped in front of her, not breaking eye contact as he held out his hand.

Ava's hackles rose. She was so taken aback by the surprise encounter with her grandpapa's arch rival, that for a brief moment, all she could manage was an 'Umm . . . I . . .'

He wasn't at all what she had imagined. Her basic manners eventually kicked in, she shook his hand and blurted: 'Ava Chiltern.'

He flashed her a movie star smile, revealing the tips of his perfectly white teeth. 'I know who you are, Madame Chiltern, it's a pleasure to meet you.' His voice soft. His accent, sexy. His gaze still fixed. 'I am very sorry for your loss. I knew your grandfather well.'

A lump appeared in her throat from nowhere.

'I hear you have inherited his vineyard.'

She nodded, cagily.

'And you will be entering the competition?'

Her eyebrows shot up.

'News travels fast around here,' she pretended not to have been rattled.

'Welcome to Flassans-sur-Issole, where your secrets are everyone's,' his eyes twinkled. His tone shifted to serious again as he continued to pay his respects. 'Your grandfather will be thanking you from heaven, it's a truly wonderful way to remember him by.' He dipped his head. 'I wish you the best of luck.'

Surely this isn't the same Ambrose that Madame Chevalier and Bernard had been bad-mouthing? Who was corrupt and ruthless? Ava was beginning to think they had got him wrong. He seemed so nice, so charming . . .

'You must come and visit my vineyard, you are welcome anytime.'

The woman on his arm, who was itching to move on, rolled her eyes and extended her pout.

'In fact, why don't you come for dinner on my yacht?'

Ava's eyes widened. She imagined he owned one of the XXL super-yachts reserved only for the super-rich like oligarchs and football club owners. The biggest boat she'd ever stepped into was a dingy on a reservoir on some freezing cold school expedition.

'I will give you a tour of the estate, which overlooks the sea, the views are breathtaking. And then we can eat lobster on my boat drinking my new sparkling rosé. I think you'll love it, it's my latest labour of love.'

It was undoubtedly a showy offer, but Victor delivered it in such an understated way he made a champagne lobster cruise sound like a trip to the local supermarket. Ava couldn't help but be reeled in, just a smidgen.

With what could only be described as a resting bitch face, the blonde on his arm trailed a hand across the back of his neck with the same determination of a dog marking its territory.

'Thank you, that sounds wonderful.' Ava replied, politely trying to dodge her glare.

'Great! I will get my PA to contact you with dates.'

He kissed her goodbye on both cheeks, his designer stubble brushing her skin. Ava could feel the woman's eyes boring into her.

He finally relented to her tug. He carried on shaking hands, laughing, joking, with the confidence of a man with status and wealth, until he disappeared from view. His expensive aftershave hung in the air.

Madame Chevalier's eyes' bulged when she saw Ava clamber into her car.

'What happened to you?' she gasped.

With all the adventure of the last twenty-four hours, and no mirror to hand, Ava had forgotten she probably looked like she had spent the night in a ditch.

She flipped the visor down to examine her reflection.

'Oh my God! Victor Ambrose saw me looking like this,' she cringed at her panda eyes. 'And he still invited me onto his yacht?'

She licked her finger and rubbed the streaks of mascara so furiously she didn't notice Madame Chevalier had slowed the car to a stop.

The housekeeper erupted. 'You spoke to Monsieur Ambrose?'

Her apple cheeks had reddened, her hands were clenching the steering wheel with such force that her knuckles were white.

'Yes, in the town, he was very friendly actually. He invited me to see his vineyard.'

'You mustn't go! You grandfather would turn in his grave if he knew.'

'I haven't gone yet. And I don't think he is as bad as you say. In fact, he seemed nice.'

'Nice?'

'Polite, and he paid his respects to Grandpapa.'

'Trickery!' she spat.

'I felt it was genuine.'

'It's all one grand performance, a smokescreen.'

'He was really quite humble.'

'*Mon Dieu!* I can't speak to you when you are behaving so irrationally.'

'I can't talk to you when you're being unreasonable,' Ava fired back.

A frosty silence fell between them.

Madame Chevalier turned on the ignition and pulled onto the road with jerky angry movements.

The pair spent the whole journey home in silence, punctuated by huffs and deep sighs from the housekeeper. Ava stared out the window, too annoyed to see the stunning views.

It was hard for Ava to believe the man she had just met could be so underhand, bribing judges, trying to sabotage her grandfather's success. He seemed so dignified and loved by the people in the town, and by women – if his girlfriend's possessive behaviour was anything to go by. She assumed it must be his girlfriend as she hadn't clocked a wedding ring. Ava spent the last few minutes of the journey wondering why she was even looking at his ring finger.

The car came to a screeching halt outside the house. They both sat there for another terse moment, stubbornly, neither wanting to apologise. Madame Chevalier unclipped her buckle and snapped, 'Bernard has fixed your car so you won't need me to pick you up again.' She slammed the car door so hard Ava felt her body reverberate with it.

"Thank you!' Ava called out after her, watching Madame Chevalier waddle into the house. She folded her arms like a sulky child who had just been told off. 'If I want to go on a lobster cruise I will,' she muttered.

# Chapter Seventeen

'Bloody hell babe, I'm booking a flight to see you, pronto. This Ambrose fella sounds hot. I hope you said yes to dinner.'

Ava knew Emilia would like the sound of Victor. She was drawn to anything flashy and expensive.

'Get in there,' she urged.

'But what about Jacques?' Do you think I've blown it with him?'

'Never mind him, he sounds like he still lives with his parents. You need to be with someone suave and rich and sophisticated.'

'And Mark?' Ava's tone suddenly dropped.

'Forget him!' Emilia shrieked. 'He's still with that tramp, I saw them at Sergio's this week. I didn't want to tell you, babe, but they looked like they were sharing a plate of dough balls.'

'We used to share dough balls,' Ava whimpered.

'Who needs stodgy carbs when you can have lobster? You need to get a bit of action with this Vineyard guy.'

'I can't, it would be disloyal to my grandpapa.'

'Hun . . .'

Emilia's pep talk was drowned out by beeping from the courtyard. Ava threw open her bedroom window, the shutters smacking against the wall.

'Oh my!' she exclaimed.

'Is it Vineyard guy? He's come to pick you up in his convertible?'

'Not quite. I've got to go, I'll call you back.'

His blue velvet suit shimmered under the light like a Christmas tree decoration. On hearing Ava approach, he spun around to reveal even more extravagance: a white shirt with ruffles, a yellow cravat and matching canary-yellow socks and brown brogues. Three huge designer travel trunks at his feet. He couldn't have looked more out of place on the dusty dirt track.

'Ava, darling!'

'Jean-Marc?'

'*Enchanté,*' he air-kissed her twice.

He pulled back, holding her with outstretched arms. '*Très belle!*' He then gently lifted her chin with the tip of his finger. 'The similarities are remarkable,' he examined her face. 'You have your grandfather's eyes.'

Ava smiled. 'That's what my mum used to say.'

'His spirit lives on in you. And in the vines.' He looked around, a flash of horror striking his face. '*Mon Dieu!* But what a job we have.' He squealed. 'And so little time. In just four and a half months we will be harvesting!'

He grabbed Ava's hands. '*Ma chérie*, you must forgive me for not getting here sooner. I had no idea things were so bad here. You poor thing, you must have really suffered.'

Ava blinked at him.

'But don't worry, I am here now. We will save this vineyard from destitution.' He clapped his hands in quick succession. '*Allez, Allez*, we must look at what needs to be done. First, to where the wine is made,' he pointed to the horizon like a commander charging into battle, leaving his mountain of designer luggage cases in the middle of the courtyard.

159

He pranced briskly ahead, listing changes at a million miles an hour, gesturing to his left, pointing to his right. His hard soles echoed like tap shoes on the flagstones, until his screechy voice became drowned out by the roar of an engine racing towards them.

Rocketing up the driveway was a man on a moped, wearing a very familiar fur-trimmed denim jacket.

'Oh my God!' Ava couldn't believe it, not after the fountain incident, surely not?

'Oh my God what, *ma chérie*?'

'That's Jacques!'

'Who?' He cocked an eyebrow.

But before she had time to explain, Jacques had skidded to a stop in front of them, vanishing into a fine mist of dust only to reappear moments later, sliding off his bike in one fluid motion. He was already grinning as he pulled off his helmet.

Ava's stomach swooped. A little gasp escaped Jean-Marc's mouth.

'What are you doing here?'

Jacques tucked his helmet under his arm.

'You said you needed an extra pair of hands.' Flashing her his boyish grin, 'So here I am.'

He walked towards them wearing his ridiculously snug-fitting jeans.

'Well at least the help has improved,' Jean-Marc noted under his breath.

*Was this really happening?* Jacques was standing in front of her offering to do heavy lifting. It seemed too good to be true.

'That's really kind of you,' she looked to Jean-Marc, 'but we will be fine on our own.'

Jean-Marc cleared his throat. 'Ava, darling, I think we could really do with an extra pair of hands. Let's not be hasty.'

'I don't have any money to pay him with,' she whispered.

'That's okay,' Jacques interrupted. 'I don't need money as I will keep my job at the restaurant. I just want to learn how to make wine. It has always been my dream, that's why I left Montpellier. I wasn't learning anything in the restaurants there. But here, I can really understand the process,' he paused, catching Ava's gaze, 'if you will let me.' He looked at her cheekily. 'You won't even notice I'm here.'

Ava somehow doubted that.

'I thought you were working at a vineyard?'

'Say yes,' Jean-Marc hissed.

'I would much rather work here,' Jacques looked around him.

'Say yes,' Jean-Marc's voice rose into a squeal.

Her eyes flickered between the two men. Her heart was telling her only one thing. She let out a little breath. 'Okay, yes.'

Jacques smiled broadly, his eyes fixed on her.

'And if we win the prize I will pay you from the winnings, deal?'

'What do you mean 'if'?' Jean-Marc scoffed. 'But we won't get first prize standing around here doing nothing. *Allez! Allez!*'

They looked like a small army squad lined up outside the barn. Jean-Marc flounced up and down, shouting instructions and swinging his arms.

'Bernard, you are in charge of looking after the vines.' He turned and pointed.

Bernard grunted.

'Jacques, you will make sure all the machinery and equipment is working.'

Jacques couldn't wipe the smile of happiness from his face.

'And Ava, darling, your job is to make this look effort-less so Monsieur Ambrose thinks we have everything under control. I want to make that man sweat with fear of losing.' His voice turned acidic. 'I've never lost a competition, and I don't expect to start now.'

Ava very nearly shouted, 'Yes sir!' as it felt like that kind of moment, but wasn't sure Jean-Marc would appreciate her attempt at humour. Instead, she stuck her hand up. 'Do I have time to nip to the toilet before we start?'

She quickly retracted her question when she saw Jean-Marc's exaggerated eye roll.

'No, okay, I'll hang on then,' she crossed her legs.

Jean-Marc put his hands on his hips.

'Listen everyone. I'm going to explain to you how we make wine. That way we can all understand our job for the summer. *Oui?*'

There was a rolling murmur across the troops.

'*Parfait!*' their leader spun around. 'So, as you can see, directly in front of us is the grape press. There is no need for people to use their feet any more,' he chuckled to himself. 'This,' he pointed, 'is where the magic begins.'

He walked up to the long white cylinder that looked like a fuel truck. Touching it with both hands, he breathed in deeply as if he were performing some holistic treatment.

Ava and Jacques gave each other a sideways glance, struggling to snuff out their sniggers.

'The grapes are picked at the end of summer in harvest time and they are poured into the press here,' he pointed to a hole in the top of the tanker. 'One type of grape at a time into the machine, and we only use red grapes to make rosé.' Ava and Bernard caught each other's eyes and she looked away quickly, stifling a grin. Jean-Marc marched to the other side of the tank. 'We don't press them straight away, we leave them to swim in their skins for three or four hours so a bit of the colour and the flavour of the skin is absorbed into the juice. It is called the maceration process and this is how we get the majestic pink in rosé. Are you all following so far?' He didn't wait for a reply. '*Bien.*'

His hand was now hovering over a giant red button that looked like an end-of-the-world destruction trigger a baddie in a Bond film might have. He lifted the Perspex encasing it. Jacques leaned forward, softly brushing shoulders with Ava as he peered over. She didn't dare look at him this time, just in case he could tell her pulse had rocketed. She wondered if he could also feel the sparks.

'When I press this, a balloon will start to expand inside the tank, gently extracting all of the juice. The leftovers – the skin, the seeds, the flesh – will be taken away,' he pointed to the conveyor belt.

Jacques' shoulder was still touching hers. Had he deliberately not moved away? She didn't want him to, she loved the feel of him brushing against her, how it made all her nerve endings tingle. Listening to the words 'flesh' and 'press' being thrown around wasn't helping matters.

'You can change the flavour and colour of the rosé depending on how long you press for.'

*There was that word again.*

'Twenty minutes less will produce a completely different juice. This is where the creating process begins.' Jean-Marc tapped the tips of his fingers together excitedly. 'So many possibilities even with just one type of grape. Magic!' He cleared his throat. 'But it needs a very good winemaker to know when to say that the juice is ready, to say let's go, lets press.' He tapped his chest, 'That will be *moi.*'

'What next?' he spun around. '*Ah oui,* I must see the cuverie.'

Jacques whispered, his breath hot in Ava's ear, 'The word comes from *Cuve*, which means tank or vat.'

She looked at him blankly.

'Where the wine is made.'

'Oh, I thought that was just called the barn.'

He placed his hand on her lower back as he guided her in the direction of the huge barn.

'In winemaking there is a special word for everything. It has its own language, a language similar to romance because so much love is put into it.'

His touch gave her goosebumps. She swallowed hard.

Her grandfather's barn, or *cuverie*, was like many others in the French countryside. Rectangular, and built from mismatched wooden planks. The pitched roof was made of corrugated iron that had rusted to a burnt amber colour. Back in the thirteenth century it would have housed the Knights' horses. Now, it was home to three huge stainless-steel barrels.

Jacques leapt ahead and heaved open the huge double doors. They whined and wobbled on their hinges, protesting against being moved. Bernard led the troop into the gigantic open space. Two pigeons flapped their wings angrily at being disturbed and rose to the wooden beams, chirping their irritation from above.

Ava hadn't paid much attention to the barn when she first arrived, but studying it now, she could see what a shabby state it was in. The roof was riddled with holes, slivers of sunlight poured down from above, dotting spotlights across the ground. Giant spider's webs clung to the corners clasping mummified insects. And something was moving to the left, making a scuttling noise. Ava tried not to think about what it could be.

'Lucky it almost never rains in summer or we would be in trouble.' Jean-Marc gazed nervously up at the roof.

Bernard started coughing. He reached out a hand to a woodworm-riddled beam to steady himself.

'Are you all right?' Ava checked.

He nodded, patting the gunk in his chest. 'He doesn't know what he's talking about. No rain, of course there will be rain. Idiot.'

Jean-Marc took centre stage again. He picked up a stick and pointed at the towering silver barrels.

What happens if it rains?' Ava whispered to Bernard.

'A storm could finish off the last of the grapes. It could damage the barrels.'

'Destroy our chances of winning?'

Bernard looked at her sideways. 'It would all be over.'

Ava gulped audibly.

'So,' Jean-Marc continued. 'When the grapes have been pressed, the juice is separated into here for the fermentation process.'

'I remember my grandfather making wine in old wooden barrels.' Ava turned to Jacques.

'This is the modern way to make rosé. It keeps the wine light and fresh, how it should be in Provence. Oak wood gives a smoky heavy flavour to the wine, nobody cares for this much any more.'

'Ah, I see.'

He smiled at her.

'I will be doing a natural fermentation using only the yeast that was living in the skin of the grapes combined with the sugar in the grapes.' He smacked the barrel with his stick. 'The fermentation process develops the flavour.'

Ava lit up. 'It turns the grape juice into booze?'

'*Oui!* But Ava, please! Into wine, not booze, that is a disgusting term, ugh. You English and your booze cruises and boozy nights out and . . .'

'How long does the fermentation last for?' Jacques cut in.

'Only ten to twelve days. It is critical that we control the temperature in the tanks to stop the wine getting too hot during this process.'

'What happens if it gets too hot?' Ava and Jacques asked at the same time, and then both laughed, shyly.

'It kills the yeast! They all die!'

'It remains grape juice,' Bernard added.

'*Oui*. No alcohol.' Jean-Marc thumped his stick onto the ground.

Ava let out a small gasp.

'I will oversee the start of the fermentation. It takes a lot of precision. You need to have enough yeast, enough sugar and the minimum temperature to start. It is only a job for someone skilled.'

Bernard coughed to conceal a laugh.

'After fermentation we just wait for the flavours to mature. That's where the alchemy begins. We wait, we filter, blend, air the wine, blend again, continuously tasting it to find that perfect flavour, recreating the exact combination of ingredients to recreate Monsieur Bellavance's wine in time for the competition in spring next year. This is our challenge.'

Jean-Marc opened the door of a barrel and poked his head inside.

'Disgusting. Filthy!' his voice echoed up the vat. 'They will have to be cleaned, they need to be, *Mon Dieu!*' He recoiled, squealing and flapping. 'A mouse! There is a mouse inside.' He sprinted across the barn and leapt onto a stool. 'Get it! get it!'

'Come on, it's just a mouse,' grumbled Bernard.

Ava stared daggers at Jacques when he gestured at her to catch the rodent.

'I was only kidding,' he gave her a playful nudge. 'I'll get the mouse. He's probably more scared of you than you are of him.'

Without hesitation, Jacques climbed through the hatch into the barrel, thrusting his pert derrière into the air.

'Oh my,' Jean-Marc quickly forgot his trauma and started fanning his face to cool off. 'Have you got him yet?' he called after Jacques.

'*Merde!*' came the echoey reply from the barrel, followed by some loud banging.

'No, don't kill him, he's only small,' Ava shouted.

Another tense minute passed before Jacques' bum re-appeared in the doorway. He wriggled himself backwards, his hands cupped, a tail dangling between his fingers.

'Keep that thing away from me!' Jean-Marc squirmed on his stool.

Bernard sniggered. 'What sort of man is afraid of a mouse?'

'I make the wine, I don't have to deal with the wildlife in the countryside,' he snapped. 'What do you take me for? I live in Paris,' he swept his hand across his brow, 'where it is civilised.'

'Shush both of you, you'll scare it,' Jacques whispered, carrying the furry creature into the open.

Ava knew it was silly, ridiculous really, but she couldn't stop her heart melting at the sight of Jacques whispering a few soothing words to the mouse before setting it free into the vineyard.

The tiny brown creature weaved through the trunks and then stopped. He rose onto his hind legs, cleaned his ears and whiskers, twitched his nose and then scurried away, disappearing amongst the vines.

'Ah-ha-hem,' Jean-Marc cleared his throat. 'If we could get back to the pressing matter of the competition.'

He straightened his cravat, pretending that nothing had happened. 'Now, in order for me to recreate the perfect blend, I will need to taste the masterpiece. Where have you hidden the wine?'

It was a drum-roll moment as everyone's eyes turned to Bernard.

The gardener studied his audience. There was one stranger amongst them, could he trust Jacques? His eyes lingered in hesitation. He then nodded, as if he'd weighed everything up in his head, and turned back towards the house.

'Follow me.'

Madame Chevalier's broom was tapping everyone's toes before they had even set foot into the study.

'Off! dirty shoes off!' she bossed, targeting Jacques and his trendy black biker boots.

'You too, Bernard, off.'

He narrowed his eyes and grumped: 'But I'm going back outside in a moment.'

His words were a red rag to a bull. She threw her hands on her hips, her pigtail swishing like the tail of an angry cat.

'Do you know how many hours I've spent this morning sweeping this place spotless, cleaning up after Madame Ava?'

Ava bristled. 'What have I done?'

'You're not a child any more.'

'I had noticed that,' Ava muttered under her breath while Jacques edged towards the door trying to dodge the line of fire.

'And you!' she pointed to him. 'Boots off now.'

Once Madame Chevalier had got rid of all her hot air, she managed a half-smile. 'So, what are you all doing in here?'

'I've come to show them the wine,' Bernard revealed.

'It's time?'

'*Oui*, it's time.'

They padded across the living room in their socks, Bernard leading the way in his thick blue ones punctured with holes. Jean-Marc was close at his heels in his traffic-stopping yellow pair while Ava was trying to hide from Jacques the fact she was wearing naff Christmas socks.

'They were a gift,' she blushed at his cocked eyebrow.

They came to a standstill next to her grandfather's reading chair, baffled as to where the big reveal was going to come from. Bernard groaned with pain as he strained to reach the top shelf of the bookcase.

'Do you need a hand?' Jacques moved to his side but Bernard was too proud a man to ask for help.

'*Non*,' he refused, running his hand along the ancient leather-bound books on winemaking.

Ava remembered how her grandpapa used to read them to her after dinner, explaining the history of winemaking in France. She would fall asleep in the crook of his arm.

Bernard began pulling out the journals, one by one, the expanding gap slowly revealing an alcove in which three bottles were secretly stashed.

'*Mon Dieu! Mon Dieu!* Is that them?' Jean-Marc squealed, grabbing a bottle from Bernard. He was almost hyperventilating with excitement as he held the rosé in his hands. He hugged it to his chest, whispering to it in French.

'What's he saying?' Ava asked Bernard.

'He's asking the wine to tell him its secrets.'

'Of course he is. Has he got a reply yet?'

Bernard chuckled. It was the first time she had made him laugh.

'I think he will be waiting a long time for that.'

Jean-Marc turned to his audience, his eyes were big, watery and emotional.

Holding it up as if it were a trophy, he said, 'This, *Mesdames et Monsieurs*, is going to win us the Golden Grapes.'

## Provence, Summer 1984

Moving the books dislodged another memory.

Ava was transported back in time to when she was nine years old, hiding in the shadows.

To when fear was coiling around her and was slowly squeezing the air out of her little lungs as she watched on helplessly.

Her mum and dad didn't know her grandpapa had sent her into the larder to fetch him some biscuits, that she was watching them from the darkness, two little eyes, peering around the door into the kitchen, seeing everything unfold, but being too young to understand why. Why was her dad interrogating her mum about who she'd met in town? The same question over and over again.

'I just went to get some croissants for the journey home,' her voice changing from defensive to frightened as he ground her down.

Ava jumped as she heard his fists slam onto the worktop.

'You were gone for an hour and a half!' his voice rising to a shout. 'An hour and a half, it doesn't take that long to go to and from town. Who were you meeting?'

'Nobody.'

'I said, who were you meeting?'

Her voice quivered: 'No one, it was difficult to find parking and then there was a queue in the *boulangerie* and then . . .'

He swatted the bag of pastries from the table, sending them flying across the kitchen.

'I didn't meet anyone, I promise.'

She was begging. Her mum was begging him to believe her.

Her father's voice exploded, like the roar of the dragon in her favourite cartoon, the angry, booming voice when he was just about to eat one of the villagers. 'LIAR!' he thumped both his fists down.

'What's going on in here?' her grandpapa burst into the kitchen, his eyes searching the room. 'Where's Ava?'

She froze, terrified her father's fury would turn on her if he discovered she'd been listening in.

'I sent her to fetch me some biscuits from the larder.'

She edged back into the dark of the room.

Her grandpapa faced her father. 'I will not have you raising your voice in *my* home, to *my* daughter.

'Mind your business, old man.'

*'À qui pensez-vous parler!'*

Her father took a step towards her grandpapa, staring him down, and snarled: 'In English! Your insults are lost on me, you interfering fool.'

'Tony, stop!'

'Stay out of this, it's between me and your father.'

Her grandpapa puffed up his chest, his belly rising. 'I said, who do you think you're talking to?'

'Tony! Papa!' her mum cried.

Ava's body was trembling under the strain of trying to stay completely still, silent as a mouse, while her fear coiled tighter and tighter around her chest. She wanted to save her mum, her grandpapa and the only way she could think of doing that was to distract her father.

Clutching the packet of biscuits in her hand, she stepped into the light. She smiled weakly. 'I found them!'

# Chapter Eighteen

**July 2018**

Ava stepped out of the kitchen into the courtyard with the tray, the summer heat throwing all of its intensity at her. She closed her eyes for a brief moment and stood perfectly still, listening to the birds chattering in the trees, to the high-pitched chirping of the cicadas, to the bees humming as they hopped between the roses that were climbing around the porch.

She was wearing a simple white vest and denim shorts, frayed at the edges from where she had cut them from her jeans, and a pair of flip-flops she had picked up in the market.

Four months had passed since she had arrived in France and her hair had grown long, past her shoulders. She'd tied it back into a simple ponytail with an elastic band she'd found in the top drawer of her Grandpapa's desk that morning. Her skin was bare apart from a smattering of freckles that had blossomed thanks to her daily dose of sunshine.

She inhaled deeply, the scents of the lavender that she had planted by the front door whooshing towards her. Life was good, in fact she couldn't remember it ever being better. Even though she had practically no money to live off she had never felt richer in inner peace.

The ice cubes clinked against the jug as she walked towards the barn, the sweet smell of the fresh lemonade heady underneath her nose.

Jacques had been working hard all morning trying to get the wine press to work so she thought he deserved something refreshing that would quench his thirst.

At the sight of him, her mouth fell slightly open.

Jacques was poised on top of the press, with a hammer, with his top off.

*It would be dangerous to interrupt him now,* she reasoned, trying to string out the perfect moment for as long as possible.

But he'd heard her footsteps crunching on the gravel. He gave one last bash of the hammer and looked up.

'*Salut!*' he shouted, waving.

She lifted the tray. 'I thought you might want this.'

'You read my mind. Hang on, I just need to get down.'

The condensation was dripping down the sides of the jug under the fierce heat.

'Okay, I'll just wait here,' she replied. *Of course, where else would you go?* Ava chastised herself for making yet another obvious remark. She'd been doing that a lot recently – stumbling over her words in front of Jacques. They'd been working side by side, almost every day, but instead of relaxing into the familiarity of having Jacques around, she'd been growing increasingly tense – concerned about what he might think of her. If he thought of her at all. Of course he didn't . . . her thoughts trailed off as her mouth fell open.

Jacques swung his legs around and slid down the side of the press, crouching as he landed in the dust. He stood up, wiping his oil-stained hands on a rag tucked into his back pocket, slinging it onto the ground as he walked towards her.

Ava had seen men with six-packs on billboards and in films but she didn't know they really existed. She'd been married to man with a belly for twenty-three years; she thought that's what all normal men had. How wrong she had been.

He even had those muscular 'V' lines pointing like an arrow in the direction of his low-slung jeans.

'It's hot today,' he said, pouring the cloudy liquid into the glass.

Ava swallowed. *You're telling me.*

He took long restorative gulps, draining the glass in seconds. He wiped his mouth and thanked her, not breaking eye contact.

'You seem to know what you're doing,' she squeaked, referring to the press.

He filled another glass.

'You forget I grew up on a farm. My parents live not far from here actually,' he hooked his hand into the distance.

'And that's where you learnt how to handle machinery?'

Their conversations always seemed to hover somewhere between formal, like now, when she felt like she was questioning him for a job interview, and very familiar. It could change within seconds, catching her off guard, suddenly the air between them crackling like static.

He smiled. 'Do you really want to know where I learnt to operate machinery?

She blushed. Searching for something to disguise her bashfulness, she pointed to a scar running across his six-pack: 'How did you get that?'

'Oh, this,' he traced his finger softly over the faded white line. His expression suddenly looking pained. 'I was knifed in the bar I was working in.'

'No!' she exclaimed.

'*Oui*, I was trying to get a rowdy customer to leave and he pulled out a knife and attacked me.'

'You're kidding?' She stared at his chest a little more. 'You're so brave to have stood up to him.'

He looked at her intensely for a long moment and then cracked a smile. 'No, come on!' Tipping his head back with laughter.

She shoved him, playfully. 'I can't believe you lied.'

'It was too easy,' he sniggered. 'This,' he pointed, 'I got when I was fourteen, when I thought piercing my own ear was a good idea.'

'When is it ever a good idea?'

'When your friends all have earrings and you want to be part of the *cool* group,' he said, using his fingers as commas.

'I can't see an ear piercing.' She moved closer. Their eyes locked.

'That's because I passed out from the pain and came crashing down on my beer bottle.'

'You're kidding? You impaled yourself on a beer bottle?'

His cheeks turned pink. 'Not so impressive, is it! Now you know why I lied.'

'How many girls have you told that story to?' she chortled, before realising what she'd said.

His eyebrows shot up; her suggestion that he was an outrageous flirt hung in the air.

She cleared her throat as he looked the other way, the frisson dying down again.

'So how do your parents feel about you working here?'

It was back to interview questions.

He shrugged. 'They're much happier about me working here than the other vineyard. They like the fact that it's a small family-run estate. Being farmers, they know what it is like to struggle against the elements and they said they admire you for trying to make this work.'

'And what about you? They must be proud of you for what you're achieving?'

He rubbed the back of his neck shyly. 'They're just thankful for the opportunity you have given me.'

Even if his parents hadn't told him, she respected his passion, the way he fought for what he wanted from life. It was strange, she'd known Jacques for only a fraction of the time she'd been with Mark, but because their thoughts, their dreams, were so much more aligned, she felt like she'd known him forever.

'I know what it feels like to be given a second chance,' she said.

He looked at her kindly, as if he understood she had suffered in her journey to Château Saint-Clair. His battle to do the job he loved had made him wise beyond his years, sensitive to the struggles of others.

She found comfort in the silence that fell between them.

And then the static started to spark up again. His gaze was like a vice, pinning her in place.

'So you have decided things are finished,' he paused, 'with your husband?' He looked down at Ava's hands, to the bright white band that shone against her tan, where her wedding ring should have been.

Ava had removed it a few days ago to protect the gold from damage, but she'd forgotten to put it back on. She hadn't missed it being there. She hadn't even noticed it was gone. But Jacques seemed to be paying close attention to her actions.

She rubbed her thumb over where it used to be and looked up at him and whispered: 'Yes.'

He smiled, but still not giving anything away.

'How does your daughter feel about it all?'

'Things are getting better between us, although,' she sighed out, 'we had another heated argument this morning. I think she still harbours anger over me not trying to fix my marriage. For not selling the vineyard to buy our old home back. It's been sold now, to a family, I've been told.'

'Are you sad it's gone?'

'No.' the word came out instantly, before she had time to process it. 'I don't miss it at all. It's funny, isn't it? How you can want something so badly and one day you just stop caring.'

The frankness and intimacy of their conversation was pulling her in, giving her the courage to ask Jacques something that had been preying on her mind.

'So tell me about you.'

'Me?' He laughed. 'I told you about me.'

'You told me about your scar! Tell me about . . .' her throat suddenly constricting, 'tell me something a little more personal.'

'More personal,' he said playfully, spinning out her awkwardness for as long as possible.

'You know what I mean,' she looked down, blushing, the heat rising inside her. In her best trying-to-be-casual voice, she asked: 'Is there a special someone in your life?' She even added a little shoulder wiggle to make it seem playfully nonchalant.

He smiled. 'Yes.'

Her heart plummeted. *Of course there was! How could she have thought there wouldn't be?* Struggling to mask her disappointment, she burbled out a 'Nice.' *Nice? There was nothing nice about Jacques liking someone else.*

He took a sip from his drink. 'But I'm not sure how she feels about me. She's not easy to . . . how do you say this in English . . . easy to read?'

'Yeah, that's how you say it. So, are you going to ask her out?' she asked half-heartedly.

He smiled again. 'I think so,' flashing her a look.

And there it was again, '*le frisson*'. Jacques was impossible to read and it was driving her crazy.

Ava was in the process of crafting another question to get closer to the truth about the mysterious Jacques, when Jean-Marc screeched out for his attention. Jacques rolled his eyes at her. 'I've been summoned.' He held his cold glass against his face for a moment, cooling himself down before he was thrown into more heavy lifting work. Ava found herself staring, too obviously, at the glaze of moisture left on his golden skin.

This was torture! she decided, watching his muscles ripple as he reached down to pick up his tools. Torture.

# Chapter Nineteen

'Wait, Ava!' a familiar voice bounced off the walls of the narrow street. Ava spun around. It was Camille, waving vigorously. Her hair was encased in layers of tin foil, her tiny frame swaddled in a giant dressing gown streaked with bleach stains.

'I've been trying to get hold of you all week, where have you been?'

'Sorry, it's been manic getting ready for harvest.'

'Come,' she beckoned Ava to follow her inside the hairdresser's.

She glanced at her watch. 'I really should be getting back, I promised I'd make lunch.' She lifted up a bag of baguettes and groceries.

'They can wait, come.'

Ava wavered some more and then smiled. 'Okay, five minutes . . .'

The salon's interior was as dated as the faded, sun-bubbled posters in the window with its parquet wooden floor, leather swivel chairs facing dusty mirrors, giant dome lamps, and a trolley heating up a set of rollers. The local radio was humming in the background and a white cat was snoozing in the warmth of the window. It smelt of shampoo and chemicals and nail varnish. There were half a dozen women inside in various states of recline. One lady was having a pedicure, the rest looked like they were there to put their feet up and have a gossip. Camille whizzed around the room with introductions before returning to her hot seat underneath the lamp to finish off infusing her highlights.

'Ava is in France to find herself,' Camille announced to the group.

'Well, that's not quite true . . .'

'She's also here to meet a handsome French man.'

'Ummm . . .'

'In Flassans-sur-Issole?' the beautician painting the toenails chortled. '*Bon chance!*'

'Of course here,' Camille smiled at Ava knowingly – knowing everything about her crush on Jacques. 'But I've been telling her, she needs to sex up her appearance, to find that confident woman hiding inside her.'

'It won't make any difference, he's not interested,' Ava grumbled. She'd stamped out all hope of him fancying her since their chat. He'd probably asked the girl out by now. She pictured some pretty leggy thing in her twenties. Someone much more his age.

'This is not about *him*, it's something for you,' Camille swiped.

'Nothing like a perm to pick you up,' the woman earwigging while flicking through a magazine suggested, without looking up.

'Perm?' Ava panicked. She hadn't seen one of those since the eighties.

'Ah, don't listen to Danielle, Marie here is a wizard with the scissors, she will transform you, won't you, Marie?'

'*Oui!*' The hairdresser stepped forward, introducing herself as the owner of the salon. She had jet-black hair that was long and glossy and swished like a show horse – they had to be extensions, Ava thought. She wore a white flowery apron, its pouch bulging with velcro rollers. Clipped onto her wide leather belt were scissors, a comb and a hairspray. She looked like a strange mix of a fifties housewife and a sexy cowgirl from a Western.

Camille turned to Ava, staring at her intently. 'It's time.'

'It is?'

'*Oui*. So, we start with the hair.' She patted the seat next to her.

Ava looked more than worried as she took a pew. 'What's wrong with my hair?'

The hairdresser appeared behind her in the mirror, grimacing as she ran her hand through Ava's limp locks.

'It's dead,' she said unforgivingly in her basic English.

'Dead?'

'*Oui*. Off!' She snipped with her fingers.

The rest of the room nodded in agreement. It was one against six.

'But I've always worn it long—'

'So it's time for a change,' Camille insisted.

'Perhaps it just needs a bit of reshaping,' Ava suggested timidly.

There was a communal '*non!*' from her panel of judges. Even the cat had looked up and was staring at her.

'She needs a drink!' Someone exclaimed. 'Get *Madame* a drink!'

Next thing Ava knew, a glass of something exceptionally pale pink and zesty had been thrust into her hand. 'Le clos', she was informed, was a special buttery, creamy-tasting rosé from a family-run vineyard called Château Peyrassol.

She took a sip and raised her eyebrow. Drawing on her expanding expert knowledge, she commented: 'This would be a perfect accompaniment to fresh white fish or just as an aperitif.' And then under her breath, added: 'Or a tasty tranquilliser when you're about to get your hair lopped off.'

Without hesitation, she tipped a huge mouthful of the sweet nectar into the back of her throat, the alcohol soaring straight to her head. It was just what she needed to take the edge off.

Marie was poised with her scissors.

'Ready?'

Ava closed her eyes, she couldn't look.

'Tell me when it's over,' she winced.

Camille touched her arm. 'Have faith.'

Ava kept her eyes glued shut for the next twenty minutes, tensing every time the scissors whistled past her ears. She soothed her angst listening to Camille's enchanting voice recounting her life in Paris.

The pharmacist told how she was once married to a wealthy businessman, living a life of luxury and extravagance. They had a huge apartment in the expensive Saint-Germain-des-Prés neighbourhood. They ate in the finest restaurants, they had tickets to all the sellout shows. She put her entire being into supporting her husband, accompanying him to his galas and charity events, massaging his huge ego, dropping everything she wanted to do for him. And then one day, she decided to abstain from her mind-numbingly boring lunch with the wives of his colleagues, only to return home to find her husband in bed with another woman.

'Screwing the secretary. A cliché if ever there was one.'

'Oh God, I'm so sorry,' Ava said softly.

'Don't be, I'm not.' There wasn't a hint of regret or sorrow in her voice but strength, with the occasional flame of anger.

'So what did you do?' Ava asked, her eyes still tightly shut.

'*Mais oui*, I screwed him too, for all his money in the divorce settlement.'

There was a mini round of applause from the ladies.

'And now I am the boss of my own life, creating my own remedies and helping other people heal, living in the most beautiful part of France.'

Her tone turned reflective. 'There is no substitute for doing something you love. And when you are happy you radiate, and a man of your dreams finds you, not the other way around.'

The room fell into a contemplative silence at her words. And then the thoughts were blown away as Marie fired up the hairdryer.

That meant only one thing, the big reveal was moments away. Ava let her hair be ruffled this way and that as the warm air massaged her neck, still not daring to open her eyes.

'Okay, we're finished,' Marie announced abruptly, wrapping the cord around the hairdryer.

There was another silence, a much more disconcerting one this time. Shouldn't someone be saying something? Ava panicked. Even an obligatory 'That's nice'? It was unbearable; Ava had to peek, just with her left eye.

'Oh my God,' she gasped.

She stroked the back of her head, where her long hair used to be.

Camille appeared behind her shoulder, staring at her through the mirror. 'You look beautiful.'

'Stunning!' The woman getting her nails painted vamp red added.

'*Magnifique*,' exhaled a voice from across the salon.

'A new woman,' Camille whispered in her ear. 'All that extra weight that was dragging you down, gone.'

Ava couldn't stop running her hands through her gamine crop. Her parting was now to the side, soft and feminine, emphasising her heart-shaped face. Ten inches of her hair lay fallen at her feet.

'It brings out your beautiful eyes.' Camille removed her dangling earrings and held them to Ava's ears.

'Some striking jewellery will be the perfect accessory. And a chic trouser suit, with heels of course, finished off with a clutch bag under your arm.'

Ava swivelled around to face her. 'But where would I wear something like that? I spend my days working on a vineyard.'

'Tsk. This is all about you feeling good about yourself. Reaching your potential, showing off that fabulous body of yours. You don't need an occasion to look fabulous.'

'I don't have anything like that in my wardrobe.'

'But I do, which you can borrow.'

'You would really lend me your clothes?' *Were people ever really that nice?* Living in suburbia for years, where people keep themselves to themselves, had made her cynical of genuine kindness.

'Of course. We are friends – here to help each other.'

'I can't thank you enough for being so kind to me.'

'*De rien.* It's my pleasure. I'm enjoying helping transform you into a swan.'

Ava looked at her excitedly. 'So what's next? Make-up?'

Camille tutted. 'That can wait. There is something more important we must do first.' Her beautiful smile curled at the corners with mischief.

'We will be asked a lot of questions, two women in our situation, so be prepared.'

Ava pulled away from Camille's arm. 'Oh no, I don't want any attention. The last thing I need is people gossiping about me.'

'It is better to be talked about than not at all. You want to be noticed, you should be noticed, and what we are about to do is essential. Trust me!'

Ava hovered by the shop entrance staring wide-eyed at the mannequins wearing black and nude corsets with stockings and suspenders.

'I've seen those monstrosities you bought in the market, remember. I promised I'd help you feel sexy and confident, that I'd find your *Je ne sais quoi*, and it begins here.' Camille tugged her arm towards the door. 'It will be fun. Come on.'

Ava stepped forward, gingerly. 'Okay, okay.'

The door jangled as they entered the Aladdin's cave of lingerie. The shop was wallpapered purple and gold and lined with row upon row of underwear sets. To the left were the intricate lace designs, understated but classy underwired bras and French knickers. To the right, the more racy twin-sets, corsets, thongs, bras with buckles, straps in places Ava couldn't imagine would be comfortable. She didn't know where to look.

'Toto, I have a feeling we're not in Marks and Spencer any more,' she squeaked.

'Pardon?' Camille turned her head.

'Oh nothing, I was just saying how, erm, decorative the designs were.'

The heavy red velvet curtain at the back of the shop rippled, and a woman emerged through it like a cabaret show.

*Bonjour Madame,* she sang, before realising who it was. In a much cooler tone '*Camille. Ça va?*'

She wasn't at all like Ava might have imagined would run a boudoir-esque shop. In fact, she looked more boarding-school matron than *Madame*. Her grey hair was pulled back into a high chignon bun. She was dressed in a long pleated skirt with a cardigan, a string of pearls and smart high heels. Her oval glasses, which looped around her neck on a chain, were perched at the end of her nose. She peered down them at Ava.

'This is my friend, Ava, she's English.'

The shopkeeper stared at her suspiciously, just as Camille warned her she might.

'It's a pleasure to meet you, Madame.' She paused, her eyes studying her. 'Are you looking for anything in particular? Is it for a special occasion?'

Ava sensed a loaded question.

'Not really, I'm just after . . .' she looked to Camille, realising she had absolutely no idea what she was there for. 'I'd like a plain bra that I could wear under a T-shirt. Please,' she smiled meekly.

'*Non, non, non,*' Camille butted in. 'My beautiful English friend is looking for something sexy.' The shopkeeper's eyebrows shot up. 'Something that's gentle to touch, so soft it feels like it's kissing and caressing the skin.'

The woman's eyes widened.

'But at the same time, accentuates her curves, screams – *undress me!*' Camille smiled mischievously, clearly taking delight in setting tongues wagging.

Ava supposed Camille must have had it up to her neck with small-minded gossips and this was her small way of taking revenge and empowering herself.

The shopkeeper was too genteel to rise to Camille's bait. Instead she smiled politely and injected a lilt of waspishness into her tone when she suggested maybe her friend would like to try something from the left half of the shop.

'What about this?' Ignoring her, Camille picked up a black and red plunge bra from the adjacent wall that had enough padding to fill a cushion.

'What am I supposed to do with that, I'll topple out of the thing,' Ava coughed away her shock.

'Nonsense! What size are you?'

'34C, but—'

'Try it on,' she thrust it into Ava's hands and gave her a pat in the direction of the changing rooms. 'And this,' she handed her a teeny matching thong.

'There's barely any material on this, it might as well be see-through!'

'Trust me, it will look fabulous.'

Ava wasn't convinced she looked fabulous at all. In fact, as she stared at her wobbly bits in the three mirrors that were cruelly angled to show every part of her body, she attacked herself for having three *pain au chocolat* this week already.

'How's it looking?' Camille called through the curtain.

'Terrible, I'm taking it off.'

'No, let me see first.'

'No, I look fat.'

Camille yanked back the curtain.

Her hands clapped with pride. 'You look beautiful, *très très belle.*'

Ava was stunned, quickly masking her breasts with her hands.

'Don't be ridiculous,' Camille pulled them down. 'Be proud, you have a fabulous figure. And great breasts, *mon Dieu*, look at them!'

'Really?' Ava was genuinely baffled. She couldn't remember the last time someone said something nice about her body. It must have been decades ago when she first met Mark, and his words were barely complimentary. As for her boobs, she didn't know it was humanly possible to hoist them so high, never mind that she couldn't breathe. Although she was enjoying seeing cleavage she never knew she had.

'*Oui!* And you need to show it off more.'

The shop owner reappeared with a tape measure. 'Do you need any help, Madame?' she asked while Ava snatched the curtain, wrapping it around her like a sari.

'My friend was worried she needs a bigger size?'

They both waiting for Ava to peel away the velvet. Realising she wasn't going to win this battle, she took a deep breath and stepped out.

The shop owner peered down her glasses, nodding. '*Oui, très belle.*' She then slipped into matron mode, pushing overspilling bosom into the balcony, yanking the straps to lift the bust, running her finger under the material to check it fitted snugly, with all the gentleness of a rider saddling up a horse.

'*C'est bon,*' she stood back, dusting her hands together, while Ava turned increasingly pink. '*Non,* the size is perfect.' She then casually remarked. 'Someone is a lucky man.'

'It's for a lover. A young lover.' Camille whispered naughtily.

Ava wanted to kill her. The woman smiled politely and said she would wrap the underwear set up.

'She'll wear them now,' Camille called after her.

'I will?'

'Yes. Those things,' pointing to her washed-out grey-infused bra and Little Miss Sunshine pants, 'must be destroyed.'

'Oh but . . .'

'Trust me. You will start feeling sexier almost immediately.'

Ava reluctantly did as she was told. She tossed her comfy go-to knickers into the bin and put her trust in the magical underwear.

The till was an old-fashioned register with buttons that went 'ping' and a tray that popped out violently. Next to it stood an ornate glass cake stand brandishing a stack of multicoloured macaroons. The shopkeeper saw her eyeing them up and lifted the lid.

'*Non merci*,' Although Ava wished she'd accepted the sweetener when she heard her fabulous new look would be sixty-five euros.

It wasn't really that expensive for what it was but Ava couldn't stop the rapid surge of guilt that had taken hold of her. It felt wrong to spend money on herself.

She shook her head. 'I should be giving this money to Sophie or investing it into the vineyard.'

The shopkeeper frowned, impatiently.

'*STOP!*' Camille held up her palm. 'Just stop for a moment and think about the last time you did something for you? When did you last buy yourself something nice?'

'Ummm.' Ava closed her eyes as she tried to recall.

'If it takes you this long to remember then it was too long ago.' Her voice softened. 'Do this for you. For all these years you've placed yourself second to your family.' She brushed Ava's new side parting from her eyes with her slender fingers. 'You need to nurture yourself to help other people grow. Your daughter will understand. The vineyard will flourish. But first, you must blossom.'

The woman waiting had an awkward smile. '*Oui ou non?*'

Maybe Camille was right. It wasn't like she could return the thong anyway.

Ava blew out her cheeks. '*Oui.*'

Dark clouds had swooped in. The sky had turned the colour of granite. A cool damp breeze swept through the alleyway, shaking the washing lines, robbing the blossom from the trees, whispering how the worst was yet to come.

But they were too deep in gossip to notice what was swelling overhead. As soon as they left the shop, Camille giggled, 'She will be feasting off this for weeks. You and your hot lover will be the topic on everyone's lips.'

'Yeah, thanks a lot for that,' Ava groaned.

Camille's voice lowered. 'Do you want to know the funniest thing of all?' Looking back to the owner through the window, 'She behaves prim and proper, but it's all smoke and mirrors. She is having an affair with an inspector in the *gendarmes*.'

'No!'

'*Oui!* You see, nothing is as it seems.' She cocked her beautifully tapered eyebrow.

Ava was so lost in laughter, she didn't notice she'd walked into the path of . . .

'Victor!' she exclaimed, bashing her nose on his shoulder.

'Madame Chiltern?' he squinted. 'I didn't recognise you. Your hair, it's . . .'

'Gone,' she finished off his sentence, putting a hand up to her head self-consciously.

'Sophisticated, I was going to say. Feminine,' he raised his eyebrows. 'I like it.' His gaze slid to her lingerie bag.

'Did you have a successful shopping trip?' A smile fluttered across his mouth.

Her cheeks flamed. She'd forgotten she was clutching a bag with her old bra inside. She snatched it behind her back, suddenly feeling very exposed.

'This is Camille,' Ava quickly moved the subject on but her friend was looking the other way, exuding frosty vibes.

'Anyway, I hope you are well,' she politely glossed over that too and then, thankfully, the strained conversation was broken by an enormous thunderclap erupting above them.

They all looked to the heavens.

'We never had that dinner,' he said.

Ava felt the first raindrops splash.

'Umm, yes, I would love that,' she replied hurriedly, her mind on thinking how far she was from her car.

'Next week?'

'Perfect.' She felt Camille tug her arm in the other direction.

The wind was building. More black and grey clouds appeared out of nowhere.

'I'll see you then,' he kissed her goodbye. She wasn't sure if it was Camille making a hissing noise or the impending storm.

'I hope this passes quickly, it's not good for the grapes,' Victor added just as another thunderclap exploded.

A lightning bolt of realisation suddenly struck Ava. 'Jesus, the vines!'

'Go, Go!' Camille hugged her quickly goodbye, whispering 'Stay away from him,' in her ear as she left. Ava turned and ran, but not before the heavens decided to open.

# Chapter Twenty

'You can do it, come on little fella.' Ava slipped into first gear up the hill, clutching the steering wheel, desperately trying to keep the teeny car steady on the road as the wind battered it from every direction. The rain was lashing so hard her windscreen wipers couldn't keep up. They swished violently from left to right as she hunched forward, glaring into the storm, telling it to keep the hell away from her vines in not-so-polite English.

It had been such glorious weather all summer she'd completely forgotten Bernard's words of warning – that a storm could wipe out all their hard work, that it could ruin her chances of entering the Golden Grapes and scupper all her chances of winning the money she desperately needed to save Château Saint-Clair.

'Go, go!' she yelled as if she were giddying up her horse and then slammed on the brakes as a branch hurtled across the road, narrowly missing her windscreen. She lifted her foot off the clutch and the engine stalled. She banged her hands angrily on the steering wheel. 'Come on!'

Ava bucked like a bronco the rest of the way along the narrow country roads, nervously braking at every turn as visibility diminished to nil. A wave of relief hit her when she finally saw the amber glow of the house lights. She couldn't believe how dark it was, she was only meant to have ducked into town for bread and cheese.

Ava caught herself thinking about Jacques. She prayed he hadn't left for work yet and was still at the château; she really needed a strong man to help her batten down the hatches. She needed Jacques. There, she said it, the words resonating.

Out of the dark, Jean-Marc launched himself into the beam of her headlights, flapping his arms, panic-stricken.

'We are ruined!' he shrieked, the wind carrying his words into the storm. 'The barrels – they will be destroyed.'

Ava leapt out of the car, only to be thrown back against the door by a powerful gust of wind. Her back seared with pain but her tears were lost in the rain running down her face. She rooted her legs into the ground, just like a vine.

'How can we save the grapes?' she shouted.

Jean-Marc hollered back through his cupped hands. 'There's nothing we can do, except pray they will survive.' His white shirt was billowing behind him like a ship's sail.

'And the barrels?'

Jean-Marc turned and pointed to the top of the barn, where a shadowy figure was balancing, precariously, on top of the roof.

Ava clutched her hands over her mouth. 'Oh my God.'

Jacques was risking his life to plug the holes.

Without thinking, she ran towards him, her beautiful new hair-do soaked and glued down to her forehead, the wind tossing her body side to side like it had the car. She dug deep, hunching her shoulders into the wind and charging on until she was right below him, her heart hammering so hard she thought it might explode out of her chest.

'Jacques!' she screamed, jumping up and down waving her arms wildly to get his attention. 'Get down. It's not safe.'

But her voice was lost to the storm.

'Jacques!'

It was pointless, he couldn't hear.

She watched through her fingers from below as he teetered along the spine of the roof, fastening plastic sheets where the rain was pouring through. Finally he looked up, and waved. 'I'm okay.'

The moment he was back on the ground, Ava threw herself at him; wrapping her arms around his neck, clutching him tightly, overwhelmed with relief that he was alive. He said nothing, just held her, their wet bodies pressing against each other, and then he pulled away.

'We have to barricade the barn door, the wind is going to knock the barrels over.'

He slicked his mass of hair out of his eyes. His white work shirt, drenched, was glued to his six-pack like transparent paper.

Somehow, Ava managed to focus. 'Tell me what you need me to do.'

Their arms were outstretched, their feet ploughed into the gravel as they pushed with all their might against the wind to force the giant doors closed. Ava swivelled herself around, pressing her back against the rough wood as Jacques hammered in slats to stop the doors bursting open.

Every smash of the hammer vibrated through her chest. The rain was licking her in every direction, burning her cheeks.

'I can't hold it for much longer,' she screamed.

'Hang on,' he bashed the hammer onto the nail. 'Just one more second,' he smacked it one final time. 'Okay, I think it will hold, now let's run.' He took her hand.

They sprinted to the house, hurdling over garden debris, running so fast her legs almost collapsed underneath her. They stumbled into the warmth. Ava let go of Jacques' hand

and fell back against the door, her chest heaving up and down, her pulse galloping. She shut her eyes to stop the world spinning, to slow the adrenaline coursing through her. And then something brushed against her skin. She jumped with fright.

'*Pardon*, I didn't mean to scare you,' Jacques pulled away half a bush that seemed to have attached itself to her vest. *Which was now just as transparent as his shirt*, she suddenly realised. *And that meant only one thing, her new black and red bra was showing through as bright as a traffic light, and his hand is still there, why has Jacques not removed his hand* . . . Ava's heart quickened again. She hardly dared to look up, but the pull was too great, Ava slowly lifted her eyes to meet his—

'You are a hero!' Jean-Marc exploded into the hallway, already dressed in an entirely new outfit.

He rushed over to give Jacques a hug and then thought better of it when he spotted the small puddle at Jacques' feet.

'You have saved the vineyard.'

Jacques reluctantly dragged his eyes from Ava. 'Really, it was nothing,' he said.

'*Mais oui*, if the barrels were destroyed there would be no wine production.' His eyes suddenly brimmed with tears, 'And no wine means no prize, and . . .' He looked away, fanning his face to stop himself from crying. He suddenly lunged, kissing Jacques briskly on both cheeks. 'You are so brave!' He turned, dramatically. 'And now I am off to bed as I must rest if I am going to be able to make this wine. *Bon nuit.*'

Jacques stood there, shell-shocked, recovering from an evening of being battered from every direction, until Ava gently asked:

'You're not going to the restaurant now, are you? It would be too dangerous to travel there.'

He nodded. 'I have to, I'm the only waiter on tonight. I'll wait for the storm to calm and then leave.'

Her stomach dropped with disappointment. She swallowed and straightened. 'Well, the least I can do is dry your clothes. I'll find you something to wear in the meantime.'

'Thank you,' he said softly.

There was another one of those confusing charged moments, as electrified as the storm, as they looked at each other.

'I like your hair, a lot,' he lifted his eyebrows.

'Oh, my hair!' She'd completely forgotten she'd had it cut with all the drama. And was now very conscious what a mess it must look. Ava ran her hands through it, raking it from her face, which, unbeknown to her, only accentuated her delicate features more.

He broke their intense stare, Ava taking that as a signal for her to find something for him to wear.

Jacques followed behind as she made her way up the stairs. The steps groaned underneath them, the house creaked around them. The rain hammered down from above. But there was something cosy about being locked safely inside an old sturdy house that wasn't going to be bossed about by a storm.

She didn't mean to stare as she placed the folded clothes onto the stool in her bathroom but he was just wearing his boxer shorts and had the most perfect back she'd ever seen. His shoulders were broad and his muscles undulating underneath his golden skin, as he ruffled his hair dry with the towel.

Their eyes locked in the mirror.

She quickly looked away, her face flushing with embarrassment.

'These are the best of what I could salvage from my grandfather's clothes.' Patting them, pointlessly. 'They'll be far too big for you but at least they are dry.' She edged towards the door. 'If you need anything else just holler.'

'Holler?' he smirked.

'Call out, oh you know what I mean. Anyway . . .' she fidgeted, 'I'll be downstairs if you need me.' She turned to leave, frustrated at herself for getting embarrassed and tongue-tied and swooning over a guy who was clearly not interested, or worse, enjoying playing hot and cold. Her thoughts were so full of regret and anger she barely felt the warmth of his hand when it first touched her arm.

But it started to sink in as Jacques clasped his fingers around her dainty wrist and gently tugged her back to him.

She frowned with uncertainty, nervous, anxious, about what was going to happen next. Jacques touched her temple with his finger, softly ironing out her worry. Ava's pulse rocketed.

They exchanged a brief look, and then simultaneously broke into smiles.

'You worry too much,' he said, and then, before she had time to reply, he bowed his head and planted a kiss on her lips.

He pulled back slightly, checking his desire was reciprocated, and when she didn't open her eyes, or change her dreamy expression, he kissed her again, slowly, gently, his lips moving between her neck and her mouth.

Ava let out a little yelp as he lifted her up into his arms and carried her through to the bedroom. He placed her carefully on the bed and brushed away the pillows, with one, swift, firm sweep of his arm, so he could have all the space he needed to be with her. He lay down on top, being careful not to smother her, his arm muscles tensing as he shifted the weight onto himself.

Her mind was wavering between surrendering herself to the moment and fretting about what she was doing. Was she touching him too softly, too firmly? She'd never been with another man except Mark.

Her skin tingled as he pulled her vest off, his eyes widening at the sight of her sexy padded bra. He smiled and started kissing her more fervently, unclasping the back in one fluid, clearly practised, movement.

*Oh God, he's slept with so many women*, she panicked. *And I bet they are all younger and more beautiful with firmer bodies than me*, and then her thoughts were lost again as he nibbled his kisses towards her nipple.

She arched her back and the next thing she knew, Jacques had scooped his arms underneath her and rolled her over, hoisting her on top of him. Suddenly, under the bright bedroom light she felt horribly exposed. She covered her breasts with her hands, turning her head to look the other way.

'What are you doing?' he said, softly, cupping his big warm palms over hers.

The words were trapped in her throat. There were so many things she wanted to say to him, but instead, she just smiled, shyly.

He guided her hands down, tenderly placing them on his taut stomach.

'You don't need to hide. You're beautiful.'

His words made her want to cry as much as she wanted him to kiss her again. Ava was relieved when he took the choice away by flipping her back onto the bed and began unzipping her shorts.

He made love to her, slowly, tenderly, while outside, the rain hammered against the roof, the wind whistled past the window and the vines shook vigorously.

Everything was calm when she woke. The rain had stopped, the howling wind had hushed, there was nothing but stillness and moonlight glowing through her roof window, and – she looked across the bed – nobody beside her.

The sheets on his side were peeled back from where he had slipped out.

She pushed herself up onto her elbows and looked around the moonlit room for clues as to where Jacques might be. The pile of clothes she had left him had also vanished.

He had gone. She couldn't quite believe it at first. But as she re-checked the evidence her heart sank. He'd really gone and without even saying goodbye.

Ava smacked the mattress. 'You idiot!' *How could she have been so stupid to let herself be used? Of course he was only after sex, what else could he possible want from her?* She suddenly felt incredible vulnerable and alone, more lonely then when things had been bad with Mark. She felt the familiar sting of tears as feelings of regret and anger swelled inside her like an oncoming tidal wave. She wished she'd never met Jacques.

Ava was hugging her knees, her face buried, sobbing into the duvet when the floorboard outside squeaked. It was a quiet mouse-like noise from someone walking on their tiptoes, trying not to make it creak.

She wriggled back under the covers, anxiously watching the door handle turn. The hinges whined and a triangle of light from the corridor flooded the room.

She let out a small breath of relief when she recognised who it was, his body silhouetted against the light. She opened her mouth to speak and then closed it as Jacques began stripping off. Instead, she lay perfectly still, trying to control her breathing so he wouldn't know she was awake, watching him. He peeled off his shirt and trousers, and stood for a moment in the centre of the room, naked, the moonlight skimming off his body, the shadows accentuating his every muscle. She couldn't quite believe how attracted she was to him.

A tiny squeak involuntarily escaped her mouth.

He startled. 'Sorry, did I wake you?'

Ava decided it was best not to disclose the fact she'd been gawping at him for the past five minutes. Pretending to yawn and rub her eyes, she said: 'I heard a noise.'

'Sorry!'

'It's okay.' She smiled forgivingly, secretly jubilant that he'd returned and it turned out, was not the love rat she had him pegged for. 'Where did you go?'

'To check on the barrels.' He walked closer to her. Completely starkers.

'Are they okay?' She managed to keep eye contact.

'The shed is still standing. The storm has passed, we'll survive.'

The storm hadn't passed beneath the sheets though, Ava thought as she suddenly felt a surge of lust. She didn't wait for Jacques to initiate things this time. As soon as he climbed back into bed she locked her legs around him and flipped him onto his back. He smelt rugged, of the outdoors.

He grinned like a Cheshire cat as she pinned his hands down, and tightened her thighs around him so he couldn't move.

He opened his mouth to speak but she told him to 'shhhh', moving her index finger from her lips to his.

This must have been what Camille meant about summoning her inner woman as every part of her felt electrified from being in charge. She threw back the sheets so not one inch of her was covered. He could see every curve and crevice on her body and she didn't care.

She leant forward and kissed him, rocking herself backwards and forwards on him until he gently slipped inside. His hands were straining to grab hold of her hips, his stomach taut as he tried to lift himself up, but she fastened him down with the weight of her body.

Backwards and forwards she rocked to her own rhythm, his eyes widening with every stroke. Backwards and forwards, slowly riding herself to ecstasy.

# Chapter Twenty-one

**August 2018**

'Mum, what's up with you? You sound different.'

'Do I?'

'Yeah, all floaty and weird. I was telling you about going sailing with Carly this summer and you didn't say anything.'

'Sorry darling. I thought you were coming to stay here.'

'Muuuuum, I said I was going to Croatia. Weren't you listening?'

Ava stared dreamily out of her bedroom window at Jacques walking through the vineyard, by Bernard's side like father and son, the pair of them laughing. She imagined they were chatting about the harvest, discussing how much longer the grapes needed to ripen. She wondered if he was thinking about her and all the different places in the vineyard they'd made love over the past month.

She gave herself a shake and tried to focus on what her daughter was saying.

'Honey, it's absolutely fine if you go, I just miss you, I wish you could come here and meet . . .' She stopped her sentence abruptly, suddenly worried Sophie might disapprove of Jacques. After all, he was closer to her daughter's age than hers. And what would she call him? Her boyfriend? Do women in their mid-forties still have boyfriends? For some reason it didn't sound right. Or was he 'a lover'? She certainly couldn't introduce him to her daughter as that. Whatever Jacques was, Ava had not long patched things up with Sophie and she didn't see the need to rock the boat by revealing how she was moving on from her dad, just yet. At least not over the phone.

Anyway, the chances of whatever she was having with Jacques lasting until she next saw Sophie were slim. Ava was already bracing herself for everything to go tits up because despite Jacques lavishing her with compliments, despite him making her feel sexier and the most desired she'd ever felt in her life – she closed her eyes momentarily, a smile creeping across her face as she thought about the incredible orgasm he had given her that morning – despite all of that, there was still a little voice of doubt inside her head questioning why someone like him would want to be with her.

'MUM!' Sophie stressed. 'Seriously!'

'What, sweetheart, what did I miss now?'

'I asked you if you had heard from Dad?'

It was such an innocent question but it was a clanging reminder of the unresolved state of her marriage. Within seconds, everything Ava had worked so hard to blot out returned, and the high she had just experienced in bed with her 'young lover' was fading off far into the distance.

She felt sick to her stomach. Even after everything Mark had done, she was struggling with the guilt of sleeping with another man whilst still married. She felt her throat constrict at the 'M' word.

She also felt horribly guilty because despite Sophie saying she was getting used to the separation, Ava knew all she longed for was her family to be together again.

She drew a pained breath. 'I know this is hard for you, honey.'

'I'm fine about it,' she snapped. 'The only reason I'm bringing it up is because Dad mentioned he had something to ask you.'

Her body tensed. 'Ask me what?' Ava hadn't heard from Mark for months, since the night he'd been too busy to respond to her in her time of need.

*Selfish prick.*

'How would I know what he wants, Mum? If you would just speak to each other and sort things out.'

*Ouch.* Another stab of guilt. This time it was deeper and more serrated – touching a nerve. She felt terrible her daughter had become the go-between. And somewhere, deep inside, she felt a failure for not having managed to make a success of her marriage. The feelings were so deeply rooted it was hard to extract them, even after a summer of sunshine, sex and wine.

Her conversation with Sophie had ended on a friendly note, talking about how she couldn't wait to show her the vineyard and tell her all about her great-grandfather, but Ava's feet felt leaden as she made her way downstairs. She questioned what she was doing, worrying if she'd upset Sophie, fretting about what Mark wanted from her.

She blinked as she stepped outside into the blazing summer heat, only to be swept off her feet, quite literally, by the man she was trying very hard not to fall for.

Jacques spun her around in his arms, his strength making her feel as light as a ballet dancer. He kissed her slowly on the lips, the heat of his mouth and the sun quickly helping her forget her worries and sending her to boiling point. He buried his face into her neck, planting dozens of little kisses across her skin until she erupted in a fit of giggles.

Madame Chevalier cleared her throat loudly as she passed the pair on the porch. They glanced sideways at each other and burst into laughter like two naughty teenagers having been caught snogging.

Despite her grumps, the housekeeper had quietly shown her approval of Jacques. She'd even commented on how Ava's complexion was glowing and how happy and carefree she seemed, although it didn't pass without a small barbed comment about how Ava mustn't let herself become too distracted from the competition and it didn't do to be so publicly 'amorous'. Bernard pretended he hadn't noticed the blossoming romance, just as a father might do of a daughter, to avoid a toe-curlingly awkward conversation about relationships.

Ava stared up at Jacques, his eyes were piquing with excitement.

'What is it?'

'It's nearly harvest time. Just a week or two and the grapes will be ripe. Jean-Marc and Bernard just tested them, they are so sweet and juicy.'

He pulled his hand out from behind his back, peeling back his fingers to reveal a huge, round juicy red grape, which he'd been clutching the whole time.

'Try it,' he passed it to her lips.

He watched her mouth intently as she slowly bit down. But Ava's attempt at a sexy eating technique was thwarted by the grape's sudden explosion, spurting juice across her chin and his T-shirt.

'Sorry,' she wiped her mouth with the back of her hand.

'*De rien*,' he dabbed his chest. 'I needed a shower anyway,' he said with a devilish smile, taking her hand to pull her upstairs with him.

She giggled, pushing away his chest. 'I can't, I have to go meet someone.'

He frowned, his eyes running over her. 'I thought you were looking dressed up. Who are you meeting?'

She sensed a flare of jealousy. Which she liked. In fact, it turned her on, this possessive side of him.

'I promised I'd have dinner with Victor Ambrose. Keep things friendly before the competition.'

Jacques' eyes narrowed. 'Victor Ambrose?'

'Yes,' her shoulders sagged as she braced herself for a lecture. 'I didn't tell anyone because I knew it would cause problems. I knew they,' she nodded her head towards Madame Chevalier and Bernard, 'would give me a hard time. But I hoped you wouldn't, that you'd understand that I'm just trying to keep the peace and bury the hatchet, for whatever supposedly happened in the past.' Cheerfully she added: 'He seems genuine, like he wants to be my friend.'

Jacques looked away, his mouth pursed.

'It's just dinner,' she took his hand but he tugged it from her.

'Please.'

He sighed deeply and looked into her eyes, with, if she wasn't mistaken, not anger, but fear.

'I'll be okay, I'm a big girl, you don't need to worry about me. And you definitely don't need to worry about me running off with him.' She wrapped her arms around his waist and pulled his rigid body towards her. Kissing his lips she whispered, 'He's too old for me anyway, I like them much younger.'

Jacques cracked a smile.

'Okay, well enjoy, it will be an experience if anything. It's a massive vineyard.'

'But not as incredible as ours? Size isn't everything.'

'Ha, no, of course not.'

She glanced at her watch. 'Bugger, I have to go.' She pecked him on the lips and walked briskly towards the car, her kitten heels smacking against the stones.

'Ava!' Jacques called after her.

She turned and smiled.

'Don't tell him anything.' He paused. 'About your grand-father's wine. How we have some bottles left.'

She rolled her eyes playfully to say 'as if.' But there was something about the way he warned her that left an uneasy aftertaste. There was something more to what Jacques had said – something he was holding back.

# Chapter Twenty-two

Château Ambrose wasn't what she'd imagined it to be.

It was the polar opposite of her little vineyard. Vast, modern, boasting all the latest state-of-the-art technology – picking machines, presses, barrels of every description. The vines even had a fancy irrigation system to make sure they had just the right amount of water to keep the grapes juicy.

A slick operation. She felt a prickle of envy.

There was a visitor centre and a shop selling Château Ambrose wine. Golf cars lined the entrance waiting to take clients out on a tour of the estate. An estate that spread all the way to the Mediterranean sea.

Victor was right about one thing though. The views were breathtaking. She arrived at sunset and the sky was an enormous mass of fiery reds and oranges, its rich colours bleeding into the sea's reflection. The small waves shimmered silver as they caught the light rolling into shore. If she closed her eyes she could hear them crashing against the beach – they were that close to the Côte d'Azur.

'You're late!' a gravelly voice startled her.

She spun around and took a little breath.

She had told Jacques that Ambrose wasn't on her radar but it was hard not to appreciate his dashing good looks as he stood before her, looking sharp as anything in a crisp white shirt, the sleeves rolled up to his elbows, showing off his expensive watch. He was wearing designer jeans and a Prada belt, loafers the same light blue colour as the sea and his tan was shades deeper than when she last saw him.

His eyes were unreadable behind his aviator sunglasses. He took a sip from the glass of white wine he was casually holding by his side.

'You look beautiful,'

'Thank you,' she replied. *Thank you?* Ava couldn't remember the last time she accepted a compliment without some internal dispute. It caught her off guard, just as Victor had.

He noticed her watching his wine glass.

'Would you like to try?'

'I'd love to,' she reached her hand out, assuming he was about to pass her his glass.

But with so much as a flicker of his eyes, a butler appeared carrying a silver tray with an oversized glass and a bottle of white. With his white gloves on, he poured Ava a generous helping into the glass that was the size of a small swimming pool. He dipped his head for Victor and made his way back to the château, his chin high, his shoulders back and poised.

Victor chortled. 'The Americans love all of that nonsense. Pomp and ceremony.' He spoke of his butler. 'I can't stand it myself, but they are some of our biggest clients.'

Ava was gazing at the 'château', which also looked like it had come straight out of the States, with its colonnades and mock-distressed blue shutters. It couldn't have been built much more than ten years ago. It was brash, gaudy and a world away from the heritage of her little vineyard.

'So what do you think of the wine?'

She dipped her nose inside the glass and inhaled. It was so intense she had to pull away for a moment.

'Ooh, it's powerful.' She returned for a second sniff. 'I'm getting spices – vanilla and cinnamon,' she closed her eyes and inhaled. 'Pepper and something smoky, hmm, what is that . . .' she breathed the wine fumes in deeply. 'Toasted hazelnuts! It's been kept in wooden barrels.' She beamed proudly.

He smiled. 'Very good, you have the touch. This is our premium white and has been aged in oak barrels for nine months giving the smoky taste you're picking up.

'It's made with two white grapes, Rolle and Semillon, a half-and-half mix. Rolle is only grown in Provence, so it is unique to the region, bringing with it its unique flavours, seducing you with its elegant aromas of yellow fruits, fresh lime leaves and aniseed notes.'

His gravelly voice was hypnotic. Ava wondered if it was an unwritten rule that if you worked in wine you had to speak so suggestively.

'It's a 2014 vintage, so very mature. Do you know how you can tell?'

She shook her head, humouring him.

'The colour. This amber nectar shows it's mature. Just like rosé, when a white is young, it's bright and pale. The older it gets the darker and more golden it becomes.'

He was now by her side. She could smell his musky aftershave.

'This is a full-bodied wine,' he stated. Suggestively. He swirled the wine and drained the last of his glass.

'Ready?'

'For what?'

'The second part of the grand tour. Follow me.'

Ava decided this wasn't the sort of place where she could knock back the remainder of her glass. She had to leave an impression. She was a rival, *the* rival by all accounts. Instead, she handed her glass to the butler who had magically appeared by her side again.

Meanwhile, Victor was preparing their chariot. He pulled up next to her in the golf buggy. Peering over his sunglasses he raised both eyebrows. 'Hop in.'

She giggled as she clambered onboard. He revved the electric engine and then pulled away at such a speed she flew back into the seat, laughing at the unexpectedness of it all.

The golf car was surprisingly zippy. They got up to speeds that had her pinning down the hem of her floaty dress, much to Victor's amusement. As they headed through the enormous estate towards the sea, he told her how Château Ambrose grew ten varieties of grapes, which produced white, red and rosé wine; enough bottles to export to countries all over Europe as well as America. Her head was spinning with numbers as he came to an abrupt stop on the edge of a deserted beach.

'Don't tell me you own this too?' She gazed at the untouched silvery sand cocooned by two rocky outcrops. There was a rickety jetty leading up to, just as she had suspected, an enormous all-black super-yacht. It was called *Grande Noir*, naturally.

Ava feigned her best *I've been on many a yacht* face, as she wanted to show Victor she was no Eliza Doolittle in need of educating about how the rich and famous live. She sensed he was the type who might try and gain the upper hand by throwing his wealth about, although he'd been the perfect gentleman so far with her.

He gently touched her back, guiding her across the beach. As her heels ploughed deeper into the sand she slipped her shoes off, dangling them from her fingers by their straps. The wood on the jetty radiated the day's heat, warming the soles of her feet as they drew closer to the *Grande Noir*.

Victor offered his hand and she pressed her weight onto him as she practised her most ladylike mount of a luxury yacht.

'Wow!' she gasped, giving the game away.

'It's pretty special, isn't it? It's my baby,' he patted the varnished wood-panelled side, as if it were his faithful hound.

The decking, the seats, the ceiling, seem to blur into one, seamlessly. The white leather sofa curled around like the soft curves on a womanly body. It was scattered with plumped pillows and someone had gone to the trouble of sprinkling purple petals. There was also a bottle of champagne on ice, with two flutes, and a Jacuzzi gurgled away on the deck. Ava balked as it suddenly dawned on her that Victor Ambrose might actually be trying to seduce her.

He popped the champagne cork, which blasted into the sun-setting sky at rocket speed. An eruption of bubbles overflowed onto the deck. He shook the champagne from his hand and charged the flutes.

'*Salut*,' he clinked her glass.

She took a nervous sip, the chilled bubbles gliding down her throat, taking the edge off.

'So . . .'

'So,' she gulped back another mouthful as he moved closer. The bubbles were rushing to her head.

The sound of the water chopping against the side of the boat filled their silence. A quiet moment that Ava was using to come up with excuses. *Victor was certainly looking sharp tonight but she wasn't going to cheat on Jacques. Even if the guy was a multimillionaire.* She knocked back another gulp to numb the pain of that decision.

'Isn't it beautiful,' he exhaled.

'The champagne?'

He laughed. 'That too. It's actually sparkling rosé. My *pièce de résistance*. He held his glass up to the light, the sun-setting red streaming through the pink. 'This *cuvée* will be served in all the bars and clubs in St Tropez this summer. Do you know the nightclub VIP Room?'

Ava shook her head.

'It will be priced 350 euros a bottle.'

Ava coughed on her bubbles. 'Three hundred and fifty euros?' she choked, but Victor was already somewhere else, looking out across the shimmering sea. His mood was shifting.

'I come here to calm my mind, when I need to think about things.' He turned to face her, hooking his elbows over the railing, casually dangling his champagne flute. He now wore a slightly pained expression as he took another sip.

*Maybe his life isn't all roses after all*, Ava wondered. 'What sort of things?' she asked, softly.

'Production costs, a bad harvest, disease that destroys your entire crop.' He drew in a sharp breath. 'So many things can go wrong.' He glanced at her sideways: 'You must know all about the struggles we can face?'

Jacques' words echoed through her head. But he seemed so nice and genuinely concerned for her, so inclusive about the strife they faced. It was nice to talk to someone in her industry, to share her problems.

'The storm gave us a scare,' she admitted.

He raised an eyebrow.

'We thought we might lose the barrels and the vines would be torn out.'

'But it was okay?'

She pressed her hands into a prayer. 'Thankfully.'

'What a relief.' He smiled. He then removed his sunglasses and looked at her, fixing her with his gaze.

She felt drawn to his warmth.

'But don't you think you could be happier?'

'What do you mean?'

'Well,' he paused, 'it can't be easy for a single woman such as yourself to run a vineyard.'

She blinked. 'Huh?'

'I was just noting how your disposition can't make things easy for you.'

'My *disposition*?' she huffed, unimpressed with the direction the conversation had suddenly taken.

Victor smiled. 'You know, you could just sell it. You'd never have to think about another storm again. Or a plague of parasites that can ruin an entire crop. Or the costs you must be haemorrhaging. Wouldn't that be the best thing to do – sell?'

Her mouth fell open.

'I promise I wouldn't tell,' he whispered. 'Admitting defeat is nothing to be ashamed of.'

'Are you having a laugh? Sell? After everything I've been through? Not a chance. I've made a promise to my grandfather,' she looked up to the heavens, 'which I'm going to honour, even if it kills me.'

He nodded, smiling, and then his lips morphed into a sneer as whatever self-control he'd been clinging onto snapped.

'You do realise that nobody takes you seriously,' he spewed.

All her hackles rose.

'You know nothing about wine,' he laughed. 'I don't know how you think you will ever win this prize. Just give up now and sell Château Saint-Clair before you fall into more debt. Use the money to buy a cottage back in your own country. You could go shopping and have lunches with your friends and busy yourself with things like that,' he waved his hand dismissively. He took an angry sip of his drink.

Just as Ava was curling her tongue around an acidic reply, a man emerged from below deck.

'*Bon soir, Madame Chiltern.*'

It was Monsieur Dupont, the estate agent who had evaluated the vineyard, his hands thrust deeply into his obscenely tight suit trousers. A sheen of sweat glistened across his forehead and upper lip.

Ava's eyes flickered between the two men, suddenly realising she'd been ambushed.

'Oh,' Ava nodded, 'I see what's going on here.'

Monsieur Dupont loosened his tie with the excitement of haggling on behalf of his client. Victor must have been the secret buyer who wanted to flatten her grandpapa's château and turn it into luxury flats. She should have known. Suddenly the truth was dawning on her.

'My vineyard was never worthless, was it?'

Monsieur Dupont snorted. 'I was just trying to get you the best deal.'

'By lying! Whatever it is you want now, I'm not interested,' she spat.

'Come on, Madame Chiltern, be reasonable. Now is the time to sell.'

'No!' She slammed her champagne flute down.

Victor stepped in, his smug smile fixed back on his face. 'Ava, my dear, isn't it time you saw sense? You could never achieve what you grandfather did. Just give up. Before you tarnish his name.'

She glared at him. With intense hatred. Without breaking eye contact, Ava slipped her shoes back on. 'Oh, just piss off!'

She straightened, swivelling her heels on the beautiful lacquered decking as she turned to leave.

She could hear a string of expletives explode from Victor's mouth as she marched back along the jetty. Her heart was pounding; her head swimming with anger.

She was furious at herself for giving him the benefit of the doubt. Smooth-talking charming men – like Mark – were clearly her Achilles heel. But at least she had seen through his façade in the end.

'I'll show you,' she muttered, at the thought of making Victor walk back to his car. She stormed up to the golf buggy. 'I can handle this all by myself, I don't need a man to help me, who the hell does he think he is,' she hissed, turning the key in the ignition. 'Bugger! Where's the reverse? There's no reverse,' she started smacking every button on the dashboard. She glanced over her shoulder. 'Bugger, bugger!' Victor was striding up the jetty after her, Monsieur Dupont trotting behind, trying to keep up.

'Sod it!' she squealed, mowing up the embankment, dinging the palm tree as she attempted to loop it. 'Crap, bugger!'

'Ava, wait!' Victor waved his hand furiously.

He was closing in on her – now only yards away.

She squealed as she stamped her foot on the accelerator, sending her lurching forward.

'I didn't mean to offend you.' He tried back-pedalling. 'We need to talk. Stop!'

She drew a circle around him in the sand. 'Not now, sorry, don't have time.'

And off she sped up the beach, spinning sand into their faces.

'Can you believe he had the audacity to tell me that I didn't have what it takes to run my vineyard?'

She stomped back and forth, ranting.

'Because I'm a woman. Can you believe he said that?'

Her audience shook their heads.

'No one takes me seriously. Ha! that's not true, is it?'

Before they could answer, she ranted on. 'And,' she waved her hand around. 'And he had the cheek to say I don't know anything about wine. What's he talking about? I can tell you if a wine has legs like the best of them. My husband tried to keep me down, telling me I wasn't up to the job; that I shouldn't bother following my dreams. Well sod him and sod Ambrose! I'll show him.' She stabbed her finger at her audience.

'We did warn you,' Madame Chevalier interrupted. Bernard nodded, his arms folded.

'Vulgar.' Jean-Marc spat. 'He has absolutely no class, that man. No style, no integrity. Simply vulgar. Have you seen that château, *mon Dieu*, it's so *nouveau*. Ava darling,' he touched her hand, 'don't even let him enter your thoughts again. We have more important work to do.'

'Like winning this prize,' she said. 'We'll show him, this is war!'

Madame Chevalier cheered enthusiastically, waving her oven glove. 'War!'

Their team talk was broken by the roar of engines in the distance. For a second Ava panicked it might be Ambrose until, from out of the tunnel of trees, emerged three young lads on scooters, tooting their horns.

'Who are they?' She raised her hand above her eyes to hide the glare.

Finally Jacques spoke; he'd been uncharacteristically quiet up until now. '*Mes amis*. They have come to help with the harvest.'

'You're kidding.'

'*Non*,' he smiled. 'I arranged it for you.'

Ava threw herself against him, practically jumping into his arms with happiness. 'I love you!' she blurted. And then immediately regretted opening her mouth – *Cringe, cringe*.

She turned her head the other way, wincing, praying he didn't hear her.

Jacques touched her chin, moving her mouth back to meet his. 'I love you too,' he whispered between soft kisses. Her nerve endings tingled in a wave across her body.

'You do?'

'Of course I do.' He doused her in more kisses. 'I'm sorry I wasn't there to protect you from Victor.' He chuckled. 'But it doesn't sound like you needed a bodyguard.' He kissed her again, this time, longer and lingering until Jacques' friends tooted their horns.

'Okay, okay,' he managed to pull himself away, greeting the lads, one of whom Ava recognised from the restaurant.

'This is Antoine, Louis and Leon.' They looked like they belonged in a boy band with their matching skinny ripped jeans, trainers and vests. Louis wore a black waistcoat and a cap. It was hard to imagine them getting their hands dirty in the field but Jacques reassured Bernard they were grafters. All local boys who had grown up on farms, just like him.

Ava didn't care how hard they worked, she was just grateful for the extra hands – they would soon have thousands of grapes to pick. That, and the prospect of ogling more young men with their tops off for the next two weeks.

Jean-Marc was keen to crack the whip. 'These grapes won't look after themselves,' he shooed everyone towards the fields to help with the watering and any last-minute nurturing, while he pulled a device out of his pocket.

'This will measure the sweetness. The grapes will speak to me, they will tell me how soon they need to be harvested. When they are ripe we must pick them immediately, there cannot be any delay or their taste will be destroyed. We must not get this wrong . . .' his voice trembled, 'we only have one chance.'

# Chapter Twenty-three

**September 2018**

She knew she was playing with fire. It was one of those off-limits conversations. The kind that you know you're going to come away from singed, but that doesn't stop you going close to the flame, asking that silly little question nagging in your thoughts.

'Have you had many girlfriends?'

They were lying in bed. This definitely counted as 'pillow talk'.

Jacques sighed deeply and pressed his head into the pillow, lifting his forearm to his brow.

'Really?'

'I'm serious,' she rolled onto her front, looking at him intently.

He glanced at her from the corner of his eye. Tentatively checking to see if it was a trap of some kind.

'I've had a few girlfriends, of course.'

She swallowed her jealousy.

'But none of them lasted very long.'

Ava perked up. 'Why?'

He shrugged. 'I don't know, they just weren't what I was looking for.'

She brushed his chest with her finger. 'What are you looking for?'

'Not much, really, just a woman who knows what she wants. Who has passion in what they do. A lot of the girls I met in Montpellier, they were fun,' he smiled wistfully.

Ava bristled.

'But they were obsessed with their appearance. Always posing, putting their pictures on Instagram and Facebook, asking me to take pictures of them for social media. They were too busy caring about what they looked like to enjoy the moment they were trying to capture. I found it irritating. *Bouff.*'

'Bouff?'

'*Oui, bouff,*' he smiled.

'So what have you got now, someone who's much more natural?' she playfully flicked her hair.

'*Oui*, actually.'

'And more mature.' When he didn't say anything, she cast out that line a little further, hoping for some reassurance. 'You don't mind that I'm sixteen years older than you?'

'Come on!'

Her eyes were wide, still searching for more reassurance. He rolled over onto his side and cupped his hand around her face, his fingers entwined through her hair.

'It turns me on. Your age. You're a woman who knows what she wants. Who isn't pretending to be someone they're not. Who's comfortable in their own skin.'

Ava glowed inside. Six months ago she couldn't imagine anyone describing her as those things.

'And best of all, being older than me means you can teach me things,' he grinned naughtily, pushing her onto her back.

'Teach me something,' she whispered.

'You want me to teach *you* something?'

'Very much.'

He ran his finger across her collarbone. '*Clavicule*,' he said in his most sexy bed voice.

She repeated the French word.

Quickly catching on to what the lesson was about, she touched her lips, 'And this?'

'*Bouche.*'

She looked mischievous, moving her finger to her breast. '*Mamelon.*'

'And this?' She drew her finger lower.

He matched her naughty smile, this time kissing where she was pointing. She loved how consumed he was by her. How much he wanted to please her. He wanted her, desperately, every inch of her. She rolled her eyes back in ecstasy.

'Jacques!'

A booming voice intruded their moment from outside. He flinched and then continued working his magic.

'Jacques.'

He looked up.

'Seriously?'

Ava pressed her head back into the pillow with frustration as Jacques walked to the window to see who was hollering his name at 2 a.m.

It was Bernard. Waving from the courtyard.

'Time to harvest. We have to go.'

'But . . .'

'Now!'

Jacques turned to Ava with a pained expression.

'Seriously?' she said.

'Yes.' Sighing deeply. 'It's better this way. Picking the grapes when it's cool prevents them from cooking in the heat on the way to the press, keeping the flavour crisp and fresh.' He threaded his legs into his trousers. 'I'll be back to finish what I started,' he grinned.

'Hang on,' she called out after him. 'If you're picking grapes, so am I. This is my vineyard and I'm not skipping duties.'

'Okay boss, come on.'

It was the most beautiful night. The sky was clear and enormous, a huge mass of violet sprinkled with thousands of twinkling silver stars.

The cool temperatures had released the sweet aroma of the grapes blended with the scents of the leaves and the rock roses, juniper, truffle oak and the musty earth.

Ava inhaled deeply as if she were smelling the bouquet of a wine.

The insects chirped and hummed, magnetised to the lights and head-lamps they were using to pick the grapes with.

Back in Surbiton Ava had hated bugs, anything that scuttled or had more than two legs would normally send her into a blind panic. But her time in the vineyard had relaxed her, made her realise that she could share a room with a spider, or a centipede, without anything terrible happening.

Tonight they danced around, caught in the headlights as the group plucked the juicy fruit from their stems.

Bernard explained it was better to hand pick grapes as that way they could select the best ones for the wine, and the machinery that Ambrose and other commercial vineyards used would harm their old vines because they would shake them too violently.

It was back-breaking stuff but Ava's pain was lost in the camaraderie they shared: laughing, joking, working together plucking nature's harvest in the dead of the night while the rest of the town slept.

They were laughing so hard, someone snorted.

Ava thought it was someone until, OINK, there it was again. This time sounding much more pig-like than human.

Ava peered through the row of vines, into the blackness.
GRUNT GRUNT.

*Jesus.* 'Jacques,' she hissed.

'Stand perfectly still,' he crept up behind her.

'Why? What is it?' Her heart rate rocketing.

'Just be very quiet.'

Ava narrowed her eyes, trying to focus on whatever was lurking that needed Jacques to warn her off making any slight movement. *Oh God, she took it all back, she was afraid of bugs and things that hide in the dark.* Caught in the headlight, the creature was staring back at her with glowing eyes.

OINK.

It was a wild boar. Big, stocky, hairy and with tusks.

'They love the grapes. He's very upset we are stealing them from him.'

'What do upset wild boars do?' She edged behind him.

'If he's very angry he might charge at you.'

The hairy pig was now facing them, head on.

'But he's more likely to run. Especially if I do this,' he suddenly lurched forward, waving his arms, swearing at him in French.

The boar squealed with fright and shot off into the darkness much faster than you'd think his little legs could carry him. Somewhere in the distance echoed a few grunts – some swear words of his own, Ava thought.

Seconds later, Bernard charged towards them waving a stick.

'Where is he?' he growled. 'He's been eating all my grapes.'

'Somewhere over there,' Ava pointed into the distance.

'Well if I catch him . . .' his words disappeared into angry mutterings as he walked away while Jacques and Ava stifled their giggles.

*

Ava angled her face a bit to the left.

'And do this with your lips,' Jacques puckered his best trout pout.

'I look ridiculous.'

'Come on, that's what everyone does.'

Ava pressed the button before he could give her any more advice on how to take her first ever selfie.

'I feel ridiculous. I'm too old to be doing this.' She gave him a look.

'Are you kidding, you look stunning,' he admired the headshot of her in the sunshine surrounded by buckets full of grapes.

Ava tapped out her message:

*Harvest done and dusted, can't wait for you to be here. Miss you so much. xx*

Seconds later, her phone pinged with a reply:

*Mum, you look HOT! Love your new hair and tan.*

Ava smiled, showing Jacques the message. 'I can't wait for you both to meet.'

'Do you think she will like me?'

'Who wouldn't, you're so nice!'

'Nice?'

'I mean gorgeous, and sexy, especially when you speak to me in French, and hot, and . . .'

Speaking of hot, Ava was roasting. Their picking had crept into mid-morning and the temperatures were soaring for September. She stood perfectly still waiting for the breeze, the famous Mistral, to pick up again. As if on cue, the gusty wind from the north swept through the vineyard, with huge force, shaking the vines, clanging the shutters on the house, sending the cockerel wind vane on the roof into an uncontrollable spin.

Ava closed her eyes, lapping up the coolness and the *garrigue* – the signature scent of the south carried with it. A floral fragrance like any other, a mix of piney shrubs and spicy herbs and sweet flowers.

The cool breeze gave the boys an injection of energy as they started pelting grapes at each other, running between the rows, much to Bernard's annoyance, who was telling them off. Meanwhile, Jacques was giving her a look.

'Come with me,' he led her away from the chaos.

'Where are we going?' She giggled.

'Do you always have to ask questions?'

'Yes!'

'It's nowhere far,' he stopped abruptly by the trailer where all the buckets were waiting to be loaded.

Her eyes flickered between Jacques and the straw in the back and the others who were only 100 metres away.

'You can't be serious?'

'Quickly,' he was already lifting her up at the waist as if she weighed nothing at all.

She was wearing a simple strappy dress that fell just above her knees. He slipped his hand between her legs, confidently parting them, using his free hand to unzip his trousers, his white bum, the only part of him that wasn't tanned, bobbing above the trailer.

A grape burst underneath Ava's bottom.

He pulled her thong aside, his eyes wild with the excitement of al fresco sex. 'I love you,' he mouthed, before grabbing her roughly.

Just as he was about to enter her the boisterous laughter suddenly grew nearer, now only metres away.

'Quick, get off,' Ava squealed.

Jacques poked his head over the top of the trailer. 'Hurry,' he pulled his trousers back up. They scrambled to their feet and jumped back to earth. Ava reached into the trailer and grabbed Jacques' mobile, which had fallen out of his pocket.

'Here,' she said, the screen lighting up with a WhatsApp message as she passed the phone to him. She hesitated. Her eyes lingered on the screen while Bernard and the boys crowded around the trailer with the last of the day's harvest.

Her happy expression slowly disappeared, as the meaning of the French words percolated.

*Jacques! What is the latest report from Château Saint-Clair?*

It was from Ambrose.

# Chapter Twenty-four

She looked up at Jacques, her whole body numb.

'What is it?' He grinned. That wonderful smile that suddenly made her feel sick to her stomach.

She tried to speak but her mouth had frozen with the shock revelation that the man she had fallen for had been working for her rival all along. Instead, she chucked the phone at him.

'Hey, what's going on?' He stumbled to catch it. He glanced at the screen and then exclaimed: '*Merde!*'

Quietly, she said: 'Leave.'

He reached out to touch her arm. 'Please, Ava.' But she shook him free.

'I said, get off my property.'

'Come on, Ava, you have to let me explain, this isn't what it looks like.'

Those clichéd words were like fuel on a fire.

Ava looked him dead in the eye, her anger rising, and then exploding into a lion roar: 'NOW!'

He edged away. Holding his hands up, only to bump into Bernard's rigid chest. He spun around and was met with the gardener's glare.

'*Alors*, what's going on?'

'He,' Ava pointed at Jacques, 'has been spying on us for Ambrose.'

Bernard clamped a firm hand on Jacques' shoulder.

'It's not true,' he quivered.

'He's lying.' She glared at Jacques with pure hatred. 'You're lying. I saw the message from Ambrose. He asked for his report on us. Don't tell me you aren't working for him when I saw the proof with my own eyes.'

'Ava . . .' Jacques stumbled on his words. 'Please listen. It's true, I was working for Victor but not how you think.'

She turned her back to him, fighting the tears.

He tried to pull away from Bernard's grip, but the gardener pinned him down.

'Oww, get off me,' he yelped. 'Ava, look at me, I love you.'

She couldn't look at him.

'I love you, I love you, please believe me. I wasn't lying about that.'

Bernard began frog-marching him towards his moped and then pushed him away, into the dust.

Jacques' friends immediately dived in between the pair, squaring up to Bernard in case there was more to follow.

'Leave him alone,' Louis barked, his arm outstretched.

Bernard charged forward.

'You heard her, she told you to leave. All of you. And don't come back.'

Jacques scrambled to his feet, staring at Ava longingly, willing her to turn around and face him.

Bernard raised his stick. 'NOW!'

The boys scarpered on their mopeds. Only when the humming of their engines had faded into silence did Ava find the heart to look at the horizon that Jacques had disappeared into.

'Are you okay?' Bernard was waiting for her.

She smiled, almost hysterically.

'I knew it was too good to be true.'

*

Ava wasn't sure how long she sat there, in a heap on the ground, staring out across the vines. Her brain was whirling with questions. How long had he been lying to her? How far was he planning to go to sabotage their success? And most of all, why? Ambrose must have been paying him. She felt gut-wrenchingly sick as she replayed their every encounter over the months, pulling them apart, dissecting them, trying to find the truth in every lie. She felt devastated that her French fairytale was over. But most of all she was angry – furious at herself for falling for his charade. For believing he loved her.

She clutched her stomach.

Of course it was a lie. Why would someone like him want to be with a woman old enough to be his mum? She should have trusted her gut instinct from the start.

She pushed her fists into the sockets of her eyes and screamed inside.

How, after everything she had suffered with Mark, had she let herself be fooled again by another filthy liar? Her hands were shaking with rage.

Madame Chevalier kept coming to check on her but Ava told her to leave her be. She needed to be alone to wade through her feelings of anger and sadness, nausea and pain.

And still not a single tear escaped her eyes. She couldn't, she was too numb to cry.

Eventually, when the sun had set and the darkness had crept in, and the night creatures had emerged from the undergrowth, Ava slowly made her way up to her bedroom. With heavy steps, closing the door behind her, she dropped onto the bed. She slipped her phone under her pillow, ignoring the dozens of missed calls from Jacques.

She lay on her back, staring up at the ceiling with the same desperate defeated feeling as when she was in Emilia's spare room half a year ago.

*Maybe some people just aren't meant to be happy?*

There was a knock on her door.

'I'm fine,' she lied to Madame Chevalier, wishing she would just leave her alone to slowly wither away.

The door opened.

'Please, I'm okay,' Ava whimpered.

But it was Bernard, standing in the doorway with a tray of food and a mug of hot chocolate. She didn't have the heart to tell him she wanted to be left alone. He walked towards her, the tray rattling between his shaky hands. He placed it by her bedside, but he didn't leave. Instead, he sat down heavily on the end of her bed. His eyes were kind and concerned.

He took a breath and promised: 'It will get better.' He said it with the authority of someone who knew what it felt like to have their heart torn apart. Someone who knew how powerful words of reassurance could be when everything seemed so bleak.

Those four simple words of kindness were so innocuous but carried such weight, triggering the release of the floodgates. Finally, Ava broke down in tears.

She sobbed into her hands until Bernard shuffled towards her and put his arm around her. She buried her face in his shoulder and let all of her hurt pour out.

**Summer 1988, Kent**

'Ava, where are you honey?'

She didn't want her mum to find her. She just wanted to be left to cry, alone, hugging her favourite cuddly toy. Brown Teddy was damp with tears as she clasped him tightly into her face.

'Ava, sweetheart, I've been looking for you,' her mum's gentle voice swam into the bedroom.

'Go away, leave me alone.' She sniffed and refused to turn her head.

She felt the bed dip as her mum took a seat beside her. She felt the warmth of her touch as she rubbed her back.

'Why don't we go to the seaside today? Would that cheer you up?'

'No. I don't want to.'

Her mum sighed deeply, the corner of the bed she was sat on sighing with her.

'Well, what's going to get you out of this mood?'

Suddenly her father's roar soared down the hallway.

'What's wrong with that child? She's always crying.' It drew closer. 'Can't you just shut her up?'

'It's okay honey, I'm dealing with it,' her mum's voice turning anxious.

Ava's bedroom door smacked open, clanging against the wall. She squeezed her eyes shut into Brown Teddy.

'It's that bloody vineyard isn't it?' His voice tearing through the room. 'She's having another one of her tantrums because she's not going there this summer. Well, tell her to shut up, or I will.' His footsteps charged towards her. Ava screwed her eyes up.

The bed lifted as her mum rose to her feet. 'I told you I was dealing with it.'

'You're not doing a good job. She needs discipline.'

'Leave her alone!'

'Did you just tell me what to do?'

The door was slammed shut with such force books came crashing to the floor. The footsteps in the hallway turned into scuffles while her parents' voices exploded into yelling and screaming.

Ava clasped her hands over her ears, her body trembling, her mind desperately trying to transport her somewhere far away – to sunny, safe Provence.

The days seemed to blur into each other after Jacques left, punctuated with painful memories from the past that his betrayal seemed to have exhumed.

Morning became lunchtime, became evening, became bed and then breakfast and so it went on for Ava, as she trudged through her life on the vineyard, slowly piecing her heart back together.

Bernard had been behaving very protectively, checking on her regularly with mugs of hot chocolate. Emilia was on the blower constantly trying to console her. She wanted Jacques' number to give him a piece of her mind.

'Who the hell does he think he is, hun?' she'd launched into another scathing attack. 'He might be hot to look at but where's he going in life? He's got no income and what did you say? He drives a scooter?' She snorted. 'Seriously babe, you dodged a bullet there.'

She knew Emilia was only saying these things to make her feel better but all it did was stir up her thoughts. Ava felt herself jumping to Jacques' defence, explaining how he had serious talent for wine making, which only upset her more because Ava was back thinking about everything she'd done to help him, only for him to betray her. 'I'm going to have to call you back,' she sniffed, falling back into her abyss of painful thoughts.

By contrast, the grapes were fermenting merrily in their barrels, transforming the juices into alcohol, oblivious to the drama unfolding around them. Ava was fed regular updates from a very animated Jean-Marc who was enraptured about starting on the wine blending.

'Soon we will open your grandfather's bottle and I will taste it, compare it, and recreate it,' he said, sweeping out of the room as dramatically as he swept into it. Ava plastered on a smile and then sagged back into the folds of the sofa where she'd been lying for the best part of the day already.

She checked her phone. Two missed calls from Jacques. She wished he would stop hounding her and just let her get on with her wallowing in peace.

She'd been avoiding going into town in case of an unpleasant run-in. She'd been ignoring all of his phone calls; his messages remained unread and archived in her WhatsApp. The only place she dared venture so no one would see her red puffy crying eyes was the local super-market – the Super-U – late in the evening when the aisles were deserted.

Dessert! That's what she needed. She pushed herself up, an image of a Ben and Jerry's Cookie Dough bursting into her thoughts. She glanced at the cuckoo clock; it was 2.46 p.m. She weighed up potential problematic run-ins against her desperation for comfort food – the latter swiftly winning over.

She wormed her feet back into her trusty Ugg boots, and grabbed her comforting cardigan, which she'd reintroduced into her wardrobe when Jacques left. 'I'm just heading out,' she called to the kitchen.

Madame Chevalier popped her head around the door with another of her commiserating smiles.

'*Bon*,' she applauded, clearly pleased at Ava's effort to drag herself off the sofa. Little did she know Ava was on a mission to gorge as much sugar as humanly possible.

Wearing big dark sunglasses that engulfed half her face seemed a good idea at the time. That was until she noticed everyone she passed in the aisle was staring at her, in the way French people do, for wearing sunglasses in the local supermarket.

She ducked her head into the freezer.

'Three tubs, that should do it,' Ava plonked the ice cream into her trolley. She trudged on in her Ugg boots, casting her eyes across the shelves for anything else that would give her an instant sugar rush.

The French rap song on the radio drew to a close and was promptly followed by the heartbreak classic, Justin Timberlake's *Cry Me a River*.

'Brilliant, just brilliant,' she muttered, making a detour past the crisps, sweeping bags of cheese-flavoured twirls off the shelves and into her trolley. As she stood devouring the biscuit aisle with her eyes, she heard a familiar voice.

'Ava?'

She flinched.

'Ava, is that you?'

She closed her eyes and squeaked: 'No,' pushing her sunglasses up her nose. Accepting the game was up, she slowly turned, clasping a packet of Oreos.

'I mean, yes, hiya,' she greeted her friend sheepishly.

Camille's eyes dropped to Ava's trolley and then enlarged by three sizes.

'Tell me you're not going to consume all of that?'

'Maaaaybe.'

'Don't be ridiculous. Do you know how many calories are in your basket?'

Obviously she didn't, and she would rather keep it that way.

Camille's eyes softened. 'Is everything okay?'

'What gave it away?' Ava snorted, followed by a sagging of the shoulders. 'Things didn't work out with Jacques.'

'Oh, *ma chérie*.'

'Yeah, it wasn't to be, turns out he's a liar and a fraud, just like my husband,' she paused, clasping onto the tears.

Camille reached out her hand and slowly removed the packet of biscuits Ava was holding, returning them to the shelf.

'If you want to eat away your misery I have a much better idea. Put them back,' she pointed to the contents of her cart.

Ava clung to the Ben and Jerry's.

'That too, now.'

Ava reluctantly returned all her treats and left the super market calorie-free, grumbling under her breath that whatever Camille had in mind, better be good.

Two hours later, the women were cocooned in the pink velvet booth of *Pâtisserie Papillon*, surrounded by little candles in glass jars, glugging an eye-wateringly expensive bottle of rosé, gorging on pink macaroons.

'If you are going to be bad, be really bad,' Camille smiled wickedly as she bit into a rose-and-chocolate-flavoured fancy.

Ava followed her example, exhaling a 'mmmm' as the crunchy shell melted into a chewy heaven. She dabbed the crumbs from the corner of her mouth.

Ava sighed. 'It would have never worked out anyway.'

'No, why?'

'You know, because of how old I am.'

Camille flicked her a look.

'Half the girls in this town are after him.'

'And?'

'And, and so he gets to have the pick of anyone he likes. He's probably dating one of them now.'

Camille shook her head.

'Then there's the problem of children. He'll be looking for someone much younger to have a family with, if not now, in five years' time.' She took a sip of her drink. 'He'd eventually have left me.'

'Really? So you had this conversation with him?'

'Not exactly.'

'So you didn't'?

'No.'

'Well then this is all fiction. You don't know how he felt about you.'

Ava's anger rose. 'I know he was lying, telling me he loved me just to get what he needed for Ambrose.'

There was a terse silence. Camille tilted her head, her voice hardening: 'Victor is a man who takes what he wants. I have no doubt he made Jacques feel he had no alternative than to do what he said. Let that be of some consolation.'

There was something bitter about the way she said it that made Ava wonder if she too had been hurt by Victor. But her expression was guarded, warding off any further questions.

Ava shrugged. 'Well, he didn't have to do it. Everyone has a choice.' She stopped fiddling with the macaroon, and stuffed it into her mouth.

'That is true. Everyone has a choice, including you.'

'What do you mean?' Ava's voice was muffled by her chomping.

'You can choose to be happy or sad.'

Ava blinked. 'Huh?'

'You can decide to let this bring you down, use it as an excuse to eat ice cream and chocolates.'

Ava blushed.

'Or you can push the bad aside and start looking at the good in your life, which there is a lot of, by the way.'

Camille had that school teacher look in her eyes, when they tell you to pull your socks up. She ruffled her hands through her wild curly hair and smiled, softening the blow.

'I know,' said Ava, thoughtfully. 'I'm just finding it hard to manage without him.'

Camille frowned. 'The vineyard?'

'Yes, he did so much to help. Lifting things, fixing things . . .'

'Okay, stop,' Camille snapped. '*Your* vineyard, the one that is about to produce the most incredible wine, is a success thanks to *you*. *You* had the courage to leave England for the unknown. *You* took a chance by staying and fulfilling your grandfather's legacy. And look at you now.'

'Yeah, look at me now,' she popped another macaroon in her mouth.

'You're still here. Fighting to make the vineyard a success. You're being creative, using your talents, fulfilling your potential. And you're blossoming,' she touched Ava's face, 'you're beautiful.'

Ava swallowed.

'You don't need Jacques. All you need is you. Have you ever been by yourself. Really alone?'

She shook her head.

'Don't fear it, embrace it. I was terrified of what I was going to do after I found out my husband was having an affair. I had spent my life living in his shadow, pleasing him, and suddenly I had to learn what it was like to please me. For when you are alone you can really understand what you want.' She breathed in deeply. 'When I first arrived here, I was scared. It wasn't easy being a woman, alone, wanting to run my own business in a part of France where the man is still very much seen as the breadwinner. In a small town where they talk. But I threw back my shoulders,' Camille straightened in her seat. 'And held my head up high,' she poised, 'and stuck two fingers up at them all.'

Ava giggled.

'And I haven't been happier.' Camille looked at her with authority. 'Now it's your turn.'

Camille's expensive rosé and macaroons were better than any therapist. Even though Ava had scoffed half a tonne of sugar, she felt lighter than she had in weeks. But just to make sure she was on the road to healing, Camille passed her a little green bottle.

'What's this?' Ava turned it over in her hand, but there was no label.

'It's my remedy for a broken heart. Two drops under your tongue before bed. *Oui?*'

'*Oui,*' she nodded.

# Chapter Twenty-five

**October 2018**

She wasn't sure if it was the potion or the pep talk or the fact that the sun was still shining well into October, but the horrid malaise that had been hanging over her lifted.

Ava began to feel strength in her solitude.

She practised yoga in the mornings by the pool, catching the sunrise. Enjoying the quiet around her and the calm of her thoughts. She began baking again, experimenting with French recipes, creating croissants and *pain au chocolate* to rival the ones Margot sold at the *boulangerie*.

Every time she achieved something, every time she enjoyed what she was doing, she gave herself a pat on the back. Building her confidence rather than knocking it. And something strange happened as a result; her negative critical voice began to get drowned out.

Ava finally started on refurbishing the house, clearing away her grandpapa's clutter. She ventured to the Sunday *brocante* in search of bargains she could restore to their former glory. She bought a coffee table for the living room and some yellow fabric to make curtains with. She wanted Château Saint-Clair to look as sunny on the inside as she was feeling.

If Jacques, and his ripped body, and their passionate nights together crept back inside her occasionally unguarded mind, she would stamp them out, immediately. She managed, thanks to her unwavering determination – a strength that had always been there, throughout her childhood and her marriage. It was a strength that Ava had only really been able to harness again since finally discovering what her purpose was.

Ava reinstated her stylish wardrobe, which she'd slowly put together thanks to Camille's advice and hand-me-downs. She wore her saucy underwear on every occasion, even when she was slogging away in the vineyard in her dungarees and welly boots, just to give herself a boost.

Whenever she did have a down day, she turned her anger for Ambrose into energy to drive her out of bed in the morning. She made a power breakfast shake out of remembering his dirty tricks and imagined wiping that smug expression off his face when he had to hand the Golden Grape award over to her.

'We are! We are going to win it!' she found herself proclaiming into the mirror on her dressing-table. Luckily no one was in earshot to judge her slightly manic behaviour.

Now the stakes had been raised she began taking even more interest in what Jean-Marc was doing, studying him as he beavered away in his 'lab' i.e. the corner of the barn. He had a table laid out with dozens of glass bottles, labels scrawled on in black marker pen, containing various shades of liquid pink. He looked like an eccentric alchemist, blending one juice into the other, trying to find the exact ratio of Grenache to Tibouren. Tasting the juice from the barrels every day to see if the flavour had developed enough. Swearing and having mini tantrums on a regular basis.

'*Merde! Merde! Merde!*' he screamed just as she pulled open the huge barn door.

Ava was carrying a big woolly jumper and a scarf as she was worried her master oenologist was going to catch a cold. It was warm in the sunshine but freezing in the shade. The seasons were changing swiftly.

Jean-Marc blinked at her. 'You're not serious?' His lips pursed.

She looked down at her grandfather's woollies. 'Why not?'

'Darling, I would rather catch pneumonia then be seen wearing *those*. It would cramp my creativity, *mon Dieu*.'

Ava rubbed her nose to hide her smile. 'How is the creativity going?'

She wished she hadn't asked as he quickly descended into a panic. 'It is nearly there but still so far to go. I have the red fruits and the citrus and the melon and guava but there are several ingredients missing,' his voice turning breathless.

'Oh!'

'Oh indeed.' He shook his head.

'But we still have a couple of months to find them?'

'*Oui, oui*, and they may develop but I just worry, I'm always worrying until I get it right, *vous comprendez?*'

I understand,' she smiled. 'I'm a worrier myself.'

'Ava darling, I'm so sorry, there is me going on about my crisis, but what about you, you poor sweet thing.' Jean-Marc shot her a condoling look. 'Have you heard from *him?*'

'He keeps writing to me, all the time. But I don't read his messages.'

'That must take a lot of discipline. I would just want to open them.'

'Nope,' she cut in. 'I'm not going to be brought down.'

'Well done. I mean, you have to give it to him, he's been trying very hard. What about those flowers he gave you?'

'Flowers?' Ava frowned.

'The bouquet of roses, such a beautiful Burgundy colour like a full-bodied Bordeaux Merlot, oh my. Bernard took them from him.'

A lump rose in her throat from nowhere. 'Jacques was here?'

'Yes, last week. Arrived on that adorable scooter of his. He was so handsome, it's such a shame he turned out to be a love rat, *oui*?'

But Ava's thoughts were elsewhere. On Jacques. Part of her was secretly flattered he was going to such lengths to patch things up with her; what woman doesn't like to be chased, after all? But mostly she was furious he had come to her vineyard, invaded her sacred space where she was healing. And why had it been kept from her?

'I'll be back,' she said hurriedly, 'I need to speak to Bernard.'

'I thought you knew,' Jean-Marc called after her, his voice fading as she sped across the courtyard to find the gardener.

Bernard looked at her protectively.

'Of course I told him to leave.'

Ava tried her best to not look disappointed. 'Did he say anything?'

'*Non*.' he coughed. 'Actually, *oui*, something about not being a spy. I stopped listening at that point, I was thinking he has probably come to spy on us again.' Suddenly looking worried he'd upset her, 'I thought I was doing the right thing?'

'You did,' she said, a little unconvincingly. A part of her wishing she'd had the option of seeing him.

'This is why I like to stay out of things.' He began collecting his tools. 'I try to help but it gets taken the wrong way. I do something good and Madame Chevalier tells me I'm doing it wrong. *Bouff*, I don't know,' he fanned the air. 'I just stick to my grapes. They don't give me any trouble.'

'Oh Bernard,' she found herself reaching to give him a hug. He stood rigid as a board, unsure how to respond. And then clapped a hand on her back. '*Bon!*' he said, awkwardly.

Quickly changing the subject, the gardener drew Ava's attention to the pressing matter of the hole in the roof. It needed to be repaired before winter took hold.

Ava let out a little yelp that sounded similar to that of an injured animal. 'I don't have any money, Bernard.' Her mind scrambled over all the other repairs that needed to be done. She didn't even have enough to pay the heating bill for the winter. She was planning on having fires in the living room and the study, but Ava couldn't bring herself to think about how arctic things were going to get. She dreaded Sophie's reaction when she arrived for the Christmas holidays. She'd decided it was best to keep shtum about the truth to avoid any cataclysmic tantrums.

'Can we patch it up for now?'

'I can try.'

'It's all going to be patch-up jobs until we start making money.' She paused, panicking. '*If* we make any money.'

'Don't speak like that, it's bad luck, eh. We will win the competition, I know it.'

His words had a calming effect on her. She had been finding that more and more of late; Bernard was becoming her rock, someone she could call on in a crisis.

'Oh, Bernard,' she turned as she was leaving. 'What happened to those roses?'

He flushed, enlarging the red across his already ruddy cheeks. 'I took them home. *Pardon, Madame.*'

243

Ava smiled at the thought of them decorating his kitchen table. Of him coming home after a long day in the fields to be met with the sight of the beautiful flowers, bringing a human touch into what she imagined was a lonely existence.

'Don't be sorry,' she reassured him. 'I'm happy they went to a good home.'

# Chapter Twenty-six

**December 2018**

The frosted ground crunched underneath her boots.

They'd spent the last month pruning the vines to small stumps. All that lay before Ava now was a giant expanse of earth and posts dusted in a crunchy coating of sugar icing.

The air was crisp and cold and burned as she breathed it into her lungs. She blew out dragon puffs of hot steam back into the atmosphere.

She was swaddled in layers of bulky clothing; a woolly hat, and a scarf wrapped around to her nose.

Ava closed her eyes, letting the blazing bright sunshine thaw her chilled body. And then blinked them open, taking in the winter colours all around her. The vineyard had come alive in December with the explosion of vibrant yellow mimosas and purple irises. The pastels of the fruit tree blossoms – the white and pink of the almond trees, the pinks of the plum tree and the pale pink of the apricot. The rosemary was in full bloom, decorating the horizon with pastel purple.

*Sophie is going to love this*, Ava smiled to herself.

Her daughter was flying into Nice airport that afternoon. She couldn't wait to show her absolutely everything. The house, the vineyard, the cellar, and introduce her to the incredible team behind it all – her French family.

She tugged off her boots next to the front door, shrugged off her coat and padded into the warmth in her thick angora wool socks. The house smelt of freshly baked bread and sweet dough. Ava had gone into overdrive preparing for Sophie's arrival. On top of the Aga was a brioche in the shape of a fat braid, sprinkled in dark chocolate pieces. That was Madame Chevalier's idea, she thought everyone needed fattening up with sugary treats. She didn't know that Ava had already been to the chocolatier in town and tucked a box of handmade rose creams underneath Sophie's pillow. Just like she used to do when Sophie was little.

'*Merde!*' A rare swearword escaped Madame Chevalier's lips. She'd been flapping all morning about the state of the house, despite having cleaned it three times over.

'I'm going to swap Sophie's sheets,' she announced, charging back upstairs.

'I like the ones with the daisies on them that used to be mine when I was a child,' Ava argued.

'*Non, non*, the cotton isn't soft enough. The pink will be better,' she bossed.

Their disagreement was interrupted by a knock at the door.

'Just leave the daises!' Ava shouted up the stairs, 'I like them.'

She pulled the door to, letting in a gust of glacial air. She turned to greet the person on her doorstep.

'Sophie! Honey! What are you doing . . .' Her stomach lurched as she stared at the man behind her.

'What are *you* doing here?'

'Darlin'! I've missed you!'

'What's your father doing here?' Ava glared at her husband.

Sophie looked at her pleadingly.

'I wanted you two to talk; we caught an earlier flight so we could surprise you.'

'I'm surprised!' she said sharply.

'Mum, he's come all this way to see you.'

Mark took a step forward with his arms wide open as he moved towards her.

Ava folded hers, blocking all chances of an embrace.

Mark tried for a kiss instead but Ava pulled back, dodging his lips like a boxer ducking a blow.

'Mum, please,' Sophie tugged at her sleeve, childishly.

'Just hear me out, love.'

'It's freezing out here, Mum, just let him in.'

Mark rubbed his hands together and made an exaggerated shiver.

Ava's eyes flickered between her husband, her daughter and the door. Her anxiety was cranking up by the second. She felt like a trapped animal, unfairly ambushed by those who had the greatest emotional hold over her. Even after a year apart, within seconds of seeing Mark she felt her strength ebb away. That familiar helpless feeling that had kept her trapped in a broken marriage for so many years, returning. It took all of her might to stop herself falling back into their old pattern of behaviour; putting her family before herself, being emotionally blackmailed into doing what they wanted.

*You've come so far, don't give up now*; she repeated the words silently in her head like a mantra.

'Just ten minutes of your time, that's all, I promise.'

*Don't give up, don't give up . . .*

By arriving with Sophie, Mark had made it very difficult for her to kick him out into the cold. That would make her even more of a villain in her daughter's eyes.

She sighed deeply and stepped aside, letting Mark pass but wrapping Sophie in an almighty welcome hug.

'Eugh, it's freezing in here,' Sophie complained, wriggling out of her arms.

Ava led them into the kitchen, which was warm and cosy with the Aga smouldering away. The windows were misted from the inside. Mark used his sleeve to rub a porthole to the vineyard. He pressed his nose against the glass and peered out.

'Cor, blimey, we should have come here earlier, love. Who would have thought your granddad had such a big gaff.'

Ava cleared her throat. 'You said there was something you wanted to talk to me about?'

Sophie was rummaging around the kitchen, opening cupboards and drawers, smelling the string of garlic hanging above the stove, squeezing the spongy brioche between her fingers.

'I've changed the sheets! Who was that at the door?' Madame Chevalier burst into the room with an armful of freshly washed towels clutched to her chest. Her eyes widened on seeing Mark and a little gasp escaped her mouth as she noticed Ava's strained expression.

'*Pardon, Madame Ava,*' she backed away.

Luckily Jean-Marc had disappeared to Paris for the weekend or he would have delivered a much more waspish remark.

'It's fine, just give me a minute,' she called after her.

Mark pulled a face. 'Madame Ava, la dee da.'

'Oh be quiet, Mark, she's my grandfather's housekeeper.' And then corrected herself. 'She's called Madame Chevalier and she works here.'

'You must be doing all right to have people running about after you.'

Ava stared at him. There was no doubt about it, he had a look of jealousy in his eye.

'What do you want, Mark? I haven't heard from you in months and now you show up at my door expecting me to welcome you with open arms.'

He held up his hands. 'I come in peace.'

He looked at her more warily. 'Mind if I take a seat?'

She shrugged.

The chair screeched across the tiles, slicing through the already tense atmosphere.

Ava sat opposite Mark, Sophie to her left, creating the most unrelaxed of family reunions. Everyone was watching each other, trying to guess what would happen next.

Ava studied her husband. He looked different. Their time apart hadn't been so kind to him. His eyes were drawn. His hair was more salt than pepper and he had let it grow longer, into waves that curled around his ears. A worry line had etched itself between his brows.

By contrast, she knew *she* was glowing. Her summer tan was still shimmering, giving her a golden freckly sun-kissed look. Her raven hair was tussled in a messy but chic way, streaked with copper from all the hours she had spent outdoors. Her eyes were bright from the country air. The worry lines that were once engraved across her forehead had lifted.

He broke the ice with a smile, one of his charming, *I'm about to offer you a deal you can't refuse* smiles. Only it wasn't a deal but an uncharacteristic compliment.

'You look gorgeous.' He squinted. 'Have you done something with your hair?'

She'd become so used to her 'new me' reflection, she'd forgotten the old Ava, with the long hair. The Ava Mark knew.

'Thanks. I cut it off. I needed a change.'

'Well, you look great . . . really . . . hot!'

It should have been immensely satisfying that Mark was finally complimenting her but suddenly it struck Ava – she didn't give a toss what he thought of her appearance. Although as it happened her look was more effortless chic today, rocking paint-stained denim dungarees over a jumper look. Those days when she first found out he was seeing another woman, when she dreaded the thought of running into them together at the Slug and Lettuce, she would have panicked about her clothes, her hair, her make-up. She would have wanted him to see her at her best, looking pretty. All she cared about now was why he had turned up unannounced and . . .

'How's Gabby?' she asked acidly.

He sheepishly looked down to his clasped hands. 'We're not together any more.'

'Oh dear. That didn't last long. So you've come crawling back?'

'I broke it off with her, actually.'

Ava's eyebrow shot up. 'Really? She didn't get sick of you then?'

'No,' he cut in. He tried to meet her gaze.

'I ended it because I realised what a mistake I'd made.'

Ava made an audible huffing noise.

'It's true. How could I throw away what we had?' More quietly he added, 'I'm sorry, for everything. I should have never put you through all of that.'

He pressed his lips together; his brow furrowed with concern.

But the mention of the debt, of losing their home, of the deceit, only triggered her anger. She couldn't look at him.

'Please, babe, you've got to believe how sorry I am.'

Mark reached his hand across the table and gently cupped hers. She wanted to pull away but couldn't. Something about his familiar warmth suddenly made her feel paralysed. Like an animal playing dead to protect itself. She needed to guard her heart from the hurt. Ava had fought so hard to get to where she was. *Don't give up now, don't give up.* The mantra returned.

Softly, he said: 'I've missed you.'

Her resolve began to crack as she stared into Mark's pleading eyes.

Sophie joined in. 'Can't you work things out?' she whined. 'I just want us to be a family again.'

That familiar feeling of anxiety returned, squeezing her chest like a vice.

Mark continued staring intently at her with his smoky blue eyes, those eyes that could be so persuasive.

'Dad loves you, Mum.'

'I love you, darling,' Mark parroted, still trying to keep Ava's gaze fixed.

Sophie sniffled with the onset of tears. Ava felt her fight draining away like a slow puncture. She sat back heavily into her chair, her arms flopping to her sides like a rag doll.

Sophie went on, relentlessly. 'We could buy a house now that Dad's got a new job. You could sell this dump.'

'Hey missy, this is not a dump,' Ava snapped.

'Come on, Mum, it's freezing, and falling apart. And there's not even a decent signal,' she angled her mobile into the air. 'I can't get on my Instagram feed.'

Mark cleared his throat. 'But seriously, hun. We could start over. Be a family again. It would be different this time, a fresh start for all of us.'

Ava closed her eyes and tried to breathe, but she could feel Sophie and Mark watching her, waiting for her to react.

*

'This ain't half bad, is it?' Mark took another swig of wine.

They'd moved next door to be by the fire. Sophie had gone up to her room to unpack, to find a phone signal and give her parents space to talk about rekindling their marriage.

Ava picked up the bottle of red and topped up their glasses. She needed some wine to dull how emotional she was feeling. As if by second nature, she breathed in the bouquet.

'Very intense on the nose. Black fruits. Blackberry. Cherry.' She took another whiff. 'Blueberries from the Cabernet Sauvignon grapes.' She tilted her glass. 'It's not young, because a young red looks ruby and purple. An old red looks like rust, with oranges and brown. So this is in between.' She looked at the bottle of Château Peyrassol, her new favourite red wine. 'Ten years old, I was right.' She smiled victoriously. She looked up. Mark's mouth had dropped open.

'How the hell do you know that?'

'What do you think I've been doing for the past year? I run a vineyard now,' she said proudly.

Mark took another glug.

'Alfie has something similar in his warehouse which he's trying to palm off on me. I was thinking of buying a few boxes, they're dead cheap. Probably same quality as this fancy stuff. All wine's the same at the end of the day, comes from a grape, doesn't it?'

Ava was screaming inside. But she knew it was pointless educating Mark. Some things don't change.

'So how're you finding this place? Can't be easy all on your own?'

'I'm managing. If you'd told me a year ago I'd be entering a big wine competition I would have laughed in your face, but here I am. Actually, I'm more than managing, we have a great team here and stand a chance of winning.'

'Entering a competition?'

'Yes.'

'Making actual wine?'

'Yes!'

'That's great,' he said, with a trace of bitterness. 'Yeah, well I'm doing all right too. I've got a new job with a construction company.'

'You do?' she cheered enthusiastically. Genuinely happy he was turning his life around too.

'Yeah, paying me double what I was earning before. So things are looking up. Not long until I clear my debt. Like I said, I'm a changed man.'

'I'm so pleased for you.'

'So how about you?'

'Me?' She frowned. 'Just busy making wine.'

'No, I meant how about you and,' he croaked. 'Is there anyone,' he struggled to get the words out. 'Are you seeing anyone?'

She dodged his gaze, overwhelmed by feelings of guilt. She weighed up the outcomes of confessing to her rampant summer of sex with a hot young guy in her head. Knowing Mark, it would only end in an explosive argument. And the truth was, she wasn't with anyone. Not any more. Jacques was history.

'No,' she replied softly.

A look of relief washed over him. 'Good. Because it would tear me apart knowing you'd met someone.'

The audacity of it, Ava thought. Typical Mark and his double standards.

'So there is no one in the way of us giving us another try.'

Ava peered into her wine glass as she took a lingering sip. A part of her had always known Mark would be back one day when he realised the grass wasn't greener and there was a time, in her darkest hour, against Emilia's advice, when she had wanted him back. But now so much had changed. She had moved on in so many ways. Is getting back with an ex ever a good idea? Monica from her old job forgave her husband for having an affair, but she never trusted him again; was forever checking his pockets for incriminating receipts and breaking into his computer passwords. But then she and Mark had more than twenty years of history together. He knew her better than anyone; knew what made her laugh, what made her cry, and he was the father of their daughter.

'Ummm, I think . . .' she started.

'Tell me, babe,' Mark shuffled the big armchair closer.

'I think . . .' she stared out of the window, yet again trying to hold off making a decision about her marriage.

She squinted. 'I think it's snowing!'

'What?'

'Look,' she pointed. She got up and rushed across the room.

A flurry of thick white flakes had descended on her vineyard. Dancing, whirling up and around in circles, sparkling as they passed the warm glow of the living room, and then settling on the ground below to form a blanket of icing sugar.

'It's beautiful,' she whispered, touching the window with her fingertips, her eyes transfixed by the mesmerising fall of the snowflakes.

She could hear his footsteps and then feel the warmth as Mark wrapped his arms around her. His big, cuddly chest pressing against her back. His familiar smell, flooding her senses.

'That's bloody beautiful,' he exclaimed.

They stared quietly out into the blizzard while the fire crackled away behind them, thinking about their future together.

Ava had missed the touch of a man; she didn't realise quite how much until she felt herself ensconced by Mark.

He might not have Jacques' ripped body – Mark's once flat stomach had burgeoned into middle-age spread. He now had squidgy love handles and a small belly, accentuated by the size-too-small shirts he insisted on wearing – but he was still handsome, with his rugged good looks; piercing eyes coupled with an easy charm. He was still her Mark. Her husband of twenty-three years. And after a few glasses of vino, the thought of cuddling seemed much more appealing than going back to her freezing cold bedroom alone.

Did he deserve another chance? Ava wondered if she was somehow also to blame for her marriage breaking down? Had she neglected him just as she had neglected herself? When children are involved should you keep trying to make it work?

Ava had been double-crossed by both the men she'd loved. Was she better off with the devil she knew?

Her thoughts whirled with the snow.

'So I was thinking.' Mark's voice, gravelly in her ear. 'This place must be worth a few bob. You know, if you sold it.'

Ava tensed.

'Not far from the beach. Holidaymakers would be gagging to have an apartment here.'

She pulled away from his grip and turned to face him. 'Why are you saying this?'

'Because I was just looking out at that stonking view and thought of all its potential.'

'But it has potential, to make wine.'

'Come on babe, that's not gonna earn you any money. I'm talking *real* money,' he rubbed his thumb across his fingers.

'Don't you get what I'm trying to do here, Mark?'

'I do, I do, have some time out. Clearing your head, but isn't it time you came home now? You could even get yourself a job in a bakery, making those cakes you keep talking about.'

Ava frowned. 'But I have a job, here.'

'This ain't a job.'

'What do you mean?'

'This ain't you, darling. It ain't us, buried in the French countryside. It's nice for a holiday and all but I can't be living with frogs for the rest of my life.'

'Well nobody asked you to live here!' she snapped.

A silence fell.

'What? I thought you were coming back to Blighty with me? Let's sell this place, make some money. We could live out our dreams back in Surbiton.'

There was a much longer silence as a cold front descended, and it wasn't the snow.

*What was she thinking?* Ava glared at her glass of wine. She couldn't believe she'd considered giving Mark a second chance. He hadn't changed; he was the same old Mark, expecting her to fit in with what he wanted.

It was *her* who had changed.

Yet again he had dismissed her dreams as trivial hobbies, and she couldn't bear it.

Ava's throat constricted as she battled with the words, her eyes brimming with tears. There was no going back. Softly, she said, 'Mark, I'm not coming back. It's . . . it's over.'

'What are you talking about?'

'This, us, it's done.'

'You're not serious?' Mark was so used to getting his way he couldn't conceive of someone turning him down, especially Ava, or the Ava he knew.

'I am. Who we are together, what we want, isn't aligned. When I look at this vineyard, I want to nourish it, make it blossom. When you look at it, all you want to do is demolish it. How can I be with a man who wants to destroy something that means so much to me?'

'Come on Ava, don't go pretending you gave a toss about your grandfather or his wine, you couldn't be bothered to see him for all those years. You've only perked up since you've inherited his gaff.'

The words burned, so deeply Ava could feel them scalding her insides. She hated him, absolutely hated him. For everything he'd put her through.

She stabbed a finger into his chest. 'We. Are. Never. Getting. Back. Together!' Her mouth contorted with rage.

'Ava!' Mark suddenly looked tearful.

'No Mark. I'm sorry I'm hurting you by saying this but you hurt me. Too many times. It's broken, we're broken,' her face cracked with tears.

'Ava, please,' he began to cry.

She shook her head. 'No, Mark, no.'

Ava looked at him, square in the eyes, at the tears he was shedding and for the first time in her marriage, she didn't feel guilt-tripped into fixing the problem. Instead she let the tension hang in the room as she confidently stuck by her decision.

And then despite her immense anger, she stepped forward and hugged him.

Mark softened into her embrace, wrapping her up into his big arms. And there they stood in silence, holding each other, in their hearts knowing that it probably was for the last time. Tears streaming down both their faces.

# Chapter Twenty-seven

Ava and Mark slept only two bedrooms apart that night but it felt like he was on the other side of the world.

Only when she had finally found the courage to tell him 'no', to express what *she* really wanted from her life, did she realise quite how far they had drifted.

'Slept' was not really the word to describe how those hours passed though, as Ava tossed and turned, her mind humming, constantly. She stared at the ceiling, at the wall, at her mattress as she rolled over onto her front, and then eventually at the beautiful snow-covered landscape when she finally couldn't take it any more and moved from her bed to the window. The wind had eased off so there was no more whirling and circling of snowflakes, just a gentle, graceful fall into an abyss of darkness.

Somehow, despite feeling colder than the inside of her freezer, Ava eventually managed to drift off in the early hours, into a dream-filled sleep.

Whether it was Mark's mention of it, or something that was still stirring deep inside her, Ava dreamt of her last summer at Château Saint-Clair, the last time she ever saw her grandpapa. That vision of him disappearing into a dust haze as her mum sped up the driveway kept replaying in her mind. As if her subconscious were searching for another ending.

She woke in tears. Breathless. Varnished in a film of sweat. The sheets underneath her duvet had become tangled around her legs like a noose. And then came the bonging and the cheeping of the cuckoo clock downstairs, echoing into her bedroom, reminding her it was already . . .

'Ten a.m.!' she yelped. 'Christ!' She'd been working so hard on the vineyard that she couldn't remember when she'd last slept in. She pushed herself out of bed, bleary-eyed, feeling weak already at the thought of round two with Sophie. She knew her daughter wouldn't take the news she wanted to divorce her father well. She felt a strange sense of calm though at the thought of divorce, which she'd decided about at some point during her sleepless night. She dreaded having to break it to her daughter though and her footsteps turned heavier with guilt as she closed in on the kitchen.

But as it turned out, Mark had clearly already delivered the news that they weren't getting back together, because Madame Chevalier was in a cooking frenzy and was trying to placate her daughter.

Sophie gave her mum the death stare as she entered, noisily dropping the knife she'd used to smother her crois-sant with butter onto the plate.

Madame Chevalier flashed Ava a look and shrugged exasperatedly.

Mark was tucking into his baguette, bacon and eggs. He didn't look up.

The tension knocked the breath from her. She decided the only way to handle the situation was to deal with it head on, in a calm rational manner – by falling back on to the universally positive conversation of food.

'Aren't those delicious, you can thank Madame Chevalier for rushing to the *boulangerie* this morning.'

Sophie continued to glare, dissecting the pastry into tiny pieces.

'No? Well you should really try the *pain au chocolat*.'

'Mum?'

'What's up, love?'

'MUM!'

Ava sighed deeply, while Madame Chevalier quickly scarpered into the pantry.

'I know this isn't what you wanted, sweetheart, but it's going to be okay. Your dad will still be your dad,' she looked across to Mark, who was hunched over his plate, shovelling the last third of a baguette into his mouth. 'And I will always be your mum.'

'That's just bloody great, isn't it!' She huffed. 'Well *my* dad is going to take me into town now.'

Mark looked up.

Ava cocked her eyebrow. 'Town? Don't you mean the airport?'

'Are you kicking him out already, Mum?'

'I'm not kicking anyone out, but I think your father needs to start thinking about travelling home.'

Mark finally spoke. 'All flights are grounded because of the snow. So you're stuck with me for now. Sorry love.'

She groaned internally. What could she say to that? Other than tell him to find somewhere else to stay, but she didn't have the heart to do that. She could grin and bear it for another day, she supposed.

'So are we going or what, Dad?' Sophie pushed her chair back.

Mark shrugged at Ava. 'It was my idea.'

'Best idea I've heard since I've got here. I'm bored out of my mind. How can you live like this without proper WiFi?' Sophie left the kitchen in a cloud of diva-ness.

Although Ava was annoyed at Mark for always indulging Sophie, she was secretly relieved for the space. She needed to clear her head, to think about something else that was now playing heavily on her mind – the snow. Had it damaged her precious vines?

'There's some really nice cake shops and cafés and a lovely restaurant to have lunch in . . .' she tailed off, suddenly thinking of Jacques.

'Whatever. Come on, Dad.' Sophie waited by the door.

Mark squeezed past Ava, barely looking her in the eye. She touched his arm and he managed a half-smile. 'See you later,' he said.

'Drive carefully, the roads will be icy,' she called after them but the blast of cold wind had already slammed the door shut.

Ava expected to find Bernard cursing under his breath and breaking his back as he dug out the vines from the thick layer of snow that had settled across Château Saint-Clair.

But everything was surprisingly calm and tranquil on the vineyard that morning. And breathtakingly beautiful, as the world looked like it had been caked in a thick layer of white icing. It was eerily silent. Not even the birds were chattering. There was just a faint howling of the wind as it picked up and dropped, taking with it a sheet of snow, spraying the icing sugar into the air.

She was grateful for the sun on her face, feeding her some much needed energy, and the stillness, to calm her mind. And then all of a sudden she heard his voice.

'Grandpapa?' she looked around her, into the thick mass of white.

She shook her head and carried on, the wind picking up again, howling, whispering. She stopped dead, swishing her head from left to right.

'Grandpapa?'

Perhaps it was the dream that had sparked it off, but there it was again; it was definitely his voice, her dear grandpapa, from an old distant memory, repeating the answers to questions she already knew.

'The snow won't harm them, my dear child.'

She could picture him next to her as he had been all those years ago. He was trying to reassure her the vines would be safe after she left for the summer, that the snow wouldn't hurt them.

She had been crying, wiping her dewy eyes on her little pink cardigan. He'd crouched to meet her at eye level and said: 'Do you remember watching Superman?'

She nodded, her eyes big and watery.

'And he had a protective red cape.'

'Yes, grandpapa.'

'The snow is like a cape. Protecting the vines because it stops the soil from freezing. Frozen soil is *très très* dangerous because nothing can pass in and out to the roots.' He pointed his finger to the sky and she followed it with her eyes. 'The snow brings the magic from the heavens, something called nitrogen.'

Ava's eyes widened. She tried repeating the long word: 'Ni-tro-gen.'

'When the snow melts it carries the magic ingredients from the sky into the soil which the vines will drink. So, my dearest Ava, there is nothing to fear. They will survive until your return.'

His gravelly voice faded into the wind as quickly as it had appeared. She breathed in deeply, smiling, feeling a sense of calm wash over her, and the certainty that she had nothing to fear.

She waded on, through the snowdrifts, the white powder crunching beneath her boots, to find Bernard studying the ground between a row of vines, emitting a low growling noise.

'What are you doing?'

Bernard narrowed his eyes.

'He's back, look,' he pointed to the hoof print.

'The pig?'

'*Oui*. Who else!'

'Why? There are no grapes for him to eat.'

'He is scavenging for food. He will eat anything that will fit into his mouth. Even the insects that live on the vines.'

'But isn't that good because insects are bad?'

'It's terrible! It means he is still here, and will probably be back next spring. If not him, his cousin, or babies or . . .'

'Oh, Bernard, isn't it wonderful.' She stretched her hands into the sky.

He looked at her sideways, suspiciously.

'Are you feeling well?'

'Me?' she exclaimed. 'I don't think I've ever felt better.' Despite being dizzy with tiredness, she felt the polar opposite – almost brimming over with life, and the slightly hysterical happiness that the burden of her past was finally lifted. Slowly, steadily, the realisation that she was now a free woman, properly unattached, was sinking in.

The road ahead was unpaved. The future of her vineyard hung in the balance. What she was certain of, though, was that she wouldn't be making a U-turn back to Surbiton.

Most of all, she felt her grandpapa's presence, keeping a watchful eye over her, guiding her safely into a new future.

# Chapter Twenty-eight

It was turning dark when Mark and Sophie finally returned from their trip into town. Mark seemed even more weary than when he had set out but her daughter looked positively glowing.

Ava was relieved. She hoped Sophie might have fallen in love with picturesque Flassans-sur-Issole as much as she herself had when she'd first wandered the narrow streets. She imagined it would be sparkling and twinkly with the Christmas decorations, the shop windows laden with treats – chocolate *Bûche de Noël*, Madeline cakes, ginger *speculaas* biscuits, towers of dark chocolate truffles.

'This place isn't so bad after all,' Sophie announced as she kicked off her shoes by the front door.

'I told you there was lots to see.'

'You're telling me,' twirling the end of her ponytail, coyly.

'Such as the cake shop; did you see those crème caramels wobbling on a plate?' Ava closed her eyes at the thought of the custard texture melting in her mouth.

'No, such as the hottie working in the restaurant.'

Mark rolled his eyes.

'I mean, phwoar! What is a guy like that doing in a place like this?'

Neither Mark nor Sophie had noticed that Ava had stopped speaking. In fact, she had stopped moving all together, her whole body was frozen. Except for her heart. That was thudding. She could barely bring herself to ask the question.

'Did he have dark hair?'

Sophie was gazing at her reflection in the huge gilt mirror in the hallway, practising her best pout from various angles. She tightened her ponytail, and smiled, pleased with her look. Oblivious that her mum was hanging on her every word, then suddenly registering the question.

'Oh, yeah, dark hair, and an incredible body,' her eyes widening, 'I mean, wow.'

Ava's stomach lurched.

'He looks like he must work out,' she smiled naughtily.

'Soph!' Mark ticked her off.

'What? I'm allowed to look!'

'Look? You couldn't have been more obvious you were checking him out. And you're supposed to let the fella do the talking.'

'Oh, shut up Dad, not any more, we're not in the dark ages now. It's okay for girls to ask guys out.'

'No, it's not . . .' Mark started, but Ava cut in.

'You. Asked. Him. Out?' Ava took a small breath between words.

'Of course I did. What else am I going to do with my time here? He probably took pity on me being stuck in this backwater town for Christmas.'

Ava's pulse had rocketed. She needed to know but she didn't want to know at the same time. She forced the words out.

'And what did he say?

'Yes?' Ob-vious-ly.' She swished her high ponytail.

'Well, you didn't really give him much option did you, love?' Mark corrected.

'Huh?'

'You pretty much forced him to write down his phone number.'

'Well, you gotta be pushy to get what you want.' She smiled sarcastically at her father. 'You taught me that.' Sophie went on. 'His name is Jacques, how cool is that. A proper French name.'

'Well, we are in France,' Mark reminded her.

Ava was nearly hyperventilating at this point.

Sophie's eyes bounced between her parents.

'What's your problem, both of you? I thought you'd be happy I was integrating with the locals.' She headed for the kitchen. 'And you don't know what really happened, Dad, you were busy talking to some French guy.'

Ava somehow managed to focus enough to ask: 'French guy?'

Mark shrugged. 'Oh, it was no one. Just someone wanting to find out more about England. Heard my posh accent.' He turned back to Sophie: 'Anyway, I hope you're not going to contact him.'

'I can do what I want,' she snapped.

'NO!' Ava cried out.

They both turned and stared at her, taken aback by her totally uncharacteristic outburst.

She blushed. 'I mean, no, it's not a good idea.'

'Chill out, Mum. Je-zus!' Sophie gave her an exaggerated eye roll.

An unsettling atmosphere had descended over Château Saint-Clair that evening. A feeling of claustrophobia and anxiety had been building and was now hanging like a thick fog in the living room where they had all gathered to be near the fire.

Mark was behaving skittishly. He was glued to his phone, checking for weather updates. Sophie was also physically attached to her mobile, but for other reasons. She had been trying to stalk Jacques on social media for the last hour, seeing if she could find his Facebook or Instagram profile.

And Ava was unable to sit still for longer than two minutes as her mind flip-flopped between extreme emotions. Jealousy that the man she'd loved might be interested in her daughter. Fear, that he might try to manipulate Sophie into telling him secrets to feed back to Ambrose. Guilt that she was actually feeling jealous. And frustration that she had to swallow her emotions and keep the toxic cocktail of feelings locked up inside so her family didn't find out what she had been up to over the summer. She couldn't confess about Jacques, not now.

*I'll just have to stand back and let Sophie get on with it. She isn't a little girl any more. I would never compete with my daughter over a man. Never.*

*But what if he breaks her heart just like he did mine? And uses her to find out what her grandpapa's secret blend is?*

*What if he falls head over heels in love with her?*

Flip flop, flip flip, went her emotions.

On top of that, she was finding it hard to share oxygen with Mark. She had to keep things civil for the sake of Sophie but it was a struggle when she really wanted him gone. *Not long now before the planes would be in the air again. Keep calm and carry on.*

'I'm going to send Jacques a message!' Sophie announced.

All the soothing and rational words Ava had silently been thinking shot out the window.

'What? You can't!'

Sophie looked sideways at her from the big padded chair that she had spread herself across, her legs hooked over the armrest.

'Don't tell me what to do, Mum. Quit controlling me. I'm not a baby. You got me out here and now you want to stop me having fun.'

'Don't speak to you mother like that,' Mark stepped in.

'She has no right to boss me about. I can do what I want, go out with who I want . . .' She pushed herself into an upright position. 'When I want.' Waving her mobile. 'And I don't need to ask my parents' permission.'

Ava lunged and snatched the phone from her hand.

'Oi! What are you doing? Give it back.'

'No,' Ava clutched it to her chest, turning her back to Sophie. 'Mum, don't be weird, give it back,' she flung her arms around her mum, trying to grab it from behind. Ava wriggled like a worm on a hook. Mark stared at them both, gobsmacked.

Recovering from his shock, he stepped in to break up the tussle. 'What *is* going on? Stop it!' He tried to pull the two women apart. When that didn't work, he snatched the phone out of Ava's hands instead.

'No one will be messaging anyone,' he said, holding it up out of arm's reach. 'Until everyone calms down. What has got into you both?'

Sophie started jumping up and down, swiping at her dad's raised arm.

'Settle down!'

'Give it back to me, now!'

They were so busy squabbling no one had noticed what was going on outside – that a blizzard had whipped up, that a dense mass of flakes had descended and an icy wind was blasting them horizontally past the window. Or the headlight beaming through the darkness, or the humming of an engine, or Bernard, shouting. Until two voices were yelling so loudly at each other they could be heard above the howling artic wind.

Mark was the first to investigate. He marched over to the living-room window and peered into the courtyard.

'Wait!' he exclaimed. 'Isn't that the guy from the restaurant?'

'Jacques?' Sophie leapt across the room. 'Oh my God, he's found me!' she swooned.

'Jacques is here?' Ava was hot on her heels.

The three of them now had their noses pressed to the glass.

'What is Jacques doing here?' Ava said to no one in particular.

'Wait, you know him?' Sophie snapped.

'What's going on? Why's Bernard arguing with him? Jesus has everyone gone mental?' Mark charged towards the courtyard. As he yanked open the door, a blizzard of snowflakes sprayed into the hallway. The three of them launched themselves into the cold in hot pursuit of one another, to where Jacques and Bernard were slinging insults.

Bernard was waving his stick and Jacques was waving his hands in frustration. Ava noticed immediately that his face was etched with worry.

'What are you doing here?' Sophie exclaimed. 'I haven't even messaged you yet?'

'Come on mate, it's not gentlemanly to be stalking a girl.' Mark stepped in front of her protectively.

But Jacques wasn't listening; his attention was concentrated on Ava. He sprang forward, trying to reach her, only for Bernard to barricade him with his stick.

'Ava, please, you have to listen to me!'

She stood there, frozen to the spot, quite literally.

'Leave now,' Bernard shoved him backwards.

But the old man was no match for the strength of Jacques. He grabbed hold of the stick and began driving Bernard backwards, clearly trying not to hurt him, but still determined to get through to Ava.

'STOP!' she screamed, terrified one or both men would get hurt.

The snow was burning her skin. She'd dived into the cold in just her jumper and jeans and was having serious regrets.

'Stop it now,' she pulled them apart.

Meanwhile, Sophie and Mark had stepped back, looking on in disbelief. Jacques' eyes were wild with adrenaline.

'Ava, you're in danger!' he blurted.

'What do you mean?'

Bernard yelled, 'He's talking rubbish.'

'Ambrose's men are coming for you!'

'What?'

'They were in the restaurant, saying how they were coming to burn down the château.'

'Don't listen to him, Madame!'

'You must believe me, they're dangerous.'

'Hang about, what do you mean?' Mark spoke up. 'Ambrose?'

Jacques turned and glared at him.

'Don't pretend you don't know him. You were talking to him earlier.'

Mark laughed, nervously.

Ava turned to her husband. 'Mark, what's going on?'

'Umm.'

'Mark?' she shrieked.

Four sets of headlights appeared on the horizon.

'Oh God,' he gasped.

'Mark, what the hell is going on?'

The car engines roared as they tore down the drive.

'I didn't know this is what he meant, I swear.'

Ava's eyes flickered between the cars and Mark, fear gripping her stomach. 'What do you mean? What have you done?'

But before he could answer the four-by-fours were upon them, circling the mulberry tree, their tyres burning, honking their horns, masked men hanging out of the windows, howling like wolves.

'We're coming to kill you,' they cackled. 'Ow ow owwwwwwwellll.'

'Get inside, now!' Ava screamed.

'Come on Sophie,' Mark grabbed her.

'No Mum, I'm not leaving you!'

'Go, GO!'

They drove round and around, skidding, spraying gravel and stone into the air, the sand flying with the snowstorm. Ava couldn't see who they were, the faces were lost in the shadows and hidden behind black balaclavas.

Jacques pulled Ava's arm. 'We need to go.'

'They're going to destroy my vineyard,' she screamed.

'They'll destroy you, now come on.'

'I . . .'

But before she could finish her sentence, Jacques had picked her up and was running with Ava in his arms for the front door. Bernard was hobbling close behind. The attackers' howls chased them into the house. They bolted the door behind them.

'Sophie, honey, are you okay?' Ava cried out.

'I'm here, Mum,' she was in the kitchen. 'Who are they? They're really scaring me.'

Ava raced through to where her daughter was hiding and wrapped her arms around her, holding her tightly. She trembled in her arms, her face leached of all colour.

The headlights shone through into the kitchen as they tore past the window, lighting up everyone's terrified faces. Around and around they went like the beam of a lighthouse, only they weren't warning them of danger but bringing it to Ava's door.

'Quick, we need to turn off all the lights,' Jacques leapt into action.

He was dressed head to toe in black, wearing an oversized leather Aviator jacket and a thick black scarf. The cold had turned his ears and nose pink. But his beautiful eyes glowed bright and alert.

'Right now it's like we're in a goldfish bowl; they can see everything we are doing.'

Without hesitation, Bernard hit the light switch and they were plunged into darkness.

'Mum, I'm scared.'

'Shhh, it's going to be okay,' Ava squeezed her tightly.

There was another explosion of hyena cackles, engines revving, tyres skidding and then the sound of exhausts fading out.

'They're leaving!' Mark trilled.

Sophie broke down into tears, sobbing with relief.

'It's okay sweetie, we are going to be all right.' Mark gave a theatrical sigh. 'We can all breathe again.'

'Oh, thank God,' Ava muttered, shaking her head with disbelief. She pressed her hands over her heart; it was pounding so hard she thought it might jump out of her chest. She then turned her gaze to Mark, took a deep breath, limbering up for an almighty inquisition, indicating to Bernard it was time to turn the lights back on, to throw her wretched husband into the spotlight.

'Wait!' Jacques hissed.

Everyone froze.

'Oh no, what now, what now?' Sophie squealed.

'I think I saw a torchlight.' He peered into the gloom. 'There,' he pointed. 'And another one over there.'

'Mum, Dad, what's happening?' Sophie's words were thick with fear.

'I don't know honey. Jacques, what can you see?'

'Nothing; they've disappeared.'

A deathly silence fell on the room as they listened for voices, for the crunching of footsteps on the snow, for the sound of someone trying to open the door.

Ava held her breath. All she could hear was her heart drumming in her ears.

*Ba boom. Ba boom. Ba boom.*

'Where are they?' Mark whispered.

'Shhhh,' Bernard hissed.

Ava tiptoed to where Jacques was keeping watch. She could hear his shallow breathing, she could feel the warmth of his breath whistling past her face as they both looked through the glass.

Silence. It was deafening.

*Ba boom. Ba boom. Ba boom.*

And then suddenly, a haunting 'Oww owwwwwwell' echoed into the night. Followed by another howl from across the courtyard, and another to the left, until they were all howling like a pack of wolves, circling their prey.

# Chapter Twenty-nine

Sophie dropped to the floor, curling into a tight ball, clutching her hands over her ears. 'Make it stop, make it stop,' she pleaded.

SMASH.

It sounded like a bottle being broken.

'What's happening?' Ava screeched. 'Jacques?'

There was a bright flame of light, and it was burning on the other side of the courtyard, on the . . .

'The barn!' Jacques yelled. 'The barn's on fire!' He leapt around the kitchen, desperately searching for something he could use to put it out. '*Merde! Merde!*'

'The bastards are trying to destroy my wine!' Ava cried. She pointed to Mark, who had dived behind the sofa. 'Call the police, now!'

'Me?' He trembled.

'Yes you, do it.'

Meanwhile, Jacques had stopped hopping from one foot to the other, and was now by the front door. Without saying another word, he launched himself into the blizzard.

The cold and the panic had taken hold of Bernard's lungs. He was hit by a fit of coughing that forced him to steady himself against the wall. It had also sent him over the edge with rage. He fought against his old body and between wheezy breaths, he announced: 'Enough!'

'Oh no, what are you going to do?' Ava panicked.

'I'm going to finish this!' With that, Bernard disappeared into the tiny cupboard beneath the staircase and reappeared armed with a hunting rifle.

'Oh my God, oh my God!' Sophie squealed even louder.

'You've got to be kidding?' Ava gasped.

'*Non!*' And with that he marched like a soldier towards the door, his rifle slung over his shoulder.

'Jesus!' Ava ran after him. 'Bernard, please, don't leave us.'

'I'll be back. Stay inside.'

She grabbed his arm, clinging to it like a crustacean. Her eyes were big and watery, her hands trembling.

'Look after your daughter.' He glared at Mark, who was cowering behind the soft furnishings, and then pulled the door open, letting the blizzard and the cold fly into their faces.

'Bernard, please!'

He gently pushed her back inside and slammed the door shut behind him.

Ava's legs crumbled beneath her. She fell with her back against the door and slid to the floor, landing on the mat in a heap. Her whole body had turned into a wobbly blancmange pudding.

'Mum?' Sophie called out.

'I'm still here, honey,' she whispered.

She closed her eyes.

'Are we going to be okay?'

She didn't know what to say. Her barn was on fire, her château was under attack, and the men had thrown themselves into the fray. She felt sick, dizzy. Exhausted with emotion and fear.

And then a gunshot fired.

Ava froze.

'Bernard?' she whispered with all the voice she had left.

Another bang went off, echoing across the vineyard.

'Mum, is that Bernard?'

'Yes, I think so . . .'

'Mum?'

'Yes, it's Bernard,' she said more loudly, with more conviction. 'It's Bernard,' a flame of anger igniting in her belly as she shouted his name.

The thought of him being hurt was unbearable. *How dare they attack her beloved vineyard, how dare they destroy all those months of hard work.*

Overcome with anger and pure undiluted rage, Ava rose to her feet. All signs of wobbliness were gone.

'No one intimidates me!' she roared.

And so, for the third time in a matter of minutes, the front door was yanked open. The cold was allowed in, for a few seconds, while Ava braced herself. She hunched her shoulders into the biting wind, and stepped into the fray.

Despite the storm hurling hail in her face she was still able to see Bernard. He was easy to spot; he was the one with the gun.

The gardener was surrounded by five shadowy figures who were taking delight in baiting him. He jerked the air rifle left to right trying to keep the wolves at bay.

The sight angered Ava even more. She charged towards them, fuelled with adrenaline and fury, her arms swinging by her side as if she were a soldier marching into battle.

The enemy were dressed in black. Black jeans, jackets, balaclavas, biker boots. She wondered if one of them, who had a much more slight appearance, might be a woman, but it was hard to make out any distinguishing features. She suddenly realised that they might have targeted her tonight, precisely because there was a snowstorm, making it harder to identify them. Her anger exploded.

'You don't scare me,' she barked.

Bernard started at her voice. 'Madame Ava, go back inside.'

'No, I'm not waiting indoors while these thugs destroy my property. The police are on their way, so why don't you leave?'

She eyeballed all of them in turn.

Her eyes shifted to the barn. She couldn't see any flames. Jacques must have put them out. She had to stamp out this fire first before she could check.

Sniggering, the tallest of the group walked towards her. He lowered his head and thrust it inches from Ava's face so his eyes were staring directly into hers.

It took all her courage not to move, but she didn't even flinch. Ava glared back at him, rooted to the spot like her vines.

'Go back to England,' he snarled. His words puffed into the cold air and he stank of beer and cigarettes.

Ava's eyes narrowed to slits as she stared at him closely. 'I'm not going anywhere.' Her hands quivering by her side. 'You can pass that message on to Ambrose.'

A couple of the gang exchanged glances.

Puffing her chest out like a cockerel, 'No one runs me off my land.' Ava thought she sounded like something out of a film; a Western!

'Ha!' he leaned in even closer, raising his hand.

'Don't even think about it,' she rallied, stressed every word. The blood was pumping through her ears. 'Like I said, the police are on their way.'

He raised his hand even higher, preparing to strike.

And then, right on cue, the blue and white flashing lights of the *gendarmes* lit up the skyline.

They shifted uneasily. One of the group grabbed the leader's arm. He shrugged him off aggressively and continued to stare Ava down.

'*Allez!*' his friend insisted, turning to run.

The whirling lights grew closer and the sirens began bleating as the officers closed in on the vineyard.

'*Allez, maintenant!*'

The car engines revved, the four-by-four skidding to a stop by the leader's feet. The thug gave Ava one last glacial stare and then dived into the jeep. The wheels spun, the smell of burning rubber charging the air, and then they tore off back up the road in convoy. Their exhausts billowed hot fumes into the frozen sky.

'They'll never make it!' Ava celebrated, cheering the police on with her fists.

'They will, they can turn left into the forest,' Bernard pointed.

Ava had forgotten about the back road through the truffle oaks and the olive groves.

'And the snow is slowing the *gendarmes.*'

'No, damn it!' she stared at the lights, willing the police to speed up. 'They're going to get away.'

There was nothing she could do; it was in fate's hands.

Suddenly her attention was diverted by huge plumes of black smoke swelling through the snow towards her. She sprinted across the courtyard to the barn, fanning her way into them, coughing, spluttering, shielding her stinging eyes with her forearms.

She could hear him before she could see him. She lifted her chin, looking through squinted eyes, and there he was – extinguishing the last of the flames with his jacket. Jacques lifted his leather coat above his head and thrashed it down. Again, and again, starving the fire of oxygen.

Ava was sure she was having some sort of déjà vu for Jacques was saving her wine barrels in just his shirt.

He stamped out the last of the embers with his boot, fanning the thick black smoke from his face. He turned to Ava, his face covered in soot. His hair was white with snowflakes. Despite everything, she couldn't help smile at the sight of him. The words burbled out: 'Thank God you were here.'

'*De rien*.' He kicked the broken glass. 'I think they must have set a bottle alight and thrown it at the barn. It probably had some accelerant in it. Perhaps petrol, alcohol, something that burns.'

She gasped. 'Like a homemade bomb!'

'*Oui*.'

She coughed.

'Come, let's get warm.'

She arched an eyebrow.

'Not like that.' He smirked.

Despite everything, the static electricity was still there, humming between them, much to Ava's annoyance.

Sophie was waiting by the door.

'Mum!' she screamed.

Without thinking, she rushed out into the snow in her socks and flung her arms around Ava, hugging her tightly as she buried her head in her mum's shoulder.

'You're okay. I was so scared.'

Ava kissed her repeatedly on the top of her head.

'It takes more than that to get rid of me.' She looked over her daughter to see Mark skulking in the background. 'A lot more than that.'

Sophie pulled back and grinned, her eyes brimming with pride. 'You totally rocked out there. Respect, Mum!'

# Chapter Thirty

Five officers dressed as though they were armed for a riot clambered out of the tiny car. They had bulletproof vests and rifles and handguns and pellets strapped to their cargo trousers. The little vehicle sighed as it sprang back into shape.

'Gosh,' Ava gasped. 'You'd never get this sort of turnout in England,' she whispered to Bernard.

They followed Ava into the kitchen where she immediately offered them all a cup of tea. *As that's what British people do in times of crisis – drink tea, keep calm and carry on.*

Although her hands betrayed her. They were still shaking as she switched on the kettle and lined up two rows of cups and saucers.

'Mum,' Sophie said.

Ava carried on flitting around the kitchen, trying to find the roll of biscuits she could have sworn she'd bought at the Super-U.

'MUM!' Sophie shouted. 'I don't think the police are worried about biscuits, you just need to tell them what happened.'

'Oh yes, right.' Ava shook her thoughts into place.

It had only just happened but why did everything seem so blurred? She narrowed her eyes straining to remember any distinguishing details. They were French, she knew that much.

'They were all wearing black.'

The police officer in charge pulled out a notebook and pen from one of his many trouser pockets. He had short cropped hair and was clean-shaven. His right cheek was pocketed with scars. He barely blinked as he listened to Ava describe how the night unfolded, while the others sipped their tea, quietly observing, every so often readjusting their armoury.

'So,' he inhaled deeply. 'You have no idea why they targeted you?'

The word gave her the chills.

'I have a very good idea why,' Ava said, her eyes chasing around the room, rallying support. 'I think they wanted to destroy my wine because I might win The Golden Grapes and knock them off their reigning title.'

'I see.' The gendarme tapped his pen on the notebook. 'And who is they?'

'Ambrose!' Bernard blurted.

'We think they were working for Victor Ambrose,' Ava explained.

The officers exchanged glances. The chief *gendarme* lifted his eyebrows and scribbled something down. His expression was unreadable. He cleared his throat. 'It's very serious to accuse someone of trespassing, of arson and damage to property. Monsieur Ambrose is a very respected member of the community. Do you know this?'

Ava rolled her eyes with frustration.

'That's what everyone says but he's not who he pretends to be.' Her voice was trembling with anger.

'Who is he then, Madame?'

'Someone who wants to ruin my chances of winning.'

'The . . .' he looked at his notes, 'the Golden Grapes?'

'Yes!'

'I see.'

Ava sighed deeply with frustration.

'Please, I know it sounds ridiculous.'

He rolled back onto his heels.

'But Victor wants to win. He sent his men to do his dirty work. I think.' She glanced at Mark who immediately looked away.

'But you didn't see them?' The gendarme interrupted.

No,' Ava sighed heavily.

'But I did.' Jacques spoke up.

Everyone turned to face him.

'And you are?'

'Jacques, Jacques Janvier.'

'I've seen you before, you work at the restaurant in the square.'

'Yes, I work there, but that has nothing to do with this . . .'

The *gendarme* studied him.

'So what did they look like?'

Jacques shrugged. 'One was tall, he had a goatee beard, a shaved head, maybe six foot two. Another was much shorter, he was wearing a grey hooded jumper, he . . . ' He kicked the table leg, annoyed at himself for not remembering more.

'And the cars, did you take a registration?'

Ava shook her head.

'Their number plates had been removed,' Jacques explained.

'Are you going to find these men?' Bernard lost his patience.

The officer closed his notebook abruptly and nodded. 'We will be investigating, but it will be difficult to charge anyone without identification.'

'I knew it,' Ava hissed. 'Ambrose thinks he's untouchable.'

'I'm sorry, Madame, but it is hard for us, you understand. If you can remember any more details then let us know. In the meantime, stay alert. Keep your doors locked. And if you have any more trouble, call us. Now you are on the system we will be able to get to you quicker.'

Ava gritted her teeth.

The *gendarme* drained the last of his cup and then indicated to his team it was time to leave.

She knew it wasn't his fault, the officer was right, there was little he could do. Ambrose had worked that one out.

'*Bon soir, Madame,*' he dipped his head and they left the château, their boots clunking, their weapons rattling as they marched out in single file.

Ava returned to the kitchen with a face of thunder.

'You!' she pointed at Mark. 'You'd better tell me everything, and right now.'

Ava knew Mark must have been involved in the attack; she'd only protected him from the police for Sophie's sake. But now the officers were gone, there was no stopping her. Hell hath no fury like a woman who'd had enough of her husband's lies.

'NOW!'

With everyone's eyes locked onto him, Mark immediately crumbled. He dropped his head into his forearms and began sobbing, huge, breathless sobs.

'The thought of anything happening to you or Sophie kills me,' he wailed. 'I had no idea . . . I just thought he was some rich guy who could help me out . . . I'm an idiot!'

'Yes, you are a bloody idiot, Mark, and you'd better tell me exactly what you've got yourself mixed up in.'

Ava stood over him at the table, her arms crossed, her jaw clenched. She was using all her self-restraint not to grab her soon-to-be ex-husband by the shoulders and shake the truth out of him.

He pushed the heels of his hands into his eye sockets and yowled dramatically.

'I'm an idiot!'

'We know that, Mark, now start talking.'

He took a shaky breath. 'Well, about three months ago I get this phone call, out of the blue, from some French geezer.'

'Ambrose?'

'Yeah, Victor Ambrose; he said he knew you and told me all about the vineyard you had inherited. Obviously I'd heard from Soph that you were there but I had no idea you were taking it seriously, I thought you'd just gone there to lie by the pool and drink wine and get over me.'

Ava bit her lip.

'Ambrose said you'd become a bit of a laughing stock in the town, the English woman trying to make wine, and thought you needed rescuing. I couldn't bear the thought of all those Frenchies talking behind your back, babe.'

She flashed him a look.

'Anyway,' he sniffed, 'Ambrose then offers me a deal.'

'You mean money?'

His cheeks flushed. 'Guess you could call it that.'

Bernard shot Mark a look of disdain from across the kitchen, while Sophie could barely bring herself to look at her dad. Her hero image of him, the man she'd always looked up to, being shattered by the second.

'He said he would pay me to persuade you to sell the vineyard and move back to Blighty.

She pursed her lips.

'And on top of that I would see the money from the sale. He said it would be millions,' his eyes widening with glee. 'It was a win-win situation as far as I was concerned. I get you back . . .'

Ava glared at him.

'And I pay off all my debts.'

'So you haven't really paid them off?'

He dropped his eyes to his hands, and shook his head.

'I knew it!' she muttered. 'I bet you're lying about Gabby too!'

'No, we have broken up, just she ended it with me . . .' he trailed off.

'How much?' she hissed.

'Huh?'

'How much did you sell me for?'

He swallowed. 'Twenty thousand.'

Ava's head rolled back with hysterical laughter. Everyone else exchanged concerned looks.

'Mum, are you all right?'

'I'm absolutely fine, darling. Your father isn't though, because he was robbed.' Turning to Mark, 'Ambrose is a multimillionaire. What he offered you was crumbs.'

Bernard muttered something in French to Jacques and they both sniggered. Mark sank even further into his chair.

'So then what?'

'I thought it was a wind-up at first but then I did a bit of research and saw this Ambrose fella looked like he might be kosher so I booked myself on a flight out to France.'

'With me,' Sophie butted in.

'I wanted to come out for a holiday with you anyway, sweetheart, honest.'

'Liar!'

He exhaled nosily. 'Give the old man a break here.'

'No,' Ava snapped. 'Go on . . .'

'I told him you weren't interested in selling, in getting back together with me.'

'You're telling me. Then what?'

'That all happened earlier today, when I met Ambrose in town, when I ran into what's-his-name-over-there too,' nodding to Jacques.

The men glowered at each other.

'And then?'

'And then Ambrose said to leave it with him; that he had something up his sleeve that would make you want to sell. I asked him about the money but he just walked off and . . .' Mark looked up, suddenly realising what he had said.

He squirmed in his seat. 'But by then I wasn't interested in the money any more.'

Bernard snorted.

Mark held his hands up. 'I didn't know he would do this. I swear. I would never have put you in jeopardy. You have to believe me, babe. Sophie?'

Ava whipped him with her eyes. 'Stop calling me babe! I always hated that name.'

'But I thought you liked it,' his voice had turned thin.

'I can't even look at you right now, Dad,' Sophie sniffed.

'Honey, I'm so sorry. I was just trying to bring us together as a family.'

'Bollocks!' Ava shouted.

'Deep breath,' Jacques whispered.

Ava composed herself. 'Just because I'm not a heartless human being I'll let you stay the night, but as soon as it's morning, you are leaving, I don't care where you go. Where you end up. I'm done with you.' She dusted her hands together. 'You're not my problem any more.'

Mark's bottom lip wobbled.

'What are you going to do?'

'Without you?' she chortled.

'About this Ambrose fella?'

Ava narrowed her eyes, a look of determination crossing her face. 'I'm going to get even.'

As the words were echoing around the room, there was a loud thud from the hallway, followed by a '*Merde!*'

With all the grace of a newborn foal, Jean-Marc skittered into the kitchen, brushing the snowflakes from his shoulders. 'It's a death trap out there! I almost slipped and died!' He looked at everyone's white and drawn expressions. 'What did I miss?'

# Chapter Thirty-one

**Provence, Summer 1985**

Ava giggled, the sweet innocent laugh of a child.

'Again, Mummy,' she said, despite having begged her to stop tickling her a moment earlier.

'Come here, you!' Her mum lunged with open arms, trying to grab hold. Ava squealed, rocketing down the cobbled path through the herb garden.

'I'm coming to get you!' Mum gave her a head start.

'Adele!' her grandfather shouted through the laughter.

Ava skidded to a stop and looked up. Her grandpapa's usual cheerful face was looking anguished, as if he was struggling with some deep internal pain. He pushed out a smile for Ava. 'Run along, child, I need to speak with your mother.'

They were leaving tomorrow for England. Ava only had one precious day alone with her mum. She wanted her mama to keep tickling her, for the fun to continue, for she knew it would all disappear as soon as they were back home with her dad.

Ava threw a stroppy face. Grandpapa sighed wearily from the terrace. 'We won't be long, I promise.' His voice hardened as he directed his gaze towards his daughter. 'Adele, please.'

It was her mum's turn to be the sulky child. She reluctantly made her way back towards the terrace. Ava crouched beside the flower bed, pretending to busy herself plucking a bouquet of lavender and herbs while she pricked up her ears.

Ava's mum crossed her arms.

Her grandpapa breathed in heavily as he mustered up the strength to reason with her, one final time.

'I want you to leave him,' he ordered.

Her mum scrunched her hands into fists. 'Please Papa, stop.'

'I need you to listen to me, you need to leave him; he is destroying you. I will not stand and watch my only daughter be devoured by this monster of a husband.' He crouched and scooped a handful of soil from by his feet. 'He will grind you down until nothing is left of you,' he unfolded his fingers, letting the grains drain between them. 'Nothing but dust.'

Her lip quivered. 'But I'm frightened.'

'Then leave him!'

'I can't leave. Where will I go?' She looked around her and shrugged. 'Here?'

'*Oui!*'

'He'll come after me and drag me home.' Her voice bled into the claustrophobic heat. 'I'm so tired of putting up a fight, it's just easier to go along with what he wants. That way I have peace. If I don't upset him, if I don't say things to antagonise him, then it will be okay.' She exhaled deeply. 'He's not all bad. Sometimes he's wonderful, he's caring, he's loving, he will do anything for me. That is the man I fell in love with and I just hope he will come back to me.'

'For goodness' sake! He's not nice, he controls you by this nasty and then nice act. It's one *grand* performance to get what he wants.' He threw his hands up. 'I can't sit and watch this happen to you, I just can't,' he shook his head.

She turned her back to him. 'No one asked you to.' Her eyes hardening. 'I will deal with this alone.'

'You're leaving me no choice!' her grandpapa threatened.

Ava jumped with fright as a warm hand enveloped hers and gave it a gentle tug. It was Madame Chevalier, dragging her away.

'Come, Ava, we need to get you out of the sun.'

'But what about Mama?' She looked back over her shoulder.

'She is busy with your grandpapa. You can help me make the bread for dinner tonight.'

Little did Ava know then it would be their last supper together.

**Provence, 2018, 4 a.m.**

'That's it!'

Ava was convinced she'd cracked it. Finally it all made sense.

The fear Ambrose's men had brought to the vineyard had driven out another memory. The one that had been the most deeply buried, knotted in the roots of the vines, but now, finally unearthed, explained the dark mystery that hung over her family.

Grandpapa had been trying to break up her mum and dad's marriage. Her mum was so fearful of how her dad would react to him interfering, she had decided when they left the next day, they would never come back. All contact severed.

Ava remembered her grandfather's words – *she needs to know*. Ava smiled as she realised how Grandpapa must have been trying to protect her. He *needed her to know* he wasn't abandoning her, that it was her mum's decision to tear her away, to split the family up. That he had done everything he could to protect her mother.

She felt a sudden surge of relief at finally being able to lay the past to rest, which was quickly followed by a crash of exhaustion. The enormity of what she'd remembered – lost in the adrenaline she'd used up to save the vineyard.

All night, she'd been up and down out of bed like a jack-in-a-box worrying about whether Ambrose's men had come back to finish what they started.

With every creak, every howl of the wind, every twitch of nature, she'd thrown off the duvet and leapt to the window, scanning the vineyards for any sign of the balaclava thugs.

And if it wasn't the noises, her thoughts about Mark and Victor's treachery were keeping her up. Nothing surprised her with Mark any more. He was an idiot, a money-grabbing spineless prick, but putting that aside, she knew he would never intentionally try and hurt her or Sophie.

But Victor – he was something else. The wine mogul was a total snake, no, worse than that; snakes weren't slimy enough. Ambrose was a cockroach, no, not evil enough. A scorpion! Yep, that was it! They were native to Provence, scuttled and had a sting in their tail. Ava scrunched up her face to stop her unfiltered thoughts turning even more evil. Severe sleep deprivation was sending her over the edge.

There was one person she couldn't get out of her head, though.

Jacques. What was he? She just didn't know any more. She thought he was a liar but he'd protected her from the man he was supposed to have been scheming with. He'd saved the vineyard – again. If she looked at it that way he wasn't far off hero status. She could feel his presence in her house, burning a hole in her thoughts. He was directly below her, keeping watch from her grandfather's chair beside the living-room window. He'd insisted he stay in case they had more trouble. It was a nice gesture. Lovely, really. Maybe he was lovely after all.

*Arrrgh!* She clamped her eyes closed again. What a night! She pressed her head back into her pillow.

*Maybe she should check to see he wasn't too cold? It was sub-zero temperatures outside after all and the château wasn't much warmer. She was desperate for a glass of water, gasping in fact, yup that was really why she was venturing downstairs at 4.23 a.m.*

Without a moment's further thought, Ava slipped into her dressing gown and tiptoed her way out of her bedroom, with a quick check in the mirror en route, just to be sure she didn't have bed head, or dribble dried to her face. Nothing to do with Jacques, nope, because she couldn't care less what he thought of her any more.

A butterfly flapped its wings through her stomach as she neared the living room. The lights were out but the moonlight bouncing off the snow sent a glow of silver into the house. She could see the back of the worn leather armchair, a tanned brown hand flopped over the armrest, and she could hear a soft whistling noise as Jacques breathed heavy in and out breaths.

She collected the throw from the sofa and crept up behind him, stepping lightly across the creaky floorboards.

So much for a guard dog – he was fast asleep. His head crooked to the side, his mouth slightly open, a faint snoring noise whistling in and out. Ava's face brightened; she couldn't help but take delight in the stolen moment, where she was able to watch his handsome face while he slept – the way she sometimes used to do when she would wake in the night and gaze at him next to her in bed.

She unfolded the blanket and placed it over him. Her face almost brushed his as she tucked the fabric around his shoulders. He stirred. She froze. He opened one eye and blinked.

'Ava?' he croaked.

She smiled awkwardly. 'Sorry I woke you, I was just . . .'

His eyes slid to her hand on his shoulder.

'I was just trying to keep you warm.'

'You didn't have to do that,' he shifted, and straightened. His face was creased from where he'd been pressed into the head rest.

'I know but it's cold out there, down here . . . in the living room.'

'*Merci*.' He looked at her.

Their conversation was as stilted and as awkward as when they first met. And just as full of sexual tension.

Ava felt compelled to stamp it out immediately. She wasn't going to fall for his charm again. Not for a second time, hero or not.

'So anyway, thank you again for staying over.' She rose to standing.

'Wait!' He grabbed her hand impulsively.

For a long moment they both stared at what he'd done. Until she tugged it free, her lips pressed together, fighting the urge to let down her guard.

'Will you please listen to me? I've been trying to explain to you what happened for months but you've blocked my calls, not read my messages.' He softened his voice. 'If you still hate me after hearing what I need to say then I will never bother you again, but just give me a chance.'

Ava glanced at the cuckoo clock. It wasn't as if she'd be able to go upstairs and fall asleep anyway. 'Okay,' she sighed heavily. 'I'll get a fire started.'

They were almost touching.

Ava's legs were curled to the side like a cat snoozing on a cushion. Jacques had let the sofa's soft leather swallow his tired body into its folds. They sat in silence for what seemed an eternity; their exhausted eyes mesmerised by the fire, watching the flames lick the wood, listening to the pop and crackle as it devoured the logs. She knew they were both silent because neither wanted to spoil the moment by talking about the past. Ava resisting the urge not to sneak glances at Jacques whenever he moved to stoke the fire.

As the sun began to rise, shooting a crimson light into the room, Jacques took that as his cue to speak, while the rest of the house still slept.

'*Je suis désolé*,' he began.

'You're sorry.'

He nodded.

'Because you were right, I was working for Victor.'

Ava gripped onto her anger; she'd promised she would let him speak.

'I had been working for him for free for six months before I met you.' He clenched his jaw. 'He promised me a future at the vineyard, which, as you know, was everything I had dreamed of, it was why I came back to Provence. But every time I finished a task, he would have another one for me, and another. I became a circus animal jumping through hoops, doing his shitty jobs for him. He had a way of making me feel like I needed to prove myself; that I was never good enough.' He rubbed his stubbly chin angrily. 'I was near breaking point by the time he mentioned you to me.' He looked at Ava intently, checking he hadn't said too much.

'Go on.'

He sighed again. 'He had heard that we had become friends. He asked if I would get to know you better, find out what you were doing on the vineyard.'

'Spy on me?'

His face flushed red.

'He promised if I did what he asked of me he would train me to become a sommelier. And he would pay me this time. He was offering me everything I had dreamed of; how could I refuse?' His voice rose with every word.

Ava kept her gaze fixed, trying to remain impartial. She had promised.

'So, I did what he asked. But pretty soon what you were offering was so much more.'

Both her eyebrows shot up.

'*Non, non*, not like that. The opportunities to make wine. To really learn how. I didn't need Victor any more. So I stopped reporting to him. The message you read was not complete. It went on to say how angry he was at me not replying to him. Demanding that I answer him or the deal was off. But the deal had been off a long time.'

Ava ran her eyes over him, studying him for signs of lying. A shifty look, a nervous gesture, a nuance in his tone of voice. It was impossible to tell but something inside was persuading her to trust what she felt instead of what she saw. Which, aside from that Jacques looked bloody hot with his rugged stubble look, was that he was telling the truth, about Victor at least. A lump had risen in her throat while she thought about the next question. She wanted to know but was afraid of the answer. Any woman in her shoes would be.

'So, all that stuff about, you know . . .'

He frowned.

'You know, about us and . . .'

Jacques looked at her through squinted eyes trying to decipher what she meant.

'Love me!' she blurted. 'Did you actually love me or was that for show?'

He promptly took her hand in his. 'Ava Chiltern. *Je t'aime!*'

Ava giggled nervously. He didn't stop.

'*Je t'adore!*'

'Ummmm,' she found herself blushing.

'*Je suis fou de toi*,' he kissed her hand. 'I am crazy about you.'

'You are?'

'*Oui, oui!*' He kissed her hand repeatedly. '*Sans toi, je ne suis rien.*'

Ava knew what that meant. Without you, I'm nothing. In English it would have sounded cheesy but in French, with his rolling 'r's and his sexy accent, it was just plain romantic.

She laughed, 'I think I get the idea.'

'But do you understand?' He drew into her face. She felt his breath on her again. 'But do you really understand what I'm saying?' His mouth was closing in on hers like a heat-seeking missile.

'Jacques, no,' she half-heartedly pushed his chest.

But he had that look in his eye, that wild flicker she'd seen many a time before, when he passed the point of no return.

'I haven't been with another woman since you,' he reached for her neck with his lips.

'Really? Or are you telling me that because you think that's what I want to hear?'

'How could I be with anyone else when my head was filled with thoughts of you.'

Ava glowed inside. 'Really?'

'Yes, trust me.'

He wrenched her closer with his strong arms. The fire crackled as a strip of bark burst into flames.

'You have no idea how much I've been thinking about this . . .'

The embers of adrenaline left over from fighting off Ambrose's men sparked again. Her pulse spiked. He leaned in closer and closer, the memories of what it felt like to kiss him flooding back.

But this time she pushed him away, with determination. 'I'm sorry, I can't, I need time.'

Jacques immediately released his grip, easing back into the sofa, fighting off his look of disappointment.

There was a moment's awkward silence.

'It's not easy to trust after everything I've been through. I need a bit of time to find that again with you.' Her voice changed to something much more matter-of-fact as she pulled herself out of the inferno.

He nodded understandingly, although she could tell from his eyes that he was feeling what she was.

'It wouldn't be right, with . . . Mark . . . being in the house.'

'*Je comprend.*' He was still adjusting to one hundred miles per hour to nought in nano-seconds.

'Do you know what I could do with now?'

He shook his head.

'A friend.'

He flinched.

She couldn't help but giggle at the look on his face.

'But more than anything, I need a friend to help me save this vineyard. I need your help. I can't let Ambrose win, not after everything he's done. I don't want to have to sell and move back to England.'

He let out a small gasping, '*Mon Dieu!*'

'Please come back and work for me here. You don't need me to promise you a job as a winemaker, the job is already yours.'

He stared at her.

She was about to say 'I need you' again and then Camille's words suddenly fired through her head, reminding her 'You don't need anyone, you can do this all by yourself.'

Ava straightened. Taking the power back into her own hands, she said: 'I want you here as part of the team.'

He nodded, fixing her gaze with his intense 'I want to take you to bed look', and then released his grip on her eyes, a cheeky smile returning to his face. He took a bow, and putting on his best haughty British accent, he said: 'Your wish is my command, my lady.'

# Chapter Thirty-two

January 2019

'He's your boyfriend, isn't he?'

'Don't be daft.' Ava turned crimson.

'It's okay, Mum, you don't have to hide it from me.'

'I'm not hiding anything,' she shrugged.

Sophie twirled the end of her ponytail. 'Well if he's not your boyfriend, something's going on between you two because you're always acting really *weird* around each other.'

Ava couldn't deny sparks had been flying around the vineyard for the past few weeks.

'I get it.'

'What do you get, honey?' She wished her daughter would just drop it. She found it hard to speak to Sophie about another man when her daughter had been so upset by her parents' split.

'I get why you want to be out here. Away from Dad.'

Ava was taken aback. She stared at her daughter.

'I really get it. At first I thought it was some kind of mid-life crisis, but now . . . now that I've seen how much happier you are . . .' her voice wobbled. She turned her head away, pinching back her tears.

'Oh honey, it's okay.'

'I'm not going to cry,' she fanned her face. 'Not in public,' she glanced up at the busy departures terminal. 'I'm fine.'

She turned back to face her mum with a determined look. Shifting gears, Sophie pouted: 'Anyway, all I'm saying is, I'd consider coming back here.'

'You would?'

'Hmm, yeah, maybe.' She smiled. 'Anyhoo, let's get this over with,' and gave her mum a hug goodbye.

Ava handed her a gift. 'Just something for the journey.'

Sophie peered inside, the paper bag rustling as she rummaged through the half a dozen pastries. 'Jesus!'

'Blame Madame Chevalier, she made them this morning. She thinks everyone needs fattening up.'

'Tell her thanks, they look delish. Okay, I really have to go,' Sophie tugged at her pink wheelie case.

Ava felt hot tears spring to her eyes as she watched her daughter strut her way towards the departures gate. They'd never been so close; she was really going to miss her.

Sophie suddenly swung around, her ponytail swooshing. 'Oh and Mum!' she yelled across the noisy concourse.

'Yes, darling.'

'You better beat that bastard!'

Instead of telling her off for cursing Ava raised her fist, like some scene from a Rocky film, and gave it a little shake.

'Mum!' And with that, she was gone.

With the Eye of The Tiger theme song bopping around in her head, Ava charged into the 'lab' – which had been moved to the pantry as it was simply too cold in the barn – only to find Jean-Marc slumped over the table, surrounded by a zillion test tubes, wailing.

'Oh no, what's happened?'

Madame Chevalier poked her nose around the door. 'What is the matter with him?'

'I don't know,' Ava whispered back.

'It's finished,' he whimpered.

'The wine, you've finished making it?'

'*Non! We* are finished.'

Ava and Madame Chevalier exchanged panicked glances.

'It's a catastrophe, I can't find the missing flavour.'

'Of course you can,' Madame Chevalier snapped.

'*Non, impossible.* The wine, it will not speak to me, it will not tell me its secrets. I am . . .' he exhaled '. . . beaten.' He stretched out his arm, knocking test tubes over. He let out a pained whine, his head still firmly planted on the table.

Madame Chevalier looked at Ava impatiently. 'I'll clean this up.'

'I've got to do something.' Ava jittered from one foot to the other. 'We can't lose,' her breath quickening with anxiety. 'I've got to go . . .'

'Where are you going?' Madame Chevalier's voice faded as Ava sprinted in the direction of the only place that might hold the answer.

She burst into her grandpapa's bedroom, frantically beginning her search, for she didn't know quite what. Tasting notes? Drawings? A notebook detailing the alchemy of winemaking? Something, anything, there had to be at least an equation of some sort written down.

She opened the drawers in turn, fingering through the contents. A packet of tissues, cigars, a magnifying glass. She pulled out the next drawer down. Pills of every description. Loose coins, a box of cufflinks, some neck ties.

The coins clattered against the wood as she pushed the drawer in and yanked out the next. A fancy shoe-polish kit from Paris. A comb clogged with grime. Some handkerchiefs embroidered with her grandpapa's initials.

The final drawer was overspilling with photograph albums. She perched on the side of the bed and began flicking through one dating back to 1973, only to quickly slam it shut. She couldn't afford the time to walk down memory lane just now.

She ploughed through the secret door into the dressing room and began checking the cupboard. Standing on her tiptoes to reach the top cubbyholes, she patted the insides down, feeling her way over socks and vests and huge underpants.

'Where is it, Grandpapa?' she asked the heavens.

She moved to the clothes rail and dropped to her knees where dozens of shoeboxes were precariously stacked on top of each other. Just one small nudge in the wrong direction . . .

'Bollocks!' she yelped as they spilled open across the floor. She had no idea her grandpapa owned so many pairs of the same shoe. As a child she thought he lived in his pair of blue loafers, but really, he had 'one, two . . . eight pairs! Grandpapa!' she exclaimed.

She shoved them to one side with a sweep of her arms, and carried on burrowing; rummaging for what else she could find underneath the musty clothes rail.

She wriggled herself backwards and flopped onto her heels, on the verge of giving up.

She closed her eyes and tried to imagine herself stepping back in time to thirty years ago.

She was in the dressing room, just as she was now. There was a lot of noise coming from outside the window.

She concentrated really hard, straining to remember, squeezing the juice of her memories out.

Little Ava was wearing her mustard-coloured dress and her green boots – she remembered how pleased she was with herself for slipping past Madame Chevalier's eagle eyes in her muddy boots.

But why was she in Grandpapa's dressing room? Ava breathed deeply, trying to excavate another memory.

She was searching for chocolate! That was it! Ava smiled as she remembered how she regularly hunted for Grandpapa's secret stash of praline whips.

She stilled her mind again, drifting back in time, hearing the scratchy music from the gramophone drift through the open window. She stepped gingerly towards the noise, her heart drumming as she was terrified of being spotted. She pulled back the curtain so only the tip of her nose was showing and peered down onto the sun-drenched terrace below.

There was her mum, twirling in circles, a long floating dress sweeping behind her as Bernard spun her around.

They were dancing.

Ava's eyes widened as she watched them laugh and chatter away in French. Every so often her mum would throw her head back in fits of giggles because she'd stepped on Bernard's foot.

She was almost unrecognisable – happy and carefree – completely transformed.

She heard her grandpapa cough. She angled her eyes down even further to find him slouching in his favourite deckchair. His book was resting on his chest, a glass of rosé next to him, waiting to be drunk.

Where was her father? Ava remembered. He wasn't there. That was the summer her mother had come to collect her on her own. The final summer.

Ava rose to her feet, into the present. Why had her memories sent her back in time to that very moment? What was her grandpapa trying to tell her? It was a sign, it had to be. A marker towards where his tasting notes were kept?

She had been in his dressing room, hunting for the chocolate.

Ava stepped towards the window.

Which he used to keep in the biscuit tin. The giant blue and white oval thing which he used to hide underneath . . .

Ava pulled back the curtain beneath the sink.

'*Et voilà!*' she exclaimed as her eyes lit on the prize. She pulled out the dented, scratched tin from its resting place, now utterly convinced her grandpapa had spoken to her from the grave.

She placed it down on the floorboards. Her palms were suddenly clammy with nerves at the prospect of unveiling the vineyard's best-kept secret.

The metal lid made wobbling vibrations as she yanked it off.

Ava let out an involuntary squeal as she clapped eyes on what was inside. She reached her hand into the tin, heart thudding.

# Chapter Thirty-three

'Where's Bernard?' Ava burst into the kitchen.

Madame Chevalier looked up from behind a cloud of flour.

She shrugged.

'Tell him I need to speak to him urgently if you see him,' she rushed back out as quickly as she had stormed in.

Bernard wasn't in the vineyard, or in his toolshed, or fixing the tractor. The only place left was his home, in the forest.

Ava tore along the track, the sharp rocks stabbing into the soles of her shoes, throwing her off kilter. She held out her arms to steady herself and kept on running.

She rarely entered the truffle forest and she knew why as soon as the tall sturdy trees swallowed her with their branches. It was creepy. Within moments of leaving the main path the trees surrounded her, muffling any sounds and making her feel like she was walking in the dead of night.

It was a goblin's play pen with its gnarly branches reaching out like tentacles. A thick carpet of emerald moss covered the forest floor, creeping over any fallen trees, devouring them back into the ecosystem. Things squawked and rustled in the undergrowth and Ava had an uneasy feeling she was being watched by many sets of beady eyes.

She kept on running. As she turned into the long bend, the forest parting into a clearing. A bright yellow lake of mimosa flowers lay ahead. Behind that, sandwiched between two sprawling oak trees, was a Hansel-and-Gretel style house, with blue shutters and in serious need of a lick of paint.

Bernard had really immersed himself in nature, Ava thought as she waded through the sea of yellow towards his porch. She had slowed to a near crawl, completely out of puff. Her need to speak to the gardener about what she had discovered was driving her on. Only he could now help her with the answer.

She landed on his doorstep, a hot mess. Her breath had reduced to rasping gasps, beads of sweat were bubbling up from her brow. Not a good look. She rapped the brass door knocker twice. Stood back, and wiped away the salty sweat that was stinging her eyes.

Nothing.

She cupped her mouth with her hands, tilted her head to the sky and hollered: 'Bernard!'

Still no reply. She peered through the window, which was coated in spider's webs clutching the limbs and wings of dead insects. Through the misty glass she could just about make out the outlines of a kitchen table and a cabinet and two candlesticks. Just as she was about to launch herself from the porch to have a nosey around the back, the door opened.

Bernard appeared, slipping his trouser braces over the shoulders of his checked shirt. He yawned and rubbed his eyes. He blinked heavily, trying to register the unlikely sight of Ava on his doorstep.

'Madame! What are you doing here?'

He rubbed his eyes some more, still battling sleep. She must have woken him from his nap.

'Can I come in?' Her chest was still heaving from lack of oxygen.

He hesitated. Bernard was clearly wary of letting anyone inside his home.

'I need to speak with you urgently,' she insisted, practically pushing herself inside.

He nodded, opening the door wide so she could pass.

The house smelt of a log fire and of the hearty beef stew that was bubbling away on the stove. He showed her into the living room, which was stark except for two armchairs, a rug and a bookcase, a glass-encased map of Provence on the wall and the smoke and embers of a dying fire.

'Is everything okay?' He watched her limp into the centre of the room.

'There's something I need to ask you.' Bernard watched Ava's gaze slide to the photograph on the shelf by the fireplace. He waited quietly for her reaction.

Ava picked it up and stared closely at the photo of her mother. She looked like a film star with her oversized sunglasses and a show-stopping smile. She looked happy. In love, as she smiled for whoever was holding the camera. Ava stared at Bernard, who dropped his eyes to the floor.

'Why do you have a picture of my mother in your house?'

A heavy silence filled the big empty space. He folded his arms without answering. The atmosphere had become vaguely hostile.

Ava pulled out her hand from behind her back, revealing a bundle of letters.

'I found these in my grandfather's room.'

Bernard shifted uneasily.

'Do you know what they are?'

He narrowed his eyes to slits as he focused on her hand. He shook his head.

'I was looking for his tasting notes but instead I found these.' She pulled out the first letter from the envelope, shaking it free into the tense air. 'It's a letter to my grand-papa from my mother,' her voice wobbling. She looked up to see his reaction, but still he didn't stir. She raised her eyebrows as she prepared to read the first line. The inside of Ava's mouth had suddenly become so dry she could barely move her tongue at first. Finally she found the courage to read out loud:

*'Dear Papa*
*If you continue to threaten me with telling Ava the*
*truth of who her real father is, then I have no choice but*
*to stop all communication with you.'*

Ava cleared her throat, her anger dissipating as the tears brimmed in her eyes. She choked them back.

*'For if the true identity was ever revealed I would*
*spend the rest of my life living in perpetual fear of the*
*repercussions, which we both know would be severe. I've*
*suffered enough pain to last a lifetime and I don't have*
*the strength or the courage to fight it any more. I know*
*you don't understand why I don't just leave him, Papa,*
*but I'm afraid. I'm terrified of what my husband might do*
*and what a life without him would be like. You've never*
*known what it feels like to wake up and not be sure*
*whether someone will love you or beat you and I hope you*
*can try and understand what that does to a person's soul.'*

Tears trickled from Ava's eyes, splashing onto the hand-written paper. She could sense Bernard's heart turning heavy but she couldn't bring herself to look up, not until she had finished.

*'I hope you will tell Bernard from me,'* she took a deep breath in, *'how much I loved him.'*

With tears now streaming down her face, her voice broke on the final words. *'And when things are bad, all I need to do is look at my beautiful daughter and I will be reminded of him. For he will always be her father, and the love of my life.'*

Ava's face crumbled as she sobbed silent tears, her mother's heartfelt words shaking between her trembling fingers. She was so lost in a world of grief and confusion, she barely felt the letter being taken from her hands. Bernard stood next to her, his breath laboured with emotion.

'You didn't know?' Ava whispered, but the answer was clear.

He stood silently next to her, still absorbing the revelation; both of them feeling the heartbreak of lost time. All those years they had spent alone – Ava thinking she had a father who didn't care for her. Bernard living in isolation because he had lost the woman he loved, not knowing he had a daughter all along.

Slowly, Ava lifted her gaze from Bernard's hands, clutching the letter, to his face. And still he said nothing, but he didn't need to, his eyes spoke for him. Tears were running down his rugged sun-beaten face.

A low murmur rumbled inside his throat as he finally spoke: 'She never told me.'

He reached a shaky hand to the wall to steady himself as his legs began to fall away beneath him.

'Bernard?' Ava rushed to his side.

She helped ease him into a chair. He sat back heavily, his arms dropping to his sides and his head rolling onto his chest. Ava collapsed onto her knees, placing her tiny palm over his giant worn-out hand.

His face was perfectly still except for the tears that continued to fall. Ava felt compelled to show him, her father, her love. She reached her arms around him and hugged him tightly, squeezing his old creaky body.

And there they remained, holding each other, weeping tears of regret, and also happiness, that finally they were a family.

The sky had turned mauve, the creatures in the forest had woken by the time they were both ready to speak of the past. They had moved to be close to the fire. Ava was nursing a cup of hot milky cocoa as Bernard stoked the flames. Quietly content in each other's company, as if it had always meant to be so.

Every now and then, they would talk, slotting the memories back into place, together.

Bernard seemed haunted by what had happened to her mother, burdened with guilt.

'I tried to rescue her,' he shook his head. 'But she wouldn't let me. At the time I was angry. I thought it was because she was embarrassed of me.'

'Embarrassed?'

Bernard cast her a look. '*Mais oui*, she was the *châtelaine*, I was just the gardener. If our affair had become known, well . . .' He trailed off, shaking his head again. 'I should have done more.'

Ava reached out and squeezed his hand.

'And then one day, she told me it was over, and she wouldn't be coming back. That she was going to try and make a success of her marriage.' His square jaw clenching as he relived the anger. 'I thought your grandfather was angry at her for this, but he had also learnt you were my daughter. I wish he had told me.'

'He was protecting her,' Ava said, realising how wrong they had both been.

Bernard nodded. 'So instead of finding happiness she ran away and hid from everyone she loved.' He slid forward in his chair, stabbing the fire with the poker.

'But why didn't she come and find you after my dad left her?'

Bernard shrugged. 'By then I imagine she had decided the past was the past.' After a long, considered silence he added: 'I understand what it is like to feel safer alone.'

His honest words gave her the courage to admit her own truth. 'My mum was afraid of being happy,' Ava said, suddenly realising the parallels of her mother's life with her own. As she too had stayed in an unhappy marriage out of fear. She too hadn't chased her dreams because it was easier, less frightening to stick with what she knew. That way she wouldn't get hurt if her dreams didn't come to anything. 'I know what that feels like . . . to be afraid of taking a leap of faith,' she confessed.

Saying the words out loud, finally, felt good – like she was performing an exorcism of the ghosts that had been haunting her. Ava could see how far she had come. How she had broken free of the curse that seemed to hang over her family. She turned to Bernard. With kind eyes she looked at him. 'You're not alone any more.'

# Chapter Thirty-four

**March 2019**

As it turned out, Ava was more surprised than anyone else to learn the truth about Bernard. Madame Chevalier boasted she had sensed it all along. Jean-Marc confessed he had spotted the similarities: 'the nose, it is unmistakable.' Jacques hadn't put two and two together, but now he knew, he observed how some mannerisms were identical.

'Like what?' she argued with him.

'Such as your stubbornness.'

'I'm not stubborn,' she crossed her arms.

'*Non?*'

'No.'

Secretly, she took delight in the insult. For two reasons. Firstly, it was wonderful to finally know where her traits came from. Secondly, she was enjoying the renewed closeness with Jacques.

Life at Château Saint-Clair had never felt better. The vineyard had taken on a new identity, it was now a 'family affair'. It was everything that had been missing from Ava's life in England. Even Sophie had perked up since hearing about Bernard, because she now had a grandfather, who she hoped would indulge her shopping whims. She had yet to learn the measure of Bernard; that said, Ava suspected he was secretly glowing inside with the knowledge that he had a granddaughter to spoil.

The only downside to their new-found happiness was that it had raised the stakes even higher. Without the prize money, her father would be homeless. The battle had become much more than beating Victor Ambrose and saving her vineyard.

That was why Ava was beside herself with worry as the deadline for entering the Golden Grapes was just three weeks away.

Jean-Marc had not been able to recreate the blend. In his words, he'd produced something 'disastrously mediocre'. He was inconsolable about letting Ava down. No one had seen or heard from him for two days since he had locked himself away in his bedroom.

As far as Ava was concerned, there was only one answer to the catastrophe.

Jacques found her sitting on the terrace on the white ornate chair, slumped, with a glass of wine in her hand.

'Is that your grandfather's last bottle of wine?' Jacques stared in horror at the rosé.

'Uh huh,' Ava knocked back another huge gulp. 'I thought I might as well enjoy it seeing that it's not going to speak to us.' She was well on the way to being drunk.

'You're giving up?'

She shrugged.

'The flavours are missing. We're going to lose. Bernard will be homeless. I'll have to go back to England.' She took another glug. 'Ambrose will win.'

She held up the glass to the light, tilting it to the left and right, the holy grail of wine sloshing this way and that.

'Be careful!' Jacques cried, one nervous heartbeat from making a football dive to the ground to catch any falling drops.

Ava continued to throw caution to the wind, carelessly examining its contents.

It would have been a bitterly cold March day if it wasn't for the bright Mediterranean sun warming the terrace. The vineyard was showing the first signs of spring. It had been a whole year since she had arrived in France, since she began work on the vineyard, but Ava wasn't in the mood for reminiscing.

Smacking her lips together, she slurred, 'You know what? This isn't half bad. In fact, I can honestly say, this is the best rosé I've tasted in my whole entire life.'

Jacques narrowed his eyes; suddenly overcome with anger at Ava for jeopardising their last chance, he made a swipe at her glass.

'Ah ha ha,' she stumbled to her feet, sending the heavy metal chair crashing onto the terrace paving. She hugged the wine glass in one hand, the bottle in the other.

Jacques sighed impatiently. He put his hands onto his hips, stretching the fabric of his V-neck jumper across his chest.

'I don't like it when you get like this,' he muttered. 'You're impossible.'

'I like it when you are like this. You're sexy when you're angry.'

He looked at her from under his knitted brow and held out both his hands. 'Give it to me,' he motioned.

'No,' she replied, stubbornly, hugging them even more tightly into her chest.

'I know you're upset. You don't need to put a brave face on for me.'

'I'm not upset,' her bottom lip wobbling.

Jacques took a gingerly placed step towards her.

'Just give me the wine.'

'No.'

'This is a very emotional time for you, but . . .'

'Don't patronise me!'

'But please, don't destroy your chances now. It's not just about you, everyone here has dedicated themselves to helping you win.'

She childishly blew a raspberry.

'You're so serious!'

He took another small step till his hands were almost within reaching distance.

'Don't come any closer or I'll drink it all!' she threatened. 'I swear.'

Cautiously he edged a little further and then one step more.

'Stop!' she yelled, just as he lunged.

The pair crashed to the ground, Jacques landing on top. Their eyes met and then Jacques snapped his shut, cringing as the enormity of what he had done sank in. He opened one eye, just in time to catch the cheeky smile spreading across Ava's face as she raised the bottle into the sky with her right hand. By some miracle, she had managed to save it from spilling. She let out a nervous giggle.

Overcome with relief, without thinking, he impulsively kissed her.

Ava was as surprised as he was, but it didn't take long for her minxy, drunken smile to return.

'Kiss me again,' she whispered.

So he did. This time with lust and intensity, showing her how much he had missed touching her lips. His tongue slowly sweeping through her mouth and then pulling away to gently suck on her lower lip. God she'd missed him.

'More,' she demanded, closing her eyes in drunken ecstasy.

So he teased her. Pulling his mouth away from hers, drawing it down, towards her neck. Tantalising her senses with small, soft kisses along her skin.

'You smell so good,' he said, diving back into her mouth, more fervently. She arched her back, not feeling the hard stones beneath her any more, just Jacques' hard . . .

He pulled away, his brow furrowed.

'Where do you think you're going?' She dreamily opened her eyes.

With all the finesse of a dog sniffing out its mate, Jacques plunged his nose back to her neck and took a deep inhale.

She giggled. 'I preferred what you were doing before.'

He pushed himself onto his heels. She grabbed his belt to try and yank him back on top of her.

His eyes were wide, excited. He shook his head, as if he didn't trust his thoughts, and then a smile danced on his lips, pushing a dimple into his cheek.

'That's it!' he exclaimed.

'Er, no it's not. This is it,' she grumped, trying to hook him with her legs.

'Your perfume!'

'What? Jacques, you're not making any sense.'

'*Pêche!*'

'Huh?'

'Peach! The missing ingredient is peach!'

He leapt onto his feet. Ava clumsily pushed herself up from the ground.

'I smelt your perfume. I tasted the wine in your mouth. It's peach.' He swept his hair from his eyes, his incredible body rigid with the excitement of his breakthrough. 'How could I have not made the connection before?'

Ava wobbled her way to standing, dusting the sand from her bum.

'The connection between my perfume and the missing ingredient?' she asked, barely making a connection with the ground. Her head spinning.

'*Non!*' he grabbed her hand. '*Allez*, we don't have any time to waste.'

# Chapter Thirty-five

Ava had hoped she would never have to relive her tractor ride experience again. Her only consolation, as she stared at the muddy trailer, was that her grandfather's award-winning wine had numbed her sufficiently that she wouldn't be feeling the bumpy ride home.

Jean-Marc, on the other hand, was on the verge of a panic attack when he discovered where he would be sitting. He had no choice but to 'slum it' because that's where the peach schnapps barrels would be – the answer to all their prayers. He had to oversee their safe delivery to Château Saint-Clair. There was no room for error. It was a life-or-death situation as far as he was concerned.

'Careful!' he squealed as Bernard and Jacques hoiked an old oak barrel into the trailer. Tempers were fraying under the stress.

'How about you give us a hand instead of shouting orders from your throne,' Bernard snapped.

Jean-Marc gasped, touching his hand to his face. 'Is he serious?' He turned to Ava. 'He can't be serious. *Non, non, non*, I don't do heavy lifting.'

In her other ear, she had Jacques apologising, profusely.

'I can't believe I didn't think of this sooner,' he kept saying. 'I just didn't make the connection.'

Jacques had forgotten that his uncle, who loved taxidermy and brewing his own liquor, not necessarily in that order, would sometimes sell his used oak barrels to Ava's grandfather when he was finished making his peach schnapps.

The wood would have absorbed the peach flavours from the liquor and then infused with the wine as soon as the juice was placed inside the barrels.

'He once mentioned it in passing, years ago. I didn't think anything of it because rosé isn't usually made in oak barrels.'

Jean-Marc tutted.

'And I was young,' Jacques stressed.

'I would never forget a detail such as that,' Jean-Marc snipped. Jacques gave him a devil stare.

'Excuse me, hello,' Ava waved. 'We only have three weeks left. Is that enough time for the flavour to infuse?'

'I hope so!' Jean-Marc replied. 'I pray to the gods it is.' He clasped his hands. 'But if it isn't, I blame him.'

'Me?' Jacques pointed to himself.

'*Oui.*'

'I've just saved the day! In fact, I would say it's me who has made the wine.'

Ava quietly stepped away from the warring men, letting them battle it out for chief winemaking status. And then she stopped abruptly, her thoughts percolating, spun around and snipped: 'Actually, I think you have me to thank. For drinking the last bottle. Because if I'd never opened it, Jacques would have never have found out about the peach.' She nodded proudly.

They stared at her, suddenly silenced.

She lightly patted the smoky-smelling barrel and smiled. 'I think we all need to thank Grandpapa. Because somewhere he's had a hand in this, guiding us,' she looked to the sky, 'from up there, making sure we found the secret. He was there all along.'

'So who would like to try some of my peach schnapps?' A booming voice sliced through the bickering. A moustached man with ruddy cheeks, who clearly had an appetite for the good things in life, appeared waving his hip flask. He knocked his head back and took a generous swig of the home-brewed liquor.

It was Jacques' uncle, Fabian.

'It's still breakfast time,' Jean-Marc's eyebrows arched in horror as he checked his watch.

'It's never too early for the good stuff.' He put one hand on his lower back, thrusting his huge belly forward, like a pregnant woman. Impervious to Jean-Marc's exaggerated eye roll, Fabian turned to his nephew and Ava.

'And this is the lovely lady in your life you have been talking about?' His eyes twinkled. *No question where Jacques had inherited his mischievous look from*, Ava thought.

Ava didn't even need to look at Jacques, she could feel him turning pink. She, on the other hand, was quietly glowing with the news that Jacques had been talking about her with his family.

'*Enchanté, Madame*,' Fabian kissed Ava's hand, his moustache tickling her skin. 'I can't believe he's been hiding you away all of this time.'

Jacques coughed. 'We're not together . . .'

Fabian wasn't listening, he was too busy charming Ava. 'I wished I had met you sooner so I could have shared with you all my stories of your grandfather. I would have told you about the time we got very, very drunk trying my pear brandy.' He guffawed. 'It must have been eighty per cent alcohol. *Mon Dieu*, we could barely stand,' Fabian rolled onto his heels, laughing heartily. 'He was a good man, your grandfather. And an excellent winemaker.' He kissed his fingers and sprinkled the excellence into the air. 'The very best.'

'I wish I had met you earlier too.' Ava smiled wistfully.

'Well you've met now, and we've learnt about the barrels, so let's get moving,' Jean-Marc grumpily interrupted their reminiscing.

Speaking over Jean-Marc, Fabian shared his wine knowledge.

'*Jacques, mon garçon*, you must make sure you regularly turn the barrels so the peach is equally distributed.'

'I know, Uncle.' He slid the second to last barrel into the trailer.

'And you must keep topping them up as some of the wine will evaporate through the wood.'

'Yes, Uncle.'

'Do you want me to do it for you?'

'No!' Jean-Marc screeched before regaining his composure. 'No *thank you*,' he pressed out a smile. 'Jacques, we need to go, time is of the essence.'

The barrels were tied in place with rope, leaving only a small gap for a single passenger. Jean-Marc winced as he took a seat, wedged into the corner. Ava was whistling a sigh of relief she had lucked out of travelling with him.

Bernard had a wry smile on his face as he closed the back of the trailer, sealing Jean-Marc's fate. 'Hold on tight,' he couldn't help himself.

'What do you mean hold on tight?' Jean-Marc's head spun around, searching for Ava. 'Ava, what does he mean?'

She giggled as she clambered onto the back of her steed – Jacques' moped. She'd grown extremely fond of Jean-Marc, he was one of the family, but it was hard to resist winding him up when he was in full diva mode.

The tractor engine roared into life, shaking vibrations across the trailer. Jean-Marc took a deep inhalation and spoke calming words to himself.

Fabian waved them off enthusiastically, between swigs of his hip flask. '*Bon chance!*'

Jacques lifted himself off the seat, throwing his weight down, kick-starting the moped into action. He looked over his shoulder. 'Are you ready for this?' he said playfully.

'Are you telling me I need to hold on tight?' she counterattacked.

'You can if you like, I won't complain,' he revved his little motor.

Under duress, Ava wrapped her arms around him, her fingers clinging against his taut stomach, her thoughts revisiting the drunken kiss. She wanted more of him. It was torture having had just a taste of what she'd been missing.

They set off in convoy down the winding mountain road. Jacques hung back behind the tractor so they could have a second set of eyes on the precious cargo. The view was as magical as it had been all those months ago when Ava had visited the hilltop town for the winetasting, only the changing seasons had created new colours and scents. The landscape was budding with spring growth, the plants itching to morph into bloom. The air smelt fresh, as if the cold winter had rinsed it clean. The sky was as blue as the azure sea, garnished with a few wispy clouds that scudded across the horizon.

Jean-Marc's eyes were clamped shut though. He couldn't bear to watch the dirt rubbing into his clothes. A sheen of sweat had developed across his face. His only consolation for enduring such pain was knowing that the suffering was almost over – they had cracked the mystery and now actually stood a chance of winning.

Jean-Marc soothed himself as he imagined the stage, the lights, his Armani suit shimmering under the spotlights as he turned this way and that for the cameras, clutching the Golden Grape statue in his hand.

# Chapter Thirty-six

## Spring, St Tropez, The Golden Grapes

Emilia stopped and stared into the window of the Dior shop.

She wasn't gazing at the stunning couture outfits though, but at her own reflection, as she adjusted her breasts, pushing them up so high they almost spilled out of her white bandeau-style dress.

'Jesus, they'll fall out!' Ava squeaked, nervously looking left to right at the horrified faces of the glamour pusses who were strutting past. She then took a quick glance at her own reflection. Her initial choice of dress had been a teal-coloured meringue, something classic, a ball dress for an award ceremony. That was until Camille had scolded her for even considering looking like a plump cake in St Tropez. 'The women there will eat you alive for wearing that!' she'd said, handing her a floor-length, lace, fitted emerald-coloured number instead.

Ava was suddenly feeling seriously self-conscious as she stroked her hand across her stomach.

'Are you kidding me, your tum is as flat as a pancake,' Emilia caught her out. Turning to face her best friend, she said: 'You look astonishing. Honestly babe, the best I've ever seen you.'

Ava returned to the Dior window, giving herself one last inspection. She had to admit, the figure-hugging dress was sexy, and complemented her elfin crop. With her huge sparkling earrings, she looked almost regal.

'When you're ready,' Jean-Marc tapped his foot, clearly anxious for what lay ahead. He was looking dashing too, in a racing green velvet Armani suit which he'd deliberately chosen to match with Ava. All the men were looking handsome – Bernard had managed to fit into her grandpapa's dinner jacket, and Jacques, well she could barely look at him without gasping out loud. He was breathtakingly handsome – the white of his shirt offsetting his tan, his tailored jacket enhancing his broad shoulders and narrow waist. His thick chestnut hair, ruffled into a perfect messy style.

Even Madame Chevalier looked a picture. Emilia had managed to persuade her to swap her skirt and jumper combo for a tunic-style dress, and to take out her beloved braid. Ava wasn't sure she had ever seen the housekeeper with her hair down but it looked beautiful and she suggested she should do it more often.

'*Non*,' Madame Chevalier cut her dead. 'Just this once and no more.'

Emilia exchanged a humorous glance with Ava. 'Let's get this show on the road then.' She gave her reflection one final pout and teetered off along the cobbles in her matching white stilettos.

There was a real sense of camaraderie as they strode together through the glamorous streets of St Tropez. Past the designer shops, Armani, Versace, Gucci, their opulent shop fronts screaming wealth and status.

Emilia was like a child in a sweet shop. Eyeing up everything, wanting to touch everything – including the men.

She pushed down her sunglasses. 'Why have I not been here before?' her eyes lingering on a hunk they passed. Spinning around to gawp at his bum.

'Do you have to be so obvious?' Ava cringed. Although she was secretly glad her friend was back in her life. She'd missed her massively.

The streets were narrow, and practically paved with gold as they meandered their way down to the sea. They turned a corner and they had arrived on the grandiose marina just as the sun was setting.

The place was like a catwalk show – skinny waifs in designer clothes prancing up and down the promenade or clinging on the arm of some extremely rich guy, to a backdrop of super-yachts.

'Je-zus!' Emilia gasped. Even she hadn't seen anything quite like it. They stopped, transfixed by the sight of a super-yacht attempting to reverse-park in between two other similarly priceless boats with less than half a metre to manoeuvre. The crew of ten, wearing matching uniforms, were hopping around, waving their hands, panic-navigating to avoid a collision. Ava didn't even want to imagine what a nick on the paintwork would cost.

They carried on, past the next boat, which had turned itself into a nightclub for the evening, with a glitter ball on deck, disco lights flashing, music blaring, the bass pumped up.

'What about if we stop in here for a cheeky drink, en route.' Emilia shimmied her shoulders.

Ava stared at the Victoria's Secret model lookalikes dancing and taking selfies and the slicked-back-hair lotharios spraying champagne, and was actually relieved she wasn't jumping around with them, but had her feet firmly planted on dry land, with her new family, who were genuine people.

'Okay, well what about just me? I'll catch you guys up in five.'

Ava threaded her arm through Emilia's and tugged her. 'You're not leaving my side.'

They didn't have much further to go; according to the directions on the white and gold embossed invitation card, the ceremony was being held at the tail end of the marina, behind the yacht club, in what looked like a carpark on the map . . .

'I thought this was just some small awards thingy . . .' Ava's mouth fell open.

The 'carpark' was one giant gleaming white marquee with a red carpet entrance, manned by dozens of security guards, all of whom looked very serious with radios in their ears, and microphones on their sleeves.

There was a traffic jam of huge black limousines pulling up in front. Chauffeurs were swearing as they attempted to reverse and turn in the small dropping-off area.

Paparazzi photographers were hustling behind the red rope, trying to get a snap of the rich and famous before they disappeared through a thick white curtain that hung at the entrance.

'Hun, I told you winemaking is one of the snobbiest industries out there. The richest of the rich will be here. Celebrities. Vineyard owners, buyers, sellers. All wanting to be seen in the pages of *Hello* magazine, or *Bonjour* or whatever they call it here,' Emilia explained, pushing her breasts up again.

'Stop doing that,' Ava hissed.

An explosion of flashbulbs lit up the sky as some stunning leggy model twirled on the red carpet.

'Oh God, I've got stage fright.'

'You look stunning. Just own it.'

Ava turned to Jacques, her eyes huge, like a rabbit in headlights.

'You don't need me to tell you how beautiful you look.'

'I do, I really do,' she trembled.

He kissed her softly on the forehead. '*Tu est belle*. Don't be afraid.'

'Here,' Bernard stepped forward, offering his arm. 'We will walk this carpet together.'

Ava smiled gratefully, hooking her arm into his. 'Thank you,' she whispered.

And for a moment it worked. She felt safe and protected and confident as she walked alongside her father. She almost started to enjoy the glamour of it, that was until she caught sight of *him*.

Her stomach clenched into a ball of hatred as she watched Victor Ambrose peacocking up ahead for the cameras. He posed to the left and then to the right, his shoulders back, his chin raised, his fake smile fixed. He had a different girl on his arm to the one Ava had seen him with at the market. She was also blonde but this one was even poutier, her lips thrusting out from her face like an inflated life raft.

Victor caught her eye and flashed her the same practised smile. And then, horror of horrors, he approached her, on the red carpet, in front of all the cameras.

'Madame Chiltern, it's so lovely to see you here,' he smarmed, angling his body to the paparazzi, so they could get a shot of them together.

Ava blinked into the blinding lights.

'And another one, smile,' Victor hooked his arm around her. Stealing her from Bernard.

'Get your hands off me,' she growled through gritted teeth. She pulled away, staring him dead in the eye.

'Play nice, everyone is watching.'

More bulbs flashed.

'You don't intimidate me.'

'I should. Because, by the end of tonight, you'll have no choice but to sell your vineyard.' He smiled again.

'I know it was you who sent those men to burn my château down.'

'How *magnifique, ma chérie*, you have quite the imagination,' he laughed. 'It's so tragic you haven't been able to use that creative mind of yours to make your grandfather's wine.'

She raised her eyebrows. 'Haven't I?'

He pretended not to look rattled. 'And one more, just for that camera over there.' He then withdrew his smile and sneered: 'One way or another, I will be winning tonight.' He replaced his hand on his date's skinny derrière and carried on up the red carpet.

'Stay calm.' Jacques touched her back lightly.

'I hate him,' Ava said under her breath.

'I know but he wants you to bite, so don't give him the satisfaction.'

She bit down on her anger instead as she stepped through the marquee curtain into what looked like the bottom of the ocean. The palatial room was illuminated in blue and purple lights. The ceiling was adorned with glowing gold chandeliers shaped like sea urchins. Everything else was white. The tablecloths, the chairs, the giant bows attached to the backs of the chairs. Even the aerial gymnasts were wearing skimpy white outfits as they twirled through hoops suspended from the ceiling.

The stage was glittering, the steps were illuminated. The backdrop was one huge television screen flashing tranquil images of tropical fish and dolphins swimming, plunging the event even further under the sea.

The people milling around were dripping in wealth and a mixture of young and old, although it was hard to decipher how old some of the women were, as their faces were botoxed within an inch of their lives and pumped full of filler. They had a waxed sheen to their skin, something straight out of Madame Tussauds. But their expressions were the worst. They couldn't move their faces, not even twitch their noses, but they could somehow still manage an arch of their eyebrows. Up and down, up and down, as they ran a critique on everyone who passed them. Ava felt the clingy material of her dress tighten even more, and suddenly craved the simplicity of her vineyard, repelled by the pomp and gloss of this superficial wine world. The divide between those who make the wine and those who drink it and profess to know everything about it becoming very distinct.

After a significant amount of champagne quaffing everyone was herded to their tables, some even helped to their seats, for the start of the awards. The raucous laughter was silenced by the loud music booming across the room. The huge screen burst into life, playing glossy panoramic views of vineyards, images of people laughing and smiling as they picked grapes.

'Have they been to a real vineyard?' Bernard snapped.

'I know, where's the sweat and the wild boar and the shouting when the wine press breaks down?' Jacques leaned in from the other side.

'Ridiculous,' Bernard folded his arms.

'Although I do like these,' Madame Chevalier tapped the plate, turning it over in her hands to examine the brand.

A tall man wearing a Tuxedo walked onto the stage, his shoes clicking loudly on the hard shiny surface. He adjusted the microphone and turned a dial that sent an explosive ear-piercing hum across the room.

'*Pardon*,' he said sheepishly. He fiddled with it a bit more and then cleared his throat. The audience hushed into a silence.

'*Bon soir, Mesdames et Messieurs*,' he began.

Ava would have liked to have said she listened intently, but she hadn't realised that there were literally dozens of wine awards, for every colour, for every category, from the best terroir prize to the best colour. It was like a Crufts but for wine. She was only interested in one prize though – the best in show for rosé. So when Emilia announced: 'Jesus, I need a smoke!' she didn't take much persuading to lure her outside, just to give her hands a rest from clapping if anything else.

Emilia inhaled so viciously on her cigarette Ava worried her lungs might combust. She blew out the plume of smoke into the last of the sun-setting sky, and also slightly angled into the path of some snotty-looking women.

'I can't take the tension, I'm so nervous for you,' she confessed.

'You're nervous! I think I'm having heart palpitations. What if we don't win, Em? I'm frightened.'

'You just need to check in with yourself. Take some deep yoga breaths. Follow me,' Emilia inhaled deeply, her cheeks puffing with air, her face turning purple as she held it in.

Several more party-goers walked past, their conversation halting abruptly at the sight of Emilia's puffer fish impression.

'Oh bugger off,' she exhaled.

They raised their eyebrows and carried on talking about her as they disappeared through the marquee curtain into the sea of bling.

'Now you try,' she turned to Ava. 'Deep breath . . .'

'I've got a much better idea,' Ava said.

Five minutes later the women were sitting by the harbour, their dresses hoiked up, their legs dangling over the water, a bottle of Château Saint-Clair next to them, talking about men rather than wine.

'I really like him, he's hot, and he's clever *and* nice . . . did I mention he was hot?' Emilia gave her honest appraisal of Jacques.

'So you don't disapprove that he's sixteen years younger?'

Emilia burst out laughing. 'Disapprove? I think you should win an award for reeling in that fish, he's gorgeous. And, what's more. you two seem so well matched, you want the same things, you complement each other, he gives you room to breathe and be yourself. When he looks at you, he has pride in his eyes.'

Ava frowned – wow, this was deep for Emilia.

'Don't let yourself feel judged.' She went on. 'Stick your finger up at them, babe, let them think what they like.'

They clinked glasses.

'Where did you get this?'

'Madame Chevalier smuggled it in her handbag. It just seemed right that I drank my own wine tonight.'

'It's bloody good, wow. I'm going home with a crate of Château Saint-Clair, try and stop me.' Emilia's face then turned serious, a rare look for her. 'I just want you to know, before we get sucked back into that awards thing, how proud I am of you, first prize or not.'

'Really?'

'Yes! Look how far you have come. Not much more than a year ago, you were crying into your cornflakes, and look at you now – beautiful, confident, running a vineyard. Kicking ass. And no Mark, you finally got rid of him. I'm so proud of you.' She took a sip of wine. 'Of course, I take full credit.'

'For what?'

'For sending you out here. If it hadn't been for me, you would still be in my spare room.'

'Ha!' Ava scoffed. But she knew it was probably true.

They fell quiet for a moment, taking in the stunning scenery. The quaint houses that lined the marina had turned golden with the setting sun. The soothing sounds of the water chopping against the hulls of the boats, the seagulls crying and . . . Emilia's stomach rumbling.

She clutched her belly. 'I could murder a fish and chips,' she announced. 'That finger food in there is killing me.' They both burst into a fit of giggles.

'There you are,' the familiar voice shouted from behind them.

Ava and Emilia turned their heads, just in time to catch the golden orb of light falling onto Jacques. He looked like a Golden Globes statue himself with the light turning his brown skin a silky warm colour. His buff body, poised; his strong triangular chest enhanced by the sharply cut dinner jacket.

'I was worried about you.'

Emilia kicked Ava's leg. 'He worries about you, that's adorable,' she whispered, very loudly.

'They are about to announce the awards.'

Ava's stomach flipped over.

'I don't think I want to listen. Can you just tell me the results when they are over?'

He ticked her off with his eyes.

'I'm serious!'

He moved closer, holding out his hand for her to take.

'Don't worry about me,' Emilia scrambled to her feet, flashing her knickers as she swung her legs around.

Jacques held out both his arms for the ladies to grab. Ava wrapped herself around him, clinging tightly like a monkey onto a branch, suddenly overcome with nerves.

'Let's do this, team!' Emilia trilled.

# Chapter Thirty-seven

They arrived at their seats just as the awards were being announced.

Victor was three tables away. The wine mogul was leaning into his chair, one arm casually slung over the back, the other stroking the arm of his pouty blonde.

The host for the evening continued his story of rosé. 'As you know, to be selected for Côtes de Provence and this award, le rosé must be a blend of a minimum of two grapes.'

There was a murmur of acknowledgement amongst the crowd.

'The standards this year were excellent. The competition was fierce, many of the wines were exquisite.'

Emilia rolled her eyes. 'Come on, come on.'

'But!' He held up his finger, speaking in a thick French accent. 'But fear not, we were able to choose and without further delay, in reverse order,' he pulled out an envelope from his pocket. 'In third place the award goes to . . .'

There was a painfully long pause. Ava's hands were clammy.

The man slowly opened the gold envelope and pulled out the thick crisp card.

'Château Ambrose.'

'Yes!' Emilia sprang up from her seat.

Jacques squeezed Ava's hand. Bernard and Madame Chevalier had never been so enthusiastic about clapping.

Ava's gaze slid across the room to Victor, who for the first time was struggling with his fake smile. She noticed how he was chewing the inside of his mouth, with curbed anger. He wouldn't look at her, not even a sideways glance. His eyes were fixed on the stage. Even if she didn't win, she thought for a moment, at least he hadn't. But that wasn't enough for her . . . she turned her gaze back to the stage.

The clinking of knives on glasses echoed across the room as everyone was hushed into silence again. All the moisture had left Ava's mouth. She hadn't noticed but her fists had involuntarily rolled themselves into tight balls.

She felt Jacques' hand on top of hers as the presenter began talking again. He carefully unrolled each of her fingers until he was able to thread his through hers. She looked across at him and gave him a small, fearful smile.

'And in second place . . .' the lanky man on stage announced. He pulled the card out of the envelope. Ava closed her eyes. Her heart was hammering. Jacques squeezed her hand again.

'*En deuxième place*,' he repeated in French. 'The prize for the best rosé . . .' he lingered on the words.

'Just spit it out,' Madame Chevalier snapped, fanning her anxiety away with the silent auction list.

'Goes to . . . Château Saint-Clair.'

The room exploded into a round of applause, while Ava imploded. She felt as if someone had plunged her head into water. Everything was blurred and muffled and she couldn't breathe.

'Ava?'

Jacques voice was somewhere far away, calling out for her. Her chest tightened.

'Ava?'

She opened her eyes. Bernard was sitting very still. Jean-Marc was white as a sheet, tears in his eyes. Madame

Chevalier was shaking her head and Emilia was knocking back the wine. She could feel Victor Ambrose's gaze on her, but she wasn't going to turn around and give him the satisfaction of seeing her defeated eyes.

Finally she spoke. 'I'm sorry everyone. I tried my best.'

'It's going to be okay,' Jacques was forcing a happy expression.

She turned, looking him dead in the eye.

'No, it won't be. We all know the dream is over.'

He opened his mouth to speak, and then hesitated, knowing that whatever he said wasn't going to fix it.

The first prize was awarded to a fledgling vineyard located somewhere towards the mountains that specialised in organic wines, but none of them were really listening. Jean-Marc had stormed off outside to cool down. Ava was slumped in her chair, her eyes had a glassy sheen as she stared into nothing. Her heart, shattered into little pieces, like the silver confetti that was now exploding from the ceiling. Celebratory music was blaring, people were milling around, laughing, clearing chairs so they could dance.

Out of the corner of her eye, she saw him approach, the lapels on his dinner jacket flapping as he marched towards her. He was a missile, seconds away from mass destruction. Ava steeled herself, rising to her feet. She knew Ambrose was going to offer her a deal and she was going to have to accept it. She needed that prize money to keep the vineyard running. Without it, Château Saint-Clair would fall into disrepair. The last remaining grapes would wither and die.

She turned to face him, inhaling, exhaling . . .

'Ava Chiltern?' A woman stepped across his path. She held out an elegant hand.

'Yes,' Ava replied hesitantly, her gaze still trained on Victor, who was rolling his eyes impatiently, desperate for the woman to move on.

'My name is Kathy Brandon.' She had the most strangled upper-class English accent Ava could imagine. 'It really is a pleasure to meet you.'

Ava shook the woman's hand, which was adorned with gold and gemstones. She thought she was probably some British aristocrat who had come to be seen at the awards. One of those types Emilia had described.

'I just wanted to say congratulations on your winning.'

'We didn't win, we came second,' Ava said sharply.

The woman looked taken aback.

'I'm sorry,' she sighed, one eye still on Ambrose, 'it's just been a long disappointing night.'

'It's quite all right, dear. And I don't want to take up your time. I just have something you might be interested in.'

The woman rummaged around in her Mary Poppins bag. Meanwhile, Victor was shifting from one foot to the other, staring daggers at the woman.

She pulled her head out of her bag and handed Ava a card which was embossed with the logo Magic Wines. She tapped it with her finger while Ava's mouth fell open. 'It's my son's company really, dear, I just own it. He calls me the caretaker,' she smiled.

'It's the biggest wine wholesaler in the UK,' Ava said. She knew that, thanks to Mark.

'That's very sweet of you to say so. Anyway, we would very much like to stock your wine, it's rather good.'

'Is this a joke?'

The others had cottoned on to the conversation and were now crowded around.

'Oh, no, I'm very serious! We'd like to buy the whole stock you produced this year, we were thinking for perhaps, £200,000 . . .'

Ava stopped breathing.

'But that's of course up for negotiation, my son likes to be involved with that side of things, dear. I'm sure we might be able to go higher.'

'Higher?' she gasped.

'And then we can start looking at the 2020 vintage.' She paused. 'Are you all right, dear? You've gone awfully pale.'

Jacques gave her a gentle shake and she let out a huge gasping breath she'd been holding onto.

'It's absolutely fine,' she squeaked, the blood returning to her face.

'Perfect, well, there's my card, so just give me a call on Monday. Lovely to meet you, dear, enjoy your celebrations.' And with that she pulled her oversized bag into her side and disappeared into the shower of confetti.

'Somebody pinch me,' Ava whispered. 'Somebody pinch me!' she shouted. 'Ow!'

'You asked!' Emilia said and then threw her arms around her best friend.

From that moment, everything morphed into slow motion – the hugging, the squeals of happiness, the shouting, mouths opening and closing with words of congratulations that were stretched out and distorted. Ava shook her head, bringing her back into real time, just when Bernard was telling her how proud he was of her, his eyes brimming with admiration.

'Thank you, thank you, thank you!' she said, hugging him. 'For everything.'

It was all so overwhelming that Ava had almost forgotten the dark shadow lurking in the background.

'Ava, can we talk?' Victor reminded her of his presence.

She took a final look at her family, of their jubilant faces, of the pride in their eyes, and then spun around with strength and fury.

'Why don't you just crawl back under that rock over there where you came from because *we won't be selling . . .*' Her voice was bursting into song; she couldn't contain her victory a second longer.

He scoffed. 'What are you going to do? Live off the grapes?'

'No!' She threw her hands on her hips, suddenly becoming all Beyoncé-sassy. 'I've been offered a very lucrative deal to sell my wine, and I'm going to accept, so you can stuff your deal where the sun don't shine, *comprendez?*'

He glared at her.

'Bye,' she waved sarcastically.

She could tell he was clinging onto his temper by a thread. His eyes flickered around him, checking to see who was listening. When he realised half his best clients were in earshot he had no alternative but to squeeze out a restrained response. Which was simply a death stare before he turned and marched back to his table, muttering under his breath.

Ava spun around, breaking into a little dance as she did so, jiggling her arms and legs around, only to smack head on into Jacques mid-twirl.

'Ouch!' She rubbed her nose. *It had all been going so well.*

'I didn't know you like to dance,' he smirked.

'Well, you know, only on special occasions,' she blushed.

He leaned in. 'Teach me something,' he whispered in her ear.

She was a little taken aback at first, but then she saw that familiar look in his eye, the same one he had when they'd been in bed. And when she felt the static crackle she couldn't help smiling naughtily.

'Well, you put your hand here,' she said, moving his palm to her bum.

He grinned as his fingers gave her a firm squeeze.

'And you hold me close with your other hand.'

'Like so?'

'Like so,' she said, his mouth millimetres away from hers.

'And then?'

'And then . . .' her pulse rocketing. 'I kiss you,' she said softly.

'And then?' His eyes were wild.

'Well . . .' She looked at him wickedly just as another shower of confetti rained down from above.

## THE END

# Acknowledgments

Firstly, I'd like to thank my agent Sarah Hornsley. I've loved your energy and enthusiasm from the get-go. You're always brimming with ideas and have encouraged me every step of the way. I can't thank you enough for helping me achieve what I've always dreamed of doing. After years of ghosting other people's stories, you've helped me find my own voice.

Next up, the editorial team at Trapeze, Orion books. Sam Eades, merci beaucoup for taking a chance on me and for all your support and pointers and helping me develop a playful tone to my writing and making me giggle, a lot, about Jacques. Phoebe Morgan – I couldn't have wished for a better editor to take over halfway through. You've been wonderful at helping me push through those last edits and offering me such sound, positive advice. It's been such a collaborative editing process, a thank you also to Victoria Pepe who helped me fine-tune my manuscript.

The wider team at Trapeze, for everything you have done. Thank you for designing such a stunning front cover. The colours pop off the page, it sums up the feel-good vibe of my book perfectly.

Mum, Dad, a huge thanks for your continuous support.

\*

Thank you, Michael, for always being ready to listen to my plot ideas and brainstorming new ones with me.

A massive thank you to everyone who helped me bring the little vineyard to life – Jack at Majestic Wines for marrying me up with the perfect Provençal vineyard to help with my 'research' and the whole team at Chateau Peyrassol where I spent a glorious two weeks last summer learning how to make wine and finding the words to inspire me. A special thank you to Aynard and Alban.

Finally, a big thank you to the readers, for buying my book, for supporting my journey into the world of fiction writing. I've found my dream job and I hope I'll be writing for years to come!